SHELLBACK

SHELLBACK

A NOVEL

for Emily and Jack Beaver

Smooth Sailing

Stu Landersman

STUART LANDERSMAN

To order additional copies of this book, contact:
Xlibris Corporation
1-888-795-4274
www.Xlibris.com
Orders@Xlibris.com
114403

DEDICATION

We were driving down the Silver Strand Highway toward Coronado Cays and Martha Morehead Landersman leaned across, planted a kiss on my cheek and thanked me for giving her such a wonderful life. What do you say to something like that? I responded with an inappropriate, "G'won with that ole stuff!" She gave me a gentle punch on the shoulder and told me to finish writing Shellback. The next morning at the Calypso Café she passed away.

I finished the book, Martha my love, for you.

Stu Landersman

PROLOGUE

The west side of San Diego Bay in southern California is formed by the small city of Coronado. Three sides of Coronado are water; the Pacific Ocean on the west side and San Diego Bay on the north and east sides. To the south lies a strip of what was a sand bar that has been built up over the years into what is now called the Silver Strand which provides the basis of a divided highway. This Silver Strand highway provides Coronado with a land bridge, which was its only connection to the California mainland until a beautiful suspension bridge was built across San Diego Bay. That bridge now links the cities of Coronado and San Diego.

Along the sides of the Silver Strand, landfills have provided areas of state and federal properties that have separated a residential area from the rest of the City of Coronado. Originally a pig farm then a city dump, a group of imaginative businessmen converted the dump into the upscale tax producing residential community of Coronado Cays, the Cays name reflecting a Caribbean theme. It includes some 1200 homes mostly on the water, most with their own boat docks, ranging from 2-3 bedroom condominiums through attached homes to large multi-million dollar individual houses.

Home owners and residents in Coronado Cays come from all parts of the country and include many retirees, many vacationers, some dual home owners and a few still employed in the San Diego area. A significant number of Cays residents are retired military like Barney Williams, a retired rear admiral who spent most of his more than thirty years of naval service in submarines. Barney and his wife Jackie have one daughter, Eleanor, who is married to Steven Shielbrock, and sometimes Ellie and Steven get a chance to visit in the Coronado Cays.

CHAPTER 1

With the sun almost overhead, slightly to the south, the large patio umbrella cast a comfortable shadow over those seated in soft chairs at the round table. A slight easterly breeze from the nearby Pacific cooled the area from the August sun as Barney Williams leaned back continuing working the short crossword puzzle in the weekly Coronado newspaper. It was an easy one for him. He worked them all the time and always completed them in ball point pen. He laughed as he wrote in a tricky final answer, tossed puzzle and pen on the table and reached forward for the ice tea glass.

Jackie looked up from her magazine and smiled. "You got another one, eh?"

"Yeah, they seem to get easier as I get older. You think I'm getting smarter with age?"

She smiled at her husband. "You should be so lucky. More likely you're just learning the tricks of the puzzles, but keep at it mister and maybe you can convince yourself about getting smarter."

They both laughed as their son-in-law opened the slider and stepped out onto the patio. "What did I miss? Is Barney telling another good sea story?"

"No," Jackie answered. "I've heard all of his sea stories by now. He thinks he's getting smarter because he did a crossword puzzle. What's Ellie doing?"

"Oh, she's puttering in the kitchen, making horses doovers I think."

They laughed and Ellie said, "Steven Shielbrock, your mother would skin you alive if she heard you say that."

"Yeah, she would," Steven laughed. "But you just said you've heard all of Barney's sea stories. Is that right, Dad? All of them?" He asked his father-in-law.

Barney smiled, "She thinks she's heard them all but no way. I've been saving the best, and the spiciest, for just the right time."

"And when would that right time be?" asked Steven. "Could it be now? I wouldn't want to say anything out of place but even a super crossword puzzle guy might forget or maybe just not be around in time to tell his best, his spiciest sea stories. After all, there are age and memory considerations and I only get to see you and listen to stories when I get leave and we can travel here. So when would be a better time than now? C'mon, let's hear some of those spicy salty sea stories you've been holding back."

"Your Dad has probably told you all the best stories."

"No, he told me lots of stories but not the real dramatic, the really good ones. When I was young I think he thought that his really good stories would have a bad influence on me and now he won't tell any stories. Over the years I picked up bits and pieces like when you and he would get together I would eve-drop, but I couldn't get the full stories that way, the really good stories."

Barney laughed again. "Well, some of them, maybe most of them, would've been bad for you to hear when you were young. Maybe you're still too young."

Before Steve could respond Jackie spoke up. "Barney! The 'boy' is thirty years old. He's a nuke submariner. He's married to your daughter. He wants to hear some of the things that his father and you did. How long should he wait? As he says, you may be a whiz at crossword puzzles and even have a little memory left but how much longer and when?"

Barney smiled. "Hey, don't be burying me at sea yet! I get the point. Okay, let's tell some Williams and Shielbrock sea stories." He paused. "Maybe we'd better call them Shielbrock and Williams. No, maybe just Shielbrock stories 'cause that's his name and now our daughter's name. But no, again, 'cause if I'm gonna tell the stories he," Barney nodded to Steven, "wants to hear, we're going to have to call them 'Shellback' 'cause that's what he was known as through his navy time and after and even now."

Steven smiled and nodded, "Great, but not just the navy and Shellback stuff. I want to hear from you the early stuff, like you guys in school, college, summers, girls, sports, y'know, the real spicy stuff and then navy stuff, too."

"Wait a minute! That's a tall order and your Dad must have told you most of that early pre-navy stuff. I shouldn't have to go over all that again."

"Oh yeah, like I said, he told me some stories and I picked up scraps over the years but now I want to hear them from you, your side of it."

"Okay. Let's start with the story of Martin Shielbrock. Get Ellie in here with or without the 'horses doovers' and we'll talk about—, let's see, maybe we'll start with how he got his navy name, his nickname 'Shellback'."

SEA OF JAPAN, MAY 1953

At night it had been cold off the coast of Korea in the Sea of Japan even in May of 1953 and the seas became rough for a destroyer as the wind picked up. During the day if the sun came out it was hot in the junior officer bunkroom as the sun would beat down on the steel deck and the small space that housed five young officers was directly under the forecastle, with thin asbestos insulation on the overhead. It heated up like an oven, under the sun, and cooled off rapidly at night, so the space was either too hot or too cold most of the time. Fortunately, from the standpoint of habitability, the sun shone hot and clear only about half of the days, the remaining were gray and dismal, and when the seas were rough the ship rolled and pitched constantly and a fine salt water spray permeated everywhere leaving a damp clammy feel.

Ensign Martin D. Shielbrock, USNR, had been assigned to USS ROBINSON (DD 562) upon graduation from Officer Candidate School at Newport, Rhode Island. Robinson's home port was Norfolk, Virginia, but Shielbrock had little opportunity to learn much about Norfolk, as the ship deployed to the Western Pacific for the Korean War a few weeks after he reported on board. A Fletcher Class destroyer, Robinson was one of 119 ships of that class built during World War II. They were known as "twenty-one hundred tonners" by destroyermen, were considered to be fast and reliable, and carried five gun mounts, each mount with one five inch thirty-eight caliber gun.

The caliber of Navy guns is designated by the diameter of the bore, or inside dimension of the gun barrel, and a number which, when multiplied by the diameter of the bore, gives the overall length of the barrel, so a five inch thirty eight caliber gun can accept a projectile five inches in diameter and the length of the gun barrel is five inches multiplied by thirty eight or 190 inches, which is fifteen feet ten inches. It could just as well be designated five inch 190, but that is never done, probably because non-Navy people would understand it. The guns on an Iowa class battleship are sixteen inch 50 caliber, meaning that the projectile is sixteen inches in diameter and the gun barrel is 16 times 50, or 800 inches, or sixty six feet eight inches long. Navy people like to use their traditional designations and refer to the "five inch thirty eight" gun, or the "sixteen inch fifty."

Ensign Shielbrock was assigned to the Gunnery Department of the ship as the First Lieutenant. Navy ranks and shipboard positions often cause confusion for non-Navy people and with good reason because in the Army, Air Force and Marine Corps, for example, a first lieutenant is a rank, an 0-2 in pay grade, meaning the second commissioned officer rank. A newly commissioned officer, typically, in those other services would be a second lieutenant and his (or her) first promotion would advance that officer to the next higher rank, first lieutenant, and a few years later the promotion would be to captain. Not so in the Navy, where a newly commissioned officer, typically, would be an ensign and his (or her) first promotion would be to the rank of lieutenant junior grade, often abbreviated as jaygee, and a few years later he (or she) would be promoted to lieutenant. Ensigns and second lieutenants wear a gold bar on their collar, jaygees and first lieutenants wear a silver bar, lieutenants in the Navy and captains in the army wear two silver bars, or "railroad tracks." It gets more confusing because a captain in the Navy is the equivalent rank to a colonel in the other services, but the position of captain in a Navy ship can be held by an officer of any rank.

The first lieutenant on a Navy ship is not a rank, it is a position or a job and the first lieutenant is responsible for seamanship; anchors, boats, line handling, cargo handling, rigging. He is in charge of the enlisted men of the Deck Division, composed of boatswain mates and seamen, and these men on Navy ships often have justified reputations as tough and uneducated sailors, frequently in trouble ashore but capable of hard physical work under adverse conditions at sea. They also serve, with others, in the gun mounts and as part of the bridge watch. Martin Shielbrock was an ensign in rank and his job on the ship was called first lieutenant.

Similarly the commanding officer of the destroyer was a commander in rank but called captain, and the executive officer, the second officer in seniority on the ship, was a lieutenant commander in rank, but called commander by tradition. Navy people have had no problem understanding these differences, but to the land-lubber it has always been confusing.

Martin Shielbrock had learned some of these professional Navy idiosyncrasies and part of a new seagoing language at OCS but much more of it was learned aboard ship. Ride to or drop the hook referred to the anchor. Unrep meant underway replenishment. Forecastle was pronounced foc'sle, boatswain pronounced bo'sun. He dealt with heaving lines, deck tread, red lead, chipping hammers and small stuff. A steel cable was called wire, rope was line, time ashore for recreation was liberty, and time aboard ship was work, duty, watch-standing or sleep. He learned about leadership and how to take care of his men and he got to know every one of the twenty-two men in his Deck Division, where they were from, married or single, fast or slow to learn, their recreational interests, their health, their eating habits. He learned to use his petty officers and to rely on "Boats," the Chief Boatswains Mate, pronounced chief bo'suns mate, remember.

A young officer's life aboard ship was one of watch standing, training, and qualifying. He stood watch as Junior Officer of the Deck, or as CIC Watch Officer (CIC was the Combat Information Center), or as Engineering Officer of the Watch, four hours on and eight hours off. Off watch time during the day focused on training, increasing the readiness of his division and on becoming qualified for watch standing positions of greater responsibility. The goal of every young officer was to be designated as Officer of the Deck, the direct representative of the Commanding Officer, responsible for the running of the ship during the four hours of such duty on the bridge, with legal status and full authority as delegated to him for that period by the Captain. Designation as a qualified Officer of the Deck required prior qualifications as CIC Watch Officer, Junior Officer of the Deck and Engineering Officer of the Watch. It also required a full understanding of every system in the ship and to accomplish this, young officers worked to complete a series of lessons in a Junior Officers Journal which covered all these systems.

They traced and drew out the ship's main propulsion system, auxiliary steam system, electrical distribution, ventilation, steering, radar, communications, gun fire control, fire fighting and ammunition handling systems. They practiced navigation, radio procedures, ship handling, boat handling, food handling and correspondence handling. Completion of the Junior Officers Journal, they called it the JO Journal, was followed by a complex of oral tests and practical demonstrations administered by other officers already qualified, and then a final exam given by the ship's Captain.

The Captain's exam could, and often did, involve crawling through little used spaces to identify specific piping, wiring or equipments. It could involve starting-up, Navy people called it "lighting-off", and operating specified equipment, drawing out and describing various systems including alternative routing and casualty modes of operation. The captain's exam had no limits as to content or time. It usually extended over a matter of days, often a week, during which the captain would ask questions of the candidate during quiet periods on watch, at meals or at unannounced times day or night.

"Explain the Rules of the Road for a crossing situation in international waters."

"Explain our internal message handling procedures."

"Explain the super heated steam system and the effect on ship's maximum and minimum speeds."

"Explain how we make and test fresh water."

"Diagram the electrical distribution system."

"Explain the various types of five inch thirty eight gun ammunition we carry."

"Show me the Mark One Able computer and tell me how it works."

"Light off the air search radar and patch it to this repeater."

The captain's exam was the climax of a process which usually took a year or two and by this exam the commanding officer of the ship made his determination as to the confidence he could place in the young officer. If, after or during the test, the captain felt that this particular officer was not ready to be given the responsibility for the ship, qualification as Officer of the Deck would be withheld and more training required.

When the captain felt that an officer had demonstrated adequate knowledge, that officer would be designated an Officer of the Deck, called OOD, and be allowed to serve as such in that ship. Shielbrock worked hard on his JO Journal. He knew there was little chance to attain the OOD status during the Korean deployment, but he hoped that during the transit home, back to Norfolk, he could become qualified. He looked ahead to the operations of the ship after the deployment and wanted to be an OOD then and for the next deployment.

Commander Steven Speakes, USN, was the Commanding Officer of USS Robinson. Called Captain by the people in his ship, Speakes was admired and respected by them all. He required high standards of performance and behavior, consistent in the application of his authority, and he knew every officer and enlisted man in his ship. He spent a lot of time talking with them, and he knew every system and piece of equipment in the ship and how it worked. Captain Speakes felt that there should never be a moment on watch with nothing to do, that if the ship's operations at any time didn't occupy the full attention of the people on watch, they should be preparing or training for what might happen. He liked the OOD to task the others on watch with potential problems or incidents, and the people in the ship called it "Playing What If."

"What if we lost lube oil pressure?"

"What if we picked up a sonar contact?"

"What if the OTC (Officer in Tactical Command) ordered us to Sasebo?"

"What if we had to put a boat in the water?"

"What if there was a fire reported in after steering?"

"What if a man fell overboard?"

For all of these questions the watch would have to report what actions they would take. Then a critique would be held, questionable procedures would be researched and the process would be reviewed for thoroughness.

Ensign Martin Shielbrock was a part of all this; busy with ships work, watch standing and qualifying so there was little time for anything else but eating and sleeping while underway. Still, he managed to take time most evenings to attend the movie in the Wardroom. Most of the junior officers passed up the movie, opting for sleep, but all agreed it was the only recreation available at sea. Well, almost all of them agreed to that but to Shielbrock it was all recreation. Tiring, demanding, challenging and at times very frustrating, he enjoyed it all and was immersed in learning the profession of a seagoing naval officer, a destroyerman. He could have had no better mentor than Captain Speakes, who had realized early that Ensign Shielbrock was a very valuable young man with great potential, that this young ensign displayed all the right characteristics of intelligence, dedication, judgment, self confidence and leadership, and Speakes was more than willing, he was anxious, to exploit this potential. Soon, Speakes reasoned, this young officer would be a valuable OOD, perhaps a department head in this or another destroyer and, even though not a Naval Academy graduate, the young officer might later elect to remain in the Navy, to transfer from reserve to regular, and to make the Navy his career. Maybe, someday, he would reach that pinnacle of achievement for destroyermen and be called, "Captain," but all that, if it was to be at all, might come later. For now the immediate goal was to teach Shielbrock all that it was possible for an ensign to learn, to get him qualified as an OOD and although Shielbrock was eager and in a hurry to reach that qualification, Captain Speakes planned a slow and more thorough process than usual.

Robinson was assigned to Support Station Charlie, twenty five miles off the east coast of Korea in the Sea of Japan, one of five such stations labeled Able, Baker, Charlie, Dog and Easy occupied by destroyers. From these stations the ships could be called in as necessary to provide naval gunfire support for troops ashore and they were also in position to maintain radar watch for North Korean aircraft which might try to fly out towards the U.S. aircraft carriers operating further to seaward. The third function of these destroyers in the Support Stations was called Search and Rescue, shortened by Navy language to the single acronym SAR. This called for them to be ready to pick-up U.S. Navy flight crew personnel returning to their aircraft carriers from combat missions, flight crewmen that might have to ditch or eject into the cold waters off the Korean coast.

Every three days the destroyers were visited by a fleet oiler, a large Navy tanker that brought them fuel and sometimes mail, and often the oiler brought personnel newly reporting and took away someone who had to leave the ship, and there were always movies to be exchanged. The oiler would steam along at a pre-arranged course and speed. The destroyer would go alongside and take position a hundred feet away as lines and rigging would be passed from the oiler, then two fueling hoses, and fuel oil would be pumped from the oiler's tanks into the fuel tanks of the destroyer.

Captain Speakes had shown the young officers how to handle the destroyer in making the approach, maintaining position and clearing the oiler's side when fueling was completed. The whole process took about an hour, longer if the destroyer needed more fuel than usual, and still longer if the oiler's pumping rate was slow for any reason. After observing the process as conducted by the Captain, the young officers took turns handling their ship alongside the oiler. Shielbrock took his regular turn and was alert for other opportunities if another officer was not available in the rotation cycle, so he got more than his share of ship handling alongside fleet oilers and became very adept at it.

One afternoon Shielbrock was standing JOOD watch, noon to sixteen hundred, four PM, and it was time to go alongside the oiler. Mike Taylor, the Damage Control Assistant, was scheduled for shiphandling but he had some problem with fuel tank soundings to deal with so Shielbrock made the approach, kept the ship alongside, cleared the oiler and returned to Support Station Charlie. It was smoothly done and he knew it, and a little later he turned the JOOD watch over to Ensign Butch Kovar, went below and worked a while on Deck Division training records. After dinner he looked over his division's spaces. Everything looked good so he was satisfied and decided to watch the movie in the Wardroom even though he had the midwatch, which ran from midnight to 0400, or four AM. After the movie he had about two hours before the watch and elected for a short nap.

It was still hot in the JO Bunkroom from the day's bright sun but he knew that soon the room would be cold. It smelled foul from sweat and poor ventilation as he lay in his bunk clad only in underwear, called skivvies by Navy men, with a wool blanket under him absorbing his sweat as always but soon it would be needed over him. His pillow case was damp and smelled with two more days before the regular weekly linen change and there was a constant high noise level as blowers tried to force clean air into the ship while others labored to draw foul air out. The smell of stale sweat and the heat brought Shielbrock's memory back to the washroom behind the dugout at the ball park in Stratford, Ontario. There he had been sweat-soaked and he ached all over. Someone was calling his name, "—Shielbrock, Mister Shielbrock!" And he returned to reality. It was the bridge messenger. "Mr. Shielbrock, the OOD wants you to call him."

"Okay. Thanks."

"You awake?" The more experienced messengers learned to be sure as often a person awakened from sound sleep fell off to sleep again as soon as the messenger turned away.

"I've got it. Thanks. I'm awake." The messenger watched him switch on the bunk light, select the correct station on the sound powered phone and crank the handle of the howler.

"A guy punched out of a corsair north of us," said the OOD. "Get both boats ready for a SAR mission. We'll be in the area in about an hour and a half."

"Roger. On the way," answered Shielbrock.

Pale filtered moonlight showed through the thin solid over cast, so that given enough time one's night vision enabled a distinction of objects. The destroyer Robinson had taken station in the center of the search area and the plan was for boat number one to search to the west, boat number two to the east and Shielbrock would be in boat number two. To the north, the destroyer Laffey from Support Station Baker was already searching with her boats.

Two corsairs had conducted a close air support mission for troops ashore and one had been hit by ground fire, made it over water and the pilot had to bail out. Punch out they called it. His wingman saw a good parachute, followed it down and stayed as long as his fuel allowed, reporting continuous positioning, but even with that much good information it was difficult to locate a man in the water at night. The seas had picked up slightly with an increase in the wind while CIC had worked out search plans and researched survival information. Wind, current and time late had been briefed as boat crews were told about survival in the water, "—this temperature—three hours senses dulled,—four hours numbed,—loss of response,—comatose, six hours, maybe eight, death." With daylight they might get a helicopter if the weather was good, but daylight was about six hours away and the weather report was not good.

The pilot had already been in the water for about two hours as the boats went into the water and Boat Two, Ensign Martin Shielbrock boat officer, moved out to the east, fifteen miles the plan called for, then an expanding square search plan. He knew they would be off the destroyer's radar on the far eastern legs of their search and ordered the boat coxswain out to twenty miles before starting the expanding square search plan. "We'll cover more area that way."

"Yes sir." The boat coxswain was Boatswain Mate Third Class Audrey Reeder from Davenport, Iowa. He was in Shielbrock's Deck Division as was the Bow Hook, Seaman Robert Anderson of Duluth, Minnesota, and a lookout, Seaman Richard Harkness from Birmingham, Alabama. The rest of the boat crew consisted of a boat engineer, Engineman Third Class Mitchell Fornier, and Signalman Third Class Kip O'Brien. The six of them; Shielbrock, Reeder, Anderson, Harkness, Fornier and O'Brien were searching for a needle in a haystack.

They had practiced this search and rescue operation a few times but always in daylight and with flat calm seas, but it was much different at night and the seas which seemed slight from the destroyer deck were magnified in the 26 foot motor whaleboat as it was tossed around in the dark. They were frightened, all of them, as they did what they were trained to do, crawling and kneeling in positions around the bouncing boat, staring into the dark, listening, waiting, hanging on. All wore heavy thick kapok life jackets, belted around their chests and under their legs and the kapok padding kept them warm and also served as cushions as they were often tossed off balance, falling in the boat. Lines, lanterns, signal flares, flags, radio, hooks, chains, life rings, blankets, and life jackets all had to be secured as the boat rose and fell over the swells and rolled first one way and then the other and Shielbrock wondered if they could ever find anything from this bouncing tossing matchbox on the sea, including their way back to the ship.

"Keep your eyes moving slowly sideways just below the horizon. Listen. Don't talk. Concentrate," he reminded the boat crew. On a small plastic board secured to his life jacket by a short cord he kept a rough search plan with a grease pencil, the Navy word for crayon, but soon he found that salt water splashing over the plastic made writing or marking impossible, so with a government issued ball point pen he kept the search plan on the palm of his hand. Five minutes due east, five minutes due south, ten minutes due west, ten minutes due north, fifteen minutes east, fifteen minutes south, twenty minutes west, twenty north, twenty five east, twenty five south. Two hours into the search and, by Shielbrock's calculations on the palm of his left hand, they had just turned north for a thirty minute leg across the general direction of their parent ship, Robinson, when a try to raise the ship by radio brought no response.

They soon learned that north headings were the smoothest for that seemed to be the direction of wind and wave movement but on east or west headings the boat rolled unmercifully and on south headings they fought the seas, banging into then over the peaks, and then down the swells into valleys on the sea surface. The diesel engine maintained a steady drone except when the boat rode over a swell and the propeller raced from lack of resistance, and equipment slid and banged from one side of the boat to the other, but gradually, piece by piece, the crew secured the loose material and after the first couple of hours almost everything was held in place. There was no way to stop the spray and the splashing as everything and everyone in the boat was soaked with cold salt water. It got in their eyes and they could feel it on their faces and taste it in their mouths and their pants were soaked and their legs were cold as they tightened their kapok life jackets for warmth.

"We got any fuckin' water?" The Bow Hook asked.

"A whole ocean of it," replied the coxs'n.

"I gotta wash out this fuckin' salt taste."

"Forget it. We open the water and the salt gets in it."

"Then what fuckin' good is the fuckin' water?"

"It ain't no good. Forget it, I said."

Shielbrock tried to explain, as young officers so often do to bring what they see as reason into enlisted men's conversation. "Look, Anderson, like Reeder said, we carry drinking water but as soon as we open it tonight it would become contaminated with salt water. So it would be best if we could all just do without for awhile. Okay?"

"Yeah, that's what Reeder said."

Shielbrock wondered why he had tried to explain what the coxs'n had said.

Three hours into the search, and five minutes away from a south heading, Shielbrock noted the increase in wind and sea. The whole Sea of Japan seemed to be moving north, he thought, and if we run our full plan, the south headings must be taking us away from the direction that these seas would carry the corsair pilot, so he decided to cut the south leg, which should have been thirty-five minutes, to fifteen. He would then search west, roughly across the origin of their search plan, for forty minutes, then north into waters not previously searched. Fifteen minutes into the south heading he ordered the coxs'n to come right to a west heading and coxs'n, signalman and bow hook were surprised, calling out, "It ain't time yet. We got another twenty minutes at least on this leg."

"Y'can't break up the square, Mister Shielbrock. Y'gotta stay with the plan."

"Yeah, Y'gotta stay with the plan."

Shielbrock listened to their protests then explained his reasoning, ending with, "—and I know I'm violating the search plan but with all this sea and wind movement to the north I want to search up there more."

Four hours they had been searching and by Shielbrock's palm of the hand plot they were over toward the west, toward Robinson, when the radio cackled, "Boat Two this is Spider. Over." Spider was Robinson's voice call.

Shielbrock grabbed the handset, "This is Boat Two. Roger. Over."

"This is Spider. Been trying to raise you for the last hour. Boat recall. Boat recall. What is your status? Over."

The men in the boat crew were instantly pleased with the prospect of going home to their ship as Shielbrock responded. "This is Boat Two. Do not understand recall. Has object been recovered? Boat Two riding nicely continuing search. Over."

The voice from Robinson grew a little more intense. "This is Spider. Object has not been recovered. Boat One terminated search due to adverse conditions. You are to terminate and return to ship. Spider is closing your search area. Over."

"This is Boat Two. I have two more key legs on present search plan. Will then close Spider. Out."

"This is Spider. Negative. Terminate search and re—," Click.

Shielbrock had switched off the radio and five wet cold tired faces stared at him in amazement. "Imagine that! Those pussies in Boat One thought that this was too rough. Some poor son of a bitch has been out here in this cold water for five hours and they're too uncomfortable to search. Fuck 'em. We're gonna find him. Turn north, Reeder." The men understood that language.

Reeder called out, "Yes, sir! All right you guys, keep a sharp eye." Then in a monotone, "—fuckin' pussies."

Twenty minutes later, the farthest north they had been, they turned east, away from their ship. Forty minutes more, they had been searching for five hours, instead of turning south Shielbrock directed the boat further north and after five and a half hours the gray light of a still distant dawn showed them a little more of the tossed seas as more spray was carried by the wind and the boat rolled more than ever.

Harkness pointed into the grey darkness, "I think there's somethin' out there!"

Four of them scrambled on their knees to his position, "I see somethin', too."

"Get a light out there."

"Yeah, there's some stuff on the water."

"See?"

"It's a bunch of stuff. It comes and goes."

"There!"

Shielbrock also saw something on the water and directed the coxs'n, "Over to the right a little more, Reeder, a little more. That's good. Slow down." A few more seconds elapsed, "Slow down some more. Okay."

All of them studied the surface of the water ahead trying to figure out what it was. Spread out over a small area, a film-like covering with only a few objects or protrusions showed above the surface but it was still too dark to see clearly and their search light was no help. Then Shielbrock saw what it was, "It's a parachute! Reeder, don't go into it. It'll foul our screw. Come further to the right. Circle it." A little more daylight helped and after a pause, "There! There's a guy over on the other side!"

They all shouted with no response. "Is he alive?" They couldn't tell. Six hours comatose, eight hours maybe death, Shielbrock tried to remember the briefing. It didn't matter. He pulled the straps off his kapok life jacket and pulled off his shoes. "Reeder, I'm going after him. He might be caught in the chute lines or unconscious. You circle around and come in from the other side. Stay clear of the chute."

"Aye aye, sir."

Shielbrock pulled the sheath knife that hung on Harkness's belt, put it in his own belt and went over the side as Harkness objected, "Hey, my Buck knife, careful!" and Reeder called out, "Your kapok—," But Shielbrock had paid no attention to either one. The water was ice cold as he swam toward the solitary figure floating on the other side of the parachute and soon he could feel the restriction to his progress as he encountered the silky nylon in the water. Easing his way through, the thin nylon wanted to cling to him, but he slipped along through it and as he could feel thin strong nylon lines he was careful not to become entwined. Even so, some spaghetti-like lines wrapped around his left leg and he couldn't push them clear so carefully he took Harkness' knife and cut the lines, moving clear once more. Getting close to the figure in the water, both of them rising and falling in the chop and swell, he could see the man's head and a portion of his chest above the water.

Pilots wore inflatable life vests, not the clumsy bulky kapok jackets worn by surface ship sailors. Pilots' vests were called Mae Wests because when inflated they resembled, with some considerable imagination, the breasts of the famous performer but in this case only the right breast was fully inflated, the left was rather more like Twiggy, but just enough to keep the pilot's head out of the water but over to one side. Shielbrock yelled to him with no response. Continuing to work his way closer, there were more nylon lines, more cutting, a little closer and he could still hear the boat engine as Reeder circled to the far side. Closer now to the pilot, close enough to talk, but no response, then close enough to touch, but no response. Was he alive? No time to find out as Shielbrock felt along the pilot's body under the water and, sure enough, nylon lines were wrapped around him. He cut them away carefully and started to pull the pilot free. A movement! Did this guy really make a movement? He didn't know, maybe it was imagination.

Working his way around and behind the pilot, Shielbrock put his left arm across the man's chest and swam clear of the parachute, using his right arm, just like he had learned in Boy Scouts, and every stroke brought a shot of pain up and down the right side of his back. Ahead was Boat Two coming toward them and as a life ring splashed close ahead, he grabbed it, hooked his right arm through still holding the pilot with his left and yelled, "Pull! Pull!" and he could feel the rapid motion through the water. Alongside the boat, strong eager hands grabbed the inert body of the pilot and lifted him clear of the water, over the combing and into the rolling boat.

"Cover him! Wrap him in blankets," yelled Shielbrock.

As the boat crew dragged Shielbrock on board he groaned with pain as they dragged him across the combing and into the boat. That damn back again. Stratford, Ontario.

"All the blankets are wet, all soaked," Fornier and Harkness were kneeling on the deck grating in a couple of inches of sloshing water, sorting through the blankets.

"Use them anyway," ordered Shielbrock, also on his knees and holding onto the rolling boat. "That's all we have. We've gotta try to get him warm. Reeder, head west! O'Brien, shoot a green flare high but generally toward the west. Harkness, get on the radio and raise the ship. Fornier, you and Anderson wrap that guy with all the blankets you can, and put him alongside the engine compartment. Get his legs up higher than his head."

All sprang to do as told and Shielbrock dug under the forward seats for a life jacket. Cold in the water, now in the wind he was much colder. By the time he strapped on the heavy padded kapok life jacket Harkness had the ship on the radio and Shielbrock took the handset. "Spider this is

Boat Two, Navy pilot onboard. Condition unknown. Comatose or dead. Heading west. Firing flares every five minutes. Find me. We may be able to save him. Over."

"This is Spider. Roger. Continue west and continue with flares. Out."

"You hear that, O'Brien? A flare every five minutes." The signalman nodded. "Fornier, any response? Any movement?" Every move from one part of the boat to another had to be accomplished by crawling and hanging on to railings, supports or seats as Shielbrock snaked over to the heavily wrapped body alongside the engine box where it was warmer.

"No movement, Mister Shielbrock, I think he might be dead."

Shielbrock put his face up close to the pilot's. Was he breathing? He couldn't tell so he pulled the pilot's eyelid open, but with the poor gray light and constant rolling couldn't detect any eye movement. Artificial respiration? It was too rough in the boat. He put his mouth against the pilot's ear, "You're gonna be okay, friend. We're gonna have you dry and warm in a little while." No response as he tried again, "Hey, I gotta know your name. I've gotta report that you're okay. What's your name?"

"He moved!" Fornier yelled.

Shielbrock held up his hand, a futile gesture signaling silence, and spoke again into the pilot's ear. "What's your name?"

The pilot's mouth moved and there was eye movement but they remained closed, but then in a whisper, "T,—t,—tale,—Taylor, Taylor."

"Okay, Taylor!" Shielbrock yelled with joy, "What's your first name?"

A long pause as the boat rolled from one side to the other and crashed crazily over one swell and down into another as the diesel engine droned on and cold salt spray covered them all.

"Dick. Dick Taylor," the pilot whispered.

"Okay Dick Taylor! Now, what squadron do you fly with?" Shielbrock wanted to get him talking but a longer pause followed as O'Brien fired another flare and the boat crashed into another swell jarring them all and more salt water splashed over them. The diesel continued to roar and Shielbrock continued to shiver. "Richard J. Taylor, Lieutenant, U.S. Navy, 564782," barely audible.

"Jesus!" Shielbrock sat up. "He thinks he's been taken prisoner or something, so he's giving his name, rank and serial number." Then to the pilot, "Okay, Lieutenant Taylor, you just rest right there and we'll have you nice and dry in a little while." On the bouncing rolling deck and in the cold wet blankets, Shielbrock thought aloud, "That is if we can find the ship."

"Spider this is Boat Two. Recovered Lieutenant Richard J. Taylor, 564782. He gave me that info. He's alive but seems to be in shock or something like it. Over."

"This is Spider. Roger. Interrogative 'in shock or something like it.' Over."

"This is Boat Two. How the hell do I know? I'm no doctor. Like hypothermia. Over."

"This is Spider. Roger. Are you still firing flares? Over."

This is Boat Two. That's affirm. Firing flare every five. Over."

"This is Spider. Roger. No joy. Out."

They bounced along a few more minutes, cold, wet and tired as another flare was fired.

"Boat Two this is Spider. Sighted your flare. Coming toward you." The men in the boat cheered. "Come to course two five five magnetic to close us. Over."

Shielbrock gave a "Roger," directed Reeder to the new course, and put his mouth to Lieutenant Taylor's ear. "Okay, Lieutenant, you'll be warm and dry in a little while. Hang on." He thought he could see a slight smile on Taylor's pale face.

Shielbrock was shivering with cold and his right shoulder and side ached from the familiar Canadian pain. He had forgotten about the knife in his belt as the boat crew had pulled him in, dragging him across the boat combing. He had also forgotten the brief warning from Harkness, "careful," and that Buck knife, so carefully honed to a razor's edge, had pushed its way through his belt and pants, into his left femoral region cutting into the thigh muscle before it fell into the sea. Blood had run down his leg and across the boat in a trail where he had crawled to the pilot alongside the engine compartment and to his present position with the radio handset. Coxs'n Reeder, cold, wet and tired yet still standing solidly driving the 26 foot motor whaleboat as he had been for the past hours, looked down at Shielbrock crouching alongside and both saw the gaping gash and flowing blood at the same time and both yelled for help.

Shielbrock started to lose consciousness but heard bits and pieces of what seemed to be continuous incoherent orders from Reeder and responses from the others as the engine droned and the boat continued to bounce, roll and pitch. He heard Reeder's orders about first aid box, largest gauze pads, rags, wrapping tight, ace bandages, tarps and helmet liners and he could hear Harkness complaining about losing his Buck knife, finding the right bandages and getting blood all over and, "We need a corpsman!" and Reeder's response, "No shit! He's in the other boat." Shielbrock felt his thigh being wrapped tightly and then himself being wrapped in a heavy canvas as he shivered and waited, thinking that this is what going into shock was like as he fought to remain conscious, managing to get out, "I'll g—, get you another knife, Harkness."

"Yeah, thanks. Ain't no more in the ship's store. That was the last one," was the seaman's sarcastic reply.

After a while Shielbrock sensed the boat turning and felt it ride a little less violently, heard Reeder calling out that the ship had made a lee for them and yelling about catching a sea painter and soon he sensed a change of light as the still bouncing boat was in the shadow of a grey steel wall. Then there were more shouts and noises of rigging as the boat jolted and he felt uplifted, raised, steadied, clear of the sea and then clear of the boat and as he lost consciousness the last he heard was Harkness yelling to his Deck Force shipmates, "—and Mister Shielbrock lost my Buck knife and almost cut his cock off and got blood all over the boat."

Crossing the line, it is called when a ship crosses the equator and those on board, officer and enlisted men, who have crossed before are called Shellbacks, where-as Pollywog is the title for a man who has not been across the equator. The ancient ritual of the sea from sailing ship days includes a rather harsh initiation ceremony administered by Shellbacks to bring into King Neptune's realm of the mysterious ocean deeps those newly ordained as real sailors. After all, a sailorman can dress and act the part, drink, carouse and fight in foreign ports, screw exotic oriental, brown, black, European, Asiatic, and African women, even get tattooed, but until he has "crossed the line" he is not a real sailor, not a Shellback.

Among Shellbacks the biggest fattest belly is bared, covered with mustard, catsup and horseradish along with a liberal dose of lube oil, and each Pollywog, clad in skivvies throughout the ceremony, must kiss "King Neptune's Belly" and to assist in this amorous event the Pollywog's face is pushed deep into the obese belly to eliminate any attempt at a tentative peck. A tunnel to Neptune's realm is formed by a twenty foot tube of canvas, three feet in diameter, filled with weeks of accumulated garbage and into this wet, hot, stinking mess each pollywog crawls, emerging at the other end covered with odiferous scum. The first few are fortunate but those transiting Neptune's tunnel later encounter, in addition to the sticky stinking garbage, the vomit left by earlier transitors, usually causing more of the same and as Ensign Shielbrock followed Seaman Harkness in the garbage tunnel late in the festivities, Harkness paused to cough and vomit and Shielbrock tugged at his leg. "Can I borrow your knife? Maybe we can cut our way out of here."

"Fuck off! I ain't got no knife 'cause a you!"

High pressure fire hoses wash down the filthy Pollywogs while salt water tubs serve for heretic christenings, and there are degrading competitive races and games, with mock drum head justice trials. Heads may be ceremoniously shaved, paint poured on private parts of the initiates and endless verbal abuse is directed at the pollywogs until finally King Neptune accepts the candidates into his realm and declares them to be forever after known as Shellbacks. Oh, but its' fun. Fun?

What is intended as fun frequently is excessive and sometimes ill feelings develop, but in the end everyone, or almost everyone, smiles, relieved that the big event is over and that the ship is rid of Pollywogs, filled only with real men of the sea, Shellbacks, all content that it is a once in a lifetime ordeal.

After six months of the Korean War they started the journey home, to Norfolk, Virginia, and while at sea Ensign Martin Shielbrock served his thirty day restriction to the ship, but at Naples, Italy, Shielbrock was able to get ashore long enough to find a new Buck knife for Harkness. The meaningless restriction (they were at sea), along with a letter of reprimand (that was removed from his record), had been imposed on him by Captain Speakes for disregard of orders on the SAR mission, failure to follow the search plan, taking off his life jacket and damaging government property (his cut leg), while at the same time Speakes submitted a recommendation for him to receive the Legion of Merit medal for the rescue of Lieutenant Taylor. When USS Robinson (DD 562) crossed the equator just south of Singapore at 103 degrees 55 minutes 16 seconds East Longitude, Ensign Martin D. Shielbrock, USNR, became a Shellback and the name stuck.

CHAPTER 2

Before Barney could go on or Steve could comment Ellie saw a chance to get into the story-telling. "So let's see, Steven's Dad came back from the Korean thing with a new name and he came to Norfolk, right?" The others all agreed. "Now, that has to be where he met Barbara. And who would know that part of the story better than Barbara's room-mate? None other than our very own Mom who at that time was known as Jackie Simpson! I've heard it a few times but Steven hasn't so, Mom, why don't you team up with Dad on this one and let's hear about what it was like in Norfolk when the newly named Shellback got back there.

NEWLY NAMED SHELLBACK IN NORFOLK

The three B's existed in Norfolk; beer, broads and in this case basketball instead of baseball. Martin Shielbrock and Barney Williams played basketball for the destroyer flotilla team along with Barney's shipmate from the destroyer Waldron, Jim Woolrick.

Barney had graduated from Officer Candidate School two months before Martin. When the destroyer Robinson returned to Norfolk from Korea with the newly named Shellback aboard, Barney was on board Waldron preparing to go to Korea. It was like an extension of college for them, except they had more spending money and although they worked during the day on board their ships, most nights they were free to play ball and to enjoy the local night life. Often after basketball they made the rounds of Norfolk area officer clubs. Often they found girls and often they didn't spend the night on their ships.

Tuesday nights were best at Oceana Naval Air Station, Wednesdays at the Norfolk Naval Base club. On Fridays the Destroyer Escort Piers club had a group of local young ladies and Saturdays saw a packed o'club at the Norfolk Naval Air Station. The sing-along at the Amphib Base attracted a big crowd on Thursday nights and was a favorite of Shellback.

In the early 1950's Norfolk, Virginia, and the area immediately around it made up the largest naval base complex in the world. Hundreds of navy ships were home-ported at the Naval Base there. It was the location at the Commander in Chief of the U.S. Atlantic Fleet and numerous other commands. There were two major naval air stations in the area, the largest naval shipyard, many Navy schools, communications stations and amphibious warfare activities. Sailors out-numbered single girls 50 to 1 and single officers out numbered good-looking college girls more than that ratio, but then all girls were pretty, some just more than others. Norfolk girls fell into two basic categories; enlisted men's' girls and officers' girls. Now, there was no agency to keep this rule and there were many that passed over and back but basically Norfolk girls stayed in one camp or the other.

Barbara Muir had come to Norfolk after graduating from the University of Alabama in 1952. Her friend Jackie Simpson had graduated the year before and had come to Norfolk as a result of job hunting as a business major. Jackie's job had been a disappointment but she stayed with it because of the great social life Norfolk offered and it was that social life that attracted Barbara, who soon found a job in a fashionable department store and shared an apartment with Jackie.

There had been boys in Barbara's life before she came to Norfolk, a couple of teen-age romances in high school at Enterprise, Alabama, and a number of young men during college had held her attention for brief periods of time. There had been sorority and fraternity parties, football weekends and proms which seemed so important at the time, sexual fumbling, experiments and wrestling in cars, on beaches and in hotel rooms but none of it had been particularly satisfying or pleasurable and she learned, if anything, to search for something better.

In Norfolk there were naval officers, countless naval officers and through her life and Jackie's they came and went in a continuous flow. Tall, short, talkative, quiet, funny and serious, they came from all parts of the country and all ethnic backgrounds. There were naval aviators who flew from the decks of aircraft carriers and tried to act dashing and bold, submarine officers quiet, serious and studious, and destroyer officers who could be anything or nothing. She learned their differences and the terminology of their lifestyle so if an officer's ship was in port for upkeep it meant that he would be around for a week or two, while overhaul meant a few months. If his ship was about to deploy he would be away for many months; forget him and find someone else, someone who would be around to take you to dinner and dancing.

In those years Norfolk was a dry town, no liquor was sold in bars or restaurants, so there were very few, if any, good restaurants. The officers clubs sold liquor, beer and wine, served excellent food, and provided the best dancing, often to name bands. There were a few, very few, private clubs in Norfolk and a few country clubs, but these were available only to members and membership was generally limited to the wealthy.

Officers clubs in and around Norfolk formed the basis of Barbara's and Jackie's social lives and often they double-dated, always they met other men; friends or shipmates of their dates. The girls knew that they could go out seven nights a week if they chose, each night to a place of their choosing and probably each night with a different officer. Rank meant nothing to the girls. Ensigns to lieutenant commanders, they dated an occasional commander, and once Jackie went out with a captain. Little sex was involved in these dates as the girls didn't allow it on a first or second date and usually more, and they didn't date these officers many times before they moved on to another admirer.

In addition to the naval officers, Barbara occasionally went out with a young man from work. Peter Tomaselli was the assistant manager of the shoe department at Loffman's, where Barbara worked in the Ladies' Attire department. Peter was fun to be with, belonged to a private club and told her a lot about the store; who was whom and how to get along. He was ambitious and hoped to rise in the store's hierarchy. Peter's club was not as large or as elaborate as the officer clubs, but the service was good, it was quiet and a small combo provided nice music for dancing.

After cocktails and dinner one Saturday night, they had just returned to their table when a tall, very distinguished looking older man approached. "Oh, Jesus, he's heading this way," whispered Peter as he rose.

"Peter Tomaselli! How nice to see you here. I thought I saw you out on the dance floor, and this is our new young lady in Ladies Attire, I believe, Miss Muir?"

"Good evening, Mr. Loffman. Yes, this is Miss Muir." Peter and Loffman shook hands. "Delighted to meet you, my dear," Loffman took the hand Barbara extended.

"It's a pleasure, Mr. Loffman, but I'm not so new. I've been at Loffman's for about four months."

"Has it been four months? I should have known and I should have met you before. I'm at fault, forgive me but I'm very pleased that you're with us. You add so much to the department."

"Thank you. I enjoy it." Barbara smiled, and she knew her smile was not lost on Loffman. God, but he had beautiful blue eyes, and his eyes were definitely on her.

"Well, it's nice to see both of you. Enjoy yourselves," and he was off.

"Jesus! That's Loffman himself, you know," explained Peter, "He and his two brothers own the store. Their father started it. I didn't know he knew me. I've met him twice but I didn't think he'd remember me and he sure knew you."

"Is he married?"

"Yeah, I think his wife has some medical problems, sick all the time."

A few minutes later the waiter brought them a bottle of champagne in an ice bucket, served it with all the proper ceremony and stated simply, "Compliments of Mr. Loffman."

"Dom Perignom!" exclaimed Peter, "The guy sure has class. Y'gotta admit that. This musta cost at least fifty bucks."

"Yes, he is rather charming," Barbara quietly agreed, sipping the champagne. "This is very nice."

Loffman returned to their table later and Peter thanked him for the champagne.

"You're very welcome. Hope you enjoy it. Peter, would you mind if I asked Miss Muir to dance?"

"Not at all."

"Miss Muir, would you do me the honor?" Those beautiful blue eyes were on her again and she was quick to accept.

On the dance floor she was surprised to find that he was an excellent dancer and he led with a firm right arm, not too close, as they glided around the small floor. They made light talk about the club, the music, the combo and the store and she was flattered by his attention.

"You are an excellent dancer," He said. "You probably get a lot of practice with naval officers at the o'clubs, I would guess."

She laughed, "I suppose that's to be expected in Norfolk, isn't it?"

"For an intelligent, good looking woman like you, sure." He moved her away from him slightly as they danced, so that he could look directly at her with those eyes, "And you are a beautiful woman."

Only slightly embarrassed, but rather pleased, she drew herself closer to him to escape those eyes. "Thank you."

The song was near the end. "Barbara, I hope I'm not embarrassing you, but I would be very pleased, I would be honored, if you would have dinner with me sometime soon." They danced in silence a few seconds and as the song ended she moved back, still in his arms and looked at him, "Why, I'd be delighted to have dinner with you."

Sunday, a dozen long stemmed roses were delivered to her apartment and a simple card read, "I hope that Tuesday is acceptable for dinner. A taxi will call for you at 8. Jules."

"Barbara, are you crazy?" Jackie was angry. "He's old enough to be your father and he's married. What the hell are you doing?"

"He's not old enough to be my father. He's charming, attractive and intelligent, and I want to see what it would be like to have dinner with him, that's all. Don't get all upset."

On Tuesday she found that he was nineteen years older than she. His wife had been in and out of hospitals for cancer operations and treatment over the past ten years and they had no children. He lived a rather lonely home life, traveled a good deal and spent most of his time with friends and his wife never accompanied him. He was even more charming than she had expected from their dance and more intelligent. An art connoisseur, he wore expensive tailor made clothing, played golf and tennis, enjoyed deep sea fishing and knew the best restaurants and clubs in most cities. He lived very well.

Dinner was at a private club that Barbara had not heard of before. Elegance, dim light and excellent food was served and continuous but discreet service was provided by a waiter who obviously knew Jules Loffman. Jules asked Barbara if she liked seafood and when she said yes he proceeded to order the entire meal. There were cocktails before dinner, wine carefully selected and sampled, after dinner drinks and soft music. In Barbara's memory it was the most elegant dinner she had ever had and she told Jules Loffman so.

His eyes, directly across the table, held her captive. "I hope that you will allow me to take you to dinner again, many times, here and elsewhere."

"I'm looking forward to it." Her own reply surprised her.

Explanation and apology for the need of discretion followed. After all, even though he had little direct contact or involvement with his wife, they did share the same house and they did make appearances of living together. Barbara interrupted his explanation, "Please. Don't, Jules. I understand. No apology is necessary." and nothing more was said on the subject.

They did have dinner again, on a number of Tuesdays, at that same club and elsewhere, and there were gifts; a gold bracelet that first dinner, a matching necklace the third. An angora sweater, a semi-precious broach and perfume followed.

Each Tuesday night dinner date started with a taxi calling for Barbara and taking her to a restaurant or club to meet Jules Loffman for dinner. He would drive her back to her apartment and usually give her a gift and after a kiss in the car, he would walk her to the door and depart.

Barbara still went out with naval officers, but not as often, maybe once a week, usually doubling as a favor to Jackie. It was fun, but not as interesting as a dinner with Jules.

They had been out almost every Tuesday night for three months, when Jules asked her to accompany him on a short business trip to Richmond. Over Jackie's protests and warnings Barbara went and they stayed one night in the same hotel, each in a separate room.

In Norfolk the next day a beautiful blue silk dress was delivered to the apartment for Barbara from Cheza-Peake Fashions, a ladies clothing store which Barbara knew to be one of the most expensive in town and later Jules told her that he owned the store and suggested that she look at it some time as he gave her a card.

Barbara entered the shop and was immediately impressed with its elegance. Donna, the manager, looked at Jules' card and showed immediate and sincere interest. For the next hour she showed Barbara dresses, suits, shoes, accessories, giving advice, discussing styles and fashions all focused on what looked best for Barbara. Whenever Barbara looked for a price tag or asked about the cost, Donna put it aside with, "Don't worry about that," or "That doesn't apply to you." In fact, Barbara learned finally that anything in the store was available to her for twenty five percent of the marked price. This meant that she could dress herself in clothing from Cheza-Peake Fashions for less than the Loffman's store, even with her employees' discount. Delighted, for her next dinner date with Jules she wore a new outfit completely from Cheza-Peake.

He told her of a hair dresser used by his store for fashion shows and she found it to be the best in town. For her the cost was small. She and Jackie had always helped each other do their hair in the past, now she found that once a week at the hair dresser was well worth it. Soon it was twice a week.

Another short business trip, dinner, dancing, a kiss goodnight and separate rooms. A few more Tuesday night dinner dates, gifts, the kisses a little more serious but nothing more. Jules took her to the most elegant places and they were a striking impressive couple. Both tall; a forty one year old distinguished gentleman with a twenty-two year old blonde beauty, both attired in the most fashionable expensive clothes. Strangers looked to see if they were movie stars.

They had flown to Atlanta for the weekend, where the Loffman brothers were involved in the purchase of a department store. After dinner and dancing, Jules walked her to her room. Pausing at the door, Barbara thanked him for a lovely evening. Another pause, "Let me show you something." He stepped into her room.

Spread out on the bed were a beautiful lace and silk negligee and nightgown in pale blue. "These are beautiful!" She gathered them in her arms. "Oh, Jules, these are so lovely, I don't have anything like this, nothing so nice, and," she went to him, "there's no one as nice as you. You are a darling." They kissed. He started toward the door then hesitated. "Look. You see this door?" Along the side wall of the room she hadn't noticed as a chair was in front of it. He moved the chair aside. "My room is on the other side of that door. The door locks from both sides. Right now this side, your side, is locked. My side is unlocked and it will remain so all night." He walked out.

Barbara stood in the middle of the room a few minutes, holding the nightgown and negligee. She looked at the locked door connecting her room to Jules'.

Slowly she undressed, showered, powdered herself, put on the nightgown and negligee, did her hair and make-up, and checked herself in the mirror. Satisfied, she unlocked the door and walked into Jules' room.

Moonlight through the open draperies at the far end of the room provided dim light. Soft music was playing.

Jules had been sitting on the sofa in front of the windows, wearing a gold dressing gown. The moonlight silhouetted him as he rose.

"You expected me?" she asked.

"I had hoped."

"If you hoped, why haven't you done more before now?"

"I wanted you to be sure. I didn't want to pressure or force you. I didn't know if there was a real attraction, for you, I mean."

"Did you think that I would go out with you as often as I have, that I would go away with you as I have, unless there was an attraction?"

"As I said, I had hoped."

Still standing, she sipped the champagne, put down the glass and went to him. Close, tightly, they held each other, kissing with a passion, releasing that which had been held back over the months. In bed, he was gentle, but not too gentle and Barbara experienced thrills and pleasure she had never known before or imagined. Hands, fingers, mouth and tongue explored her, excited her, lifted her to magnificent heights. Released, she immersed in pleasure and it started again. At the top of her mountain of pleasure his tongue caused her to leap with joy and again when she thought it had been the ultimate, there was still more.

Not realizing that she had been expressing her feelings she heard him whisper, "Oh, no, my darling, that is not the ultimate. There is more for you, much more," and he continued kissing, stroking, handling. He was right. Climbing even higher she was plunged into an abyss of pleasure and delight beyond those before. He entered her then, deep, strong and hard, with long slow strokes and just when her delight and pleasure had taken her into ecstasy, she felt him release and gasp with pleasure and she too released. Tightly they held each other, trying to maintain the moment as long as possible, then fell exhausted, complete.

Dislocated, not caring what time it was or where, she felt him come to her again and thrilled as in the beginning. She loved the feeling of his tongue. She loved what he did to and with her. She loved him as he very gradually brought her down from the clouds in which she had been floating to the restful comfort and warmth of his bed. His kisses worked across her stomach, her breasts, her neck, to her mouth and she delighted in the taste of her own pleasure that it carried. To her ear his mouth moved and he whispered, "You are an exquisitely delightful woman, Barbara Muir, and I am hopelessly, desperately in love with you."

His ear was next to her mouth, also. "I'm in love with you, too, you darling foolish man. Please, I beg you, don't deny me this togetherness anymore."

"I promise, my darling. There'll be this and more."

There was more. One weekend each month they went away together, no longer staying in separate rooms. From Jules, Barbara learned the myriad lovemaking activities she could perform which conveyed pleasures to him comparable to those he imparted to her.

In Norfolk their Tuesday night dinner dates continued with discretion and reserve. Never entering her apartment, Jules often sent flowers and other gifts. Barbara had stopped dating naval officers, but Jackie continued to urge, even harass her to join the social activities at the officers clubs.

She had been seeing Jules Loffman for almost a year when his wife went into the hospital. It was serious. Visiting his wife every day at the hospital, Jules saw nothing of Barbara for over a month. During that time, under constant pressure from Jackie, Barbara started to question in her own mind her status and future. When finally she and Jules went to dinner, he discussed his situation. In spite of the age difference he wanted to marry Barbara but couldn't divorce his ailing wife. Her case was terminal but there was really no time estimate. His wife was out of the hospital, at home with daily nursing care and it could go on for months or even years. Barbara would marry him immediately if he was free and still wanted her, but if all she could have was their part time love affair she would settle for that, but deep down inside Barbara had her doubts.

At work, in the Ladies Attire department of Loffman's, Barbara was very successful and very popular. Hired as a college graduate into the store's Executive Development Program, she was expected to work in a department for an unspecified time after which she could expect to become an assistant manager of a department, then a manager and possibly on to positions as a group supervisor or in purchasing, or marketing.

Very quickly she demonstrated a keen sense of business, style and taste. Customers asked for her advice. Never too busy to explain color coordination, fabrics and proper accessories, she gave advice on what would be appropriate to wear to specific events. Older wealthy women valued her recommendations, young women sought her advice. Girls marveled at her charm and poise. When a few of the more discriminating and wealthy customers were unable to find what they wanted at Loffman's she sent them to Cheza-Peake. When an opening came for an assistant manager in the Housewares department she refused, electing to remain in Ladies Attire.

Barbara had wanted a car for some time. The bus was convenient to and from work and grocery shopping was within walking distance of the apartment. Always there were young officers with cars to help with the errands that Jackie and she needed. Over the past few months, though, she had developed a desire to have her own transportation. After a number of visits to various dealers she settled on a Ford two tone convertible. Jules insisted on arranging the transaction and the financing, he brought her a pile of papers which she signed without reading and a few days later she had her convertible, financed with reasonable monthly payments, licensed and insured. Jules had offered to buy the car for her but Barbara insisted that she pay. Each month she sent $110 to the First Bank of Norfolk.

To Barbara, choosing a car was like selecting a dress or a coat. It had to match her hair and coloring and it had to go well with her other clothing. The car was a part of her apparel. Light blue and cream, the convertible driven by the striking blonde wearing a blue and cream ensemble caused heads to turn wherever she went, as surely as they did when she walked into a restaurant.

Often Barbara and Jules discussed marketing, advertising, merchandise display, convenience of charge accounts, fashions and sales technique. Amazed at the depth of understanding Barbara displayed, Jules sought her views and advice and was never disappointed. To Barbara, Jules was a fascinating resource of knowledge on the business of store management, buying and finance. Together their discussions covered the full range of interests in the running of a modern fashionable department store. Barbara understood what the customer wanted and had learned well the sales aspects. Jules had experienced and studied the management aspects.

Once, Jules tried to convince Barbara of the value of "selling up", that is getting a customer to buy an item more expensive than originally intended. Barbara laughed at the idea. "Jules, that's simplistic. It's easy to sell up and its good basic sales procedure but I like to think beyond that. Rather than up, I use a more sophisticated technique. I call it 'multi-dimensional'."

"Multi-dimensional?"

"Yes, Mister Know-it-all. Let me give you an example. A few weeks ago an admiral's wife came into the store for a dress. She needed it for an afternoon garden party and had fifty dollars available. We found two, one was forty dollars, the other sixty. It would have been easy for me to sell her the sixty dollar dress and she would have left the store pleased and only slightly guilty with having exceeded her budget by ten dollars."

"Sounds like you missed, or the store missed out on twenty dollars."

"Foolish man. I am not finished yet with Mrs. Admiral."

"Sorry, go on."

"I accompanied her to the shoe department, then for a purse, gloves, earrings, a hat, total one hundred thirty three dollars, all but the forty dollar dress on a newly opened charge account."

Jules was truly amazed. "That's great!"

Barbara continued, "That's not all. First, the customer was delighted, second the store did more business, third the husband was pleased because his wife was such a hit at the garden party (maybe it helped get him promoted or something), and fourth another admiral's wife came in last week, sent by the original wife, asked for me by name and wanted an outfit herself."

"And what did you sell her?"

"Nothing. She had more money so I sent her to Cheza-Peake where Donna sold her over three hundred dollars worth of merchandise." They both laughed.

Their Tuesday dinner dates and weekend trysts continued and were delightful. Never tiring of the elegant restaurants and plush hotels, Barbara enjoyed being treated as a lady and had assumed an outwardly casual attitude, as if she took all the elegance and attention for granted. Expecting proper treatment, she could identify laxity or incorrect service and had developed the most subtle means of expressing discomfort or dissatisfaction; a hand gesture, a raised eyebrow, a movement of the head. Barbara had become, in brief, and elegant snob at the age of twenty three, and for her twenty third birthday Jules gave her a full length mink coat.

"Jules, the coat is exquisite, it really is, you know that, but I told you when I was buying the car, you've got to stop these gifts. I adore you and I love the thought, but how do you think it makes me feel? I am, in fact, your mistress. Please, let me keep just a little self respect. I get along well enough on my salary at the store, and I do work well and hard and earn it on my own. Please,—" Jules interrupted. "You are not my mistress, Barbara, please don't say that."

Then it was Barbara who interrupted, "What would you call me, if not your mistress? What do you think other people call me?"

"I don't care about other people. I love you and I like to do nice things for you, to you and with you, and—."

"—and I love you, too, and enjoy being with you but please, Jules, stop the gifts." Then after a short silence she added, "Being with you, whenever we can, is gift enough." But to herself, deep down, Barbara was asking herself if that was really enough.

Doubt grew and enabled Barbara to yield to Jackie's pressure a few weeks later, agreeing to join Jackie and her officer friend and attend the Supply Corps Officers' Ball with an officer she had gone out with a year before. Lieutenant Richard Maverhill was a supply officer on the aircraft carrier Intrepid. His ship was scheduled to deploy to Korea for many months, departing Norfolk two weeks after the Ball and Barbara reasoned that she could go out with Richard and then he would leave for a long time soon after so that she would have no lasting problem with him.

At the Naval Operating Base the Ball was a huge success and Barbara had a wonderful time. She had almost forgotten the attention that she attracted from the young officers and was very pleased and flattered. She danced almost every dance with Richard or his friends or shipmates, and they all looked and acted so gallant in their white uniforms as they asked about her, flattered her and talked about their impending involvement in the Korean War.

The following week, just a few days before his ship was scheduled to deploy, Barbara and Richard joined Jackie and some friends for a very informal dinner and evening at the Amphibious Base Officer's Club. Downstairs, the club did not require coats and tie and was known as a haven for junior officers. Often the large room was filled with noise and smoke and a piano player led songs, rowdy at times, and for some unknown reason Thursday nights had developed into the most popular night to "sing-along", as it became called. Barbara, Richard and their friends had chosen this particular night at the Amphib Club and it was as expected; crowded, noisy and smoky. All joined in as a club habitué, Joe Sullivan, belted out his favorite, "Steve O'Donnell's Wake."

"There were fighters and blighters
an' Irish dynamiters.
There was beer, gin, whiskey, wine and cake.

There were men in high positions,

There were Irish politicians,

And they all got drunk at Steve O'Donnell's wake."

Joe sang out the chorus in a loud clear tenor accompanied by the two hundred or more club patrons, then by himself in the same voice but with an exaggerated Irish accent, "Oh, Stevie bie, why did y' die, the weepin' widow cried, and they all got drunk at Steve O'Donnell's wake—." The singing continued.

Through the noise, singing and smoke Jackie leaned across the table and asked or yelled to Barbara, "Have you seen those three standing at the bar?" She had to repeat it before Barbara replied.

"Yes. The one in the middle, in the red sweater is okay, but forget the other two." They laughed and turned their attention back to the singing.

The three at the bar had just come in and ordered a pitcher of beer. Feeling fortunate to find space at the bar on a Thursday night, they drank fast and a second pitcher followed. In the middle stood Jim Woolrick, six foot three and 180 pounds wearing a red sweater. This was Jim's last night as an active duty Navy officer for tomorrow he would be released to the inactive Naval Reserve, free to return home and find a civilian job having completed three years of active duty in destroyers including a deployment to the Korean War and another to the Mediterranean Sea.

On his right was his shipmate Barney Williams, five foot ten and a hundred ninety pounds, wearing a tan summer sport jacket, beige shirt and maroon tie. The night out for the three of them was Barney's treat because of Jim's last night in the Navy and also it was the birthday of the third officer, Martin Shielbrock.

Shielbrock was to the left of Jim Woolrick, was six foot three, weighed 180 pounds and wore a white shirt, light blue tie and dark blue lightweight blazer. His hair looked awful, being in a confused state somewhere between a crew cut that had been and a longer hair style that was not yet there.

"Okay," Barney Williams declared. "The dinner was on me because Jim is leaving us and the Navy." He raised his glass, "To my shipmate and team mate Jim Woolrick; Smooth sailing and a following sea." The other two followed suit and they all drank as Barney continued. "Now for my lifelong pal and team mate Martin Shielbrock on his birthday I offer a special gift. For tonight and only tonight, you Martin Shielbrock get to pick out from this room, not one, not two but three, yes three women of your choice. Any three, and I will get you their names and phone numbers." Barney started to look around the club.

"You're crazy as hell. I'll get my own women."

"No, no, really! This is a special deal for you," insisted Barney, "and I've already spotted the first one. That blonde over there is just for you. She doesn't even have to stand up. I can tell she's tall and she fits your 'heels, hose and turned up nose' specification."

Martin Shielbrock had seen her, also. "If you're going to make a move for yourself, good luck, but for me, stay away from that one. I'll take care of her myself."

"With all respect, close brother of mine," Barney's drinks were starting to show, "I have seen you in this kind of action before, with some success and many a failure, but that woman I think is out of your league."

"We'll see."

"Now if you don't want me to arrange her for you, pick another. You have to use your birthday present; three women."

"Okay," Martin looked around and in haste indicated a good looking woman far across the room at a table of four couples. The noise, smoke and singing continued as Barney headed across the room and Shielbrock turned to Jim Woolrick and asked, "What do you think of that one?"

Woolrick leaned over and put his elbows on the bar, looked across his right shoulder toward the blonde and then left toward Shielbrock, "That's a great looking woman. Maybe the best I've seen in here. Do you suppose she's an actress or model or something?"

"Maybe so," Shielbrock's elbows were also on the bar. "I'm going to find out. What do you make of the group she's with?"

"Seems to be with the guy to her right, the one in the camel hair jacket. I don't know any of them at the table. The gal directly across from the blonde is pretty good, too. Saw her when she turned around awhile ago. If I had to guess, I'd say the guys might be supply. One of them yelled something about 'out of stock' when his glass was empty."

"Uh, huh," Shielbrock thought awhile. "You going to try?"

"Not me. I'm leaving tomorrow. Good luck," replied Jim.

"I think I'll catch her coming out of the ladies room." Martin Shielbrock thought aloud.

The noise, smoke and singing continued and over in one corner a glass dropped and broke with a "clop" sound indicating that it had been full as people in the area exclaimed, laughed and moved around. Loud voices and laughter almost drowned out the piano until a popular song was offered and the voices joined in.

A scuffle across the room caught Shielbrock's attention and moving toward it he left Jim and the beer at the bar. Barney was standing face to face looking up at a guy, their mouths running and their facial expressions showing anything but pleasure. Shielbrock couldn't hear the words through the noise but continued to push through the crowd toward the table with the attractive woman that he had earlier hastily indicated to Barney. Facing Barney was a guy clearly very angry as Shielbrock arrived at the table and asked, "What seems to be the trouble?"

"What's it to you? Butt out!"

"This guy is a friend and I'd like to keep him out of trouble if I can."

"Well somebody ought to keep him on a leash. He thinks he can make passes at any woman in the place and this one happens to be my wife."

"Well, I can see why you're mad. I can't blame you for that but you know that a lot of bird-dogging goes on down here. He's had a lot to drink and probably couldn't see her ring. I'll take care of him. Barney, apologize to the man." Shielbrock was between them and started to guide Barney away but he resisted.

"Shiel, this is the woman you pointed—."

"Okay, Barney, that's enough. Let's go."

"Wait," Interrupted the stranger. "The woman you what? What's your part in this?"

"Nothing, nothing. Just a misunderstanding between a couple of guys who both admire a good looking woman, that's all. My compliments to you," and Shielbrock guided Barney away from the troubled table.

"Shiel, I was trying to set her up for you. You pointed her out from the bar."

"I know, Barney, I know. My fault. Just keep moving back to the bar. Everything's okay."

"But I told you I'd set you up with any three women in the place and—."

"I know, Barney. We'll pick out another one." They continued through the crowd back to the bar, passing near the table with the great looking blonde. She and Shielbrock made eye contact for a second and he smiled as she quickly looked away.

Halfway through the next pitcher of beer, the blonde left her table and headed toward the stairs to the ladies room.

"My move," said Shielbrock a couple of minutes later as he left the bar and headed toward the stairs.

Off the lobby at the top of the wide carpeted stairs was the ladies room and halfway up was a landing where the stairs reversed direction. From this landing Shielbrock could see the top of the door to the ladies room and after a few minutes the door opened. He started up the stairs but it was someone else so he returned to the landing. Again the door opened and he started up the stairs but it was false alarm once more so back to the landing. The door swung out again and he started up the stairs and there she was walking toward him, an elegant woman in heels and hose with turned up nose. She walked with an air of feminine confidence announcing clearly, I am a woman. Taller than he had expected, she was almost six feet in heels, nice.

"Excuse me." He stopped as did she. "I know this sounds corny and you've heard it a hundred times, but I really do think we've met before. I'm Martin Shielbrock."

She looked at him and thought she would have preferred a pass from his tall friend in the red sweater at the bar. Look at this guy, she thought. His hair's a mess. His face is sunburned and peeling. His clothes are very plain. His line is as corny as they come. "You're right. It is corny and I have heard it before. If we had met it wouldn't be very flattering if you didn't remember my name or where we met, now would it?"

"Yes," And she started to walk away. "But I mean it. Really. I think we've met." Shielbrock was desperate. He was losing her attention so he gambled, "I'm a Supply Officer in the Medford."

She stopped and asked, "Were you at the Supply Corps Officers Ball last week?"

"The Supply Corps Ball! Sure! That was it! You were with," Shielbrock pointed down the stairs, "what's-his-name, there. You were wearing that beautiful gown and everyone wanted to dance with you. I was one of those not lucky enough to get a dance with you." He hoped the lie would work.

She looked at him again, this time with a little more interest. There was a certain sincerity, intensity, strength, and then she saw his eyes. Those steel blue eyes were fixed on hers. God! Was she going through this again, as she had with Jules Loffman? Would she allow herself to be captured by big beautiful intense blue eyes again? "That could have been it" she replied. "I was with 'what's-his-name' as you say, and it was a lovely ball. His name is Richard Maverhill and he's on the Intrepid. What ship did you say you're on?"

"Medford," Shielbrock lied and continued. "And if what's-his-name is on the Intrepid he's about to go away for a long time. Maybe I can have another opportunity for a dance with you, after all." He paused and she hesitated so he continued. "I wonder, that is I hope, uh. Would you do me the honor of allowing me to take you to dinner sometime very soon, like tomorrow night?" His blue eyes were on her.

Deja-vu? Still she hesitated. He's not all that great, he's corny, she thought, but there is something about him. She didn't want to get involved with anyone just now, nothing serious, but Richard was leaving and this guy could provide transportation, meaning an opportunity to meet other officers. Even her previous transportation officers were better looking or had more to offer than this one. Should she? She hesitated and looked straight into those captivating blue eyes and was surprised to hear her own voice, "Why, I'd be delighted to have dinner with you tomorrow night." Shocked with her own reply, she wondered, what the hell am I doing?

"That's great! And now if you'll give me your address and your name I'll pick you up at seven."

Barbara still thought it best to provide a way out, an escape in case she changed her mind. "Call me at six and we'll work out the details." She gave him her phone number. "I'm Barbara Muir and what did you say your name is?"

"Martin Shielbrock. Thanks. I'll call you at six tomorrow." He stood there smiling and watched her walk away, Jesus, what a beautiful walk.

The beer pitcher was almost empty, again, and Barney ordered another as Shielbrock returned. "Get to bat?" Jim asked, his eyes still looking straight ahead, elbows still on the bar.

Shielbrock took the same position, staring straight ahead, elbows on the bar, "One for one."

"Nice!" Jim dragged out the long "I" sound. "Is she good, now that you've talked to her?"

"She's great. I'll bet her shit doesn't even stink."

"That's good, 'cause I'd bet you're gonna hafta eat a fathom of it just to see where it came from." Sailor talk.

Shielbrock thought awhile, then smiled. "Might be worth it."

The noise, smoke and singing continued and the place was more crowded than before as Barney moved around the room with a glass of beer in his hand, talking to friends, some newly made. His glass almost empty, Barney returned to the bar. "Shiel," Barney only used that name in times of crisis or when he had too much to drink. "Shiel, I found this great looking gal over near the windows. She's with Allerton from the Huntington. You know him?" Then continuing after Shielbrock shook his head indicating no, "Doesn't matter. She's good looking, nice body, smart. I got her phone number." He extended to Shielbrock the back of a torn match book containing the name Alice and a phone number but Shielbrock held up his hand in a stop gesture.

"You keep it Barney, I've just hit one."

"But Shield, I told you I'd get you three tonight and this is the first, here."

"Thanks, Barney. I appreciate it but I release you from that offer. You've done enough. You keep Alice. I'm all set. No more please."

"But Shiel," Barney would not let go. "It's your birthday. Jim's leaving the Navy and I'm deploying—."

"Barney, I won't be lonely, honest. I'll miss you both to be sure, but lonely I will not be."

"Barney, he won't be lonely," Jim added.

"Well, what are friends for?" Slurred Barney, still not satisfied as he wandered off again, into the noisy crowd, staggering slightly with beer glass in hand.

"There were fighters and blighters and Irish dynamiters, there was beer, gin, whiskey, wine, and cake—," Joe Sullivan was leading his Irish song again, louder than before, with more singers, each having consumed more drink. The noise level of the singing did not allow normal conversation and one had to yell to be understood. Jim and Shielbrock turned away from the bar, leaned their backs against it and each placed the heel of one shoe on the foot rail as they sang along, beer glass in hand and looked over the crowded, smoke filled room. Jim nudged Shielbrock with an elbow and nodded his head in the direction of Barbara Muir's table. There was Barney, beer glass in hand, crouched down in his stance as a baseball catcher, leaning into the space between Barbara and the vacant chair formerly occupied by Richard, who had gone to the head, Navy talk for men's room. Barney was talking a mile a minute, his mouth close enough to Barbara's ear so that he could be heard by her amid the noise and Barbara listened, smiling, with a patient and tolerant expression, nodding in acknowledgment at appropriate times. She was looking at Shielbrock and Jesus, he thought, how long had this been going on and what the hell could Barney be telling her? He made his way through the crowd toward the table and after gently but firmly helping Barney to a standing position, he eased him toward the bar and apologized to Barbara. She indicated that she couldn't hear so kneeling, he put his mouth near her ear. She smelled good. What perfume! "My apologies," he almost yelled. "Sometimes he gets out of control."

Barbara laughed and motioned him to bring his head closer and with his ear close to her mouth she said, "Either you're an amazing guy or he's a bigger liar than you. I gather he's a very close friend."

Again their heads changed position, "Right on all charges. He is a close friend, a bigger liar and I'm an amazing guy but more on that tomorrow."

Their heads shifted so that she could speak. "I'm looking forward to it."

What a woman, he thought as he guided Barney back toward the bar. Jim was over near the stairs, having intercepted Richard returning from the head and engaged him in conversation, then the three met back at their places at the bar and ordered another pitcher of beer.

"Thanks for the pick," Shielbrock said to Jim, referring to a play in basketball in which a player blocks the path of an opponent to free a team mate for action. Jim nodded and Barney slurred, "Hey, Shiel, that blonde is okay." He emphasized the long O sound in okay and continued. "She listened to me. She is smart. I told her all about you. She was interested. Did you see she was interested? You got somethin' good there, Shiel, real good."

"Barney, thanks. I appreciate it but if she was smart she wouldn't listen to you." They laughed and Shielbrock gently punched Barney on the shoulder. There was more noise, more smoke, more singing and another glass dropped but few heard it as they drank more beer.

"You're not a supply officer and there is no such ship as the Medford and you were not at the Supply Corps Ball and your name is something like Shielbrock but everyone calls you Shellback." Barbara had answered the phone when he called promptly at six.

"Hey you know an awful lot about me and we've hardly talked. Do I get a chance or is it all just Barney?"

"He had a lot to say about you last night, and I don't like to be lied to," Barbara was angry.

"Can't blame you for that," And Shielbrock went on to explain how he thought she was going to walk away and in desperation he had come up with the Supply angle. It had worked, after a fashion, and now he would tell all with appropriate modesty and honesty if only given an opportunity. He would have the opportunity as she gave him directions to her apartment and an hour later, at seven, he arrived at her door.

"What happened to the tall good lookin' guy in the red sweater?" Jackie had answered the door, seated Martin in the front room and gone into the bedroom where Barbara was in the final steps of dressing. "Barbara, have you seen this one? He is definitely not for you. Ugh!"

Barbara laughed, "Don't worry. He's only transportation. You've been after me for a long time to date naval officers again. Okay? Here's one. The guy in the red sweater left town, got out of the Navy, I think, so I settled for this one. He'll be fine for one date and he knows a lot of others."

"Well if you're going to re-enter the officer social circles I wish you'd have been more selective."

"I will be in the future." Barbara was almost ready.

"Listen to that!" Jackie pointed toward the front room. They could hear a plink-plink of the ukulele which normally took up space on an otherwise empty bookshelf.

"Hmm," Barbara listened. "Third Man Theme, see, good taste in music. That's encouraging."

"Good taste? Wait 'til you see his clothes"

"Why? What's he wearing?"

"Same thing he had on last night."

"Blue blazer, white shirt and light blue tie. Not particularly exciting, is it?"

"No, and he isn't either, if you ask me. He's just a plain crude athletic guy. Not at all your type."

"Well, we'll see. There was something about him when we met last night, an intensity that sort of fascinated me, but it's probably nothing."

"Barbara, you had a couple of drinks last night. Now you're going to see him with a clearer mind. Remember, you can go out there, take a quick look and tell him you're ill and you can't go out tonight."

"Jackie, I just talked to him on the phone an hour ago and told him I'd go to dinner with him."

"Okay. I've warned you and given you an out. It's up to you."

Barbara was ready and she laughed. "It'll be all right. Just one date."

Jackie hung her head, her arms crossed in front. "He'll probably take you to Shoney's Big Boy for a hamburger for dinner."

"Or maybe Joe Philly's for a beer and a pickled egg?" Barbara continued to laugh as she went out to the front room.

It wasn't Shoney's or Joe Philly's. It was candlelight, tablecloth, two forks and wine, and it wasn't just one date. They talked, they laughed, they danced, they joked and they talked more and more. They went out a number of times as he flattered her, asked about her and Barbara was interested, then intrigued, then captivated. Martin was attracted, enchanted and then he too was captivated as she questioned him, discussed issues, focused on him, was attentive, interesting and flattering.

"What's this thing about `heels, hose and nose'? Barney mentioned it that first night we met at Little Creek." Barbara asked as they drove from her apartment for dinner.

"Nothing, it's just the way Barney and I describe the kind of women that I'm attracted to."

"What does it mean?" Barbara knew it some how applied to her and insisted on knowing how.

Martin was hesitant, "That's all there is to it. I like women in high heel shoes and hosiery, you know, like, err, silk stockings, nylons."

"Yes, I know what heels and hose means. What's the nose part?"

"Just a rhyme part, you know. I like poetry. `For though from out our borne of time and place the flood may bear me far, I hope to meet my pilot face to face when I have crossed the bar.'"

She laughed and insisted, "Don't try to change the subject. What's the `nose' part?"

He laughed, also, and gave in. "Okay. Barney and I long ago developed this little saying which describes the kind of woman I like. It goes, `Heels and hose and turned up nose.' It means a woman who wears, and is comfortable in, heels and hose, and is sophisticated, confident, stylish and up to date. Barney calls it stuck up, a snob. I can't help it. I like women who are stuck up."

"And am I stuck up, a snob?"

He knew he was on sensitive ground and answered slowly. "Well," He paused, "That may be someone else's definition. To me you are sophisticated, confident and stylish. You're very good looking and you know it.

You dress well and you know that, too, nothing wrong with that. I don't know if that qualifies you for the title of snob, but it's very attractive to me to be with a woman who is good looking, dresses well and is confident of her actions. The old fashioned term is `carries herself well', but that's what is meant by `Heels and hose and turned up nose'."

Barbara was silent for awhile as Martin drove in silence.

"Then it has nothing to do with the shape of my nose?" She asked.

"No," He laughed, "Nothing to do with your nose which like the rest of you, is perfect."

"God!" She shook her head, "Still the same corny line." They both laughed.

"How about Barney? Is there a saying for the women he likes?"

Martin paused a moment, "Uhh, no. No, we don't have a saying for Barney."

"You're lying to me, Martin Shielbrock!" She turned and moved closer to him in feigned anger.

"You do have a saying for Barney. What is it?"

"Hey, okay, okay," He held up an arm in self protection as he drove. "There is a saying, but you don't want to hear it. Honest. Really."

She sulked for a moment, "I want to hear it."

"No, really, you don't. Did you see September Song with Joseph Cotton?"

"Stop trying to change the subject! I want to hear the saying that describes the women that Barney likes. Tell me, please." She put her hand on his arm and imitated a sweet little girl, wide eyed look, with cocked head and smile.

He looked at her briefly, then back at the road, smiling. "You don't have to fake that little girl look. You're beautiful enough to get whatever you want just by asking."

"That's not fair. Thanks for the compliment. Now tell me."

"You won't like it."

"Tell me, please." She was turned toward him with both her hands on his right arm, smiling.

"Okay," He took a deep breath, hesitated, and exhaled. He started to speak and hesitated again, "Now don't get angry."

"Tell me! Tell me! Tell me!" She accentuated each with a gentle punch on his arm.

"Okay," He made a motion of gripping the steering wheel for support. "Tits, long hair and hips that bear."

Barbara sat back in the car seat, staring straight ahead with no smile. "That's awful!"

"I told you, you didn't want to hear it."

"Why does it have to be ugly?"

"It isn't ugly. It just describes the kind of woman Barney wants. He wants to have a big family, lots of kids, so he wants a woman with—."

"I know, I know. I heard you," She thought for awhile. "Couldn't it be descriptive without being crude?"

"Well, it's only crude or ugly if you think of it that way. It is descriptive and clear, and it's verbally economical."

"Verbally economical." Barbara sulked in silence for awhile then said, "Jackie."

Martin glanced at her, away from then back to the road. "What about Jackie?"

Barbara continued to look straight ahead, "Jackie wants to have lots of children."

"Oh!" Martin drew out the exclamation, smiling, "And she has—."

"Martin!" Barbara interrupted him with feigned anger, smiling and a gentle punch on the arm as they both laughed then she thought a while, smiled and looked at him. "Heels and hose and turned up nose. I like it."

Martin returned the look seriously, "I do, too. Looks like I found her."

Four months later they were married.

CHAPTER 3

The sun was dropping down towards the western horizon and the "horses doovers" were all gone. Ellie had refilled the ice teas and Barney paused in his story-telling, looking to the west, contemplating.

Steven broke the silence. "It sounds like those were some great times in Norfolk then, right?

"Yeah, right, those were good times. Right, Hon?" Barney looked at Jackie and got a smile and a positive nod.

"Well, I sailed away to Korea. Martin married Barbara, finished his tour in Robinson and moved on to another destroyer. Department head, I think it was gunnery then ops, did real well, good fitness reports, then had a two year tour with the TYCOM staff, got to know some high level people, y'know, senior, who helped him along.

"Probably his big career boost along that time was when he got detailed as executive officer of a destroyer, Stickell, when he was still a lieutenant. That was a big break, y'know, because XO of a destroyer is a lieutenant commander billet. There were no other lieutenant XOs then, not in destroyers. None of us knew then that it was virtually the eve of the Cuban Quarantine."

CUBAN QUARANTINE, SEPTEMBER 1962

Lieutenant Martin Shielbrock was known as Shellback by all his Navy friends when he reported on board the radar picket destroyer USS Stickell

(DDR 888) at Norfolk, Virginia, in accordance with his orders and four days later he relieved the Executive Officer. He was delighted, still a lieutenant yet serving in a destroyer as Executive Officer, a lieutenant commander billet.

Stickell was a World War II destroyer, a Gearing Class, 2250 tons, 390 feet long with 40 foot beam, four Babcock and Wilcox boilers providing 600 pound steam to two turbine engines, the ship was capable of 34 knots. Seventy-seven of these ships had been built right at the end of World War II and most of them were commissioned in 1945 and 1946. Gearing Class destroyers carried three gun mounts with two barrels of 5 inch 38 in each mount, a total of 6 five-inch guns, and Stickell was one of 26 ships of this class that had been converted a few years before to radar picket destroyer and designated DDR. The DDRs were primarily anti-air warfare ships, because the main feature of their conversion had been the addition of special air search radar, including a large clumsy antenna which provided the altitude of air contacts while other radar gave only range and bearing.

Her anti-submarine capability was archaic by modern Navy standards of the day and like most of the DDRs, the ship was scheduled for a long ten month period in a naval shipyard during which a modernization and conversion would take place, changing her to a DD and upgrading the anti-submarine equipment including new sonar.

The commanding officer, Commander Lawrence Wolder, called Captain by Navy tradition, was friendly and easy going. He could afford to be relaxed as for the next two months Stickell would be alongside the pier at Norfolk. Then the ship would make a trip to Earle, New Jersey to offload ammunition, and then on to the Philadelphia Naval Shipyard where Shellback would take over the command as the ship commenced a ten month rehabilitation and modernization process.

Ten months in a shipyard was Shellback's rather dismal future, hardly the way to spend a valuable sea duty tour. He could only hope to get the ship through on time, no small task, and be involved in some at-sea operations during the second half of his expected two year tour of duty. As a senior lieutenant at this point, he would probably be a lieutenant commander before the ship completed the shipyard work, and then a commander would take command and Shellback would be Executive Officer again.

Captain Wolder had orders to Washington, to duty on a high level staff, was very pleased with the prospects of working with people on that level and was anxious to leave but the trip to Philadelphia was all that stood between him and his departure for Washington.

On the second week of Shellback's duty as Executive Officer of Stickell, events moved quickly. The captain received a message from the Bureau of Naval Personnel changing his orders to "detach immediately". He had to be in Washington not in a few months but right now so Shellback took command, Wolder departed and the plan was now for Shellback to take the ship to Philadelphia in two months. No problem, rather a good deal for Martin Shielbrock, a lieutenant, to command a destroyer at sea, even if only for transit to a shipyard.

On a Saturday morning in September 1962, Shellback, as the youngest and most junior commanding officer of a destroyer in the Navy, left his home in Norfolk and went on board to see that all was well for the weekend. He intended to be home for lunch but he didn't get home for six weeks.

Shellback received a phone call on the ship from the squadron operations officer informing him that Stickell might be sent to sea for extended operations. "Make preparations for getting underway on short notice."

"Where am I going?"

"I'm sorry, I can't say on the phone."

"How long will I be gone?"

"—don't know."

"Will other ships be going with me?"

"—can't say," and so it went.

Shellback notified his department heads; four lieutenants ordinarily, but on this, a Saturday morning in port, only two of them were on board. They and the duty people from the other two departments started a crash program of recalling people, checking supplies and gathering parts and equipment which were spread out in the various maintenance and supply activities around the naval base.

Shellback himself went to see his destroyer division commander, Captain Steven Speakes, the same Speakes he had served under in the destroyer Robinson and again on the type commander staff. Although it had not been mentioned, Shellback suspected that it was due to the direct influence of Captain Speakes that he, Shellback, had been ordered as a lieutenant into a choice lieutenant commander billet in a destroyer of Speakes' division. It had to be. It couldn't just be a coincidence with over two hundred destroyers in fifty divisions.

After explaining the rather informal alertment he had received, Shellback reminded Speakes that his status in the ship was, more or less, one of "caretaker" and, after all, he was only a lieutenant.

"Who is the commanding officer of Stickell?" asked the division commander.

"I am, sir."

"Do you feel that you are not capable, some how not competent or not qualified to command the ship?"

"No sir. I am fully capable, competent and qualified."

"Do you think that I would have allowed you to take command if I thought otherwise?"

Shellback smiled, "No, sir."

"Now you get back to your ship, Captain Shielbrock, and do whatever you have to do to accomplish your mission." Speakes used the title "Captain" given to any officer in the Navy in command of a ship. It was, and still is, one of those Navy traditions that defy time and legality. Navy people have no problem with it.

"Yes sir, Commodore," responded Shellback. "I'll let you know when I sail."

The ship was a beehive of activity as sailors came and went with parts, provisions and equipment. Many, called back to the ship from home or recreation were immediately put to work helping the ship make ready for sea. Every hour a "muster on station" was held, an attempt to find out who was present and who was missing, but these were futile gestures, as it was impossible to count a crew constantly running errands off, on and around the ship. Each hour, also, the squadron operations officer would cross the nest of four destroyers of the division and ask in each ship, "How many men are you missing?"

Before he would answer each time, Shellback would ask how the other ships were doing. "O'Hare is missing a hundred and sixty. Corry is missing a hundred and thirteen. Cecil is missing a hundred and twenty-two," would be typical status. Shellback, unaware of his exact status, would reply, "I'm missing a hundred and five." Always his status a few less than the lowest of the other three ships. As the outboard ship in the nest of four destroyers, he knew that he would be the leading candidate to depart first for any assignment, and Shellback wanted to go on the assignment no matter what it was.

Finally, by the six PM visit of the ops officer, 1800 in Navy time,

Shellback found out about the task. Soviet missiles were in Cuba and the President was considering a blockade. Navy ships were being alerted to head toward Cuba in case the blockade was ordered and in his 1800 status report Shellback told the ops officer that he was missing seventy men.

"Okay, you're the lowest, Captain," This from one lieutenant to another but the squadron ops officer was speaking for his commodore. "You are to get underway, now. Proceed to the lightship and rendezvous with the oiler Tuscaloosa and escort her south. All this will be confirmed by message after you're underway."

Shellback sent word to his division commodore and got underway for what became known as the Cuban Quarantine, the youngest in age and most junior in rank of any captain of a destroyer in the Navy. Finally, with an accurate muster after getting underway, he found that he was missing a hundred and fifty men, more than half the crew.

Six days later in the Caribbean the Norfolk based destroyer Bearss showed up with seventy-three of the Stickell crew. For three hours the two destroyers steamed alongside each other transferring the men by "high line", a process in which one at a time a man rides across the water between the ships in a small seat suspended from a tight line. Stickell took on board 73 of her crew plus 18 others belonging to her division-mate, Cecil.

Enroute to rendezvous with Cecil that night, Shellback was on the bridge when the Combat Information Center of his ship reported that a small radar contact had just disappeared from the radar. It had originally been picked up off to port at eight miles but binoculars showed no lights and so it was thought to be an unlighted fishing boat. Now at four and a half miles and still no radar contact, Shellback came out of his bridge chair, checked the bearing and ordered the Officer of the Deck to turn to that course. Then in rapid order, "Combat, mark that fishing boat as a datum. Get it on the DRT. Alert Sonar. Set ASW Condition One." Shellback had ordered his ship to the highest degree of readiness for an anti-submarine operation as he closed the last known position of the radar contact.

"Shall we slow, Captain?" asked the OOD as the ship was making sixteen knots.

"Not yet," answered Shellback. Then, thinking aloud, "Sixteen knots. Sixteen hundred yards in three minutes. Four and a half miles to go. Nine thousand yards in about sixteen minutes." Then, into the squawk box,

"Combat, let me know when we're four thousand yards from datum." Nine minutes later the Combat Information Center reported, "Four thousand yards to datum," and Stickell slowed to ten knots. Three minutes later on the squawk box, "Bridge, Combat, this is Sonar. Sonar contact bearing two nine three, range two eight zero zero, solid echo, no doppler, evaluate possible submarine." It was twenty minutes past midnight.

An immediate message went out from Stickell, giving the latitude, longitude, course, speed, echo quality, contact evaluation and the destroyer's intention, "to remain with contact."

Stickell circled the contact, maneuvering to keep the range at about twenty three hundred yards, constantly tracking the movement to determine and to refine the course and speed of the "possible submarine" and to detect any change of direction.

"Course zero seven zero. Speed three knots," continued to be the contact's movement as Stickell circled.

An hour after his initial contact report Shellback was handed an immediate message from the Fleet Commander stating that there were no U.S. submarines known to be in the area. This meant that Stickell's contact, if it really was a submarine, was a "stranger," possibly a Soviet submarine, or else it could be no submarine at all. It could be one of those many anomalies of acoustic detection; a school of fish, a knuckle of disturbed water, a mass of kelp in a slight ocean current or a ghost of electronics in the ship's sonar, any one of and many more of which would be called a "false contact" or "non-submarine."

"Possible submarine" was upgraded to "Probable submarine" after an hour of contact with solid echoes, course and speed, but still no evasion attempt by the contact.

Every hour Shellback sent out a situation report, called SITREP, giving the details of the action. These were serialized starting with number one for the first hour, so that SITREP Three meant three hours of continuous contact, still solid echoes, "Course zero seven zero. Speed three."

Three hours of continuous contact was very rare as U.S. ships often gained sonar contact with strangers or schools of fish and, either one, the contact took evasive action or disappeared in a few minutes. For Stickell, especially with her out-dated sonar, to hold contact with a "probable submarine" for three hours was suspect, and Shellback knew it as he called the Chief Sonarman to the bridge.

"Chief Petrovsky, if this is a submarine as we circle it we should get more solid echoes from its beams, weak echo from directly ahead and soft echo from its stern. Can you detect any of that?"

"I already have, Captain. I can tell the aspect from the echo quality. It's a submarine. At three knots I can't get doppler and I don't know why it's not evading, but there's movement and good echo. It's a submarine."

"Okay. Go back to sonar and call out target aspect as we circle." Then to the Operations Officer, "Tell CIC to compare the Chief's aspects from Sonar with the DRT heading of the contact."

In this manner Shellback confirmed that the experienced sonarman could tell the beam, bow and stern of the probable submarine. He had already designated one of his officers as "recorder" and he made sure that every step, every order, every report was recorded in a logbook; a detailed diary was being kept of the entire operation.

Just after SITREP Four had gone out from Stickell, Shellback received a message from his task unit commander, who was the commanding officer of the oiler he had been escorting. "Break off and return," the message read. Shellback disregarded it. SITREP Six described the same gradual movement, echo quality and solid contact, and soon another electronic message from the task unit commander included, "—lack of evasion tactics, lack of significant movement, doubtful validity,—break off and rejoin. Acknowledge."

Shellback responded with, "Your message acknowledged. This is a Soviet submarine. I intend to remain with it."

After nine hours of continuous contact Shellback was still on the bridge of his ship as daylight had broken and another message from his task unit commander had been received after his acknowledgment and it had been disregarded. The hourly SITREPs continued. A message from the task group commander, a captain in rank and one step higher in the chain of command, was brought to Shellback by a radioman. The message included, "—appreciate initiative and dedication—, lack of contact evasion or movement—, evaluate non-submarine—, break off and proceed on duty assigned." Shellback put it on his clip board.

In the early afternoon a fleet oiler escorted by the destroyer Miles C. Fox came over the horizon and by flashing light Shellback asked them to remain clear as he was holding a probable submarine. They complied as neither Fox nor the oiler had seen the messages on Stickell's contact as they were not addressees.

From Fox came by flashing light, "Can I help you?"

"Affirm. Come on over," also by flashing light.

Fox left his escort role and closed Stickell as CICs on both ships exchanged information and soon Fox reported sonar contact which correlated with Stickell's contact. Shellback told Fox that he would continue the SITREP submission and asked Fox to hold the contact for awhile and of course Fox readily agreed and continued circling what he, too, evaluated as a probable submarine.

After catching up with the deliberately slow moving oiler, Stickell went alongside, refueled and rushed back to the probable submarine. Regaining sonar contact, Shellback sent by flashing light to Fox, "Appreciate your help and confirmation. Recommend you catch up with oiler."

"Thanks for letting me join in. Best luck," by flashing light as Fox departed.

SITREP Fourteen described the turnover of the contact between two destroyers, confirmation of the evaluation by Fox and refueling from the oiler.

Each hour the ship measured and recorded the temperature of the ocean water at depths to two hundred feet using a bathythermograph, called BT, a device lowered by wire from a short boom on the port side of the fantail. Sound in the ocean water is significantly influenced by variations in temperature, and as sonar is an acoustic system it is important to know the profile of temperature versus depth.

"Afternoon effect," said Chief Sonarman Petrovsky to Shellback as he showed him the smoked glass BT slide, as a thin barely visible line scratched in the carbon showed the changes in temperature at the various depths.

"Yes," agreed Shellback. "There's a layer, all right. What do you make that depth to be, Chief?" Shellback had looked at many such slides as Anti Submarine Warfare Officer, Gunnery Officer and Operations Officer in previous destroyer duties.

"A hundred and twenty feet, Captain. If that submarine ducks under the layer we'll probably lose contact."

The Officer of the Deck, Lieutenant Pete Botazelli of the Gold Team, asked the question on the minds of all. "Then why doesn't he?"

"That's the big question, all right," responded Shellback. "For sure, he would if he could, and if he knew. He's a BT himself and would only have to vary his depth to get the profile."

"But, if we assume that he knows there's a layer, why doesn't he use it and get away?" Pete asked.

The question was rephrased as Shellback thought aloud. "Yes why? It has to be that he can't go deep. He can't evade. He has to have some problem, maybe mechanical, and if he can't evade he'll just try to wait us out. He's trying to make us think that a real submarine wouldn't just go zero seven zero at three knots indefinitely. He hopes that eventually we'll say 'non-sub' and break off."

"Or," added the OOD, "our superiors will say 'no evasion equals non-sub' and order us to break off."

The "layer" they spoke of is called the thermocline by oceanographers. It is a sharp change from the water temperature near the surface which has been warmed by the sun, hence "afternoon effect," and the colder water beneath. In this case the BT showed that the water had been warmed down to a depth of a hundred and twenty feet. Sound energy sent out by the destroyer's sonar would travel relatively straight until it reached this layer of cold water and then it would be reflected or refracted at an unpredictable angle. With no return echo there would be no contact and a submarine could hide under such a layer; a basic ASW problem.

SITREP Seventeen described how a P-2 Neptune anti submarine patrol plane had come by and after establishing radio communications, Shellback asked the P-2 to make MADVEC runs over the contact and the aircraft agreed. MADVEC is an acronym for a procedure in which an ASW aircraft makes passes over a ship's sonar contact as vectored by the ship, to confirm the presence of a contact with the aircraft's magnetic anomaly detector (MAD). After six successful MADVECs the P-2 had to depart.

After twenty hours of contact Stickell received a message from the task force commander, a rear admiral commanding the carrier task force and another step higher in the chain of command, "—admire dedication and tenacity,—unlikely Soviets would have submarine in these waters during quarantine,—lack of evasion by your contact—, low probability—, probable anomaly—, break off and proceed on duty assigned."

Shellback sent back, "—confirmed by another destroyer and P-2 MAD,—gradual movement consistent,—solid echo,—contact I hold is a Soviet submarine,—intend to stay on it."

Twenty four hours after first gaining contact, Shellback had not left the bridge. Meals had been brought to him, what little he ate, and coffee was being consumed in copious quantities. A voice spoke behind him as he picked up half of a grilled cheese sandwich, "I've got a sharp Buck knife you can borrow to cut that sandwich but only if you promise not to lose it or get cut."

Turning, yelling and smiling, Shellback called out, "Richard Harkness from Birmingham, Alabama and the Robinson." He grasped the sailor's right hand and forearm. "What the hell are you doing here?"

"I'm trying to get back to my ship, Cecil, but you got other things to do."

Still obviously pleased, Shellback answered. "Well, it's great to see you and we'll get you back to Cecil soon," then looking at Harkness' sleeve, "First Class, what?"

"Quartermaster. Remember, you let me go from Deck to OC and I struck for QM?"

Shellback really didn't remember but covered it with, "Right, and now I need you here."

The sailor replied, "Oh, I've already started helping your QM watch standing," and the two former shipmates discussed days in Robinson and what had become of former associates. Then Harkness went back to the chart table and told a group of assembled Stickell sailors much exaggerated sea stories about their young skipper including how Harkness and the others had saved the life of a navy pilot, how Ensign Shielbrock had lost Harkness' sharp Buck knife, how the ensign had almost lost some of the most important bodily parts and, "—got us all medals,—tossed his cookies crossing the line,—I pulled him through,—that's why they call him Shellback."

Shellback had done some calculations concerning the Soviet submarine. Starting with a ninety percent battery charge, the most likely class of Soviet diesel electric submarine which this might be, a Foxtrot Class, could maintain three knots speed for forty-eight hours. This submarine, if it was a Foxtrot Class or a submarine at all, had now been down twenty-four hours. He had about another twenty four hours to go before he might reach a dangerous condition, dangerous because of lack of propulsion, but also difficult to breathe and difficult to tolerate the stench and the heat inside that submarine, if it was a submarine.

If it was a submarine, and he was held down "to exhaustion," which is what Shellback hoped for, would he come finally to the surface docile and panting for breath, or would he be angry, his common senses numbed by fatigue and distorted by humiliation, and would he then perhaps do something foolish and fight before he came to the surface?

Both wore the two silver bars of a navy lieutenant, railroad tracks they were called; Shielbrock, the captain of the ship with nine years of commissioned service, and Pete Botazelli, the Gunnery Officer with five years. Not much separated them in years of service but a vast difference in responsibility. "Captain, may I speak with you for a minute?"

"Sure. What's on your mind?" As if Shellback didn't know.

"Well, sir, it's a little sensitive. It's about this hold down we're doing. We, uh, you've been told to break off and proceed on duty assigned. That's a direct order, sir, and you've disregarded it. Now, Captain, I think we've got a Soviet submarine here. I agree with you on that and I understand why you want to stay on it, but with all respect, sir, you're disobeying direct orders."

"Yes. I know I am, but as you say, this is a Soviet submarine we're holding and I really don't think any of my superiors would want me to break off if they knew that. They just don't believe me."

Botazelli continued, "But, captain, you've got a very fine career going, if you don't mind me saying. Hell, everyone knows you're a front runner and all that. Look, you've got a command, a destroyer and you're only a lieutenant. No other lieutenant in the entire Navy has command of a destroyer. Aren't you blowing that career over this contact? Is it worth it?"

"Do you think I should break off and leave this contact?"

"Jesus, I don't know, Captain. I hope that you don't break off, but I don't want, and I know the others here feel the same, we don't want you to ruin you career over this. You might get court martialed!"

"Yeah, I might, but not if I can prove it's a Soviet submarine."

"Well, I don't think Ivan there will be available to testify at your court martial."

"Probably not, so we'd better force him to the surface and expose his ass to the outside world, to the doubters."

"We, all of us, want to surface him, but Captain, why are you willing to risk so much? If we had sailed away when first ordered, no problem. Carry out our duties. Get home. Nice job, Captain Shielbrock, and now on with a bright career and future. Now, orders disobeyed, bad feelings. Hell, even if we surface the red bastard there'll be bad feelings. You would have embarrassed not only the Soviets, but our guys who ordered you away. So you won't be court martialed, you'll only have influential enemies in high places."

"Maybe so, but maybe no. I may make some enemies but if we surface this bastard I'll make some allies, too, or at least I hope so. At any rate, though, I've got to see this thing through. The way I see it, the Soviets put a guy in command of a submarine, give him a crew, train and equip them and send them over here to operate undetected under our front porch. The CO of that Soviet submarine is a product of his country, as are his ship and crew. They're all products of their country. We're products of the U.S.. Me, I'm a product of the U.S., you are, our crew and this old ship. We're not at war in a combat sense, but we're in a conflict of influence, this Cold War, and the Soviets want to influence the world to advance their political, economic, social, cultural, what have you system. We want to curb that influence. You and I can't contribute much in peacetime toward that effort, but this much we can do, this little bit. We can show the Soviets that they can't send their submarines to operate undetected near us, not all the time they can't, because this one time at least we caught him and for whatever reasons he can't get away. It may be the fault of their product, their system, I don't care. That Soviet bastard is here and I'm here. He has to work with the ship and crew he was given, just like I have to, only I got his ass and I'm not letting go. I want to force him to do what he was told not to do; get caught. I want a picture of him on the surface. And another thing, while we've been holding him these past," Shellback looked at the clock, "twenty four hours, he hasn't been able to communicate with his higher ups, so they don't know what he's doing and they can't get word to him. Our leaders do know what we're doing but if this 'quarantine' blows up into a hot war, we'll know it first and we'll get the first submarine kill of that war. Now, I don't expect that to happen, but he has to think about that, too."

"Are you sure that perhaps, that is, could it be, Captain, that maybe this whole thing is a bit more personal with you, like you against him?"

Shellback hesitated, "You may be right. I can't say it's not personal."

The watch in Stickell changed every four hours. Two teams constituted ASW Condition One, so that Shellback saw his Blue Team then his Gold, then his Blue again and so on as his officers and men changed the watch, but he stayed on, sitting in the captain's chair in the Pilot House on the bridge, coaching the Officer of the Deck but letting him maneuver the ship and coordinate with CIC and Sonar to hold contact.

Stickell had departed Norfolk missing 150 men. Even with the return of 73 men and the additional 18 of Cecil who were put on the watch list, every underway watch station had to be manned on a two section basis rather than the three or four sections usually used for peacetime steaming. It was called "Watch on Watch" or "Port and Starboard." For special events ships sometimes used "Blue and Gold" to designate the watch sections. It meant four hours on duty and four hours off, and during the time "off" duty men had to eat, sleep and do essential ship's work as sixteen to twenty hour working days were common in a two section watch basis.

"Contact range—, bearing—, on course zero seven zero, speed three knots—," every few seconds from the squawk box, along with continuous ping-echo, ping-echo from the underwater phone speaker.

"What the hell is going on here?" Demanded Rear Admiral Richard A. Meyer, commanding the carrier task force consisting of the aircraft carrier Forrestal and eight other ships in the Cuban Quarantine. The fleet oiler Tuscaloosa kept his ships in fuel, which required the oiler to run around to the various ships as each required "a drink," as they put it, and one destroyer had been assigned to escort the oiler, but now after a full day, that destroyer was wasting valuable time with an obvious false sonar contact and Meyer would have to give up another one of his valuable destroyers to escort the oiler. "Who is this guy in this can?" Meyer again demanded.

His Chief of Staff replied, "He's Commander Lawrence Wolder, Admiral."

"Don't know him. Well, get him off his ass and on his way. What does it take to get him going?" The admiral was angry.

"He's been told a number of times but he insists he's got a Soviet submarine."

"Bullshit! If it was a Soviet submarine it would be evading, deep and fast, and an old can, a Gearing like Stickell couldn't hold it for five minutes. It can't be a submarine!"

From the rear of the briefing room the Assistant Surface Operations Officer, a lieutenant commander spoke up, "Uh, excuse me Admiral, Chief of Staff, we may have the wrong CO. That is, I think there was a change in that ship just before the Quarantine was declared. I'd like to confirm that with our screen commander. He'll know even if it isn't one of his ships."

"Okay," The admiral was still annoyed. "Get on with it, but I don't give a shit who the CO is, get him back where he should be."

The Assistant Surface Operations Officer went to the ship's phone and called the signal bridge and ten minutes later a messenger from the signal bridge of the carrier Forrestal handed a paper to Admiral Meyer in his command center in the ship.

"Como to flag. Present CO Stickell LT Martin Shielbrock," the admiral read aloud. "Lieutenant? A God Damn lieutenant has command of a destroyer and deliberately disobeys direct orders! Fire the son of a bitch!" The admiral tossed the paper to his Chief of Staff.

"I'll write the message, Chief of Staff," volunteered the Assistant Surface Operations Officer.

"Thanks, Dan. Get right on it," and as he left the command center the Chief of Staff turned to the admiral, who was still fuming, and said slowly, cautiously, "Just as a thought, sir, as a 'what if', if you'll forgive me, what if it really is a Soviet submarine?"

Even though angry, Admiral Meyer smiled at his Chief of Staff and responded with the old time Navy disclaimer. "If that's a Soviet submarine I'll kiss his ass, and yours, on the foc'sle and give both of you a half hour to muster a crowd."

Martin Sheilbrock half dozed, was half awake in the elevated captain's chair on the starboard side of the Pilot House. In his half sleep he was on the mound, hot summer day, soaked in sweat at the ballpark at Stratford hearing, "C'mon, you've done enough. It's time to quit."

"Bullshit. I'm not through. This is my game."

"You'll ruin yourself,—career,—future,—call it quits,—you've done more than enough."

"No! Get out a' here and le'me finish!"

The smell of pastry intruded into his half sleep along with ping-echo. His head and shoulders ached. His neck ached and a familiar pain extended down the right side of his back to his hip and his legs felt heavy. What was that odor, pastry? Ping-echo. He came fully awake to, "—on course zero seven zero, speed three knots—." Still holding contact.

He slid out of his chair and made his way across the darkened Pilot House to the coffee pot. Nine years. It was only nine years since that day in Stratford but it seemed like more.

Lieutenant Bill O'Conner, Blue Team Officer of the Deck, looked at him carefully.

"You okay, Captain?"

"Fine, thanks, any changes?"

"No sir. Captain, if this is a Soviet submarine, why do you think he hasn't tried any evasion? The same course and speed for over twenty four hours, and probably the same depth, too." The question was still on all of their minds.

"He can't evade. I'm sure he's had some kind of a mechanical casualty. I don't know what that casualty is, but I'm sure he can't maneuver or go deep, or else he would, as you suggest. I'd guess he has some kind of water tight integrity problem, a leak, and if he goes fast, turns, or goes deep it gets worse. I'm hoping that's what it is, because if it is a leak than he has to run a pump, and that means more load on his battery, which shortens his battery life."

"So he has to come up sooner," added O'Conner.

"Right. If we had better, or maybe more modern sonar we could listen and, just maybe again, we could hear a pump."

"How about the Gertrude?" O'Conner asked about the underwater phone, using its nickname and pointing to the remote unit on the forward bulwark of the pilot house.

"I guess it's not sensitive enough but a few hours ago I thought I heard a very faint chunk-chunk-chunk sound in among all that background noise. Then I didn't hear it. I dunno, maybe I was just hoping and imagining things, like that pastry smell. Do I imagine that, too?"

"No sir. That's for real," O'Conner smiled. "We got our baker back with that group from the Bearss, and he's baking sweet rolls for breakfast."

Shellback looked at the clock. Four AM. Twenty eight hours of contact. "Let's send the messenger down to get us some samples of those sweet rolls."

Early on Shellback had developed a procedure for maneuvering to hold contact. He circled the slow moving contact while Stickell made eight knots, maintaining the range at about two thousand to twenty five hundred yards. It took about an hour to make a complete circle around the contact and after three or four circles he would reverse direction by turning toward the contact after opening the range. Turning away from the contact to reverse direction would put the contact "through the baffles," or through a deaf area directly astern of Stickell, with temporary loss of contact. Similarly, the reversal took place when the destroyer was directly astern of the contact where the submarine's propeller and engine noises masked the sound so that for a few moments the submarine would not know Stickell's exact location.

A message came to Shellback from Commodore Speakes, his division commander, "—have confidence in you and would like to help,—give me something to go on."

Shellback drafted a long message to Speakes describing the events and emphasizing that in his evaluation the contact was a Soviet submarine, "—lack of evasion due to mechanical problems,—estimate battery capacity,—expect exhaustion limit in about eighteen more hours."

SITREP Thirty left Stickell at dawn including, "—no change; solid echoes, course zero seven zero, three knots." Ping-echo.

It was the second dawn since gaining contact thirty hours ago as Shellback went to the tiny cramped sea cabin just aft of the Pilot House, removed undershirt and khaki short sleeved uniform shirt, brushed his teeth and scrubbed his face, neck, arms and chest. With clean undershirt and uniform shirt, without bothering with rank insignia, Shellback felt a little better as he left the sea cabin. God, but that bunk looks good, he thought as he closed the curtain that served as a door. It had been forty-eight hours since he had really slept, the last thirty of those hours holding contact.

"Stand up straight, look the part, look like a pitcher," he could hear Coach Jordan.

FROM: COMDESDIV TWO SIX TWO
TO: COMCARDIV TWO
PERSONAL FOR CHIEF OF STAFF FROM SPEAKES
SUBJ: STICKELL CONTACT

PARA I CAN APPRECIATE THAT YOUR PLATE IS MORE THAN FULL OF OPERATIONAL CONSIDERATIONS AND THAT STICKELL REPRESENTS AN UNNECESSARY PROBLEM STOP CO STICKELL IS AN EXCEPTIONAL INDIVIDUAL WITH CONSIDERABLE EXPERIENCE AND MATURITY OF JUDGMENT DESPITE HIS RANK STOP

PARA IF AT ALL POSSIBLE COMMA WITHIN THE DEMANDS OF OPERATIONAL TASKING VERSUS RESOURCES COMMA I HOPE THAT YOU COULD ALLOW STICKELL A FEW MORE HOURS TO PROVE OUT THIS CONTACT ONE WAY OR THE OTHER STOP AS HIS ISIC COMMA I WILL TAKE THE

APPROPRIATE ACTION WHEN AND IF YOU CAN NO LONGER
TOLERATE ACTIONS STOP

PARA HE WAS THE BOAT OFFICER WHO PICKED YOUR
WINGMAN OUT OF THE WATER OFF KOREA STOP THAT WAS
TWO HOURS AFTER I TOLD HIM TO GIVE UP THE SEARCH
AND RETURN TO THE SHIP STOP

PARA VERY RESPECTFULLY COMMA SPEAKES STOP

"So, he saved your wingman's ass and now you owe him one. Okay, we'll give him a little more time and let Speakes handle it, but you guys are wasting my time. It can't be a submarine." Admiral Meyer handed the message back to his Chief of Staff. "Dawson prepared this one," added the admiral, "but just hold it for now. Maybe we won't need it with Speakes stepping in."

The Chief of Staff read the message that had not yet been sent:

FROM: CTF 20
TO: USS STICKELL
INFO: CHAIN OF COMMAND
SUBJ: RELIEF OF COMMAND

PARA IAW NAVY REGULATIONS COMMA OFFICER ON
BOARD NEXT SENIOR AND ELIGIBLE FOR COMMAND IS DI-
RECTED TO RELIEVE AS COMMANDING OFFICER IMMEDI-
ATELY STOP

PARA MAINTAIN ALL RECORDS AND LOGS FOR INVES-
TIGATION CONCERNING SHIPS OPERATIONS AND COMMU-
NICATIONS OVER PREVIOUS 48 HOURS STOP

PARA READ ARTICLE THIRTY ONE RIGHTS TO FORMER
CO AND SAME FOR OTHERS WHO MAY HAVE BEEN PARTY
TO ALLEGED LACK OF DISCIPLINE STOP ADVISE ALL CON-
CERNED NOT TO SPEAK OF SHIPS DISCIPLINE PROBLEM
AMONG THEMSELVES STOP

PARA ACKNOWLEDGE RECEIPT OF THIS MESSAGE AND
COMPLETION OF ACTION ASAP STOP

The admiral frowned, "I don't really like this message. There's some legal issues involved here that I don't feel comfortable about. Did the JAG see it?"

"Dawson went over it with the ships JAG Officer," explained the Chief of Staff. JAG stood for Judge Advocate General; a navy lawyer.

"Well, it seems more tidy to have his ISIC handle it," replied the admiral. ISIC was Immediate Superior in Command; the regular reporting senior for official administrative purposes. Every officer in command had one as it was the person who wrote his fitness reports, the official "boss."

0800. Thirty two hours of holding contact with no change, no evasion. The destroyer Stribling came over the horizon at high speed and at near maximum range for daytime flashing light Shellback sent, "Can you join me for some ping time?"

The reply came back just before the ship was out of flashing light range, "Sorry, have important promises to keep and miles to go before I sleep."

Shellback never found out what his poetic promises were, nor did it matter but another confirmation would have been valuable. The P-2 patrol aircraft that came by that day at 1000 did not respond to Stickell's radio calls, and Shellback wondered whether he was being ostracized or maybe his radio gang was too tired to set up their equipment properly.

1100. Another brief terse message from the task unit commander was received:

FROM: CTU 20.3.5
TO: USS STICKELL

BREAK OFF AND PROCEED ON DUTY PREVIOUSLY AS-SIGNED STOP ACKNOWLEDGE STOP

FROM: USS STICKELL
TO: CTU 20.3.5

YOUR DIRECTIVE ACKNOWLEDGED STOP HOLDING CONTACT WITH SOVIET SUBMARINE STOP

Commander Second Fleet was the most senior naval officer afloat and from his flagship at sea, this vice admiral was the operational commander of the fleet conducting the Cuban Quarantine. He directed the movements, positioning, readiness and response of 160 ships and as many aircraft, including aircraft carriers, submarines, cruisers, destroyers, amphibious warfare ships and auxiliary ships. He controlled the employment of carrier based as well as land based Navy airplanes; hundreds of them. Four times a day this three star admiral received a series of briefings in his command center, in front of a large display of the entire Caribbean and Cuban area which showed the locations of all his ships and the flight paths of his patrol planes. The Second Fleet Flag Plot also showed various merchant ships of particular interest, mostly Soviet or other communist block ships, and on a separate map of Cuba, known or suspected military facilities were displayed while status boards surrounding the charts and maps gave details of the symbols.

COMSECONDFLT ran his fleet from this command center, issuing directives to, and receiving reports from his task force commodores, each of whom in turn worked through their own subordinate task group commanders. Each task group commander had task unit commanders and some of the task unit commanders had subordinate task element commanders. All of the ships and aircraft served at the bottom of this long chain of command, or task organization. A normal directive, for instance, would go from Commander Second Fleet down to his force, group, unit, and element commanders, then to individual ships. In a crisis or if urgency demanded, a directive could go from any of them direct to the ship, with all those commanders who were bypassed being notified as "information addressees." In reverse, reports from individual ships and aircraft generally made their way up the task organization ladder, but in emergencies a higher up could be notified directly from the ship with "information addressees" covering those bypassed.

Stickell's reports of the initial contact and all of the SITREPs went directly to the fleet commander, COMSECONDFLT, with the entire chain of command included as information addressees. In addition, the format for Stickell's reports required inclusion of the Commander-in-Chief, U.S. Atlantic Fleet, known as CINCLANTFLT, the Norfolk shore based commander of the Atlantic Fleet, a four star admiral.

At the noon briefing for COMSECONDFLT in his flagship command center, the Operations Officer detailed the complex disposition of ships and aircraft, demanding concentration to follow missions and assignments as each task force, group, unit and ship was positioned and studied, missions and tasks discussed, fuel, ammunition, provisions, material status and personnel problems were considered. Contact reports were plotted and tracked or erased as ships reported, with some changing evaluations.

"Mership on course two six zero, speed twelve knots."

"Sonar contact evaluated non-submarine."

"Surface contact evaluated fishing boat DIW," meaning dead in the water, not making way, zero speed.

"Air contact evaluated commercial airliner."

"Sonar contact evaluated marine life," a school of fish.

"And Stickell?" asked the vice admiral from among the hundreds of reports.

"Still reports holding contact, same course and speed, Admiral."

"Didn't you tell me he'd been ordered off, that his task group commander evaluated it as non-sub?"

"Yes sir. He's been ordered off by force, group and unit commanders, but he insists that it's a Soviet submarine and he's hanging on."

The admiral turned to his Chief of Staff, "What do you think?"

"Sir, we have a problem with discipline versus operational necessity. From the message traffic it appears that he's not going to obey his orders. I think that we should give Admiral Meyer some more time to work it out before we step in."

The three star admiral thought for a few seconds. "Okay, I'll wait awhile, but I don't like the sound of this. The guy's in direct disobedience of orders."

Ashore in Norfolk, the four star admiral commanding the Atlantic Fleet was receiving a similar operations briefing with some-what less detail as symbols at sea represented task groups with very few individual ships represented. His display showed a larger area of the Atlantic and the east coast of the U.S., with shore based logistic activities represented by symbols. As an individual ship reporting contact every hour, USS Stickell (DDR 888) showed on the CINCLANTFLT display along with a symbol representing his evaluation of Soviet submarine.

"That destroyer, Stickell, he's still reporting his contact?" Admiral Dennison asked.

"Yes sir, and still evaluating it as a Soviet submarine. He's been ordered to leave, to proceed on duty assigned, but he's still on it."

"You mean he's disregarded his orders?"

"Yes sir, a number of times, at least six from the traffic we've seen."

"How many other unidents have we had from the Second Fleet units in the quarantine?" Unident was a contraction of unidentified contact. An intelligence officer from the staff responded, "A total of eight since the quarantine was declared, Admiral."

"And their evaluations?"

The intelligence officer looked into a folder on his lap. "Four were evaluated non-sub within the first hour. Four were possible-sub with contact lost in, let's see; 43 minutes, 17 minutes—." He summarized, "Contact was lost in less than 45 minutes on the four possible-sub contacts."

Admiral Dennison interrupted, "—and this guy claims he's holding contact with a Soviet submarine for over thirty hours?"

"Yes, sir," responded the Operations Officer. "He claims the submarine he's holding has a mechanical casualty and can't maneuver."

"Could be, I suppose, but highly unlikely. If he had a casualty he'd have to report it to the Soviet Northern Fleet headquarters. Did we have any indication of that?"

The Operations and the Intelligence Officers looked at each other, questioning, and each responded at the same time with some variation of, "I'll have to look into that."

The Operations Officer continued, "Although it's unlikely that this is a submarine, if it is, he can't report home if he's being held down."

The Commander in Chief of the U.S. Atlantic Fleet was not pleased. "Right, but what about before he was held down? Could he have made a report before then? Let's do some research. Back up this thing to where it started and see if we had any indicators before then from the area where they started."

Shellback had another cup of coffee with his sandwich in the Pilot House. Ping-echo. Contact on course zero seven zero, three knots. Thirty eight hours of contact. No change.

An hour later Chief Sonarman Petrovsky came up to Shellback and stated bluntly, "We got a problem."

"What problem?"

"Sonar. We're having trouble with the receive side. We can put out a ping okay but we're not processing the echo the way we should. We must have a weak amplifier or some other segment of the receiver."

"And to fix it you've got to go into the receiver cabinet, right?"

"Yes sir. Now, we're still getting the echo most of the time, but it's been very slowly getting worse. Four hours ago I noticed we missed one out of ten or twelve echoes. Now we're missing maybe one out of five or six. We can still hold contact, but like I said, it's getting worse."

Shellback felt the pain in his side and back. His head and shoulders ached a little more and his legs were heavier than ever. Fifty seven hours without real sleep and he tried a little harder to think, to concentrate. "Okay, here's what we'll do." He called the OOD over to join them. "Chief, you work out a plan to secure power to the receive side so that we can continue to transmit. Then, when the sonar gets bad enough so that we're not getting echoes, we'll secure the receiver and continue to transmit. That way, you'll be able to work on the receiver. Bill," he continued to the OOD, "you get Combat ready to track on the extension of our contact along zero seven zero at three knots. To the Red bastard he'll hear our sonar just like before. He won't know that we're not getting echoes. We'll use his constant zero seven zero and three knots to our advantage. The only thing is, Chief, we can't keep that up for too long or else we'll wander off, too far from the contact, and be circling empty water. So—"

"Yes sir. I understand. I'll do the best I can to rush it up."

"That's why I want you to plan in advance what you're going to check out in there. Set up a priority. This first, then that. Okay?"

"Aye, Captain, I gotcha. I'll get together with my guys and work out a plan. We already suspect the GS 178 module, had trouble with it before. I'll let you know when we're ready."

"Good,—and Chief, let me know as we go along how the sonar is acting. When you reach the point of having trouble holding contact, we'll do this false tracking plan."

SITREP Forty included the sonar problem and described the repair plan.

He was soaked with sweat on a very hot humid day in the bright sunshine and it was between innings in the dugout. "C'mon, you've done more than enough. Le'me get y'out of there and pitch Halloran. He's fresh and ready. You're dead."

"He's dogshit and you know it. This is my game and I'm gonna win it. Get off my ass."

"You'll ruin your arm,—future,—career,—course zero seven zero, three knots," Ping-echo, ping-echo.

"No!" Shellback jumped up from his chair. He had been dozing again, more heavily than before and his neck and head still ached with pain running up and down the right side of his back. The legs were heavy, cobwebs clouded his mind and foul taste filled his mouth. The bridge watch had changed while their young captain had dozed in his chair and they all looked at him as he jumped up asking, "Any changes?"

"No, Captain," replied the OOD. "Same course and speed. Sonar losing about one out of five echoes. Still holding contact, though."

Shellback went into his sea cabin again, washed, changed his shirt and brushed his teeth. Then, a little refreshed, he looked at himself in the mirror. He hadn't shaved in about 58 hours and his eyes were bloodshot. "Jesus, you look lousy," he said aloud to himself, then went back into the Pilot House. The radio messenger brought him a message from his task group commander, "—lack of evasion,—non-sub,—sonar deterioration,—direct you to break off and proceed on duty assigned." He handed the message to the OOD, "Put this in the `little faith' file."

Lieutenant Peter Hamil, the Supply Officer, was appalled at the sight of the captain as he answered the summons to the bridge. Peter had heard what the captain was going through from the other Stickell officers but this was the first he had seen the young skipper since before the hold down had started.

"Pete, there's a good chance this guy will surface during the night. He could recharge in a few hours and submerge again before dawn. If that happens we may not get a picture of him and there are some, there are many people, who won't believe us. So, I want you to check through the ship. See who has the best quality cameras. Then give them the best film, whatever we have that's best or most sensitive, from the ships store. I'll pay for the film. If this guy surfaces at night, I'll light him up as well as I can and maybe with the best cameras and film we can get a picture. What do you think?"

"Well," the Supply Officer hesitated, "I have a pretty good camera to start, and I know of a few others. I'll check for more. Film could be a problem. We've reduced our ships store stock to get ready for the shipyard and I'm not sure what's left."

"Okay, check it out and let me know."

He had dozed off again and it was almost dark when the radio messenger awakened him at 1900 with another message from his task group commander ordering him to break-off.

Shellback prepared a reply.

FROM: USS STICKELL
TO: CTG 20.3

PARA STILL HOLDING CONTACT WITH SOVIET SUBMARINE STOP

PARA IF YOU ARE STILL CONFIDENT IN YOUR NON SUB EVALUATION OF MY CONTACT COMMA AM SURE YOU WOULD HAVE NO OBJECTION IF I WALKED OUT THIRTY FATHOMS OF ANCHOR CHAIN AND STEAMED OVER MY CONTACT A NUMBER OF TIMES STOP I COULD DROP A MK FORTY FOUR TORPEDO ON THE CONTACT COMMA BUT YOUR NON SUB EVALUATION WOULD NOT JUSTIFY EXPENDITURE OF THIS EXPENSIVE WEAPON STOP EITHER OF THESE PROCEDURES WOULD PROVE THE EVALUATION STOP

PARA DO NOT RECOMMEND EITHER OF THE ABOVE AS THE SOVIETS WOULD CONSIDER THEM PROVOCATIVE AND THEY COULD LEAD TO A VERY EMBARRASSING SAR INCIDENT COMMA OR WAR STOP

PARA THIS IS A SOVIET SUBMARINE REPEAT THIS IS A SOVIET SUBMARINE STOP I INTEND TO CONTINUE HOLDING CONTACT WITH THIS SOVIET SUBMARINE STOP WOULD APPRECIATE AT LEAST ONE DD OR DE FOR SUPPORT COMMA AND CONTINUOUS VP ON STATION STOP ANTICIPATE SURFACING DUE TO BATTERY EXHAUSTION AROUND MIDNIGHT STOP

"What do you think of this?" Shellback handed the message he had just prepared to Pete Botazelli, Gold Team OOD.

After reading the message at least twice Pete handed it back. "Captain, with all due respect, sir, I don't think you should send this"

"Why not?"

"Well, you've stuck to a professionally modest action and reporting procedure so far. You may have disobeyed orders but you haven't shown disrespect, not directly. This message comes close to insubordination. It has a nasty flavor."

Shellback thought a moment, "You're right," and he balled it up and threw it in the trash can in the corner of the Pilot House.

"Nice shot," said Botazelli.

"Nice advice. Thanks for the advice. My mind must be going."

2100. The watch had changed again and Shellback had dozed off again and dreamed again with the same dream, break it off, come out of there, call it quits.

He drank more coffee and looked over the bridge watch in the darkened Pilot House. They were very quiet and he knew they, too, were tired. They had all been through a lot and no one knew how much longer this could go on, no one but a Soviet submarine commanding officer out there a hundred feet under the dark sea. How tired was he? What strain was he under as his battery capacity and oxygen supply were reduced, with no communications with his outside world for almost two days, with some kind of significant defect or casualty in his submarine and what was he going to do?

"—course zero seven zero, three knots, losing one echo in four."

The Commander in Chief of the U.S. Atlantic Fleet was receiving his 2000 briefing in his center at Norfolk. Four star Admiral Dennison had been home four times over the past ten days, and each of those times for less than an hour. Home was a mile away on the other side of the Naval Station, but he had a bunk room near his office, and stayed on the job through periods of crisis such as this Cuban Quarantine. The briefing had progressed through most of the fleet's operations in the vicinity of Cuba when it was interrupted by a telephone call from one of the staff officers of the Joint Chiefs of Staff in Washington, calling about the readiness of an aircraft carrier. The admiral was impatient and abrupt on the phone, then hung up and turned his attention back to the briefing that ended shortly.

"Now, Admiral, we have an additional item. You asked at our noon briefing that we reconstruct this Stickell contact and compare it with special intelligence information." The admiral had not exactly put it that way, nor had he wanted a full reconstruction, but he decided to withhold his comments until he heard and saw the results of this little project.

"As of 1800 today, about two hours ago, Stickell has been holding contact for forty four hours. The initial point of contact was here." The briefing officer pointed to a symbol on the chart. "The 1800 posit reported by the ship is here, one hundred and fifty four miles between these points in forty four hours. With the addition of a favoring half knot current prevalent in that area this time of year, that supports very closely the three knot speed being reported. Initial sonar contact was gained at 0020 yesterday. The contact had been held by Stickell as a small surface radar contact for fifty minutes. It became a sinker at time 0007. Our HFDF people," he referred to the shore based high frequency direction finding system which intercepted and analyzed high frequency radio transmissions worldwide, "had an intercept at time 2306 on a frequency seldom used by the Soviets but suspected of being reserved for emergency or high priority reports."

"Like a submarine with a casualty?" asked Admiral Dennison.

"It could be, Admiral. We're not sure because we couldn't break the code and the transmission was in burst mode, so that it was on the air a very brief time. We were able to get an AOP," he used the acronym for area of probability, "but it was larger than is our reportable standard, so this intercept was not reported."

"How large and where was it?" the admiral asked, frowning.

"The usual elliptical shape, 300 miles by 150 miles located here." The briefing officer taped a plastic overlay on the large vertical plot. The ellipse included the symbol of Stickell's initial contact, just inside the northeast corner. "Our standard is to report only those detections which can be located to AOPs 250 miles by 100 miles or smaller. This AOP exceeded that standard."

"So," the admiral was not at all pleased, "we had an intercept on a suspected Soviet emergency freq which could have been a submarine reporting a casualty, and that intercept was at the time when Stickell's contact was on the surface, and Stickell's initial contact was within the AOP of that intercept, and that poor bastard in Stickell has been fighting off his entire chain of command because nobody believes him?" It came across as an angry question that needed no answer, but the Operations Officer replied with a faint, "Yes, sir."

The Intelligence Officer had something more to contribute, "Admiral, there's one more thing. If we project the contact's reported course of zero seven zero over to here," he pointed to a point on the vertical chart, "we come to an area in which a Soviet Atrek Class ship has been operating for the past two weeks."

"Atrek Class?" the admiral asked.

"Converted freighters. They are submarine tenders and replenishment ships." After a few seconds the Intelligence Officer continued, "Also, the initial contact report from Stickell said that prior to going sinker his radar contact was being tracked on course zero seven zero, speed ten. So it looks like both on the surface and then submerged, this contact might have been on his way to get some help. It's consistent with the casualty theory."

"Well," the Commander in Chief of the U.S. Atlantic Fleet broke the stillness that followed his Intelligence Officer's statement, "I suggest that as a very high priority of business here, we get a message out to Stickell and to his entire Doubting Thomas chain of command explaining what we have just explained here, informing them that I have re-evaluated the Stickell contact as probable submarine," he emphasized the I, "and suggesting that just perhaps that poor tired and harassed bastard on the bridge of that destroyer might need some help. And one more thing, the skipper of that destroyer might just be in the process of pulling off the greatest Cold War ASW coup of all time. I want a preliminary report from his ISIC by message and a more complete report whenever he has time."

The admiral started to leave, then stopped, "And still another thing, when we get this sorted out let's look into our 'standards for reporting' policies for HFDF and other systems, too. We can't afford to let these things fall through the cracks."

On board the aircraft carrier USS Forrestal, Rear Admiral Meyer was still in his command center. He got little sleep as he had a lot of ships and aircraft to control, and a lot of ocean to cover.

"That was sixteen hours ago, admiral. How long can we tie up this destroyer in what we know is a waste of time?" The Assistant Surface Operations Officer had already talked with his Ops Officer and the Chief of Staff and was now trying to convince Rear Admiral Meyer to send out the "Relief of Command" message.

"I told the Chief of Staff that we'd give this guy some time. I hadn't realized it was sixteen hours ago. Also, I'd rather have his ISIC handle it. It's more legal that way, more neat. If I do it it's an outsider, an aviator, relieving a blackshoe for cause. Bad politics."

"Yes sir. Then let me draft a message from you to his DIVCOM asking that he relieve this guy."

"Okay, Dan. Draft the message."

On board Stickell, SITREP Forty six had just gone out when the CIC Officer came up to the Captain on the bridge. The Combat Information Center was run by this young officer and this is where information from the ship's sensors such as radar, sonar and lookouts is brought together, displayed and analyzed. Tactical message traffic is processed in the CIC, also as it is the focal point, the nucleus, of tactical information.

"Captain, over the past few hours, the last three to be precise, I can't be real sure at this point, but this contact may have reduced speed. Not much," he was quick to add, "but maybe a knot. We're dealing with three knots maybe down to two, and with our relative motion and a very slight current here, it's hard to tell the difference."

"If he has slowed that could be very significant," the Captain replied.

"That's why I wanted to tell you. We've been plotting him along at three knots for so long it's almost automatic, but if I were to start a new plot three hours ago I'd say the contact was making something closer to two knots."

"You've tried a larger scale?"

"Yes sir. I shifted to a larger scale a half hour ago and back plotted as well as I could, but it's not accurate enough to be sure. In a couple of more hours it might be."

"Okay, keep at it and let me know how it shows up. If he did actually slow three hours ago, you may not have a couple of hours left."

Shellback asked the OOD to get the leading signalman to join them for a conference. "If this guy comes up at night, as I suspect, we'll have to illuminate him. So, Sigs, I'd like you to be ready with all our signal lights, no night filters. I wish we had one of those big searchlights, but we'll have to do with what we have. Be ready, but don't illuminate him until the OOD or I tell you."

"Yes, sir, but that won't be much light for picture taking," the signalman contributed.

"I know. We'll get as close as we can and hope the pictures come out."

To the OOD Shellback continued, "We should have some small portable searchlights in our boats. Let's get them up to the signal bridge." Then, back to the signalman, "Even though it might be dark, as soon as he surfaces I want the international flags that ask if he needs assistance."

"In the dark?" the signalman asked.

"Yes. It might be near dawn and with any light I want him to see, if he can, that we're asking him if he needs help. He may take our picture through his low-light-level periscope, if he has one, and I want that signal showing."

"Yes sir."

"Soon after he surfaces, night or day, the OOD or I will direct you to start calling him up by flashing light, but don't start until one of us tells you."

"He won't answer, Captain. He won't even have a signal light rigged."

"Yeah, I know, but he might rig one after awhile and whether he does or not I want to be calling him. I want to be the one initiating communications, rather than waiting for him to call me, and if he does reply send him, 'Are you in need of assistance?' and 'May I help you?' and 'What is the nature of your problem?', stuff like that. Mr. O'Connor will write them out for you." O'Connor nodded.

"I want nice polite stuff, nothing nasty like, 'We got your red ass you communist bastard.' Nothing like that. Just simple and polite, and don't wait for a reply. If he responds by light just keep sending until, well, until you can't send anymore, Okay?"

"Yes, sir. We'll be ready."

"Good. Oh, one more thing Sigs, if you will please, let's show holiday colors for this event. I believe in older times it was called 'battle colors'."

"Yes sir, Captain. It was battle colors and we'll show our biggest and brightest." The signalman was really pleased as he made his way back to his flag bags aft of the Pilot House.

Battle colors went back into the sailing ship days, when ships engaged in battle flew their largest national flags from every mast for clear identification amid smoke and fallen masts and rigging. It became a symbol of pride to prepare for battle with extra large national flags prominently displayed and the red, white and blue national ensign flown by a destroyer such as Stickell was large enough to be identified many miles away.

At 2300 Captain Speakes received a message from COMCARDIV Two, who was the task force commander, asking him to take whatever action was appropriate, including, if necessary, relief of the CO for cause, to return Stickell to assigned duties. Time had run out even though his friend the Chief of Staff, whose wingman Shellback had picked up eight years ago, had bought all the time he could. There wasn't much more to ask for and the worst part was that Speakes thought it really might be a Soviet submarine. How long could he stall, and would it do any good? Maybe he could give Shellback another hour or two at the most.

"—course zero seven zero, speed two and a half knots," losing one echo in four, one echo in three."

Shellback had been dozing again and was awakened by the sonar report which changed to "one echo in three," representing a significant reduction in sonar capability. The receiver was failing noticeably now and they might have to go through the "tracking a false contact" drill and try to repair the receiver. He wished he could think more clearly, but was so tired. Had he forgotten something? Was there something else he could do? Could he get help from anyone, anywhere? All he could do was stick with it even as a little voice way in the back of his clouded mind struggled to be heard; break off, call it quits, take the easy way out, you're too tired to go on. No! I can't give in now. Push that voice out of mind. Don't think it!

He had fallen back into a half sleep almost as quickly as he woke up a few minutes ago and as the radio messenger called he looked at the clock, 2330. It was an immediate precedence message from the commander of the patrol plane wing at Key West to his subordinate at Roosevelt Roads, Puerto Rico, with Stickell among the many information addressees. Most of it made little sense through his fogged numbed mind, but a few lines leaped out, "—matter of high priority,—divert first available flight,—report to SAC CO Stickell—." SAC was scene of action commander he realized.

"Pete, Bill, who's here?" He asked the darkened Pilot House from his chair.

"Lieutenant Botazelli, sir," Came the reply from the OOD rushing over.

"Look at this, Pete! Am I dreaming? Tell me if it's for real."

Botazelli read it carefully, then read it again and laughed. "It's got to be real, Captain, 'cause I'm sure not dreaming. This tells Rosey Roads to send us a P-2, the next available one, and says we're Scene of Action Commander. I'll have Combat check the position and set up the comms." He went quickly to the squawk box.

On legs invigorated by adrenalin, Shellback jumped up. "This is great! Jesus, what a break! I shouldn't look a gift horse in the mouth and all that, but why is this happening? Why a P-2 now after forty eight hours? Something has changed. We must have an advocate out there some where."

The OOD was still giving orders to Combat but stopped long enough to respond. "Well, Captain, who cares? We're getting help and someone out there believes us."

"Right. You're right. Let's get set up to receive our air support. This is great!"

At midnight the watch changed and SITREP Forty eight was sent out.

"—course zero seven zero, speed two and a half, losing one echo in three." Forty eight hours of contact and how much battery could Ivan have left? Not much by Shellback's calculations, but those were based on a number of assumptions any one of which could be wrong. He couldn't have much battery left and the slowing down might be indicative of low battery but how far down would this guy dare take his battery? Where was this P-2? When would it get here? How much longer could the deteriorating sonar hold contact? All of those questions were constantly going through Shellback's mind and he didn't even know of another problem, that of his own command position. How much longer would it be before a message arrived on board Stickell directing his relief for cause?

At 0100 sonar started losing one echo out of two pings, but even worse there was no consistency. Sometimes three or four pings produced echoes then three or four with no echoes and Chief Petrovsky reported that it was very difficult to hold contact and they were holding only because of the consistent movement of the target, so if the submarine took even a simple turn Stickell would be unable to maintain contact.

"Okay," Shellback thought aloud into a darkened Pilot House. "We have our problem with the sonar and Ivan has his with the battery and the casualty. He has two problems to our one. We've got help on the way and time is now on our side. We'll try to keep contact as long as we can and hope that either he surfaces or our P-2 arrives before we lose contact. If we lose contact we track his DR and try to fix the sonar." DR meant dead reckoning, which was the projected track, in this case zero seven zero, two and a half knots.

Later the watch changed and Shellback heard Lieutenant Bill O'Connor, the OOD, on the squawk box with CIC. "Get the surface radar tuned for best periscope detection and make sure those fire controlmen are wide awake with their radar. If this guy has to surface he'll put up his scope first. I want to be able to pickup anything he puts up, a whip antennae, a periscope or a broomstick. Understand? I don't give a shit what's ten or twenty miles away, concentrate on that sonar contact and get that periscope on radar as soon as it comes up, surface search and fire control."

"This is Combat, roger."

"And Combat, wake up those girls in EW. As soon as this guy puts up an antenna he's going to report to his brass. We want to know when that happens, too."

Two clicks on the squawk box meant, "This is Combat, roger." EW was the electronic warfare section of CIC, where radio and radar signals could be detected.

Twenty minutes later Combat called out, "I got a radar contact over this sonar contact! Small contact! Fire control radar reports locked on." O'Connor rushed to the bridge radar repeater and Shellback came out of his chair, grabbed his binoculars and headed for the port wing of the bridge.

"Bridge, Sonar. Contact's getting weaker. Something's changed. Maybe surfacing."

"Bridge, Combat. Good surface radar contact bearing two six two, range two two hundred, correlates with sonar contact and fire control radar."

"He's coming up! He's coming up!" yelled O'Connor.

Shellback had his binoculars glued to his eyes, peering into the black darkness on the bearing of two six two, but seeing nothing. "Go closer! Use the radar. Keep him well up on the bow to the beam," ordered Shellback.

"Come left to two seven zero—." Shellback heard Lieutenant O'Connor start a maneuver to close the radar contact.

"Captain," The radio messenger was standing behind him. "I have a message for you, sir."

Shellback's response was abrupt. "Not now. Not just now. In a few minutes."

The messenger would not be turned away, even by his captain. "Chief says you'll want to see this right away, no matter what. Told me to wake you up or interrupt you, sir."

More abruptly, "Okay, okay, but just stand back a minute. I'll be right with you." Still he stared into the darkness. Nothing.

"I hear some noise out there, Captain," yelled the signalman peering through the "Big Eyes," the ship's twenty power binoculars mounted on a carriage.

"Come right to two seven five—." O'Connor continued to maneuver.

"Bridge, Combat. Radar contact two five one, range one eight hundred."

"Bridge, Sonar. Sonar contact two five zero, range one eight hundred, soft echoes, losing more than half of the echoes."

"Bridge, Combat. I have voice radio contact with P-2 aircraft, voice call Four Billposter, closing our posit, ETA five zero minutes."

"Come left to two six five—," from O'Conner.

"Bridge, Combat, Radar contact one two five, range one five hundred."

"More noise out there, skipper, could be diesel engine starting up," from the signalman who had left the big eyes and placed a megaphone to his ear.

"Come left to two zero zero—," the OOD continued to conn the ship.

"Range?" asked an impatient Shellback.

"Twelve hundred yards, Captain. How much closer do you want?" O'Conner was watching the radar repeater as he conned from inside the Pilot House.

"Try to keep it at a thousand yards."

"Yes sir. Come left to one seven five—."

Shellback estimated that Stickell was almost directly astern of the submarine, assuming that Ivan had maintained a heading of zero seven zero. He ordered the Boatswain Mate of the Watch to call Lieutenant Peter Hamil and his camera crew to the bridge and alerted the signalman that in a few minutes they should be up on the submarine's starboard side.

A few seconds more and Shellback barked, "Range and bearing?"

"Three four zero, one thousand yards," called O'Connor from inside the Pilot House.

Shellback thought he could see something in the slight moon and starlight. "On the port beam, Sigs, Illuminate!" and two signal lights without night filters and two portable searchlights shot out beams of bright light into the blackness. They could all clearly hear the roar of diesel engines as each light moved left and right, up and down. First one than another then all four found a low black object from out of the darkness.

"There it is!" "Right there!" "I see it!" They all yelled.

"Peter!"

"Yes sir."

"What do you think? Can we get a picture?"

"Captain, I wish I could say yes, but there really isn't enough light. We can try, but I'm pretty sure we'll be wasting our time."

"Okay. Bill, go up ahead and down the other side. Try for five hundred yards on his beam."

"Yes sir."

"Cease illumination," Shellback ordered and the lights went out and they were all plunged into a total blackness having lost night vision to the bright lights. Shellback felt his way into the Pilot House and to the squawk box. "Combat, ask that P-2 if he has flares and if he can illuminate a surface contact, and Combat, please patch in his circuit on a bridge speaker."

Two clicks on the squawk box was the affirmative response.

Back out on the port wing of the bridge and still blind, Shellback heard Pete Botazelli's voice, "You got him, Captain! You held him to exhaustion."

"What're you doing up here? You're off duty. You should be sleeping. I'll need you rested and ready in a little while."

Pete laughed, "I'll be ready, Skipper. You don't think I could miss this, do you?"

"No, I guess not. Well, make yourself useful. Help Bill with a maneuvering board to get us into position."

"Yes sir. Uh, Captain, about this business of holding to exhaustion, I have to ask, who held whom to exhaustion? You were really out the past few hours. You look like you've been in a big fight."

"Maybe I have been in a fight, but as the saying goes, 'If you think I look bad, you ought 'a see the other guy!'"

"Captain?" The radio messenger was still waiting with clipboard and red filtered flashlight.

"Oh yeah, sorry. Let me see what you have."

The immediate precedence message was from the Commander in Chief of the U.S. Atlantic Fleet re-evaluating Stickell's contact to probable submarine and explaining the HFDF intercept, AOP, and movement toward the Soviet submarine support ship. The entire operational and administrative chains of command were action addressees on the message and they were directed, "—to lend every support and encouragement to prosecution of this contact."

Tears were running down Shellback's face and his knees buckled as he made his way, rubbing his back, to his elevated seat on the starboard side of the Pilot House, and he sat alone in the dark.

The Chief of Staff walked into Rear Admiral Meyer's cabin with two messages, "I think you'll enjoy these, Admiral."

"Well, why the hell didn't he tell us all this spook shit a couple of days ago? Let's get some help to this guy."

Smiling, the Chief of Staff took back the CINCLANTFLT message. "We've started that already. Rosey Roads has a P-2 on the way and we're sending a destroyer. CTF 23 is sending two DE's. But you ain't seen nothin' yet, sir. Here's another message."

"Surfacing report! Surfacing report!" The admiral yelled with pleasure. "He held the bastard to exhaustion by himself? Jesus! He did it all by himself!"

"Yes sir, and Admiral," the Chief of Staff was still smiling, "When would you be available for the ceremony?"

"What ceremony?"

"A certain ceremony on the foc'sle with a half hour to muster a crowd."

The Commander-in-Chief of the U.S. Atlantic Fleet was at his desk in Norfolk, Virginia as his Chief of Staff entered the four star admiral's office as directed. "Come in Stan and have a seat. There's something I want to talk over."

Rear Admiral Stanley had learned from his first few days in this job that Admiral Dennison used the expression, "I want to talk over" with him whenever the old boy intended to give some direct orders. This would be no exception and Stanley was prepared to receive his admiral's directive and would see it precisely carried out, for that's what good chiefs of staff did and Stanley was a very good chief of staff.

"This surfacing of the Soviet submarine by that lieutenant in Stickell." Admiral Dennison's inflection made it into a question and Stanley mouthed a silent, "Yes sir."

Dennison continued, "It has the makings of great PAO material and I'm sure the press would have a field day with it; very junior CO, old ship, antiquated sonar, everyone against him, he hangs on, defies everyone and comes up smelling like a rose, or more likely the Soviet sub comes up and our hero becomes a golden boy, a golden eagle."

"Yes, sir, it has that." The Chief of Staff noted to himself that the admiral had used "would have" referring to the press rather than "will have" and he wondered where his admiral was going, when the direct order would emerge.

Dennison continued, "Well, this situation could serve us well, you know, show that the Navy gives responsibility to young guys and these young guys have what it takes, there's glamour and drama and success in the face of adversity, but—." Dennison paused but continued before Stanley could comment. "But this all could, and even more likely would backfire on us, make the Navy look bad. Higher ranks didn't believe him, intell botched on a technicality, and maybe even why was such a junior officer in command of this ship?"

Stanley was nodding, waiting for Admiral Dennison to make his point but was surprised to hear, "Now, we're also faced with a budget issue—."

At that point the Chief of Staff couldn't resist and asked, "Budget issue? What kind of budget issue could there be in this Soviet submarine surfacing?"

"Why, Stan, I'm surprised at you," Dennison was almost laughing. "You of all people! A guy right out of OP 96, a budget guru! I thought you guys could see budget in everything. Hey, I feel good about this now, because I saw a major budget involvement before you, I beat an OP 96er to a budget factor."

Stanley was also smiling and nodded as he admitted with exaggerated contrition, "Okay, admiral, it looks like you got me there, so what's the budget consideration?"

"Look, we're trying to include funding for new sonar in the Gearings, trying to replace the SQS-4 with the SQS-29/32 series. CNO's been telling Pucinello on the House Armed Services Committee that these old sonars can't do the job, lots a' bucks involved—."

Stanley was nodding, mouthing, "Right."

The CinC continued, "Sure you can see it now. We gotta have those bucks for new sonars and if this Soviet submarine was brought to the surface by an old Gearing with old SQS-4 sonar, even though someone might point out that the Red bastard had a casualty, that won't matter, than why spend money for new sonar? 'What you have is good enough,' the budget boys on The Hill will say." Stanley nodded as Dennison continued, "Look, Stan, I want this lieutenant to be properly rewarded, awarded maybe, that's up to his ISIC and I don't want to interfere with that. What I do want, though, is as little press circus on this as possible, no big ceremony, press conferences, books or magazine feature bios. See that he's recognized quietly and bury it. See that his ISIC gets that word and understands it. I don't want to see this young guy interviewed on national TV. Understand?"

"Yes, sir, I understand. WILCO and so will his ISIC. If I may, admiral, I'm embarrassed that I didn't jump on that budget issue right away." They both laughed as the Chief of Staff got up and left Admiral Dennison's office.

CHAPTER 4

The family had just heard Barney Williams tell the story about Martin Shielbrock's involvement in the Cuban Quarantine and his subsequent ASW feat. Seated on the Cays patio they continued the reminiscence.

"Now just a minute," Jackie spoke up. "It's one thing for you guys to sail away over the horizon to glamorous adventures, but when you're married we young brides have to shift from an exiting social life and romance to a quiet lonely life style. It is not easy, gentlemen." She looked from Barney to Steven and back again. "And here was young beautiful Barbara, a life of romance and social activity. All of a sudden she's all alone and—."

Barney interrupted, "What do you mean 'all alone? You were there in Norfolk. She still had her job. There were friends. It wasn't exactly alone."

"You men!" Again she looked from Barney to Steven. "You never understand the women's point of view in this thing we call marriage! I'm talking about a total commitment, dedication, and then 'poof'. Take in all lines and bye bye baby, I'm off to the other side of the world for a year. Take care of yourself. That's where newly wed Barbara found herself."

"So why don't you tell us about how Barbara dealt with that first deployment and the separation?" Ellie asked.

"Great idea," Barney offered.

"Hey, hold it," Steven stepped in. "I was ready for some baseball. We're way ahead of the story. We haven't even gone over the early Shielbrock story, the pre-navy stuff. What about college days and summer baseball in Canada?"

Barney shook his head, "You've heard all that stuff. Let's let the girls have a chance."

"Yeah, I've heard it from my Dad but I want to hear it from you, your angle on it."

"Okay," Barney smiled and conceded. "Let's let the girls have their story and then I'll tell you about Canadian baseball." He bowed from his seated position. "Ladies, please, if you will, the story of Barbara, the new navy wife, alone, her man away at sea."

Jackie was not pleased. "Okay, you can make light of this but later I'm going to tell a connected story and you'll be out of your seat. Just wait and see!"

Barney looked at Steven and nodded. "We men are anxious to hear about Barbara waiting at home and Barbara later. The floor is yours."

BARBARA WAITING IN NORFOLK

Martin Shielbrock's first deployment after they were married was very difficult for Barbara. Norfolk life had transitioned from frequent dates with various Navy officers, to her romance with Jules Loffman and to her romance and marriage to Martin Shielbrock. Then there were four months of excitement as a new bride. She was involved in finding and setting up an apartment as their home, learning to live with this new man she loved. With partying, sharing, loving and enjoyment, and then he had sailed away from Norfolk for the Korean War four months after they were married. There were no parties and she came home each evening to their apartment, to spend the evening and the night alone. She saw Jackie on occasion and met some of the other officers' wives once a month for dinner and bridge. Jackie and Barney Williams were dating then and twice she joined them for dinner, but her life had changed from an intense fast paced social activity to a lonely, slow process. There was her job, still, and that was very important to her, and then there was the lonely apartment.

She got a letter from Martin about once a week and he always explained the ship's employment and there were words of love and affection. She wrote him at the same frequency, explaining her work, giving the local gossip and adding words of endearment. She enjoyed his letters as he described the war from his limited perspective as a shipboard lieutenant junior grade.

The deployment had been scheduled for six months but the ship soon learned that they would be extended and eight months would be more realistic. Also, there was a very strong possibility that they would transit home from the Western Pacific across the Indian Ocean, through the Suez Canal into the Mediterranean Sea and then across the Atlantic to Norfolk. Martin's letters showed that he was excited with the prospect of this return route. First, because it made the deployment a round-the-world cruise, and second, some of the officers talked about having their wives join them for one of the Mediterranean port visits. It gave them something special to look forward to, so the primary considerations were the ship's schedule and each couple's individual finances. With Barbara still working at Loffman's the money problem was less for them than some of the other young couples, but even so, Martin wrote that he was saving money in case they had the opportunity for Barbara to fly to Europe.

Weekdays were bad enough but weekends were worse as the months went by slowly and lonely for Barbara. She deliberately worked at the store most Saturdays, often passing up the weekday she was supposed to be off to work an additional day and she wished the store was open Sundays.

Martin had been away seven months and his ship had been further extended with an uncertain return date as Barbara walked into the apartment, sorted the mail and sat in the living room chair staring straight ahead at nothing. No letter from Martin today and tomorrow was Saturday but she wasn't scheduled to work this time. Then there would be Sunday, so she had Friday night, Saturday and Sunday to face, alone. She would finish the novel lying on the end table and there would be laundry, ironing, housework; the apartment was immaculate but she would clean some more. Then what? Loneliness.

The sharp ring of the telephone shocked her and she let it ring again. "Hello."

"Barbara?" She recognized the voice of Jules Loffman even after all this time. "This is Jules."

"Yes, I know. How are you, Jules?"

"I'm fine, thanks, but the more important question is, how are you?"

"I'm fine, thanks." There was silence for a moment and she added, "Really."

"Barbara, you don't sound fine. You sound upset, troubled."

"Well, I'm not upset or troubled. I'm fine. I just—, I only—, I—." She was silent another moment. "Damn you, Jules! You could always tell what I was thinking, how I felt, and now, now, even on the phone you—." Her voice quivered and tears welled up in her eyes. "Even now you can tell—." She cried openly for a while.

"Barbara, do you want to tell me about it?"

"No. It's nothing. You just caught me at a bad time. I'm all right. I'll be all right."

"What can I do to help? Barbara, please, you know I'd do anything for you. Is there anything I can do for you?"

She was silent for awhile, trying to regain her composure. "Jules, I—." She fought back her tears.

"Yes?"

She hesitated and then just blurted it out, "I am so God Damn lonely, Jules, I just, I don't know." She paused again, "I'm just so lonely."

"Well, I can understand that, Barbara. I know loneliness, and in your situation—. Well, loneliness can become pervasive, encompassing, controlling. Like most problems, you have to face loneliness and say 'I'm going to tolerate it, put up with it!' That's okay if you can see an end in sight, if it's not permanent. But if loneliness is to be permanent, well, then you have to take a step, or steps, maybe bold steps, to eliminate the loneliness or at least to make it tolerable."

"Jules, what does all your amateur philosophy mean?"

"Now, don't be nasty. Loneliness can have that effect, also, and I know that you don't want to be nasty, not even because of loneliness."

"Okay. I won't be nasty. Sorry. Run your philosophy past me again but shape it for my simple and confused state of mind."

"Your mind is never simple but often confused. Okay, my dear; loneliness has to be either tolerated or eliminated. Tolerance means put up with the discomfort. Live with it. You can do that because you know it isn't permanent. Elimination requires the lonely person to seek diversion, find a remedy and get rid of the loneliness. A show, a ball game, a church bingo game, dinner with a friend, move in with relatives; those actions must fit the situation. A person facing permanent loneliness seeks permanent elimination. A person who cannot tolerate a temporary loneliness seeks temporary measures."

"I didn't know you went to church bingo games." They laughed.

"Hey, now, that sounds better. Your laughter, a happy Barbara, is the most important objective in my life. If I have brought laughter into your life score one for me today."

"Jules, you know you have always brought enjoyment into my life."

"And now, faced with the lonely problem, or any other problem, is there anything I can do for you?"

She didn't answer.

"Barbara?"

"Yes."

"Barbara, I can't see your face. If I could, I could tell what you're thinking, but with only your voice and the absence of it I am somewhat handicapped in reading your mind. I know that you want or need something, and believe me, whatever it is, I will do everything I can to provide for it, but you have to give me something more to go on."

"I know—. I know I'm being difficult but this isn't easy. For you everything is easy but for me—."

"Yes, I know. For you this is difficult, but darling, please know that many things are difficult for me, especially when they concern you, like making this call to you."

"Where are you?"

"I'm in New York."

"New York?" Her voice had a clear note of disappointment.

"Yes, New York. Why? Does it matter where I am?"

"Well, I guess not. Not really. It's just that—. No, it doesn't matter." She changed to a forced cheerful tone. "It was sweet of you to call though. It was perfect timing. I needed someone to talk to and you call. What could be better? You're right. Loneliness has to be dealt with. 'A talk with a friend' has to be one of the best ways to dispel loneliness."

"I'm glad I was able to help. Now, are you sure that after we finish this phone conversation you'll be able to tolerate the loneliness? You haven't eliminated it, of course, but then you don't have to. You only have to do whatever it takes to allow you to tolerate it."

"Damn you again, Jules! I thought I had it under control and now—. No. It won't be any better after we hang up."

"Well then, what can we do to put the loneliness away for a longer time?"

"We can—," She hesitated. "Nothing. The phone call was very sweet, Jules."

"Barbara, even without your cooperation may I make a try at reading your mind over the phone?"

"Jules, I—."

"Hush and listen. I'm in New York. There's a flight from Norfolk to La Guardia in an hour and a half. We could have dinner at Maxim's at nine tonight. Pack a bag. Go to the airport. There will be a ticket in your name at the Eastern counter. Take a cab to the Biltmore. There will be a separate room reserved in your name. I'll call your room at eight thirty. We'll go to dinner. Tomorrow we can visit the Fifth Avenue shops, the Empire State Building and the Bronx Zoo. Dinner and a show, Saturday to be determined. Sunday brunch, Central Park and return to Norfolk. As the saying goes, 'no strings attached'."

"Oh, Jules, that sounds so—." She hesitated. "Jules, I'm married."

"Darling, there are only a few people in this world who are as aware of that fact as I am, but thank you for reminding me. My concern is your loneliness. I would like to change it to joy. If I can do so, I stand ready to serve. The extent of my effort is and will always be up to you. Now, I am going to terminate this telephone conversation with a simple goodbye. I use the common term in its generic form, implying no time frame and hoping with deep sincerity that you will answer my next call at eight thirty at the Biltmore. Please look at your watch." She did. "I suggest that you remain seated for fifteen minutes after you hang up. If, after that much consideration, you would like to have dinner with me, jump up, pack and rush to the airport. If you decide otherwise, remain as seated beyond the fifteen minutes. Remain as seated until you determine what to do about your loneliness. Either way, I wish for you much happiness."

"Thank you, Jules."

"Goodbye, Barbara."

"Goodbye." She hung up and looked again at her watch. Five minutes later she ran into the bedroom to pack.

Sunday night she burst into her apartment, threw her bag toward the bedroom and let out a whoop of joy as she kicked off her heels, sat and stretched on the same soft chair that had held a lonely, sulking Barbara two nights before. It had been marvelous! Everything had been perfect; the dinners, the show, the shopping, the sight seeing, everything.

Just as he had said; he called at eight thirty and there had been cocktails, dinner, after dinner drinks, everything with elegance. At the hotel he kissed her on the cheek and she went into her room, alone. She showered, powdered, brushed her hair, put on her make-up and a beautiful blue lace nightgown and robe, and in high heeled slippers she stepped through the door separating their rooms.

Jules was wearing a gold lounging robe and the room was dim in candlelight. It was deja-vu for Barbara, but even more delightful then that first time in Atlanta as this time Barbara knew how to respond, how to enjoy and how to share. She delighted with everything Jules did to please her and was just as pleased to thrill him in so many ways. She had almost forgotten that Jules was such an appreciative lover and every pleasure she conveyed to him was returned to her ten-fold.

They made love again Saturday morning then spent the day shopping and sight seeing like young tourists as they laughed and sang, held hands and danced. The musical show that night was the current hit of Broadway and Barbara knew that only through a heavy scalper could Jules have gotten tickets. Dinner was even more magnificent and elegant than the previous night and lovemaking was as perfect as before, and just as it was on Sunday.

As she sat in her living room Barbara still tingled all over just thinking of the touching, kissing, earlier that day and she got up and busied herself putting away her things, showering and getting ready for bed. Then she sat on the bed thinking still of the delights in another bed the past two days. Tomorrow, Monday, was a work day and she looked forward to it. Looked forward—, the mail! Saturday's mail should be in the box and she threw on a robe and ran downstairs to the mailbox.

An envelope from Martin thicker than usual dragged her back to reality and back in the apartment she held the envelope, hesitant to open it. God, where was she? What had she done? For a half hour she looked at the envelope, walked away, came back, even smoked a cigarette but she couldn't reason. Nothing seemed right, but everything was all right, she talked to herself. Look, you're in love with two very fine men and both of them are in love with you. You've just had a wonderful time with one of them and now here's a letter from the other one. This one you are married to so change roles now and share your love with your husband.

A round trip ticket to Rome and a brief letter came out of the envelope. Martin explained that the ship was enroute to the Mediterranean and would be at Naples, Italy, Sunday. She looked at the calendar to verify the date. That's today! He would meet her flight at Rome Tuesday and he had ten days leave, reservations at a reasonable second class hotel and three paydays in his pocket.

Forty eight hours after leaving Jules' bed at the Biltmore in New York, Barbara was in bed with her husband at Hotel La Fontana in Rome, Italy, across the plaza from the Trevi Fountain.

CHAPTER 5

"Barbara wouldn't want that romance story told but we're grown-ups here now so I think you should hear this. If not now, then when?" Jackie was looking at the setting sun. "How about dinner? Should we do some planning on dinner?"

"Not so fast! Don't be so anxious to change the subject." Steven looked hard at Jackie. "There must be a lot more to that story; this guy Loffman and my mom. I think I heard some whispers a few years ago. You've got more on that, haven't you? "

Jackie smiled and shook her head at Steven. "Well, maybe, but not now. Maybe later. Maybe tomorrow. It's getting late, and besides, I thought you were anxious to hear baseball stories."

Steven nodded smiling. "Oh, sure, you tell a story that leaves us hanging and then you run and hide behind a baseball story. That's a cop-out or maybe a foul ball!"

Barney interrupted. "Well, you're just going to have to stay tuned for the future adventures of Barbara Shielbrock. Remember, you asked for baseball and now you'll get baseball. 'If that's what you wants that's what you gets.' I remember saying that to your dad in Canada that summer. Jackie will be back on stage soon with more on Barbara but for now let's go back to 1952 and summer baseball. This is your dad and me in Canada and what great times we had there."

A SATURDAY AFTERNOON OF CANADIAN BASEBALL

Martin Shielbrock graduated, Class of 1952, from St. Lawrence University in Canton, New York, where he majored in Math but spent more time on the three B's; Beer, Broads, and Baseball. Barney Williams had been his classmate, close friend and team mate from grade school through high school and college. In high school they played on the same football, basketball, and baseball teams and Martin had been class President, Barney class Treasurer. Both were Eagle Scouts in the same troop and both belonged to the same Junior Achievement Company; one year Barney was President and Martin Vice President and the next year they exchanged roles. Both were honor students in high school.

The three B's came easily to them as they drank beer often and in large quantities. "Broads" is the crude expression for girls and there were always girls around, some of them crude, and baseball was their real passion. They participated in other sports as the seasons progressed but always looked forward to baseball season. Early in high school it became apparent that Barney Williams was a catcher and Martin Shielbrock a pitcher and in their senior year with Shielbrock pitching and Barney catching and hitting they took Arlington High School, in Poughkeepsie, New York, to the Dutchess County Scholastic League Championship. Their coach Fritz Jordan was on his way to becoming a legend in the Hudson Valley as that year he had also won county championships in the two other sports he coached; football and basketball. Barney and Martin had played on those teams also, so it was no surprise, with their good grades and sports achievements, that both of them obtained athletic scholarships to St. Lawrence University.

Schoolwork continued to be easy for them in college and both were popular. They belonged to the same fraternity, which they never took seriously, as they partied at all the fraternity houses, and athletic participation gave them access to all social events on or near campus.

Professional baseball scouts were clearly interested in Barney Williams, an excellent catcher, could hit well, had a good arm, could control the pitchers and was solid enough to protect home plate. Martin Shielbrock was a big right handed pitcher with impressive college baseball credentials but was considered erratic by the scouts. Against Colgate with pro-scouts looking on he gave up only three hits and struck out eleven, and two weeks later at Cornell he was knocked out of the game in the second inning. His coach and the scouts never knew Martin had been drinking and partying until four AM that morning.

Barney had berated him after the game. "Jesus Christ, Shiel, you knew there were going to be pro-scouts at the Cornell game! Couldn't you lay off the beer and broads just this once and impress them?"

Martin Shielbrock responded with, "I think that I have more to offer society than a trained monkey. Most professional ball players would have a tough time holding a job in a gas station. Baseball has given me a chance to get an education and I'd like to do something more responsible, challenging and rewarding than to 'play' the rest of my life. I don't know what that something will be but it will not be as an entertainer, a trained monkey. This country, the U.S. of A, has been very good to me, so good in fact that I may just owe my life to it, and it has been a very good life so far. Depending on how you figure the genetics, I could have been either burned in an oven or frozen on the Eastern Front, if a few poor and uneducated peasants hadn't made it from Europe to this country. Somehow I have a debt to pay, a service to give to this country, a pay-back for this fine life and I'll get to it."

At St. Lawrence, Martin and Barney learned that many baseball players from colleges across New England, New York, Pennsylvania and Ohio went to Canada when school was out because there they could get paid to play baseball and, by Canadian law, still maintain their amateur status.

The Ontario Senior Baseball League had teams in nine small cities and towns, all of them included in a roughly triangular shaped area of southern Ontario Province running from Sudbury in the north 300 miles to Kingston in the east near Watertown, New York, and then 500 miles down to Windsor in the south just across the border from Detroit. The biggest cities, Ottawa and Toronto, were not in the league, having professional baseball teams. In the semi-pro league the teams consisted of former professional baseball players, college players and local kids with hopes and dreams of making it in baseball.

After graduation, Martin and Barney signed up with Stratford, whose colorful manager Dutch Van Rosche had played minor league professional ball many years and twice had "a cup of coffee" in the majors. Dutch described the Ontario league as consisting of the shits of baseball; "Old shits who don't know when to stop, hot shits from colleges and young shits who don't know how ta' play."

Barney and Martin got rooms at Mrs. Drollinger's house and soon learned that the college players used the Maple Leaf Restaurant and Bar as their hangout. The high school kids had a meeting place of their own and the former professional players, all older, each had his own favorite place.

The league allowed payment up to twenty five dollars a game to players still considered amateurs. So, the college players got fifteen to twenty five dollars a game. The local kids played for whatever they could get, some nothing, others got five to ten dollars a game depending on how good they were. The former professional players were washouts from years in the minor leagues and a few of them, like Dutch, had very brief and unsuccessful visits to major league teams.

The Stratford Indians had three starting pitchers; two college boys and a forty one year old minor league washout. In addition to Shielbrock there was Dan Zetti from Cornell and John Dietrich with almost twenty years of some kind of organized or semi-pro ball behind him plus five years in the Army. Dietrich was drunk most of the time he wasn't playing and sometimes when he was. His salary was a secret but everyone suspected that he got about thirty five dollars a game plus some "under the table" from Stratford business men who were loyal to their town teams and bet on the games every weekend.

A typical weekend had a game on Saturday and a double header on Sunday; three games, three starting pitchers. John Dietrich was loved by the fans, so Dutch catered to their desires and often Dietrich would pitch on Saturday, Zetti would start the first game Sunday and Dietrich would be out there again to start the second Sunday game. Shielbrock seldom got to pitch and most of the fans didn't know him nor did they trust him and sometimes he filled in by playing first base. On the few occasions Dietrich failed to show up on Sundays, still drunk from the night before, Shielbrock pitched the second game of the day. He did fairly well; three wins and two losses, but the fans either moaned softly or were silent when he was announced as the starter. One of his losses had been against their big rival Kingston. As the season drew toward the close the Kingston Giants had a one game lead over Stratford. Popular thought in Stratford was that Shielbrock was to blame for the one game deficit. The fans either didn't know or chose to forget that Kingston businessmen had gotten together in August and for one weekend three game series they paid heavily to bring in four ringers; pro-ballplayers who beat Dietrich on Saturday. Zetti had been able to scrape out a close win in the first game on Sunday and Dietrich never showed up for that second Sunday game, choosing to remain drunk rather than face the loaded Kingston team again. Shielbrock got the call to start, pitched the whole game and lost 2-0 against the loaded team and a Kingston pitcher who was right out of Class A minor league ball the season before. Stratford bettors had lost heavily that weekend.

Barney Williams caught every inning of every game. He knew the league's hitters better than anyone and he knew the Stratford pitchers as well. On nights when they drank together, Dietrich, usually drunk, would tell the young players how his best years had been spent in the Army and he could name major league ball players that he pitched against. He struck out Chuck Connors, later with the Dodgers, and he got Marty Marion to fly out to left, but his favorite story was about getting Stan Musial to hit into a double play. Marion and Musial, can you imagine that? All-stars from the St. Louis Cardinals, Musial who led the National League in hitting! John Dietrich had faced them, had done well and now here he was years later with nothing; no arm, no money, no career, washed up. He liked to say that he left his arm in the army and all that was left was me, a little play on words.

Barney told Shielbrock one night after listening to Dietrich, "Y'know, Martin, that guy gets by in this league with nothing on the ball but control. He doesn't have a fastball. His curve is hardly a wrinkle. He seldom throws a knuckler because he can't control it."

"How does he get them out?" Martin asked. "He's got to have something."

"Sure, he's got control and patience. He's easy to catch 'cause he's always where he wants to be. Control, placement, the low corners, inside, outside, just across the knees, nothing more. The batters are mesmerized studying the ball and trying to figure out if he'll catch the corners. Inside corners, outside corners, always low, never a high pitch, seldom a good pitch. No speed. Control, Shiel, control. Nothing more. If you had that control, with your curve and fastball, you'd go to the Hall of Fame."

The league had a rule that the season must end on a particular Saturday in mid September and by that time Zetti had returned to Cornell to start his senior year, leaving only Dietrich and Shielbrock available as starters for the final game with Kingston. Stratford was one game behind Kingston in the league standings, so if Kingston won the last game the season would end with Kingston as Champs but if Stratford won, the league would be tied and a second game would be played that same day to determine the league championship. Dietrich would start that first game and, if Stratford won, Shielbrock was the only other starter Dutch could use in the second and deciding game, if there was one. They had to take the games one at a time and Dietrich was the logical choice to start the first game at noontime Saturday. Kingston would start their ace Mel Grieves out of Class A ball to win the championship.

As game time approached Dietrich was not at the ball park in Stratford and Dutch called to Shielbrock. "Okay, hot shit, I got no choice. Dietrich must be drunk somewhere. I don't like it, but you're gonna hafta start. Get warmed up."

Shielbrock started to warm up and there was an immediate and loud response from the early arrivals at the game. Soon, catcalls, yells and groans came from the Stratford fans and one yelled, "Dutch, you son of a bitch, you can't start that rag arm." From another, "Not Shielbrock, Dutch, you're givin' the game away," and "Get that bum outa there." They had money bet on the game.

Kingston fans that had driven over for the game were ecstatic, they cheered the choice. "We gotcha now! Money in the bank." By game time Dietrich had still not appeared and Shielbrock went to the mound for his final warmup pitches as Stratford fans groaned and Kingston fans cheered as their first batter stepped to the plate.

"Shortstop Mario Le Clerc," was announced and four pitches later he walked to first base. Center fielder John Luca hit a fly ball to right field for out number one. "Right fielder, Buster Branch," was announced and Barney went out to talk with Shielbrock because Branch was one of the best hitters in the league. "Look, Shiel, this guy can really hit but he can't handle a low inside pitch. Keep it low and inside. You got good stuff today. You can get him."

"Okay," and Barney went back to the plate.

The umpire called, "Ball one," low and inside. "Ball two," again low and inside. "Strike one," caught the low inside corner. Branch swung at the next low inside pitch and bounced it to the shortstop, to second, to first, double play. They were out of the inning and the Stratford crowd applauded.

Mel Grieves was the Kingston ace pitcher from Class A ball, and he was good as he struck out the first two Stratford batters. Barney Williams then came to bat and hit the first pitch over the left field fence; home run. Stratford Indians one, Kingston Giants zero. The next Stratford batter grounded out to end the first inning.

Shielbrock walked the first batter in the second inning and Barney threw him out trying to steal second. The second batter hit a grounder to second and was thrown out. Shielbrock walked the next batter and Barney came out to the mound. "This guy on first takes a big lead and gets back fast. Give him some encouragement like you used to in high school then nail him, remember?"

"Okay."

"Now the batter can't judge low balls, inside or outside. Keep it low. You got good stuff. Keep it low."

"Okay," Barney trotted back to the plate.

Martin stretched and paused, looking over at the runner on first base. Pretty good lead. He turned and fired the ball to his first baseman. The throw was directly toward the first baseman's mitt and the runner dove for the base with his arm outstretched but was tagged.

"Yer'oot," called the umpire for the third out.

Three Stratford batters failed to reach base. End of the second inning.

Billy Adrianne had been at bat for Kingston when Shielbrock had picked off the runner at first base to end the second inning so he came to bat to start the third inning and Barney reminded Shielbrock to keep the ball low.

"Ball one," low and inside. "Ball two," low and outside.

His fast ball caught the outside corner with a sharp thump in the catcher's mitt and Barney went out on the mound and asked, "What did you just throw?"

"Fastball, that's what you called for, wasn't it?"

"Jesus, Shiel that was the fastest ball you've ever thrown. Bob Feller doesn't have a better fast ball. Where did you get that from?"

"I dunno. Get back there and I'll try it again."

The next two pitches were blazing fast balls that both missed the outside corner and Stratford fans moaned as Adrianne walked to first and Barney trotted out again to the mound.

"Now listen, Shiel, I don't know where you got it but that fast ball is great. Don't worry about that guy on first. He can't run. Put that fast ball over the plate. Keep it low and they won't even see it. Y'got great stuff today, now use it."

The next Kingston batter, second baseman Sam Whipple, never saw the ball as Shielbrock threw him four fastballs, all low. Three found the plate and Whipple was out. Next came the pitcher Mel Grieves and Shielbrock struck him out with three fastballs as his bat never moved.

With two out the leadoff man Le Clerc came to the plate and a fast ball got him looking at strike one. Shielbrock waved off Barney's signal for another fastball and threw a curve as Le Clerc swung and missed. Another curve broke cleanly over the plate for strike three as the Stratford crowd cheered.

In the dugout Barney grabbed Martin. "Shiel, that fastball, I told you it was great but the curve broke around the corner. Jesus, you got great stuff today. I've never seen you so good. Keep it low and you're golden today."

"I feel real good Barney, I feel in charge."

Stratford left fielder Bill Jarelski grounded out to second and Shielbrock rolled an easy one to third base and was thrown out. Dominick Pallazio flied the first pitch to the center fielder to end the third inning.

Shielbrock couldn't catch the corners and walked Luca to start the fourth inning and the fans moaned as Barney trotted out to the mound again. "Y'got this next guy, Buster Branch, to hit into a double play last time, but he can hit. If he lays wood on it he can drive it into Quebec. Remember, low and inside, remember, low and inside."

Five pitches later the count was full at three balls and two strikes and Shielbrock sent his fast ball low but it wasn't inside and Branch cracked a towering drive down the right field line. The fans all came to their feet and as the ball curved foul they made sounds like a long U and a satisfied ahh. The next pitch was a curve, but with Branch expecting another fast ball he swung hard and the ball broke away from him for strike three.

Kingston third baseman Eric Stoddart had walked his first time up and had been thrown out trying to steal second by Barney so he was angry and pounded the bat on home plate. As the fourth in the line-up and batting behind Buster Branch, Stoddart was considered a good hitter. Three fastballs later the count was one and two and he expected another fastball but Shielbrock threw him a big curve and he swung at empty air.

Luca still waited at first as the Kingston first baseman Vito Morabelli came to the plate with two outs. He had grounded out in his first at-bat and this time he never moved his bat as Shielbrock threw three fastballs low across the plate.

In the Stratford half of the fourth inning third baseman George Franko, Barney and right fielder John Temple went down in order.

Kingston didn't do anything in the top of the fifth and in the Stratford half of the inning second baseman Roger Hunsey flied to left, first baseman Jack Moore struck out and shortstop Jon Fontaine grounded to first, ending the fifth inning.

Kingston pitcher Mel Grieves came to the plate to start the sixth inning and Kingston fans gave him a loud ovation as he was pitching a fine game. He had given up only one hit, Barney's home run, and had not let another Stratford batter reach base. Shielbrock fanned him with four pitches, Le Clerc popped up to the second baseman and Luca Struck out looking at fast balls.

Jarelski led off for Stratford in the sixth and topped a roller to the shortstop who threw him out at first. As Shielbrock came to the plate, instead of the usual silence he had drawn as a batter in the past there was a smattering of hand clapping, then yells and whistles which grew into a loud roar from Stratford fans that realized he had pitched six innings without giving up a hit and had struck out nine Giants. Maybe, they thought, with some encouragement he could hang on and win this game, maybe there was hope, and even though he went down on strikes they cheered. A tall fly ball to center field by Pollazio ended the sixth inning.

Buster Branch was a well known ball player in Ontario as one of the veteran former minor league players who had been up and down the alphabet of classes, once reaching Rochester in triple A with promise and potential to make it into the major leagues. The potential had not materialized and promise with hope faded each year until he found himself playing semi-pro. Still, he had his pride and that was being seriously damaged in the hot summer Sunday at Stratford facing an unknown unheard of kid called Shielbrock, a Jew or a Kraut, or both. First he had hit into a double play, next he struck out. Angry and humiliated he led off the seventh inning determined to hit as never before. Shielbrock's first pitch was a fastball so fast it surprised the veteran Branch as he watched it catch the inside corner at his knees for strike one. So he was ready for the next fastball but Shielbrock gave him a curve which broke away from him so far he missed his swing, strike two. The next two were tempting off speed but outside pitches which he took; two and two. Branch knew the fastball had to be next because this kid wouldn't want to take him to a full count but Shielbrock's fastball looked like a bullet shot from a gun as Branch swung and missed for strike three. He was furious as the Stratford crowd, nearly delirious with delight, heaped as much verbal abuse on Branch as they gave encouragement to Shielbrock. Branch stepped quickly back to face the plate umpire. "He's doin' somptin t'd' ball! He's doctrin;' it! Check d'ball!"

"Only thing he'd doin' is throwin' the ball too fast fer you t' hit," responded the umpire.

"Check dat ball! He's doctrin' it," insisted the enraged Branch. The crowd didn't hear the issue but roared with delight at the angry batter facing the umpire and they screamed even more as the umpire stepped in front of the plate and asked Shielbrock for the ball, which had already made it's ceremonial rounds in honor of the strike out around the infield, back to third and then to the pitcher. Shielbrock lobbed it to the ump who looked it over carefully and muttered, "The ball's okay, nothin' on it but smoke." Then he tossed it back to Shielbrock. "Play ball!"

Eric Stoddart was the next batter, a big strong third baseman also a veteran of the minor leagues. Also, he had been humiliated, first thrown out stealing by a college catcher, then striking out. Maybe Buster Branch couldn't hit this punk but he, Eric Stoddart would. Once, in triple A ball at Atlanta he had hit a home run off Johnnie Sain and this kid was no Sain, but like so many others, Stoddart would never admit that he, Eric Stoddart, was not the hitter he was years ago when he hit Sain, and he proved it by striking out and threw his bat into his own dugout.

Vito Morabelli was a college kid from Boston who kept his cool, worked Shielbrock for a full count, fouled off two more pitches then lifted a fly to left field for the third out. Shielbrock had a no hit shutout going for seven innings.

In the Stratford half of the seventh, Franco walked, the first base on balls given up by Greives and the first base runner since Barney's home run in the first. With Barney at bat, Franco stole second but Grieves met the challenge, striking out Barney, John Temple and Roger Hunsey to end the seventh inning.

In the top of the eighth Shielbrock had trouble controlling his fastball and walked Arnell. Billy Adrianne, the next batter, was a local kid but he had enough patience to wait for a good pitch and as none was offered, he too walked. Sam Whipple, a college kid from Pittsburgh, hit a grounder to Jon Fontaine in what should have been a double play but Fontaine couldn't grab the ball as he blocked it in front of him and all runners were safe. Bases loaded with no outs and pitcher Mel Grieves at bat. Grieves was a fine pitcher and was pitching a great game and the Kingston fans were on their feet roaring encouragement, but a hitter Grieves was not and Shielbrock struck him out. Some Kingston fans yelled that manager Victor Parcell should have used a pinch hitter but, as fans do, this was after the out. No one had suggested it before and the Kingston manager had decided to stay with Grieves.

Mario Le Clerc was a Canadian kid who had been in the Ontario league three seasons, he could run, was a good fielder and a fair hitter and could see his chance to be a hero. Shielbrock threw him four curve balls for a two and two count, then a fastball just above the knees that Le Clerc never saw. With two out and the bases still loaded John Luca came to the plate and lifted a pop-up foul ball toward the home team dugout. Barney threw his mask aside as he raced for the ball, got there, dove for the ball and crashed into his dugout. When he emerged holding the ball high the Stratford crowd went wild and Kingston manager Parcell and three players stormed the umpire yelling, "He never held it! They gave it to him! He never touched it!" The umpire barked back at them, "I was there with 'im. He caught it n' held it. I seen it," as the crowd continued to roar approval of their Indians and to heap derision on the Giants. Most of the people in the crowd had been drinking beer for eight innings in the hot sun and the Stratford Indian fans were very happy but the Kingston Giant fans were mighty glum.

In the Stratford half Jack Moore struck out and Fontaine grounded out to second. Bill Jarelski hit an easy grounder to the shortstop but the ball went right between his legs for an error and Jarelski was on first as Martin Shielbrock came to the plate. The crowd came to their feet and yelled approval, not because of his hitting potential, but in salute for his pitching; a no hit shutout through eight innings. They cheered, cried and stamped their feet. They clapped their hands, whistled and then started a chant, "Shiel—brock, Shiel—brock, Shiel—brock,—," and they kept it up as he struck out, went to the mound and took his warm-up pitches for the ninth inning.

Buster Branch was first up for Kingston in the ninth; a seething, angry, frustrated, embarrassed Buster Branch, figuratively foaming at the mouth. Before even the first pitch, Barney called time and went to the mound." Okay Shiel, this is it. You're gonna face the heart of the batting order, their best hitters. They're pissed off and they'll be over-anxious. Now is the time for patience, lots of patience, they'll be over-anxious. Don't go for three pitch strike outs. Don't give them anything to hit. Low balls. Low balls. Inside and outside corners. Nothing good. Remember, they're nervous. Make them wait. Take a lot of time between pitches, okay?"

"Okay, Okay, but if you think they're nervous, how the hell do you think I feel?"

"You don't have to be nervous. Make them wait. You're in charge!"

The umpire yelled, "C'mon, play ball!"

Buster Branch pounded his bat on the plate, dug in his cleats and took his stance to hit; the epitome of determination as Shielbrock stood at attention on the pitcher's rubber waiting, waiting. Branch called time and stepped quickly out of the batters box. "Make 'im throw, c'mon," He yelled at the umpire.

"He can't throw when yer out of the batters box. Get back in there." Responded the umpire.

Again they faced each other; the determined angry batter, the poised pitcher, both waiting as Branch wiggled his bat and mumbled, "C'mon throw it. I'll kill it." Only Barney and the umpire could hear him and as Shielbrock started his wind-up Barney said in a loud voice, "You won't even see it!" Branch did see it but swung and missed the outside curve ball. "God damn you!" He yelled at Barney as he stepped out of the box.

"Why me?" Barney replied with feigned innocence. "It was him that threw it and you that missed it like y' done all day."

A curve ball too low followed and next a blazing fastball caught the inside corner for strike two and Shielbrock felt a sharp pain on the right side of his back. He kept Branch waiting a long time for the next pitch, walking behind the mound, wiping his forehead on his sleeve and handling the resin bag before finally stepping on the rubber. Then he waited and waited some more and Branch was furious. Shielbrock fired a fast ball and the sharp pain in his back caused him to cry out, but the ball shot across the inside corner for strike three and the crowd screamed approval.

Eric Stoddart stepped to the plate and quickly the crowd quieted, aware of the threat he posed, the closeness of success, the fragile one run lead where one stroke of the bat could tie the score and erase the no-hitter.

Barney called time and went out to the mound. "Why did you yell on that last fast ball?"

"I had a pain in my back. It's okay. I'm all right. Don't worry."

"Bullshit. If you had a pain it's time to get out."

"No! We're almost there. I'm gonna finish it. Don't worry. I'm gonna use fewer fastballs. I'll set 'em up with curves and finish 'em with a fastball. It'll be all right."

Barney gave a negative head shake and trotted back to the plate where big Stoddart waited outside the batters box. They took their places. Standing at attention on the rubber, Shielbrock remembered his high school coach Fritz Jordan who spent so many hours with his young pitchers teaching them fundamentals; stand up there tall, look confident, look like a pitcher even if you haven't got all your stuff one day. Look the part. Shoulders back and head held up he nodded to Barney's signal for a curve ball. Stoddart spit a big brown cud of chewing tobacco across the plate and it hit the dirt with a splat and as Shielbrock started to wind up Barney said out loud, "Same shit comes out of both ends of you, Stoddart." The big batter started to turn toward Barney, then back to his regular position and with a weak swing he missed the curve ball and jumped out of the batters box, beet red with anger. "You son of a bitch!" He yelled at Barney.

In position again, Stoddart spit hard and defiant and the crowd was silent. As Shielbrock started his wind-up Barney almost whispered, "When all you got is shit for brains you shouldn't be spitting them out." Stoddart started to swing at an outside pitch but held back and the ball curved over the plate just above his knees for strike two. He was livid and even more so as Barney held up the ball between his thumb and index finger to show him. Without saying a word the message was clearly, "See, here's the ball. You haven't seen it all day," and reading it also, the crowd roared approval.

On the next pitch Shielbrock lobbed the ball toward the plate but well outside and Stoddart, experienced player that he was, couldn't resist the temptation as he reached out his bat in a futile ill-timed swing, missing for strike three. The crowd roared with joy, all on their feet and then they remained standing, quieted with apprehension, with two out, ninth inning, score one to nothing, one out away from a victory that would tie the league, one out away from a no-hitter shutout.

Vito Morabelli came to the plate. Twice before he had put wood on the ball, one a grounder, the other a fly ball and Shielbrock kept him waiting a long time, then took his place standing erect on the rubber, soaked with sweat but every part of his uniform in place. Look like a pitcher, he could hear Coach Jordan saying, look confident, as he threw a curve that hardly broke. Morabelli swung and nubbed it at first baseman Jack Moore who picked it up, ran five steps to the bag holding the ball over his head and leaped high in the air screaming with joy. He was not alone as all of the Stratford players yelled in victory and leaped in the air, running toward the mound and the crowd roared and surged onto the field. The players mobbed Shielbrock who was being held high in a bear hug by the powerful arms of Barney Williams. They dragged and pushed their way, still hugging, through cheering players and fans toward their dugout. It was chaos, bedlam, old men gave throaty yells, women screamed and men whistled. Drunks, and there were many, opened their throats, threw back their heads and emitted weird animal sounds while war cries came from little boys. Girls screeched as it was victory like VE Day, VJ Day, the Fourth of July, New Years Eve and winning the Irish Sweepstakes all at once.

Stratford Indian manager Dutch Van Roche stood in the dugout, hands on hips shaking his head in disbelief. "That hot shit did it. Who'd ever thought it? A no hitter!" Even as he stood there watching the celebration he knew that in just a few minutes those crazy Stratford fans would calm down enough to realize that it wasn't over, not yet, because in the Kingston dugout, quiet and angry, waited a team ready to go at it again and they had a capable experienced pitcher ready. All he had were two teen-aged kids, relief high school pitchers, hardly used all season. Dutch looked at the sky hoping for rain but there was not a cloud in sight, only the bright hot sun and he wished for Don Zetti or even that drunken John Dietrich, but realized that rain was more probable, no chance for any of that.

The team finally made it to their dugout and fans started to go back into the stands as grounds keepers began to ready the field for the next game. A river of beer had been sold that day and the vendors set another record for beer sales in the time between the games. As the fans returned to their bleachers a chant started. "Shiel-brock, Shiel-brock, Shiel-brock,—," until he stepped out of the dugout and lifted his ball cap. They roared approval and drank more beer, exclaiming among themselves over the great pitching job he had done and how they always had confidence in him all season.

There was no dressing or shower room, only a small wash room and toilet behind the dugout where Shielbrock took off his soaked uniform shirt and sweat shirt, washed off his torso with a wet towel, put his head under the faucets, dried himself and put on a clean tee shirt. He rinsed out his uniform shirt, squeeze-twisted it and put it on still wet, then hair combed, he put on his cap and checked himself in the mirror. Look like a pitcher, he remembered Coach Jordan saying.

Dutch had just told the two kids to get warmed up when Shielbrock returned to the dugout where an older man in street clothes waited. Dutch introduced him as Ace Hobson, former major leaguer and now a scout for the St. Louis Browns and after congratulating Shielbrock on the fine game, Ace explained that he had come to look over some players.

"What are your plans?" Ace asked.

"Well, the draft is after me and I've been accepted by the Navy in their officer candidate program and I expect to go into the Navy in a couple of months."

"What about after that?"

"Well, I'll be in the Navy for three years. After that I don't know. Maybe I'll like it and stay in." Shielbrock smiled.

"Okay, kid, but keep me in mind." Hobson went to talk with Barney Williams.

Deep in his own thoughts, Shielbrock sat in the far end of the dugout as the team got ready for the second game and after a while he went to Dutch. "How are you going to pitch them?"

"Well, you're a rightie so I'm goin' to start our lefty McKenzie and when he gets bombed I'll try Halloran. How else kin I do it?"

"That's all you can do, I guess." They were silent for awhile watching the warm-ups until Shielbrock said, "I was thinking, Dutch, maybe if you let me start—." Dutch interrupted, "No, no, you're through for the day. No!" Shielbrock continued, "If you let me start and go just a little while, maybe just an inning or two, just until I get roughed up, maybe they can take it the rest of the way."

"No. What're y' tryin' t' do, give them Kingston guys a chance t' get even with ya? You'd ruin yer arm. No." There was a certain lack of determination in his final "no".

"Just an inning or two, not enough to hurt. I can handle it Dutch and it could be just enough." Shielbrock came on with more emphasis and eagerness. Dutch thought for awhile. "Maybe just the first inning," Dutch thought aloud quietly, then with more enthusiasm, "Maybe if you put them down the first inning again, like the other game, they'd be so pissed they couldn't hit McKenzie."

"That's right! Dutch, let's do it! Start me!" Dutch thought awhile more, "Okay, you start."

"No! Bullshit! Dutch, you can't pitch him." As soon as he heard, Barney was angry. "He's had it! How much more do you think you can squeeze out of him. You'll ruin his arm."

"He says he wants to and he can give us one more inning," Dutch explained.

Barney looked at Martin angrier than before. "Are you crazy? You know you've had enough. This game isn't worth ruining yourself for. Sit it out Shiel! You've done great today and that's enough." Martin took Barney by the arm to the far end of the dugout. "I want to do this, Barney. I feel I have to. There's something inside me telling me to do it. Please. You took me through that first game and now I'm gonna start this one. I gotta try it and I need you to help me Barney. Please."

A pause, "Okay Shiel, but only one inning."

"Barney, I'm not gonna lie to you. I lied to Dutch cause I don't give a shit about him, but not you. Barney, I'm not coming out of there after just one inning."

"Shiel! God damn!"

"Barney, please, I want to do it. Help me. I have to do it and I can't do it without you."

Barney looked at Shielbrock then at the ground and kicked some dirt. After awhile he smiled and looked back at his friend. "Okay, Buddy, if that's what you wants that's what you gets," and they went out of the dugout on to the field.

Mel Grieves was sitting alone at one end of the Kingston dugout and Shielbrock made sure that all the other Kingston players were out on the field as he stepped into the opponents' dugout and made his way to where Grieves sat. Grieves looked up and smiled as he approached and Shielbrock held out his right hand and said, "You pitched a great game out there today, Mel. No one should lose with that kind of stuff."

Grieves shook his hand and replied, "You were the one with the great game, Shielbrock. That's the first no hit game in this league in years. You were somethin' else today."

"Well, maybe between us we gave them some kind of historic event, huh? Like when are they ever going to see a one hitter and a no hitter in the same game?"

"I guess maybe they never will," replied Grieves, who then asked, "Did I see Ace Hobson over there talking to you?"

"Yeah."

"You interested in the Browns?"

"No. I don't want to get drafted into the army so I'm going into the Navy in a couple a' months, and I want to do something else with my life than play ball. He must have talked to you?"

"Yeah," Said Grieves. "He's talked to me before, too. I'd like to get back into pro-ball and this might be the way. There's another scout around here today, Dave Jenkins from the Philadelphia Athletics. He'll be after you, for sure, with the job you did today."

"Well, Mel, I wish you the best of success. Hope you make it fast and big in the majors."

"Thanks, Shielbrock, and good luck to you in the Navy. I think they say 'smooth sailing'." The former adversaries shook hands and parted.

"Hey Shielbrock!" Martin stopped and turned back toward him. "You going out there again?"

"Yeah, just for a little while, just to start it off."

Grieves shook his head negatively and said, "Y'gotta be careful about that. Y' can ruin yer arm trying to do too much, y'know, and in these bush leagues they don't give a shit if y' live or die. Y'gotta look after yerself, y' know."

"Thanks, Mel. I appreciate that. I'll be careful." Martin started to turn away, then added with a smile, "Now don't let what I'm doing give you any ideas. We had enough of you in the last game. You just sit right there and relax."

Grieves laughed, "Good luck, sailor," and gave Shielbrock a mock salute.

CHAPTER 6

By the time Barney Williams finished the story of Martin Shielbrock and him playing baseball in Canada it was past dinner time, too late for the ladies to prepare a meal. "Let's cut out the stories for now and go over to the Calypso Café and get something to eat, and no stories for dinner." Barney offered.

Jackie liked the idea. "And no more stories until tomorrow at breakfast, at least."

They all agreed and left the condo patio to enjoy the convenience and fine food at the nearby deli restaurant on the San Diego Bay side of Coronado Cays. The Calypso owner, Hanan, asked what they had been doing this beautiful day and Steven replied. "We've been telling long kept secret family history tales of adventure and romance and Jackie is saving the spicy ones for tomorrow."

"Oooh, that sounds really good!" Hanan laughed. "When can I hear them?"

"No way!" Ellie was first to reply. "These are family secrets like highly classified, just like these navy guys deal with." She nodded toward her father and her husband.

Hanan laughed as she walked away. "Oh darn. Bet those are good stories."

Steven frowned at those at the table. "You know, there is some of this stuff available to read. That woman, the writer McManus, she wrote that book about the Indian Ocean - Iraq thing and there was a lot of stuff about Dad in that book. It was all about him."

Barney replied, "Yeah, but she had no way to find out and so she didn't go back into the real good stuff that we know of. She just wrote about what she saw and some info from the few that she was able to talk with. But still, it's a good book. She even interviewed me and some others. And she did first meet your dad some years before the Indian Ocean thing. That was when he was at the Naval War College with the Strategic Studies Group. I'll tell that story tomorrow morning."

"Wait a minute." Steven was not pleased. "How about the baseball game? You left us with my Dad trying to start the second game in Canada."

"Yeah," Barney laughed. "And I'm going to leave you there, waiting to hear how that went down. I think you already know from what you've heard your Dad and me talking about over the years, but I'm going to make you wait until I tell these gals about your Dad with the SSG at Newport.

"That summer baseball in Canada, though, that particular Saturday," Barney continued, "is just another and early example of how that father of yours would defy authority and do what was right, always what HE thought was right, regardless of what any authority or anyone else thought was right, even into and through his Navy time. Most of the time it worked out fine for him, but not always, 'cause there were times when he got in trouble for defying orders, defying convention, and it cost him."

"Okay but you've already passed over most of his Navy career. The SSG was at the end of his career, wasn't it? How about all the ships, staffs, schools he served in and the commands he had before the SSG? Are you going to go back over those?"

"You've heard all about those and grew up through most of them; the Viet Nam times, gun line and gun strikes, search and rescue in the Gulf of Tonkin, you know all about that stuff and the gals have heard it all, too. And the commands; ships, destroyer squadron and the tactical training group, we don't have to go though that stuff, we all know about those duties, his career and the adventures that were part of them."

Steven could see that he wasn't going to get his way. "Yeah, I guess I've heard about that. Okay, so we're going to skip over most of Dad's thirty year career and jump to that last of his active duty; at the Naval War College with the Strategic Studies Group. That was, as I recall, the first SSG and they're still going strong, a new group every year, right?"

"That's right." Barney was anxious to get on with his story but he paused *a short while as he got his thoughts together. "Let's see now; Newport, Rhode Island, the Naval War College, the very first Strategic Studies Group—. "*

Jackie interrupted him, "Hold on sailor! That's for tomorrow morning. For now it's dinner."

STRATEGIC STUDIES GROUP, NAVAL WAR COLLEGE, NEWPORT, RHODE ISLAND

Dr. Alfred Meyerhoff had been on the staff of the Naval War College in Newport, Rhode Island for six years as a professor in the Department of Naval Strategy. Teaching courses on naval history and naval strategy to professional military officers had been interesting for Dr. Meyerhoff, even though the students were somewhat less of a challenge than he had originally hoped. When Dr. Meyerhoff first came to the Naval War College he expected to deal with active demanding minds of the higher intelligence levels, but soon he learned that this was not to be.

Over the years he had found the students to be of a lower mental capacity than he had expected, "Jocks" for the most part, more interested in playing golf and tennis, and in following football, than in doing hard research and study into the philosophy of the military profession. Oh, there had been a few exceptions and these actually had decent educations at Ivy League schools, as had he, and why in the world these few had chosen a military career he couldn't understand. Maybe even the best colleges produced some that hadn't quite reached that upper level of academic achievement or appreciation, and perhaps it was best for those to go into the military, where clearly these few could help to raise the intelligence, academic, cultural and professional level of the overall military officer corps. Most of the officers, it appeared to Dr. Meyerhoff, had little to offer or to gain from an opportunity to participate in a high level academic program.

When offered the position of Assistant Director of the newly formed Strategic Studies Group, Dr. Meyerhoff quickly accepted because he knew that this would be a high visibility group working directly under the Naval War College President with a separate direct line of influence to the Chief of Naval Operations. In fact he had heard that these officers of the first Strategic Studies Group were personally selected by the CNO.

The director was to be Richard Murphy, presently Under Secretary of the Navy, and Dr. Meyerhoff would act as the director until Mr. Murphy could be relieved as Under Secretary and move to Newport. Here, surely, in this new group there would be the vital minds to appreciate Dr. Meyerhoff's high level of intelligence and his knowledge of military philosophy, history, application and interaction with economic, social, political and cultural factors. Here his writings and lectures would gain the attention he was due which would lead to the kind of political appointment he sought in the Department of Defense, or Navy, or State, or maybe even on the White House Staff.

Dr. Meyerhoff had prepared a short welcoming talk for this, his first meeting with the eight officers of the SSG; four Navy captains, two Marine colonels, and two Navy commanders. He had seen brief resumes of their Navy and Marine Corps prior duties but to Dr. Meyerhoff these were not important, as aviator, submariner, surface ships, artillery; these were insignificant involvements. The important factor was education such as what college did the officer attend? Did he have an advanced degree and if so from where? Had he attended any of the service colleges such as the Naval War College, National War College, Industrial College of the Armed Forces, even the less significant Armed Forces Staff College? What special academic studies had he worked on at these schools and what had he written, published and lectured on? Dr. Meyerhoff assumed that if hand picked by the CNO for strategic study, these officers, particularly the navy captains, must soon be selected for promotion to rear admiral and favorably impressing admirals now or for the future could be a great advantage for a thirty-five year old Ph.D. seeking political appointment.

The eight officers of the SSG sat around the conference table relaxed and in no discernible positions of priority or preference. They were all in uniform, which disturbed Dr. Meyerhoff because he had left word that as they individually reported for duty the previous few days, they should be told to wear civilian clothes, for after all, Dr. Meyerhoff felt, this was an academic organization and if he was to teach and guide them in the study of naval strategy, a mind clear of artificial military encumbrances was a necessity. The uniform would only complicate and obstruct academic freedom of thought.

The officers had been in the conference room for about an hour and Dr. Meyerhoff had pictured them meeting each other and discussing their expectations and concerns over what they could expect of their professor prior to his arrival. He knew they would be apprehensive about the demands he would make of them, the amount of outside study and research and deadlines for written material. He assumed that at least some of them had looked into Meyerhoff's writings and publications and they had read his *Clausewitz Then and Now* or his *Utilization of Naval Power in the 1990s.*

As Dr. Meyerhoff opened the conference room door a captain was saying, "—so I told him to fly the damn thing himself," and the group laughed, and even more as he added, "and he did." Then, turning to the door, "And this must be Dr. Meyerhoff."

"Yes, I am." The doctor entered and then shook hands with each of the eight as he moved around the table. A marine colonel," Don Rogerson." Next to him another colonel, "Hoss Hartell." Then to a navy commander, "Joe Carpenter," followed by the navy captain who had been telling the story as Dr. Meyerhoff entered, "Sid Debway." Next a short captain, "Fred Grolish," followed by a tall one, "Martin Shielbrock." Strange, thought Dr. Meyerhoff, no nicknames. Another captain, "Frank Peoples," followed by the last, a commander, "Carl Orbath, fighter pilot and never last."

Well, thought Dr. Meyerhoff, they don't all have nicknames after all, some have that peculiar false macho sense of humor and they seem relaxed in the presence of their professor. He addressed the group from his rough notes, welcoming them to the Naval War College and to the Strategic Studies Group, pointing out that he was the Assistant Director and would act as Director until Mr. Murphy's arrival, probably in two weeks. A program had been worked out for them, to familiarize them with the resources of the Naval War College in the first few weeks of their one year fellowship program and that they could wear civilian clothes here. Now it would be good to learn a little more about each other and Dr. Meyerhoff would tell about his background. Then each of them would do the same. No one moved or said anything and he looked at eight passive faces.

Dr. Meyerhoff gave his education, where he had taught and what, the books and articles he had written and his special lectures, as still eight passive faces never changed. "And now perhaps each of you would tell us about yourself. Let's start with Colonel Hartell." Hoss Hartell was sitting next to Dr. Meyerhoff so it seemed logical.

"Captain Shielbrock is our senior member, Dr. Meyerhoff, so I would defer to him," said Hoss.

Dr. Meyerhoff felt uncomfortable as all eyes shifted to Shielbrock who spoke in a baritone, almost gutteral voice. "We already know each other and our backgrounds but we'll be glad to go over them for you, Doctor, to help you get to know us. I'm Martin Shielbrock, surface warfare officer." He pointed to the surface warfare badge above his ribbons. "My last duty was CO of TACTRAGRUPAC and before that I was COMDESRON Twenty Three." He turned to Captain Peoples who started to speak.

Dr. Meyerhoff interrupted, "Before we leave you, Captain Shielbrock, could you tell us your educational background, schools and such?"

"Education?"

"Yes. If you don't mind." Dr. Meyerhoff half expected but hoped that Shielbrock wouldn't say, "I do mind," and he didn't.

"Masters in IA and EE, Naval War College, National War College, PG School, sozmark."

"What is sozmark, Captain?" asked Dr. Meyerhoff as the officers all smiled.

"Senior Officers Ship Material Readiness Course. S-O-S-M-R-C. Sozmark. It's taught by the nuclear power people to us non-nukes at Idaho Falls. It's like a crash course in mechanical engineering."

Dr. Myerhoff was disappointed in the brevity of the report but pleased with the implications and he planned to find out later more about the Masters in International Affairs and the particular areas of study. Perhaps the others would be more forthcoming. Shielbrock turned to Peoples who spoke, "Frank Peoples, VP aviator." He pointed to the gold wings on his chest above his ribbons. "Last duty commanded PAT Wing Three, prior to that in NAVAIRSYSCOM. Masters in management. PG school."

Before Dr. Meyerhoff could ask for amplification the next officer spoke. "Sid Debway, fighter pilot," pointing to his badge. "Last duty COMNAVAIRLANT staff, prior CO Forrestal, Test Pilot School, PG school, sozmark. Masters in EE.

"Fred Grolish, surface warfare." Again the badge. "Mostly amphibs. Last duty MIDEASTFOR staff, prior CO La Salle, Masters in I.A., Naval War College, SAIS, sozmark."

"Uh, Captain Grolish, please," interrupted Meyerhoff. "Sais?"

"School for Advanced International Studies in Washington. It's part of John Hopkins University. The Navy sends officers there once in a while."

"Aren't we on your turf here?" asked Shielbrock to Meyerhoff's embarrassment.

"Yes. Sorry. Please go on." Somehow this was slipping away felt Meyerhoff.

"Joe Carpenter, submariner." He pronounced it submareener, with accent on the long double e as he pointed to the dolphins on his chest. "Last duty CO Pogy, prior XO Lewis and Clark Blue, Sub school, nuclear power school, Mummmum, Masters."

"Carl Orbath—," was interrupted.

"Excuse me, Commander Carpenter, what did you say before 'Masters'?" asked Meyerhoff.

"Oxford," replied Carpenter.

"You went to Oxford?" Meyerhoff was incredulous.

"Yes. The Navy let me go for a special program."

Oh, thought Meyerhoff, some seminar or symposium for a few days. "I see." A few officers smiled.

"Carl Orbath, fighter pilot," indicating his wings. "Last duty CO VF 104, prior OP-96, PG School, Top Gun, Masters in EE."

"I don't understand 'Top Gun', Commander," stated Meyerhoff.

"Advanced school for fighter tactics at Miramar. That's a Naval Air Station."

"Thank you."

"Don Rogerson, artillery, last duty CO Second Battalion Eleventh Marines, prior JCS staff, Naval War College, Advanced Amphibious School, Masters in IA."

"Hoss Hartell, aviator, helos. Last duty CO VMH 109, prior Marine Corps Headquarters, Naval War College, Masters in IA."

Dr. Meyerhoff was bewildered because they had done as he asked, but he knew little more about them then he did from the resumes. Had they really done what he wanted? He wasn't sure and was lost in a maze of acronyms.

"Okay," Dr. Meyerhoff started anew. "Let's hope that your academic studies here are marked by achievements which convey considerably more expansive depth, clarity and detail than the meager background descriptions just delivered through your filters of modesty. I will now outline for you the program I have laid out for you to provide you with the expertise of the Naval War College. This is a program designed specifically for your one year fellowship time here. You will see that it focuses on exposing you to the history of military strategic concepts, the international situation of today, the effects of military concepts on that international situation and then you will each be given a chance to develop your own impression of a Naval role in this broad concept." He never got any further.

Shielbrock interrupted, "Excuse me, Doctor Meyerhoff. As Hoss pointed out earlier, I am the senior member of this group so whether I, they or you like it or not, I am the spokesman. Even though this is not a democratic process I speak for all here as we have already briefly discussed our role here among ourselves. We have, also, each talked with the CNO or the Commandant of the Marine Corps about what they want us to do here. So, we appreciate your efforts and concern but we'll determine our program and where it will be focused.

"Now concerning civilian clothes, we are professional naval officers serving in our professional naval duty. We wear the naval uniform as it is part of our profession and we are proud of it. We have been at this profession long enough, all of us, so that we are not encumbered by the uniform. It does not complicate or obstruct our thought. We each know the rank, seniority and background of every one of us, so that no matter what we wore we would still know these things. We are comfortable in the uniform and if you see us in civilian clothes it will be our decision, not yours.

"We're not here as students or toys for your academic process. We're here because the CNO wants us to look at a practical naval strategy. We don't want or need what you described to us as your program. What we do need could best be filled by the hard practical mind of a New York cab driver, certainly not by ivory tower academic snobs. Please see to it that our office spaces are properly equipped and we'll let you know our other logistic requirements in good time.

"Now, Doctor Meyerhoff, if you would please excuse us we have a lot to discuss as we begin to put together a program that will follow the CNO's and the Commandant's guidance. We will be working in private in this conference room for awhile."

Meyerhoff was embarrassed and humiliated as he left without a word.

As the door closed Hoss asked, "Joe, what was that Oxford shit?" Before Carpenter could answer Shielbrock responded, "Oxford, like Oxford in England, Hoss. Joe was a Rhodes Scholar."

"Jesus Christ, Shellback, I'm glad Joe didn't tell Meyerhoff that! He'd think we're all long hairs," as Hoss ran his hand over a bald and shaved head.

"No, Hoss, he'd never think that of you," and then to all, after they stopped laughing, "By the way next time we 'show and tell' let's integrate seniority."

Heads nodded, "Good." "Right." "Aye Aye, Captain Shellback."

Meyerhoff never realized that the officers had responded in order of seniority, Navy then Marine Corps.

In the weeks that followed the SSG developed a plan to gather and review the war plans of the various fleet and theater commanders. This, they hoped would give them the overall plan for the employment of U.S. naval forces in a NATO-Warsaw Pact war and tying together these plans would provide a picture of how the Navy and Marine Corps would fight what could be called World War III. To obtain these plans a series of trips were planned, trips to each major command wherever located in the world, to brief that commander on the project and to gather his views. It was an energetic program and the travels had to be accomplished promptly, because the information thus collected had to be assembled and analyzed by the SSG back at the Naval War College. But that was to be only the start as the group then intended the most ambitious of projects. They would, after analysis of the existing plans, formulate one coherent and comprehensive plan to be called "The Naval Strategy" that would be presented to the Chief of Naval Operations, modified if necessary and then with his approval, taken to those same commanders around the world and briefed to them.

Mr. Richard Murphy arrived as planned a few weeks after the Meyerhoff meeting and he immediately became a close associate, sympathetic advocate and loyal confident of the members of the Strategic Studies Group. He gave his full support to their program and his very recent status as Under Secretary of the Navy provided the group with ready access everywhere in the military. His presence, and often just his name, opened doors and made travel easy, and there was much travel and many high ranking, influential and authoritative people to see. As their Director, Dick Murphy led the group with a loose rein, recognizing that their professionalism carried a dedication and thoroughness that required very little, if any, overt direction.

In a few months Dick Murphy knew all eight members of the Strategic Studies Group very well, and they knew him, trusted him and treated him as if he, too, wore a uniform. They had traveled together, eaten and drank together, and there were often stunts and harmless "con" jobs played during their travels. Once Murphy found that the airline people had been told that he was a U.S. Senator on a familiarization trip to Japan, another time he was Vice President of the American Medical Association enroute to a symposium on herpes. On a plane to Rome he was a representative of the America's Cup Committee of the New York Yacht Club on the way to talk with Italian financiers about the next challenge series. In all of these and others he was "set up" without knowing how, why, or as what by his team of the SSG and always the first he would know was when approached by a stranger who discussed or questioned his views on a peculiar issue, but it was not all play.

They developed a Naval Strategy and their lives were filled with operation orders, operation plans, logistic plans, contingency plans, charts, maps, graphs and interview notes.

Martin Shielbrock was sitting in his office surrounded by a myriad of planning documentation when Jim Bailey, The Public Affairs Officer of the Naval War College entered accompanied by a very good looking, well built, nicely dressed young woman. It was easy to stop work for such pleasant intrusion and Shielbrock took off his reading glasses and stood up.

"Captain Shielbrock, I'd like you to meet Kim McManus. Ms. McManus is with the Washington Times. She's here with CHINFO approval to do a story on the Strategic Studies Group."

"How do you do, Ms. McManus." Shielbrock shook hands.

"It's nice to meet you, Captain." Her hand was warm and soft, the grip was firm.

Jim left the reporter with Shielbrock who offered a chair and coffee. The chair she accepted after Shielbrock removed from it a stack of directives, and they exchanged pleasantries until he asked about why she had come to Newport, Rhode Island, to the Naval War College, from Washington.

"Well, I think Lieutenant Commander Bailey said that I'm doing a story on the Strategic Studies Group and I have CHINFO approval."

"Yes, he did say that, but what makes you think there's a story here?"

"My editor showed me an item from Navy Times which said that the CNO had hand-picked this group of officers to create a Naval Strategy at the War College. It sounded to us like this must be a very special group, so," she paused, "a story."

He stared at her a few seconds. "No, no story," and shook his head.

She was bewildered. "What? Why, no story?"

"No story for two very good reasons. First, it's not newsworthy. The public is not interested, nor should they be, in the routine planning process that the military in peacetime is involved in on a continuous basis. We always plan. We're great planners. We plan for wars, battles, crises and most events that never come about, which is a good thing. It's a routine process, very dull and of interest to no one outside the military. We have trouble even getting some of the military interested."

Kim McManus hid her anger well. "And second?"

"Second, even if it was of interest to the public, which it is not, the work we do here is classified. Some of it very highly classified. It involves the security of our country. Now, we really wouldn't want to hand over to a potential enemy any classified information, would we?"

Kim leaned forward angrily in her chair and he noticed her nicely shaped ample breasts. "Captain, let's get a few things straight. I am here as a journalist with Navy authorization to do a story. I do not need nor am I interested in your evaluation as to the newsworthiness of the story. You are not qualified to make that judgment, I am. That's my business. If there is nothing worth reporting it won't be published. I do not expect to get anything that is classified but that's your business. I'm sure you know what is classified and what isn't. So, if you'll just give me unclassified information I won't jeopardize the security of the United States."

Her eyes sparkled with anger he thought, wondering if they sparkle like that when she's—, no, forget it, they are beautiful eyes though. "Okay, what do you want to know?"

She opened her notebook and placed it on the lap created by her crossed legs, nice legs. Hose and heels, he thought to himself and it had been a long time since he had noticed; heels and hose and turned up nose. She had it.

"How many of you are in the Strategic Studies Group?" She asked and he told her.

"For how long?" He told her, and the routine questioning went on as to the composition and timing of the organization. A while later the questions shifted, "Are all of you married?"

"Yes."

"And children?"

"Do you want a list of all of us with ranks, addresses, nicknames, wives names, children's' ages and names, hobbies and copies of our last income tax returns?"

She sighed and looked at him, "I'm trying to get just a little personal background for some human interest."

"Why?"

"Because, Captain, the public is interested," she emphasized the word is, "in the personal background of their military leaders."

"I'm not the CNO."

"I am aware, and I might say greatly relieved, to learn that you are not the Chief of Naval Operations but would you mind answering just a few questions about yourself?"

"Ask."

"You're married."

"That's not a question."

Kim sighed with resignation, "Are you married Captain Shiel-brock?"

"Yes. Are you?"

"Yes. Do you have children?"

"Yes. A daughter Nancy age twenty-seven and a son Steven twenty-three. Do you have children?"

"No. Do your wife and children live here in Newport?"

"No. My wife lives in Alexandria, Virginia. My daughter lives in Atlanta. My son lives in New London. Where does your husband live?"

She was somewhat stressed by the counter-questioning but tried to hide it. "He lives, that is, we live in Fairfax. Does your wife work, or is she involved in any interesting activities, and the same of your children?"

"My wife works for Saks in Washington, my daughter for a store in Atlanta, my son graduated from the Naval Academy last year and is in submarine school. I don't know of my wife's activities or if they would be of interest to your readers. What does your husband do and what kind of activities does he engage in?"

"Captain, please! I'm interviewing you, remember."

"Oh yes, I'm sorry. Go on."

"Your wife, that is, well, she lives in Alexandria and you're here?"

"You haven't asked the question and it's none of your business, nor is it the business of your readers, if there are any, but I'll provide the answer. Yes, I am married. My wife and I maintain our home near Washington, where she works. I go home on some weekends, most weekends, depending on work and weather. Being in the Navy I have been transferred around a lot and we have moved a number of times but we try to keep our home in Alexandria. This is a one-year tour in Newport and then I'll either retire or get duty in Washington, maybe, or maybe somewhere else." He paused and thought awhile, "And your husband?"

"He's a major in the Army Corps of Engineers. He works in the Pentagon on the Army staff. All of his duty, except one tour, has been in Washington and he expects to be there for most of his career. He's a graduate of West Point. Okay?"

"Hey, okay, okay, so you're an Army wife, nice."

For the first time Kim smiled at him and the smile went well with the eyes, the breasts, the figure, the legs,—forget it, he thought. Her questions continued and he showed her some charts as they discussed the political issues surrounding military spending, ship construction problems and strategic weapons.

It was mid afternoon when Shielbrock took her to Don Rogerson so she could get the views of the senior Marine Corps officer on the Strategic Studies Group. Then, back at his desk, Shielbrock looked out at Narragansett Bay, the bridge, the sailboats. Nice girl, sharp, forget it. He read awhile then spent the rest of the afternoon looking through reports and charts but was unable to concentrate. For a while more he looked out on the Bay, then closed up his desk, locked up the classified papers and went to this room at the BOQ.

Bachelor Officers Quarters had been long ago reduced by Navy people to the three letter acronym BOQ and at times the hotel-like accommodation was referred to simply as "the Q." In spite of the bachelor term associated with it, the Q was used as a temporary place to live by married as well as single officers as married officers away from home were considered geographic bachelors for that purpose. Once a Secretary of the Navy had tried to change the name from Bachelor Officers Quarters to Unaccompanied Officer Housing Accommodation, but Navy people found the new title cumbersome and BOQ continued to be used, along with the Q, so the next Secretary rescinded that directive and the traditional title returned.

Shielbrock's room at the Q was nicer than most as preferential treatment was given to the more senior occupants but even so the size, furnishing and decor would fall far short by comparison with any first rate motel. It was adequate, convenient and reasonably clean and even had a television set and tiny refrigerator. With a beer he sat in the one soft chair watching television news. Some of it was interesting but most of the broadcast didn't hold his attention. Gee, she had nice eyes, and legs, and tits, forget it. After showering, he put on civilian clothes, finished his beer and drove to the nearby officer's club.

Most late afternoons and evenings the bar and cocktail lounge at the club were empty but Fridays were different. They came from the Naval War College, the Officer Candidate School, the Surface Warfare Officers School, the Naval Hospital, ships visiting or home ported at Newport and from dozens of other commands and activities. Officers young and old, regular Navy and reserve, male and female filled the bar and the lounge on Fridays and a woman played the piano and sang in one corner. Heavy hors d'oeuvres which were consumed rapidly by the young people from OCS and SWOS and bowls of popcorn were plentiful at the bar and on the individual tables. By five PM the bar and lounge were usually filled with people talking, laughing, drinking and smoking, and an hour later it was nosier. There were more people with more to drink, more smoke, more noise, more laughter, even some singing as Captain Martin Shielbrock hung his coat in the room off to one side and walked through the carpeted lobby into the bar and lounge. It was dark, noisy and crowded, as he expected and a voice yelled, "Hey Shellback, where ya' been?" He waved toward the voice and looked around, moving slowly toward the bar. A jaygee came up to him. "Evening Commodore," and they shook hands. "Hi Charlie, how's it going?"

"Just fine, thanks sir." The jaygee moved on as Shielbrock continued to the bar. A couple of lieutenants smiled in their conversation, nodded to him and moved over enough to make room for him at the bar. A Navy lieutenant nurse on a barstool was on the other side, deep in conversation with a lieutenant commander wearing wings. The barmaid came over disregarding shouted orders from other customers. "Eve-nin Capm' Shellback. Y' didn't go home this weekend, huh? What'll y' have?" with a marked Newport accent.

"Evening Angie. No. I've got some work to do this weekend. How about a vodka and—."

"Vodka and tonic for you," she interrupted, "One or two?"

Shielbrock looked around as he answered. "Well, one for me, and is Colonel Rogerson here? I don't see him."

"Right over there with a group," She nodded her head to indicate direction as her hands were occupied mixing the two drinks.

Shielbrock looked in the designated direction, through the dim light, the crowd and the smoke. "Oh yeah, there he is. What are those others drinking?"

She handed him two drinks. "More than you can carry. Here's your usual; one for you, one for Colonel Don. I'll send the waitress over to the table."

"Thanks." He left some money on the bar and made his way around, through and between the customers toward the table.

"Uh, Commodore," A lieutenant stopped him but with a drink in each hand he couldn't shake hands.

"Hey, Bill. How are things going?"

"Great, Commodore. We're starting ship handling next week, y'know, and they've given us some stuff to read. Your book is part of it, y'know, the ship handling book for the Gearings."

Shielbrock laughed, "Well, Bill, I hope it won't get you into trouble. Good luck with it."

"Thanks, Commodore. See ya'."

"Yeah, Bill." He looked across the lieutenant's shoulder at the table where Don Rogerson was sitting with a group. "See ya'."

Hoss Hartell was there and Frank Peoples. A lieutenant commander from the OCS staff and his wife were there but Shielbrock couldn't remember their names. The Public Affairs Officer Jim Bailey was at the table and so was she, Kim McManus, looking directly at him as he made his way through the crowd toward the table.

"Evening, Commodore," someone said.

"Hey, Shellback!"

"Hi, Captain Shellback."

Calls to him were acknowledged with a smile and a lifting of one glass or the other in the direction of the caller as Shielbrock approached the table and she hadn't taken her eyes from him. He placed one drink in front of Don Rogerson and took a seat across from Kim, between Frank Peoples and the OCS guy, saying hello to everyone, smiling.

"Hey, Shellback, thanks for the drink. Where you been? You know everyone here?"

Shielbrock was saying yes but Rogerson continued anyway, "This is

Burt and Margie, you remember them, and Jim Bailey, here, and Kim. You talked to her today."

"Yes, Don thanks. Nice to be here. Are any of our other guys here?"

"Not now. Sid and Joe were here earlier but they went home." They had to talk in a loud voice to be heard over the noise as Shielbrock turned to Burt, the OCS guy. "Well, how are things going at your school? Keeping you busy these days?"

Oh yeah, we've got a big class—," and he went on to explain what was happening at the Officer Candidate School, the problems, the solutions, the people involved. Shielbrock kept looking at Burt, nodding at appropriate times and giving little remarks like "that so," "imagine that," and "uh-huh," but really he was not listening at all.

The waitress came and took their order, Shielbrock offering that it was his round for being late and the others laughed. Separate conversations went on around the table, piano music was drowned out by voices and laughter as a commander stopped at the table to tell Shielbrock that he heard a rumor that a particular admiral would be the next OP-90 and Shielbrock discussed that situation. An officer in civilian clothes came over to the table and discussed an article from the last issue of the Naval Institute Proceedings on command and control of carrier battle groups and he made a tentative appointment to meet with Shielbrock next week to discuss it further. A lieutenant came over from the bar and discussed his next duty assignment and Shielbrock asked him to come to his office next week to talk about it.

Kim had been talking with Jim Bailey who was sitting next to her as Shielbrock ended the often interrupted conversation with Burt. "Well, I hope you'll be able to get that straightened out before this class finishes."

"Oh, we will, we will. I'm sure of it."

"Good. And Ms. McManus," he turned toward her, "How did your interviews go today?"

"Fine Captain." She smiled at him. "Everyone was very cooperative. Well, almost everyone, and I got a lot of material. It's been very interesting and I'm sure there's a good story here."

"Well," he had to yell across the table so that she could hear him above the noise, "I'm glad you found it interesting but I doubt if there's any story here. Anyway, I'm glad you can see us in this 'human interest' environment, away from strategic considerations, before you leave."

"Oh, but I'm not leaving right away. I'll be here a few days. I still have to talk with Mr. Murphy and Dr. Meyerhoff." She looked at Jim Bailey who added, "Yes, and with the Admiral, too."

An officer in civilian clothes interrupted them. "Evening Captain Shellback. I wonder if I could talk with you next week about carrier battle group ASW. I'm doing a paper on VS-SSN coordination and I'd like to get your views."

"Sure, Andy, be glad to talk with you. Give me a call 'cause I might have to go to Washington around mid-week. Only one day though. Okay?"

"Yes sir. That'll be fine. I'll call you." Andy, the visitor, then looked at Kim. "A new member of the SSG, Captain?"

Shielbrock looked at Kim then back at Andy. "Yes. This is Kim Mc-Manus. She's taking over as the Director of SSG. Dick Murphy was appointed as Secretary of Defense yesterday. Did you know that?" They all laughed and the visitor responded, "Yeah. Great idea. You'll have them lined up and falling all over themselves trying to get into SSG with Kim, here, as director." Then to Kim, "What do you really do, Kim?"

"I'm a professor at the University of Maryland. I teach in the weapon systems curriculum at the School of Engineering, specializing in air and submarine communications."

They all let out whoops, whistles and laughter.

"Hey, all right! Sign me up. Nice meeting you." The visitor departed laughing.

Shielbrock turned to Kim, "Hey, that was all right. Where in the world did you get that air-submarine communications thing from?

Her eyes had that sparkle, just like when she was angry, but this time she was pleased."I do my homework, Captain."

The OCS staffie Burt and his wife excused themselves and left the table and a few minutes later Hoss Hartell departed. Frank Peoples had been talking with Don Rogerson but now turned to Shielbrock. "Hey, Shellback, I've hardly seen you all week. What have you been working on?"

"Oh, that under the ice study, you know, the one that Joe got from OP-02?"

"Is it any good?"

"Yeah. I'll show it to you next week. We've got to fold that into the plan. It's got a lot of good stuff for us."

"Okay. I've got to go now. Got to take Marylyn to dinner and I'm late. You're not going home this weekend?"

"I decided to stay and work on that under the ice study. Besides, I'll probably go to Washington Wednesday or Thursday with Mr. Murphy."

"Okay. Have a nice weekend. Nice to meet you, Kim. Bye Jim. See ya, Don."

They all said their good-bys to Frank. The place had thinned out considerably and there was less noise so the piano could be heard clearly. Another round of drinks was brought by the waitress for the four remaining at their table and Jim finished telling Kim about Naval War College history as Shielbrock slid his glass across the table and moved around next to her.

"Jim is right, of course, but the real reason the Naval War College is in Newport goes back to the days when the millionaires had their summer places here. You know, the mansions on Bellevue Avenue?" Kim nodded. "They're called cottages. Well, the millionaires left their wives and kids in the cottages every summer and they went back to New York to spend the hot summer being entertained by their mistresses. Meanwhile, back at the ranch, or in this case the cottages in Newport, the wives tried to outdo each other with elaborate parties. There being a shortage of appropriate gentlemen for their parties, someone got the idea to invite officers from the Navy ships that visited here. That worked nicely but the ships weren't always here. So, the ladies pressured their husbands to pressure the Navy to see to it that there was an adequate supply of officers for their parties. Now, the husbands were having a great time avoiding the hot summer days in New York with their cool companions and they, the rich husbands, would do anything to keep their wives happy in Newport. So, the millionaires leaned on the Secretary of the Navy, a school for officers was started at Newport and a constant supply of stiff starched white uniforms was available for the gracious elegant lawn parties on Bellevue Avenue."

"You're a cynic."

"What do you mean? I'm not a cynic, I'm a romantic. Think of all the romantic fantasy that could be developed from that story line. A rich wife abandoned by her husband for the summer in Newport falls in love with a Navy officer. He takes command of a new ship made of steel from the husband's plant. The ship falls apart. See the possibilities? Now there's a story for you."

"That's your judgment of a good story? It reinforces my statement that you can't judge the newsworthiness of anything. A much better story is centered on why the CNO would bring together a group of top officers to form a Strategic Studies Group. To build or create a Naval Strategy? Didn't we have one before? If the Navy is developing their own strategy, how does that tie in with the other services? Does each service have its own strategy? How does a new strategy bear on the budget? Do we need fewer submarines, aircraft carriers, cruisers, or more?" Her eyes were sparkling again and her tits were nice as she leaned forward, but then as she finished the last question she sat up with her shoulders back and her tits were even more beautiful. Shielbrock took his eyes from them.

"Well, those are a lot of questions which you," He emphasized the word you, "are interested in because, as you said, you did your homework. But the public has no interest in this dull planning process."

"Maybe the public would be interested to know if in time of war the Navy would go forward to find and fight an enemy or stay back and fight wherever and if ever needed."

"Maybe they would like to know that and so would Gorshkoff. So now you're into my second reason, remember, classification, national security."

"Yes, I remember. You remember I told you that was up to you. Why don't you just tell me the unclassified parts and let me do a story on it?"

"Cause there's no story here. I told you."

Don Rogerson stood up a little unsteadily. "Okay, Shellback, you guys can argue about this all night if you want but I've got to get home. Bye, Jim. Stay calm, Shellback. Kim, you are a lovely lady. Don't let him get you down." He paused, "Gosh maybe I shouldn't have said it that way. What I meant to say was keep your chin—, I mean, have a nice evening." They laughed with him.

"Drive carefully, Don. See you Monday."

Jim Bailey and Kim added their good-bys and Kim asked, "Is he all right to drive home?"

"Sure. He'll be fine. Don't worry about him."

Jim got up also, said his farewell and departed, leaving Shielbrock and Kim at the table in the cocktail lounge. Only a few other customers remained at the bar and the tables.

"I thought Jim Bailey, there, as the PAO would be taking you to dinner."

"There you are, wrong again. See. There's no such strategy."

"That's not strategy. That's common sense. Why would a bright young guy like that pass up a chance to have dinner with a girl like you?"

"You'll have to ask him, I guess. But, Captain, I believe you just flattered me." Her eyes sparkled again and they were looking directly into each other's eyes as he lowered his to look at those beautiful tits, then back into her eyes.

"Yes. It was meant to be flattery, but you don't need it. You know you're a beautiful woman."

"But praise from Caesar—, and woman, not girl?"

"How old are you?"

"Oh, so now you're doing the interview?"

"And getting no answers."

"Thirty-one."

"Jesus Christ, I'm twenty years older than you."

She stood up and picked up her purse. "Well this has been very interesting but I've got to eat. So if you'll excuse me I'll leave you here to ponder your advanced age."

He stood and put some money on the table. "I'll walk you to the door," and they made their way around and past the other tables as he acknowledged a call from an officer in civilian clothes. She stopped in the lobby, near the coat room and looked up at him. "Shellback, you make a hell of an entrance. Did you know that?"

"What do you mean?"

"Earlier tonight that place was packed, noisy, smoky," She nodded toward the bar and cocktail lounge. "You walked in and half the people in there focused on you. `Hey Shellback. Hi Commodore. Good evening Captain. Have you seen this. Did you know that,'" She imitated the greetings with a false masculine voice. "Some call you Shellback, some call you commodore. They all know you. It looks like they worship you. It's like John Wayne walking into the Long Branch Saloon."

He laughed, "No, John Wayne is much older than I am and it would be Matt Dillon from Gunsmoke walking into the Long Branch. But that's too long ago for you to know about."

"Listen—."

"No, you listen," He interrupted her. "That PAO maybe isn't so bright to have passed up a chance to take you to dinner. I wouldn't want to make the same mistake. Would you have dinner with me?"

"Well," she hesitated, "Only if we can talk about the story."

"No story."

"Then only if you don't feel too old."

"That's a deal." They got their coats and left the club.

Shielbrock explained the history of the restaurant when they were seated. The place had been a gambling hall and speakeasy in the days of old Newport. The millionaires of Bellevue Avenue came there to gamble and to drink when both were illegal. The place was closed by do-gooders and fell to ruin until it was restored and made into a restaurant in modern times. "Newport is a summer resort town, and in the summer there are probably a hundred restaurants. But in the winter, when the hungry tourists aren't here, only the best restaurants can survive because the year round inhabitants quickly learn which ones are the best."

"So this is one of the best?" Kim's eyes were glued to him and she listened to every word.

"One of the best, for sure, maybe thee best."

"Let me ask you something."

"Okay, but no story on the SSG."

She laughed, "Well, we'll see about that. What I wanted to ask you, back there at the officers club, the men that spoke to you, they called you different things, different names, like Shellback and Commodore, and you're a captain. Why do they use those different names, or titles, I guess they are?"

He laughed, "Well the young officers are lieutenants at SWOS——." She gave him a questioning look.

"SWOS is Surface Warfare Officers School. They're training to be department heads in ships. The ones I spoke to were in ships in the destroyer squadron that I commanded. In the Navy, anyone who commands a group of ships, like a squadron, is called commodore. So, they still call me commodore. Shellback is a nickname I got as an ensign when I crossed the equator. Anyone who crosses the equator and goes through a ridiculous initiation is a Shellback. In my case Shellback is close to Shielbrock, so the name stuck. So, some call me commodore, some call me captain, some call me Shielbrock, some call me Shellback." He stopped and looked at her, "What are you going to call me?"

She thought awhile, returning his look, "I like Martin."

"I'm glad."

"Why? Do you prefer to be called Martin?"

"Oh, I don't care either way. I meant that I' m glad that you like," he paused, "Martin."

"I meant the name, not the person. Remember, I'm the journalist with whom you will not cooperate?"

"Yes, I remember."

"Another question."

"Yes."

"Subjects. The men who came over and talked with you asked you about ship handling, battle group command and control, ASW and some others I can't recall. Why do they seek you out on all these subjects?"

"Well, there aren't really so many subjects—".

"Cut the modesty, Martin."

"Well," He thought awhile, "I wrote a book on ship handling a hundred years ago, or so. It was never really published, but it's used quite a bit for the class of ship that it was written for. Those SWOS students are just about to start their ship handling course, and they have been given my book along with lots of other more valuable literature. They were anxious to tell me that they got the book, that's all."

Kim was very impressed with the book and she pursued the issue of writing and publishing and the conversation drifted into literature and then into her own writing. A half hour later she brought the conversation back to Shielbrock and his many subjects at the officers club, "—and that one man in civilian clothes asked to talk to you about battle group coordination."

"Okay. That was Andy Zornack. He is a commander, a student at the Naval War College and he's writing a paper on carrier aircraft coordination with submarines."

"Why does he want to talk to you?"

"I've done a lot of carrier battle group ASW, that's anti submarine warfare—."

"I know what ASW means!"

"Okay. I've done a lot of ASW and he wants to talk with me."

"Why you? There must be others."

"Sure. There are lots of guys who know a lot more about ASW than I do but I'm here and available."

"Somehow, Martin, I don't believe that. It's not the full story. He could find a lot of others. Why you?"

"Okay. A lot of people in the Navy think that I created the command and control doctrine we use for carrier battle groups. That's not so, actually. I didn't create it but I used it at a time when others didn't understand it. You might say I helped develop it and that I promoted it. Anyway, frequently Navy guys talk to me about battle group command and control because of that background. Okay? Is there a story there?"

"Well, there might be. You've just told me you wrote the book on ship handling for the Navy and you developed the Navy's carrier battle group command and control doctrine. That just might be a story."

"That's typical journalistic distortion and exaggeration. I didn't write thee book, I wrote a book," he used the long a pronunciation, "One of very many. Mine's not very good and it applies to only one class of ship. The battle group command and control doctrine was originated by Bernie Schneiderman and developed by dozens of others, maybe hundreds of others. I'm only one. That's the trouble with your so-called journalism. You, all of you, collect bits of information, scraps, threads and you put together a so-called story which turns out to be a fantasy, a fabrication. It's misleading, poor representation, shallow and just plain inaccurate."

She was angry and her eyes sparkled. "Well maybe if our sources would be more forthcoming, if we were given the facts instead of the scraps, the background instead of the smoke screen, we could put together something which might satisfy your evaluation of proper journalism. You—, you, you're the perfect example of an uncooperative subject and you have the nerve to criticize journalists for not getting facts. Give me, give us, facts and the stories will be accurate!"

The arguing went on through the meal.

In the parking lot of her motel he got out of the car, went around to the other side and held the car door for her. Her legs came out first, both together, nice, and he held her hand as she got out of the car. She thanked him and he closed the car door and facing each other they stood a moment, then she turned toward the motel and walked slowly as she spoke. "That was a very nice evening, Captain. You were not at all cooperative with the interview but the dinner was wonderful." He walked up beside her and stopped as she turned again and walked slowly, he walking alongside her.

"I really think that you could be a little more cooperative and tell me more about the SSG. I know that there are things that you can't talk about, but just the basics, the answers to the obvious questions of why—." She continued talking as they walked together across the parking lot, up the stairs, through the double doors and down the hall. She was still talking, he had not said a word, as she stopped in front of the door to her room and in silence she found the key in her purse and unlocked the door.

He broke his silence. "I would be glad to talk to you about the relevant items concerning SSG but it really is of interest to no one." She walked into the room as he talked. Following her inside the room, he took her coat and continued to explain the lack of interest and the classification problems and she turned toward him, standing close. He looked down at her, at her eyes sparkling and at her beautiful breasts as she looked up at him, her face very serious.

He spoke slowly, "I haven't really paid a bit of attention to anything you said or I said since we got out of the car here."

"I haven't either but you really are a bastard, Shellback."

"Why do you say that?"

"You're so God Damn charming and all that but you won't cooperate. You object to a simple interview to gather some innocent information."

He didn't say anything for a few moments. Then he put his arms around her and she came close to him, pressed against him and they kissed long, deep and with a release of tension. Their mouths opened eagerly. They clung to each other.

They drove to Cape Cod the next morning and spent the rest of Saturday walking on the cold, wind swept, lonely beach. Staying at a small inn on the beach, all day they argued, not only about the SSG story that Shielbrock refused to give but dozens of other subjects as there was little they agreed on. He was a Republican, she a Democrat. He was a conservative, she a liberal. She liked musical shows, he liked drama. Classical music or modern, spicy food or bland, large cars or small, formal or informal dining; they differed on it all. He liked all sports, she thought them foolish. She thought that the only worthwhile television was the public broadcasting channel, he never watched it. But in bed they agreed on everything, enjoyed every bit of each other, and so their night again was magnificent and in the early morning they walked again on the lonely beach and argued until in bed in mid-morning they shared that ecstasy each gave the other. Then it was back to Newport Sunday afternoon, an intimacy at her motel room and each went their own way.

One day Dick Murphy asked Shellback about TACTRAGRUPAC,

what it was and what it did. "Almost everywhere we go Navy officers comment to you about TACTRAGRUPAC. Tell me about it, please."

Shellback described the Tactical Training Group Pacific, which he had started as the first Commanding Officer. He had been asked by the Commander in Chief, U.S. Pacific Fleet to start a school in San Diego similar to the Royal Navy's Maritime Tactical School near Portsmouth, England, "Go over there, visit the British school and get whatever paperwork they'll give you. Then give us a school like it but modified so as to be best for us." That was the CINCPACFLT's guidance, along with, "We need a school to teach battle group tactics to our battle group commanders."

Shellback had been selected for this role by CINCPACFLT because the admiral had heard so much about his accomplishments as a destroyer squadron commander in fleet exercises involving carrier battle groups. The admiral had promised him and delivered Shellback's choice of four officers with which to start the new school. The first class was to be taught in three months, a six week course on battle group tactics, but Shellback negotiated for a two week course to start, with intention to expand it to four weeks, and eventually six. He got the four officers; a fighter pilot and a helicopter pilot, both having had command of squadrons; a destroyer officer and a submarine officer, both with previous command of their respective ships, all four with experience on a battle group staff; and all four with the rank of commander. They formed a very successful training activity, teaching admirals and officers going to admirals' staffs, ships' commanding officers, and officers going to key operational jobs in ships as TACTRAGRUPAC quickly became recognized as the authority in battle group tactics. A year and a half later the Atlantic Fleet started a similar school.

"So you see, wherever we go and talk to Navy people someone there, often the admiral, has been to my courses," summarized Shellback.

"They've been students of yours?" continued Murphy.

"Yes."

"You've taught battle group commanders how to fight their battle groups. The admirals of the navy, at sea, learned their tactics from you." The statements were partial questions, partial summaries.

"Well, not all the admirals and not all the tactics. A lot of them knew a lot of tactics before TACTRAGRUPAC and it wasn't just me. I had a great team of real experts, y'know."

"But a lot of them didn't know much tactics before you and your team taught them." Murphy wouldn't let go.

"Let's say some of them needed some improvement or maybe refreshing of the memory."

"Why aren't you an admiral?" asked Murphy.

"You know the system. You were Under Sec-Nav. It's a complicated process. Not many make it. I haven't been selected. Why? I don't know. It's complicated. What do you want me to say? 'I'm a dumb shit.' 'I'm incompetent.' 'I don't know the right people.' 'I haven't had the right jobs.' Take your pick. We don't get a report card, y'know."

Murphy pursued it further. "You know better than that. You've been in all the right places, you're not dumb, you know the politics and you have to have some good idea as to why you haven't been selected. I'd like to hear why and I have a real reason for knowing, not just curiosity."

"Tell me your reason and maybe I'll tell you why," responded Shellback.

"I want this Strategic Studies Group to attract the best the Navy has to offer. If the guys here get selected for flag it helps get the best officers for subsequent years. Don't you agree? Doesn't it add prestige to the organization?"

"Well, you asked two questions. First, flag selection will attract those seeking future flag selection but they might not be the best for strategic development. Second, it does add to the prestige but not necessarily to the product. Prestige could help sell a product which is really of lesser value."

"Why were you not selected?" insisted Murphy.

"There are probably a lot of reasons and I don't know them all." Shellback's vague response didn't satisfy Murphy so he tried a new approach.

"What do I have to do, what can I do, to get the eligible guys of this SSG selected? You, to start with. I've gotten to know you real well these past months and I know that you should be an admiral. You're a fine leader. Everyone respects you. You're sensitive, demanding, intelligent, practical and everything else. You're probably the finest officer I've come across. So tell me."

Shellback went through an explanation of the selection process, not the legal or formal procedures well known to Murphy, but the real world practical process. "Selection by a flag board is by community; aviators, submariners, and surface ship guys. Except for the few specialities you have to be 'in' with your own community, one of their very own super achievers. There are a few jobs in the Navy, specific billets from which selection probability is very high, almost certain. Commandant of Midshipmen at the Naval Academy, Executive Assistant to the Secretary of the Navy or to CNO are examples. A few other billets have a reasonable chance of selection, such as some of the other EA's to senior appointees and four stars. From most captain billets, and I mean most, no one has ever been or probably will ever be selected for flag. A captain ordered into one of these simply will not make flag rank. He knows it. The detailer knows it. Everyone knows it. Legally he's still in the running but practically he's not going to be selected. In defense of this seemingly inequitable situation, the guys sent to those high and highest billets are super achievers. They've done it all and done it right so selection is not from the entire population of legally eligible captains, it's from among those who are in, or who have been in, those few right jobs. Then it gets to support within one's own community.

"In my case I've had all the right jobs and done them all well, if not the best. I've commanded two destroyers and a DESRON, with all the right operations. I've served in the Surface Warfare section, OP-03, in Washington. So, I have all the right tickets for the surface warfare community but I spent my most valuable promotion time, that is after my DESRON, teaching carrier battle group tactics. That's not first line surface warfare community. Maybe it should be, but that's academic. The community promotes.

"I've told our younger SSG guys that this duty here cannot be looked upon as being away from their community. Each of them reports to 02, 03, or 05 whenever they're in Washington to maintain clearly that loyalty line to their community." 02, 03, 05 were the sections of the CNO staff responsible for submarine, air and surface warfare respectively.

"Now, we have two others in the SSG eligible for promotion this year, Sid Debway and Frank Peoples. You should talk to them, for sure, but I can tell you this; both are aviators and both have excellent chances for selection. Frank is VP," Navy abbreviation for land based maritime patrol aircraft, "and Sid is VF," navy for carrier based fighter aircraft." In aviation, selection gets into sub-communities. Frank is a super achiever hot candidate of the VP sub-community and Sid is the same among the fighters. With the right help they could both make it this year."

"What kind of help?" asked Murphy.

"I'd suggest that you write to the sub-community leader of each, explain your position here, point out that you feel responsible for this particular guy's career because this is a new and unknown organization and ask him for a recommendation as to what you can do or whom you should contact to ensure that this 'hot prospect' remains competitive. Your letter will flatter the guy that gets it and he'll be in sympathy with you for looking after a guy from his community but most of all, if you pick the right sub-community leader, you've already influenced him toward selection if he ends up on the board."

"Gee, that's brilliant! Can I do it for all three, or would a phone call be better?" asked Murphy.

"No, no. No phone call. That's too easily forgotten. The written word is more valuable."

"And how about you, can I do it for all three of you?"

"Well, I'm a tougher case than the other two. You can try. It can't hurt."

"I'd like to try for the three of you. Could you rough out a letter for me and maybe suggest whom they should go to?" asked Murphy.

Shellback smiled and thought of the simple administrative process of "completed staff work" to which he had always adhered. Murphy would soon have three smooth letters ready for signature and mailing, but only after Sid Debway and Frank Peoples had concurred with the project.

"Yes sir. I'll get right on it."

Sid and Frank readily agreed that it was a smart move and the letters went out. Sid Debway and Frank Peoples were selected for promotion to the one star flag rank of Commodore but Martin Shielbrock was not selected for promotion and a few months later he retired from the Navy.

CHAPTER 7

"Oh you men and your Navy stories!" Jackie had listened carefully to the story of Martin Shielbrock's duty at the Naval War College and of his brief encounter with the female journalist. "So here we have the sailor bedding a beauty far away while his loving wife waits patiently at home, 'Keeping the home fires burning,' we might say."

Her husband Barney spoke up. "Excuse me, Steve, for intruding into this very sensitive family situation but, after all, we are family aren't we?"

Steven agreed, "Yes. Go for it! I'm just as interested as you are."

Barney turned to his wife, Jackie. "Well, we might say that but with all due respect, if any respect in this case is really due, you can't really say that Barbara had always been at home 'keeping the home fires burning,' now could you?

Jackie thought for a moment. "Well, maybe this is the time for me to tell you of a very serious family event that Barbara told me about. It happened when she and Nancy were at home in Virginia and while Martin was in Newport with this SSG thing.

LOFFMAN'S WILL

Daylight crept through the trees and found its way into the windows of the Northern Virginia home and Barbara Shielbrock looked at the window in surprise. God! How long had she been sitting here reminiscing? Hours. The ashtray was filled with cigarette butts and her throat was dry.

The thoughts that had been running through her mind had been so long ago; they were thoughts of that weekend in New York and of that trip to Rome. She had not seen nor spoken to Jules Loffman again.

She recalled that about five years after those very special rendezvous in New York and then in Rome she had heard that Jules' wife had passed away. Jackie was married to Barney Williams by then and they lived in Norfolk while Barney was serving in a submarine. The Shielbrocks were living in San Diego at that time. Jackie had called Barbara with the information about Jules' wife passing away and Barbara had sent a simple formal sympathy card to Jules. A couple of weeks later a formal card acknowledged the Shielbrock consideration.

Barbara hadn't seen him nor heard the name of Jules Loffman mentioned for over twenty years, until the same year that Martin retired from the Navy. Again, it was Jackie calling from Norfolk where Barney, just selected for promotion to rear admiral, had command of a submarine squadron. According to the Norfolk newspapers Jules Loffman had died at the age of seventy-six and Jackie read the article over the phone to Barbara in Alexandria, Virginia. Martin was in Newport at the time with the Strategic Studies Group at the Naval War College.

After thanking her for the news, they had chatted briefly, said good bye and Barbara had sat and thought about dear sweet Jules Loffman, whom she had loved. She cried as she thought of the poor lonely man, of his charm and wealth, his good looks and intelligence, and of his lonely, lonely life.

Three days later it was early morning and Barbara was about to leave the house for work as the ringing telephone stopped her. "Mrs. Shielbrock?"

"Yes."

"Mrs. Martin Shielbrock, maiden name Barbara Muir?"

Annoyed, Barbara replied, "Yes. This is she. Who is this and what do you want?"

"Excuse me, Mrs. Shielbrock, for being so abrupt. Let me explain." She detected a soft southern accent, different from her own, probably Virginian. "I am Donald Brown. I am an attorney and I must speak to you on a very important matter."

"What is this important matter?"

"Mrs. Shielbrock, would you be willing to come to Norfolk?"

"Norfolk? Why should I want to go to Norfolk?" A little twinge of concern crept into her mind, a little reminiscence.

"Well, uh, let me start at the beginning."

"Please do."

"Mrs. Shielbrock, have you known Jules Loffman?"

Barbara's heart jumped. She took a quick shocked breath, paused and slowly exhaled.

"I knew Mr. Jules Loffman years ago."

"Are you aware, and please pardon me for being so direct, but are you aware that Mr. Loffman passed away three days ago?"

"Yes. I heard. I'm very sorry."

"Mrs. Shielbrock, prior to his death Mr. Loffman retained me to represent certain portions of his will, of his estate. Let me clarify. I am not the executor of the will but I am very familiar with it. Mr. Loffman retained me to represent certain particular features of his will."

There were a few moments of silence as she thought. God, no! He couldn't have included me. He wouldn't. It must be something else, but what? Very slowly she asked, "And what is that to me?"

"Well, Mrs. Shielbrock, in simple direct terms, you have an interest in the will and I have been retained to look after your interests." He went on talking about the importance of an early get-together to discuss the terms of the will which would be read in ten days - she to Norfolk - or he to Washington - when - where - soon - important - Nancy - details - affidavits - depositions - statements. He was still talking when she interrupted.

"Just a minute, hold on. Mr. Brown, is it?"

"Yes m'am, Donald Brown."

"I'm having a difficult time putting this together, Mr. Brown, but did you mention Nancy?"

"Oh, yes. Your daughter Nancy is in the will. That's why I was saying that we must get together very soon, immediately if possible, that is the three of us."

His office in Norfolk smelled of old wood and was old dominion as in the old Virginia motto; wood paneling, heavy molding, plank wood flooring, antique furniture, lots of leather and wood, all in dark tones. Donald Brown was older than Barbara had imagined from the phone conversation the day before and he was slightly overweight, smoked cigars and wore a rather poor quality, ill fitting dark gray suit. Obviously, clothing was of no concern to him as some of this morning's breakfast showed on his tie and suit lapel.

Two beautiful women sat in front of his desk, one in her early fifties, the other in her late twenties and both were dressed very businesslike, as if they had just stepped out of a fashion magazine. After an exchange of pleasantries with appropriate southern courtesy, Donald Brown turned to business. "Let me explain, first, that Jules Loffman was a rather wealthy man. The total value of his estate is about ten million dollars. Now, second, I was a personal friend of his, and so I consider it my duty to my friend, as well as my professional responsibility to see that his desires concerning his estate are met.

"Let's discuss your involvement in this first, Mrs. Shielbrock." Brown opened a file and turned some papers. "You opened a bank account at the First Bank of Norfolk in 1951."

Barbara looked puzzled, trying to remember. "I financed a car if that's what you mean. What could that have to do with why we're here?"

"Well, according to Jules' notes it was in connection with a car that he bought for you—."

"No, no," Barbara interrupted, "He didn't buy it for me. I bought it. I financed it with the First Bank of Norfolk and made payments for three years."

Brown looked at her and smiled. "Yes. I see from the record of the account that you paid a hundred and ten dollars a month, every month for three years."

"That's right."

"Mrs. Shielbrock, the car had been paid for by Jules. Your monthly payments went into a savings account which was administered by Jules. Some of the papers you signed at that time established the account. He continued to administer the account in your name until three years ago when he named me to administer it. On three occasions he made deposits to the account. No money has ever been withdrawn and you are the only one with that authority."

Barbara was bewildered, confused. "Do you mean that for all these years, almost thirty years, that money has been in a savings account in my name?"

"Yes m'am, and as I said, there were additional deposits made three times. Jules' notes say that you would recognize the dates of the deposit."

Brown read off the dates as Barbara struggled with her memory. The dates were two days after her wedding to Martin, her weekend in New York with Jules and Nancy's birthday, but she didn't share these connections with Brown and Nancy as she sat passively listening.

"And would you like to know the balance in your savings account?"

Barbara just stared at him without answering as Nancy replied for her. "Yes, we'd like to know."

"One million five hundred and fifty three thousand dollars." Brown smiled as he looked from Barbara to Nancy and back.

"Jesus Christ!" Nancy sat back in her chair but Barbara had still not moved or changed expression.

"You must understand," Brown continued as he looked at both of them, "That this sum is not a part of Jules Loffman's estate. This is money in your account, Mrs. Shielbrock. It belongs to you and is not mentioned in the will. Now, there are tax complications, of course, and I will help you with those problems, also in accordance with Jules' instructions."

There was silence as Brown waited for some response from Barbara and finally Nancy spoke. "Mother, do you understand? Are you okay?"

"Yes, I'm fine and I understand," then turning to Brown, "That money is really not mine."

"Mother!"

"Mrs. Shielbrock, legally the money is yours. However, Jules anticipated a problem like this and instructed me to give you this letter." He handed her an envelope, stood up and came around the desk.

"Miss Shielbrock, may I suggest that we allow your mother to read her letter, that is of course unless she would prefer for you—."

"Oh, no, I'll be outside, Mother if you—." Barbara smiled as Nancy left the office with Brown.

The letter was handwritten by Jules in his bold easy-to-read style. He poured out his heart to Barbara in this letter, telling her that she was the most beautiful meaningful person in his life and even their brief times together were memorable enough to sustain him. No one meant as much to him as she and he wanted her to have some small token of his affection when he was gone. He begged her to accept what he was offering and he went on to describe his brothers, nephews and nieces, all of whom were nice people, had been nice to him and were very well taken care of.

Tears streamed down her face. She sobbed as she read his plea to accept what he offered in death. The final portion of his letter confused her as it referred to injured feelings, pride, his will and Nancy, and he offered deep apology for interfering with their lives.

The office door opened after a long time, tentatively, as Nancy looked in and found Barbara completing the repair of her make-up, composed and ready to resume the talks.

Donald Brown pointed out that Jules had six nephews and nieces, the sons and daughters of his two brothers. The will provided very nicely for the six, each receiving stock in the Loffman stores which at present market value came to a little over a million dollars each.

"And remember, ladies, these nephews and nieces of Jules are the sons and daughters of his brothers. Those brothers own the remaining stock in the Loffman stores so each of the six would be well provided for by their fathers.

"Now this is the sensitive part." Brown looked at the two ladies in front of him, then continued, "Jules wanted Nancy to receive some benefit from his estate—."

"Me?" Nancy looked from Brown to her mother, "Why me?"

Brown continued, "He was concerned that if he merely included Nancy in the will it might be contested by the nieces and nephews. It probably would unless there was good reason, legal reason for her to be included."

"Legal reason?"

"Yes. That's where I came in. Jules asked me, directed me, now this is the sensitive part, to assemble legal evidence if not proof, that the woman known as Nancy Shielbrock was, in fact, his daughter."

"His daughter!" A shocked and angry Nancy stood and looked from Brown to Barbara. "Mother?"

Barbara looked at her angry daughter, "Please Nancy, sit down and let's hear the rest of what Mr. Brown has to tell us."

Nancy withheld her question and did as her mother asked.

"Thank you," Brown continued. "It is not an issue to me, and strangely enough not even to you at this time, as to whether or not Nancy is Jules' daughter—."

"Well," Nancy could not remain completely silent. "It certainly is an issue to me!"

"Please," Brown held up his hand. "What I mean is that's a separate issue to the more immediate issue of whether the Loffman nieces and nephews believe it."

"Who cares what they think!"

"But my dear, I don't believe you understand—."

"I understand that this man claims to be my father!"

"Yes. He claims that he is your father and I have his legal evidence of that possibility. This evidence with his statement that you are his daughter would be very convincing. A supportive statement to that effect from your mother would be incontrovertible. It would in effect be proof of that paternity."

"My mother—?"

"Just a minute, I just said that whether or not he is or isn't your father is not as important, at this time, as how the nieces and nephews view it. By that I mean how their attorneys see it." Nancy started to interrupt but Brown continued. "If their attorneys see that you, I, we have proof of his paternity, then you are his sole heir and could contest the will. On one end of the spectrum of possibilities they could get nothing and on the other end it could be tied up in litigation for years before it reached any settlement."

Nancy sat back, listening as Brown continued. "Now, Jules was very aware of these possibilities and so he made up another will, after the known will. I hold the second will. It names you as his daughter, with all evidence as his sole heir. If this will is processed, you would get all of his estate. We can expect the nieces and nephews to challenge it but they would have a difficult time. What Jules has put together is now up to you, Nancy. That's why his instructions were that your mother be here to help you."

Nancy looked at Barbara, searching, asking. "I'm not sure I understand all this. Why me? What choice? What so called evidence, proof?"

With no response from Barbara, Brown continued. "We must first decide if you want me to come forward with this will or go along with the first will." Before Nancy could answer he spoke again. "Bearing on that choice is the strong probability that the nieces and nephews will challenge your inclusion in the first will and if that happens we would have to show the evidence that you are his daughter."

The two ladies looked at each other a few moments then back at Brown.

"Now, as your attorney I can offer this as a possible course of action. This is what you might call the middle road. It's a conservative procedure and it is what Jules had in mind as he explained all this to me and had me put all this together."

"Go on," It was the first Barbara had spoken in some time.

"I could take copies of some of the paternity evidence to their attorneys, just enough I would hope, to convince them of the credibility of the claim. If I am able to convince them of, well, not the proof but the reasonable validity, they would probably recommend to their clients that they accept the terms of the will including you."

There was silence in the office as the ladies stared straight ahead, then at each other, then at Brown, until Barbara broke the silence. "Mr. Brown, how much of the estate is to go to Nancy in this, as you call it, the first will?"

Before Brown could reply an angry Nancy spoke up, "Mother, we've just heard that this man claims to be my father. That means he says he had sex with you, and, and, and all you question is 'how much money is there?' I find that God Damn strange."

"Let's hear what Mr. Brown has to say. There's plenty of time for explanations if they are necessary."

"If they are necessary? You're damned right they're necessary. We're talking about who is my father and who you've had sex with. I'd say it's necessary!"

"We haven't heard the full story yet from Mr. Brown. We can discuss private matters between ourselves."

Brown was clearly embarrassed, but prepared. "Let me make one point very clear, ladies. I do not know, nor is it my affair, as to whether Jules Loffman is really the father of Nancy Shielbrock. I have assembled evidence, in some cases maybe even created evidence, to convince attorneys out of court that the paternity might be valid. A statement from Mrs. Shielbrock admitting to this paternity along with my evidence would be very convincing." He stopped to emphasize the next few words. "Whether or not Jules Loffman is really your father."

"Then you're saying he isn't my father?"

"No, I'm saying to you that I don't know but to anyone outside this room I'd say that I'm sure he is your father."

"But you'd say that just to convince the attorneys for the nieces and nephews?"

"Or anyone else that asks. I can't take the chance of a leak." He turned to Barbara, "Which makes it very important that you of all people do not deny it."

"Jesus Christ," Nancy sat back in her chair as Barbara turned to her.

"Let's not confuse what we must do in your best interests with what might be truth or fiction."

"Or lie, don't you mean?"

"I mean, as I said, we might have to say and do as Jules Loffman desired and as Mr. Brown suggests. Now," Turning to Brown, "how much of the estate would go to Nancy?"

"Okay. Let me answer your question in this way because this is how Jules wanted it explained. Mrs. Shielbrock, were you ever in Atlanta?"

Barbara was taken by surprise with the question and she held the quick breath a moment; Jules and she in Atlanta, their first time, so long ago, so beautiful at the time, the blue negligee, the adjoining door, "Yes, I've been to Atlanta."

"Are you familiar with a store there, The Magnolia?"

"Yes," And Jules had taken her to Atlanta because he had to be there to look at and to buy a store. The Magnolia?

"Yes," Nancy interrupted. "That's where I work."

Brown turned to Nancy, "Yes, I know. Are you aware that Jules Loffman is, was, the majority shareholder in The Magnolia?"

"No, I had no idea who owned the store. I guess, that is I assumed that there were many stockholders and that the manager, Mr. Tomaselli, was one of them, maybe the biggest—."

Barbara interrupted, "Who did you say?"

"Mr. Tomaselli. He's the General Manager of the store."

"Is that Peter Tomaselli?"

"Yes. I mentioned him to you after I went to Atlanta for the interview. His was the final interview of the store officials." Nancy turned to Brown, "I received a letter just before graduation inviting me to come to Atlanta and interview for a position with the Magnolia," then turning back to her mother, "I told you about the interviews. Why?"

"You never mentioned Peter Tomaselli."

"Yes I did, Mother."

"No, you didn't. I would have remembered."

"Why? Do you know him?"

"Yes. He was at the Loffman store in Norfolk when I worked there." Barbara stopped and looked at Brown, who responded.

"Yes. Jules hired Tomaselli from the Norfolk store where he had been an assistant manager, to be the General Manager of the Magnolia in Atlanta about, oh, twelve years ago, and gave him stock options as incentives which today give Tomaselli about two and a half percent of the outstanding stock." Brown looked at Nancy and hesitated, then went on.

"Your credentials were perfect for the Magnolia position for which you were hired so please don't take this wrong," He paused, "Jules Loffman directed Peter Tomaselli to contact you and to hire you."

"Directed him to hire me?" Nancy was confused, on the edge of anger. "You mean I really didn't get the job on my own?"

"Miss Shielbrock, please, I just said that your credentials for that position were fine, perfect. You would have been hired without question if you had applied as a stranger."

"But we really don't know that for sure, do we? Why was Jules Loffman interfering with my life?"

No answer was given and then Brown continued, "Jules Loffman owned sixty percent of the stock of the Magnolia. That is completely separate from his stock in the Loffman Stores, Incorporated. His first will gives all of his Loffman Stores stock to be equally divided among the six nieces and nephews. The stock in The Magnolia is to go to his daughter, Nancy Shielbrock."

The two ladies inhaled deeply and Barbara asked, "And the value of the stock in The Magnolia?"

"At present market value, which can be expected to drop some because of this transfer, the Jules Loffman holdings in The Magnolia are worth four point three million dollars."

A long period of silence followed until Barbara turned to look at Nancy and found her staring at her. Barbara turned to Brown. "I believe Nancy wants you to try to convince the other attorneys that you have solid evidence to support the claim in the first will that she is the daughter of Jules Loffman. I will make any statement, or sign any paper—."

Nancy whispered, "Mother?"

Barbara continued, "—or sign any paper stating that Jules Loffman is the father of my daughter."

"Mother?"

"Nancy, you have absolutely nothing to be ashamed of. You are going to be a wealthy woman. You will own one of the best stores in Atlanta. You can and will enjoy all of the best things in life. Marry the man you love. Share those things with him. Your children will also share in those benefits."

"Mother?"

"Yes?"

"Do you have anything to be ashamed of?"

CHAPTER 8

The four sat quietly under the large umbrella on the patio of the Coronado Cays condo. A soft breeze from the west, from the Pacific Ocean, cooled the mid-day August air. Barney Williams had just gone into the house to refill his ice tea and returned to his soft seat. He looked from one to the other of his family and smiled. "So, my dear, if what you say about the Loffman will, the inheritances and the—, what can we call it, the lineage perhaps? Those and the questions they raise, if they are facts and not fictions of yours, then we do have a very dramatic situation, as you said earlier.

Jackie was angry. "What do you mean 'fiction'? I didn't, I couldn't make up any of that. That's exactly what Barbara told me. Fiction? I don't do fiction, mister, and don't you ever accuse me—.

Barney interrupted her. "No, no. Honey, I didn't mean to accuse you of making up that story. I know you wouldn't do that, never. I just meant that, uh, that it was sensational, for them and even for us, because it explains how and why the Shielbrocks," He nodded to his son-in-law Steven, "are living well. Good."

Steven was not so sure. "Yeah, it's a great story. I've heard bits and pieces and hints over the last few years but not the full story like Jackie just told us. I thought I could detect a certain tension in the family about the time my dad retired from the navy, but I thought it was because of the retirement, not because of any monster skeleton in the closet like my sister Nancy's real father."

"Steven!" Jackie was still angry even with the near apology from her husband. "Don't even think that way. Nancy is your sister, full sister. She is the daughter of Martin and Barbara Shielbrock. There was a lot of money that came to them through some paper shuffling. That's all it was, paper shuffling. A nice man left some money and property to your sister and to your mother. Very nice. Think of it that way."

"Yeah, I suppose you're right." Steven stared out across the water. "Probably best that we leave the Loffman will and drop the subject all-together, huh?" He turned to Barney. "Let's go back to summer baseball in Canada. You left us dangling with a second game coming up."

"No, no. No more baseball just now" Barney shook his head. "I'm saving the baseball finale for later, letting you salivate over that final game. For now though, let's take a look at what your dad got involved with after he retired." Barney was determined to regain control of the tale telling.

Barney continued, "After the whole Indian Ocean action was over I had opportunity to talk to some of the participants, actually talk with them, all of the people who were with your dad and some of those that had worked against him. You see, I was in OPNAV at the time, as a command center guy, but because Shellback used me as a pseudo secure communications path during the operation, the CNO asked me to follow up on the entire operation and work with our intell folks and see if we could put it all together. So if we're going to tell the full story of Shellback we have to start out with what the bad guys were doing.

Steven was interested. "Sounds good but how did we, or in this case you, find out what the bad guys were doing?"

Barney smiled. "By reading the reports and talking with the participants, as I said. Of course it was easy to talk with those on our side but the real info, what should have been the most valuable had to come from those bad guys."

"And did they talk?"

Barney grinned. "Did they talk? They sure did talk. Too much. Our intell people gave me their interviews and told me that there was no problem getting them to talk, the problem was to figure out from all they said what was fact and what was fiction. Clearly, they could mix lies with truth so that it all sounded reasonable and all conflicted."

"So where does that leave us now, long after but still searching for the facts?"

Barney shook his head. "Well, where it leaves us is still in doubt, but maybe, just maybe even after all this time we can put together enough *wheat from the chaff to make a probable set of scenarios or stories that make some sense, some continuity."*

Steven was even more interested. "Okay, let's hear some of that wheat from chaff."

Barney paused for a while, deep in thought. "You know that where they actually came from and who sent them was then and still are questions. All the early analyses pointed at Iran. I happened to be one of the few that thought it really was Iraq. I still think so.

"Anyway, as a small part of this, we found that most of the bad guys used a name, Moses Farscian, as one of the guys who seemed to be a main man, or maybe just the most interesting, in the drama and they all talked about him. We couldn't find him. They talked about a lot of others but the name Moses Farscian came up most often. So let me start by telling you a little about what we were able to derive about this Moses Farscian guy and the operation as it unfolded for him."

BASRA, IRAQ

Moses Farscian sat on the pier, legs stretched out, back against a piling, his head wrapped in the old style desert ghutra and the early morning sun felt good with his face turned upward to the sky. The soft breeze from the Shatt al Arab waterway off the Persian Gulf was clean and pleasant, much nicer than the frequent land breeze which carried the foul smells of the city. Five other young men lounged similarly on the pier as two of them talked quietly and he easily recognized the dialects from various parts of Iraq. Was that southern Kurdish or Pashto? No, couldn't be, just country boys they were, speaking Farsi but from the west, low lives, none of them with his background of family and culture.

They had all served their leader Saddam Hussein in the holy war against Iran and even though in their twenties, each had the air of mature confidence as they were combat veterans who had faced death, been wounded, had killed and had seen friends killed, and now they found themselves hundreds of miles from the front, selected for some special assignment of which they knew nothing.

One of them grunted and nodded his head toward a warehouse as two officers in starched camouflaged uniforms approached and the six got to their feet and stood at attention. The shorter older of the officers barked, "Why are you here at this end of the pier? You were told to be at the seaward end of the pier. Get out there, now!" And the six army veterans walked briskly toward the seaward end of the pier.

"Run!" Commanded the officer, and they did. At the far end of the pier they lined up and stood at attention, waiting, as the officers walked toward them.

"What are they?" One of the army men asked in a whisper.

Moses had easily recognized the uniform and accent. "Navy. He's from al Basra."

"How can you tell?" Another whispered.

"Shoulder patches say navy, dialect al Najaf," Still in a whisper so that the officers approaching could not hear.

Another whispered, "I've never seen a navy man before, didn't know we had a navy."

"They're boat riders, sailors. What in Allah's eyes are we doing with them?"

"We'll soon see."

The officers were close now and the short one barked, "Your orders were to be at the seaward end of the pier. You did not carry out your orders. I should send you all back to the front to get your heads blown off but I need you for a special operation. The next time any one of you disobeys an order, he goes!"

Maybe that wouldn't be so bad, to go, rather than this special operation, what ever it was, with the navy, each silently thought. Does he think we volunteered for this?

The short officer continued barking. "Now, the reason we are out at this end of the pier is that we are away from the dockworkers and others. I don't want anyone to hear what we talk about." Taking a small notebook from his breast pocket, he turned a few pages and called six names; "Abolqazeri, Ghoroudi, Farscian, Mossaheb, Azhari, Montasem," and each young man yelled "Sir" in response to his name.

The officer frowned and looked from his book to those standing in front of him. He studied his book a moment, wrote a brief note in it and returned the book to his breast pocket. "You are to keep your mouths shut, say nothing, ask no questions unless you are asked and do exactly what you're told to do."

The shorter officer looked at the other, who seemed to be in charge, and at a nod the one that had thus far done all the talking looked confused for a moment as he then fumbled in his pocket and recovered his small book. Apparently he had a few pages of data on each young man as he questioned each one, commenting as he went along. Moses was the third questioned. "Farscian, your name is Moses Farscian?"

"Yes sir."

"That's sounds like a Kurd name."

Moses remained silent. Here it is once more, he thought, the Kurdish thing. I'm going to have to go through this again. Will there ever be an end to this?

"Well?" The officer was angry. "Are you a Kurd? I asked you a question."

"It's an Islamic name, sir. I was born Sunni, am now Shia. I was born in Rayat in the Arbil Region, the home of Salah al Din Yusuf ibn Ayyubi, known as al Nasir, The Victorious and also as Saladin, and I am descended from him. As was Saladin, I am Kurd."

"You are shit! Your father kissed the ass of Talibani. Your mother was his whore."

The others looked at Moses with surprise and Moses' stomach twisted into a knot. He felt the flush of rage and humiliation, swallowed and breathed deeply, exhaling with a quiver. Long ago he had learned to control himself in these situations. "Sir, my father was a grounds keeper, a gardener for a rich man in Kirkuk. My mother was a seamstress for his wife. They had nothing to do with the rich man's business. My father had nothing to with Talibani."

"Your father was one of Jalal Talabani's trash pigs of what he called the Patriotic Union of Kurdistan," He sneered at the name, "that opposed our leader Saddam Hussein's elite Baathist army when they were successful in restoring order to northern Iraq!" The officer was red faced, yelling.

"No sir. My father was a humble, poor man who earned a very meager living as a gardener. My mother did some sewing."

The officer grew angrier, "And when the righteous true Iraqis chased away your foul and dissident Kurdish pigs and cleansed the land of the stench of Talibani supporters, your father opposed these purists and fought for a divided nation." He was screaming now, pointing to his book then at Moses in accusation.

Moses waited a moment before replying. "When the wild mob

stormed our home my father's employer and his entire family had long since departed the country. My father was not at our home and we hid in the tool shed. The mob broke into the shed and raped my mother and my sister. My brother and I were beaten and left for dead but we survived and then all of us, my family and the other Kurds that survived, were sent to the south. Later, my brother and I both served in combat in the war against Iran. He was killed. I have served Allah and my country as well as any man here. I have been four times cited for valor in combat." Moses' voice was quivering, and he shifted to the dialect of the north. "I am an Iraqi soldier, a pure Kurd from a family of more than ten centuries, descended from Saladin himself and I am here to serve."

The officer stood red faced and his anger slowly faded with the realization that they were all staring at him, waiting. "You dare to call our elite army a mob? We'll see about that. We'll see if you can be trusted," And he wrote some notes in his book, then added, "All you Kurds claim the Saladin thing. He must have had a thousand bastard sons! Ha! Next you're supposed to tell us you come from the jinn of the holy land." He exchanged forced laughs with the other officer and before he turned to the next soldier to continue his interrogation added, "I didn't know there were any Shia Kurds." Both officers smiled and the taller one nodded. Oh, but he's a slick one, Moses thought.

Moses paid no attention to the public interviews of the other army men as he thought only of his own humiliation and of the many times he had been forced to explain the untrue and unjust accusations against his parents, to relive the horror at his home when, before his very eyes, his family was attacked, his home destroyed. True believers! Elite army! Dog shit! They were a mob, robbing and raping with no higher intent than the personal gain or perverse pleasure of each, trying to rid the land of the Kurds and each no better than an animal. This officer was probably no better than they and he might even have been one of them. How dare he question Moses' background!

Moses had survived the horror of that day, recovered from his injuries and with his family survived in the wreckage of what had been their town. He, with his mother, sister and brother had been sent, along with other Kurdish survivors, to the far south of Iraq to live in an area inhabited by Arab Shiites, where they were ostracized and further humiliated. A priest had told him that to overcome the stigma of his family association with the hated devil Kurdish rebels, Moses should join the most active fundamentalist Shiite group, that only in this way could he demonstrate his loyalty to Islam and to Iraq and compensate for the sins of his father, but Moses had trouble accepting this course of action. He was being asked to join the people who had killed his neighbors, raped his mother and sister and destroyed his home, the very people that his father opposed. Moses and his brother were being forced to change religions, change the things they were raised to believe in and they rejected the priest's recommendation for a while. Then, after repeated insults and abuse, hungry and homeless, unable to find work and ostracized by everyone, Moses and his brother joined the Shia Sons of Allah.

He had not been completely honest with the navy officer, not completely. His father had been a humble, poor man who earned a very meager living as a gardener and his mother was a seamstress for a wealthy businessman's family, but his father had actually first served in the small rebel army of Rasoul Mamend of the Kurdish Socialist Party, an army that had fought against the Iraqi army until driven into Iran. When the Iranian army drove them back into Iraq, Moses' father left the small disintegrating Socialist force and joined the Kurdish Democratic Party, serving under Massoud Barzani as one of the Pesh Merga, the Death Facers, fighting against the regime of Abdel Karim Qassem and then against the Baathist army of Saddam Hussein. Moses had not seen his father in over ten years and didn't know whether he was alive or dead.

Once joining the Shia Sons of Allah, overnight Moses and his brother had employment, food, clothing, shelter and were promised a future of success proportionate to the dedication and effort they put forth. Moses was able to take care of his mother and sister and took full advantage of this opportunity, becoming one of the most dedicated and hard working Shia Sons. Then came the army, the war with Iran and his brother's death as Moses' world for eight years was one of fighting and surviving. He had been wounded six times and so many friends made quickly had died that he had learned to avoid friendships. Often Moses was the most experienced man in his unit, a group of strangers, soon few would be left alive and they would join other decimated units. Awards were given the survivors, awards which quickly were recognized as meaning little else but survival. Moses never ran away as did so many others under fire, but he knew and expected in each attack that now his time had come to die, but it didn't and he survived, was picked for this mysterious special mission hundreds of miles from the Iran War and in the first few minutes faced insult and reminder of past horror. Why? Why was he being so tested? Was there really an Allah putting him through all this? He caught himself questioning Allah and murmured the prayer, "La-ila-ha Il-lah-lah." (There is no God but Allah.)

"Was that you muttering, Farscian?" The harsh voice of the officer intruded into Moses' thoughts. "Do you have something to say to us, Kurd?" He emphasized the name Kurd with a sneer, intending it as an insult.

Moses was brought back to reality, "I have nothing to say, sir."

"Then pay attention!"

"Yes sir."

The officer turned a page in his notebook, "Now that we've seen what a group of trash we have here, let's see what kind of experience we have. Have any of you ever fired a TOW missile?" All of the six young men raised a hand. Moses was surprised and could see that the others were also surprised because on the battle front Moses had been one of very few in his units who had used the American made anti tank weapon called TOW, but here all six of them had that experience.

"Well," the officer looked pleased for the first time. "Now, how many of you have ever fired a Sagger?"

Again, all of them raised hands and Moses was more surprised than before as he had not served with anyone else who had fired the Russian made anti tank missile and had thought that his own experience with it made him somewhat elite. Apparently the others had similar thoughts as he noted the surprised looks.

"Very good, maybe there's hope here." The officer, still pleased, made notes in his book. "How about the RPG-7?" All of them, again, but that was easy, a common weapon, Moses thought.

"How many of you have ever been in a ship or a boat?" The officer pointed out toward the Persian Gulf as he asked. Nothing. Then a tentative hand went up from one of the young army veterans.

"What kind of boat?" Challenged the navy officer.

"A barge across a river one night for an attack against the Iranians and a boat back across."

"No, idiot, I want to know if you've ever been out on real water in a ship or boat." Again, he pointed south toward the Gulf.

The army man lowered his hand and his head and none of the others responded.

"Okay, so you're not sailors. We'll take care of that as soon as it's dark."

That evening he led them to a fishing boat at the next pier, ordered them aboard and they went down the Shatt al Arab waterway and out into the Gulf.

It was late at night when the fishing boat made-up to the pier back at Basrah. Two of the army veterans had been sea sick most of the time underway and the smell of vomit was still present in the boat so all of them were anxious to get away from the stink, to get ashore, but the officer kept them waiting in the boat alongside the pier. "You two sick goat tits will have to learn not to get seasick. Now, you two clean up this boat and when you're finished all of you can go and sleep in that warehouse tonight." The two navy officers turned and walked away.

For the next two weeks, the six army veterans followed the same routine; mornings and afternoons in basic simple small arms training, which they didn't need, and evenings in boats out in the Gulf. The warehouse was their barracks; six ground cloths on a dirt floor. Food was scarce; tea and bread in the morning, fish at lunch and a fish stew with rice at the warehouse each night after the fishing boat cruise. Each day the weapon instructor was a different member of the Iraqi Navy, instructors that knew less than did the army veterans and each boat ride was in a different fishing boat with a different crew. No one was friendly and the six army veterans had learned from their combat experiences not to make friends so it was a lonely life for them; isolated, individually aloof and exposed to different people briefly each day.

After two weeks of training the officer explained a little about what the mission would be, just enough to lend relevance to the training but not the entire mission. "The hated Americans have some large ships which carry the major weapons for an invasion force. These ships are anchored some distance away, ready to sail here, to invade our beloved Republic of Iraq. The stupid Americans think we do not know about these ships and even if we did, the Americans think we could not reach them." He paused and looked at the six soldiers closely, leaning forward, lowering his voice, "So they do not give adequate protection to these anchored ships." The officer smiled and stood up straight. "Now, you see what we must do?" He looked at each of the six, waiting for a reply but the veterans had learned long ago not to volunteer. Still, to this direct question at least one of them had to respond and Moses Farscian finally spoke up. "Can we reach these ships in a navy boat or fishing boat," Pointing to the one alongside the pier, "and hit them with TOW or Sagger?"

"That's close but not the right response!" The officer yelled pointing at Moses. "You should have said, 'We *can* hit them, we *will* hit them, with whatever our leader Saddam Hussein gives us to hit them with, and you are ready to die if necessary to save the Baathist regime of Iraq from the American invasion.'" The six stood silent as the red faced officer slowly calmed. "Now, on this final day your training will be directed at hitting a ship with a TOW missile. Your instructor, Assadoman, is the most experienced of the Iraqi Navy in using the TOW."

Before they were turned over to the instructor the youngest of the army veterans, Emani Abolqazeri, asked the officer a question on the minds of all six. "Pardon me, sir, but if the Iraqi Navy has such experience why do you need us?"

The officer was angry again, "Wart hog! Bastard son of a bitch! I told you not to ask questions. Not that it's your business but higher-ups, very high, close to our beloved leader Saddam Hussein himself, have decided that the Iraqi Navy is to continue operating as they have done so well over the years. A new unit is to be created for this special assignment and you, you, you—," he paused looking for a word, "—you mud-rutter ingrate. You dare to question your good fortune in being honored for selection to this special unit? You dare to question our leader Saddam Hussein himself? I should send you straight back to the Central Sector to get your balls blown off." The officer paused, breathing heavily, red faced again as they all waited as he slowly calmed. By now they knew he would calm down and they had given him a title, The Braying Donkey.

"Originally I only needed four of you mud-rutters for this magnificent assignment. Then, because of the dedication the six of you displayed, I prevailed upon my higher-ups to use all of you. Now I question my own initiative. You, Abolqazeri, I should get rid of you. Do either of you others question this assignment?"

The others muttered, "No sir," as they quickly glanced at each other. They had stood before officers in similar situations countless times and it was obvious to these veterans that the officer had already promised six soldiers to his higher-ups and he was committed. Mohami Mossaheb spoke up, "Sir, you asked if we had any questions." The officer started to interrupt but Mossaheb continued, "How many times has this most experienced navy instructor attacked a ship using the TOW missile?"

Immediately the officer was red-faced fuming angry and his usual crisp style was shattered as he tried to respond. "You, you, I—, that, I did not ask you for questions. That's none of your—. You dare to question, he,—I." The Braying Donkey caught himself and stood in silence a few minutes as he calmed. "Well, now I think you can ask Assadoman that yourself. He's the expert. Get around now to the other side of the warehouse where Assadoman is waiting for your final morning instruction. Dismissed."

They sat on the ground that served as the warehouse floor, cross-legged, listening to the tall thin bearded instructor. Assadoman wore the loose baggy tan and black camouflaged pants and shirt of the Iraqi Navy with a black falcon badge of Gulf Defenders on his left shoulder, but rather than the more common beret, a head cloth was draped around his neck and shoulders. A TOW missile launcher was set-up in front of them.

The atmosphere around the six young army veterans and the instructor Assadoman was much more relaxed than with the officer. Mossaheb had been quick to ask about the instructor's status or rank, "—and so you see, sir, we are not familiar with the rank or positions of your organization. Are you an officer or something like a sergeant, or what?"

"Well, I suppose in your terms I am, as you said 'something like a sergeant.' We call it Senior Petty Officer, but I'm not an officer. I'm an enlisted man like you."

"Good!" The six army veterans looked at each other smiling. "We're sergeants, too. So what do you want to know about this TOW?"

Assadoman was first pleased then confused. "Want to know? I—I thought I was supposed to tell the six of you about it." They laughed and Abolqazeri spoke up. "We're all familiar with this TOW. We've used it in combat and had to go through training for it and even taught it."

"Well maybe they thought you'd forgotten and needed a refresher, could that be?"

The six laughed again as Moses Farscian replied, "We had to memorize the training manual and then teach others." Then Moses asked the others, "Do you still remember the manual?" and they replied with nods, smiling and indicating that they still remembered and couldn't forget.

"Then perhaps, just to take up the time so that lieutenant will think we're doing what he wants, would one of you give us a run down on the system?" Assadoman asked.

Moses, the last to speak, looked at the others and they nodded again, smiling, as Mossaheb and Abolqazeri gestured toward the missile launcher while still looking at Moses. "Okay, I guess I'm nominated," and he walked over to the mount as the instructor sat down to listen.

"The TOW weapon system is a crew-portable or vehicle-mounted anti-tank weapon. It consists of a launcher which has tracking and control capabilities," Moses put his hand on the launcher, "and a tube launched optically tracked wire command link guided missile." He picked up the case which carried the missile. "The American name TOW comes from the first letters of their words for tube, optical and wire. The system consists of six major parts; tripod, traversing unit, launch tube, optical sight, guidance set and battery." Moses pointed to each part as he went along. Then he went to each part and explained its function in detail. He then went to the missile and described its components and functions. By the time he had covered the operation of the system he had been talking for an hour. He stopped and asked his two associates if they could or if they desired to add anything.

Mohami Mossaheb spoke up, "I've only seen it used on the ground and I've heard that it can be mounted on a vehicle, like a truck, or even in a helicopter but I've never heard of a TOW being used in a boat."

The six looked at Assadoman and he replied, "I haven't heard of one being fired from a boat either. We've talked about using one for years but never had the chance. All of the attacks that I've been in we used RPG-7 and we've hit some ships. But you don't do much damage to a big ship with a little grenade. One time I hit a tanker eleven out of fifteen shots. I was close enough to see the faces of the people on the ship's bridge looking down at me. Five of the eleven were good detonations and the ship kept right on going. With a bigger warhead, like this TOW, I could have blown a hole open big enough to matter."

The army veterans nodded thoughtfully, trying to imagine what it was like bouncing along in a boat at night, picking out a target and running in at it, firing the light Soviet designed rocket propelled grenade at a large ship. They knew that the grenade was designed to penetrate light armor such as the side of a ship, scatter hot gases inside and the grenades should be effective in starting fires in ships they hit, but most of the RPG-7 available to them in Iraq were copies of the Soviet design manufactured by a company they all knew as El Fateh in Egypt, and they all knew the El Fateh version was very unreliable.

Yasir Ghoroudi spoke up, "You said that you've never had a chance to fire a TOW missile at a ship," Assadoman nodded as Ghoroudi continued, "so you're a navy guy who had never fired a TOW missile, teaching us army guys who have all fired them in combat? Isn't there something wrong here?"

The navy senior petty officer did not respond and Moses broke the silence. "Well, let's take this one out in the Gulf and fire it at a barrel. Then we'll know it works from a boat." The other army veterans nodded but Assadoman spoke up. "No! No! We can't use this on a barrel and we can't go out in the Gulf at daytime, only at night. We have strict orders from Mohsen Rezai himself, the head of our navy, that the few TOW missiles we have will only be used against enemy targets."

The army veterans looked at the navy man in disbelief and talking all at once asked how anyone could be expected to go a long distance to carry out an important mission with an untried weapon.

Assadoman, standing now, held up his hand and shook his head in denial. "Don't talk to me about the mission. I don't want to hear about it and I didn't make the rule, our leader did. We, you, me, all of us serve Allah as we can. We do as commanded by our Baathist leaders and Allah will look after us or call us to Jannah, to his side, martyred." And with that the tall Revolutionary Guard instructor walked away.

The army veterans looked at each other, questioning in silence. Then Mossaheb asked, "Now what the hell was that all about?"

Abolqazeri looked at the rapidly disappearing instructor. "Goat shit! Every time there's a fuck-up the religious freaks blame it on Allah or the Baathist leaders or even Saddam Hussein. In American terms it's a 'fuckin cop-out'. I saw it in a movie once on al Jazeera television."

"Hey, be careful!" Mossaheb looked around with concern. "Somebody might hear you."

"Yeah," Abolqazeri was smiling as he stood up, "and I might get sent back to the front or on a special mission." They all laughed.

"Hey, Abolqazeri, have you really seen television?" Sadoon Azhari asked in surprise.

They were still laughing as they stood up and Moses responded. "Yeah, country boy, he's seen television. We all have. Now let's get something to eat," and the six army veterans walked away laughing as Moses thought that maybe he wasn't the only one who questioned Allah.

In the early morning of the next day the six army veterans were carried by truck to a naval base at Umm Qasr where there was a cot and a foot-locker for each of them in the barracks. Training was light, the food was good and they had bunks upon which to sleep, a big improvement over the ground cloth and dirt floor of the warehouse at Basrah and the fish stew. Afternoons were physical fitness time, usually pick-up soccer games but sometimes just calisthenics or distance running.

On their first morning at Umm Qasr the six had been on their way to breakfast. "Look at those boats!" Mohami Mossaheb had been the first to see the dark gray hulls alongside the pier. "Six of them! Now why couldn't those boats be used to hit the American ships?"

"They must be much faster than the fishing boats," Emani Abolqazeri added with admiration, "and look, they've got guns and deck space for a missile launcher!"

Three of the boats being admired by the army missilemen were 140 foot former Soviet submarine chasers purchased by Iraq in 1962 and used as patrol vessels. The other three were 82 foot torpedo boats, also from the Soviet Union, capable of 40 knots.

"Let's ask someone what those boats are and why they're here. Maybe they could be used for our mission," Abolqazeri suggested.

"In a goat's ass are they for us," Mossaheb spoke convincingly. "Those are navy boats, all right, but if you look at them carefully you can see they're in bad condition. I'll bet they haven't moved in months. Look at them." Moses and Abolqazeri looked at him and then at the boats, realizing that Mossaheb knew of what he spoke as they had been together long enough so that most of the combat veteran aloofness had worn away and they had become closer friends than they had intended.

One night, weeks ago, Mossaheb had told them that he had held back when the angry officer at Basrah, the Braying Donkey, had asked if any of them had been in a boat or ship. Mossaheb had worked on his uncle's fishing boat many times and it had been one of the best dhows, usually making a good catch as his uncle generally sold his fish to the navy base at Basrah. So Mossaheb had seen more of the navy than did any of the army veterans and he had been exposed to Iraqi navy men before. "They're nice boats, all right, but maybe they can't cruise that far 'cause if you don't use a boat and if you don't take care of it, it's no good. Those boats have not been used or maintained."

Before Moses could reply Mossaheb continued, "Now why would they bother selecting and training us for this mission if the Navy could do it? They wouldn't need us."

Moses didn't feel that the issue was settled. "Which brings us back to the questions of why army men in fishing boats and why not navy men in navy boats?"

They didn't have any answers and the six of them looked at the patrol vessels and the torpedo boats, wondering, as Moses spoke what was on the minds of all. "Here's the navy with three patrol boats and a few torpedo boats with weapons, all Russian, now why would they bother with us in fishing boats?"

"There's something else," Mossaheb paused, thought a moment and then continued. "I think maybe the navy can't do it, can't do anything because I think they can't even take a single one of those boats out of here."

"Why?" The others asked.

"I'll tell you why," Mossaheb was more animated, "because there's the Iranian navy on one side of our navy and the Kuwaitis on the other side and our elite goatshit navy can't even get a boat out to the Gulf, that's why. 'Why us,' we've been asking? It's got to be us because the navy can't do it, can't do a damn thing and maybe only a fishing boat can get out of here and travel far enough. Remember, Assadoman? That senior petty officer told us that even in a fishing boat we could only go out at night." The others shook their heads in lack of understanding.

Each evening they listened on the radio to the news broadcast by the Baathist News Agency from Baghdad. There was news of the war with Iran and the army veterans listened eagerly for mention of their former units and most of the time they could relate the news reports with their own experiences and they could see in their imagination what their former comrades were going through. At times there were doubts and they looked at each other during the broadcasts, questioning if it really could be so, but the news reports sounded so positive, so much victory, so much Iraqi success and glamour. In their own experiences there had been death and mutilation, heavy losses, dirt, hunger, thirst and fatigue, but the news reports spoke of success, destruction of the enemy, achieved objectives, so the young veterans decided that the war must have taken a turn for the better since they left the front. Why question success? Maybe now their former comrades had enough food, ammunition, clothing, weapons, fuel and maybe even some medical support.

A Baathist news analyst described the success of, "our dedicated loyal martyrs fighting evil on the Sumar and Meimak border areas and in the Central Sector. Many have gone to meet Allah, to share in hoor al-ain," the ancient Islamic dream of joining virgins in paradise, "so that those of us remaining in our beloved Iraqi Republic could enjoy our bountiful life."

Other times they listened to religious leaders scream oaths and insults at Iran, the United States and the Soviet Union, demanding more rigid Islamic adherence while a few spoke quietly of dedication and tolerance, others stressed that each individual owed loyalty to his faith and also to his leader Saddam Hussein. Every evening there was news, sermon and prayer, always echoing success, promise and bright future, always there were appeals for more dedication, more sacrifice.

Their worn and dirty dark olive combat clothing had been discarded and replaced with the crisp new tan and black worn by the Iraqi Navy and when they were issued the new uniforms the supply official told them, "These uniforms are to replace your army rags. Make no mistake, by Allah, just because you wear these clothes you are not members of the Iraqi Navy. Do you hear me? You are still army pigs but we can't stand your filthy clothes so we issue you these fine uniforms. You mud-rutters could never be navy men, remember that!"

The three veterans looked at each other and Moses wondered aloud, "By Allah, if this mission is so important, why do they hate us so?" They had been issued blue berets but had chosen to keep their desert cloth headgear if only as a reminder for themselves that they were army combat veterans. Moses wrapped his fatiah around his head and as they walked away carrying their newly issued uniforms Mossaheb offered a thought, "Maybe they're jealous that we've been picked when they're supposed to be the ones that operate from boats."

"Maybe," Moses Farscian added, "but what in Allah's eyes does this navy do? As you said, they talk about how important they are and special, and we haven't seen one of their boats move. What do we have a navy for?" The others shook their heads and shrugged with no answers as Abolqazeri suggested, "We should form the whole navy into a couple of companies of infantry and send them to the Central Front."

As they smoked and talked one night a few weeks later, looking again at the unmoved navy boats, the army veterans discussed the possibility that the full moon might have something to do with the higher tide than normal. "You know something, Farscian," Mossaheb said seriously and as Moses responded the others continued the tidal discussion of which they knew nothing.

"That first day at Basrah when we were being mustered by that Braying Donkey?"

"Yeah, what about it." Moses had tried to forget.

"Well, the Braying Donkey really tried to take you apart and I knew I would be next and—," Mossaheb hesitated and thought a moment. "Well, you remember he made it clear that he hated Kurds." He paused again and Moses nodded adding that he remembered very well. How could he forget?

"Well," Mossaheb seemed to be trying to overcome his hesitancy. "You know all the officers are Sunni, all of them in the army so I guess in the navy too?" Moses nodded as did the other army men, all now listening to Mossaheb. "Well, you see, apparently it wasn't in his little book with the stuff about us, you see, and so he didn't have the right stuff about me, but you see, I'm a Kurd, too, originally from Arbil." Moses and the others just stared at Mohami Mossaheb, silent in the understanding that this was a serious confession, an important and difficult act by the veteran army missileman, usually the most cautious of the group.

Moses Farscian broke the silence. "I don't blame you for keeping that from the officer, Mohami, it would have done you no good, or me, or any of us, but thanks for telling me now." Mossaheb smiled as Moses continued. "Now I know there's two Kurds caught up in this crazy mess."

They all laughed and even more as Yasir Ghoroudi added, "Guess I make three of us Kurds here!" And before the laughter subsided Sadoon Azhari spoke up, "No, no, I make it four," And pointing to Abolqazeri and Montasem, "Will anyone make it five? Or six?" But the other two shook their heads in denial and the group got up and walked to their barracks with the knowledge that four of the six were Kurds, each asking himself, again, why?

After four months of good living at Umm Qasr the six missilemen were ordered to a paint stained warehouse where about 25 navy men were already assembled in a large shabby meeting room. With windows painted over, the poor lighting caused difficulty seeing details on what appeared to be a large map of the Indian Ocean and Persian Gulf area. "Looks like we're finally going to find out about our operation," Emani Abolqazeri observed.

"Yeah," Mohami Mossaheb responded, "And they're all officers, well, almost all."

Yasir Ghoroudi spoke up, "And look who's up front!" They all saw the officer at the front of the room. "It's the other officer from our first days, the taller younger one, the one that didn't talk but let The Braying Donkey squawk all the time." They laughed and took seats in a row that apparently had been reserved for them.

"I am Major Abdul Tryak abd al Razaq of the Iraqi Navy," And the army missilemen realized that the other officer, who was now sitting in the first row, had never told them his name or rank. Also, they had learned that Iraqi Navy officers used army ranks, "—and I am here to explain our special operation and brief all of you on the details." Moses Farscian could tell that this polished officer was Arab Sunni and spoke in the dialect of Baghdad.

"The name of this operation is Najaf and that is the last unclassified word you will hear from me." Major Tryak paused and looked at the group seated in front of him. "Everything else I say is classified and that means you will be killed instantly for repeating anything about this operation to anyone who is not in this room. Look around you. Remember who is here and remember that you cannot discuss or mention one word about this operation with anyone who is not here. And every one of you is charged with the responsibility of immediately executing anyone who violates this holy security."

He paused again and again looked at the individuals, eye to eye, along each row. "There are five large American ships carrying vital war materials and seven other large ships with support supplies anchored a thousand miles away at a remote atoll in the Indian Ocean called Diego Garcia. Those ships are vital to any American military action in this part of the world. If we had what those ships carry we could wipe out Iran and if the Iranians had them they could wipe us out. The Americans are preparing to take over this entire part of the world, our beloved Baathist Iraq as well as the hated Iran. The Americans want to eliminate all Islam and take all the precious oil that Allah has placed beneath our sacred land. This is Jihad. We must stop them. We will stop them. Operation Najaf will stop them. We in this room today are Operation Najaf and we will stop the Americans even as we might share in hoor al-ain, in this jihad."

Major Tryak then turned over the podium to the still unidentified first row officer, who described the organization of three fishing boat assault groups with the routes they would take and introduced captains, crewmen and army missilemen of the boats as each stood when his name was called. The briefing described a complex cover of Iranian identification and flags and detailed navigation, weapons, attack date, targeting and logistics including speeds and fuel considerations, food, water, communications and contingency port availability, above all stressing the extreme importance of mission security and mission accomplishment at any cost. No matter what happens during the operation, it must be made to look like the attacks are from Iran. He emphasized this; Iran. No matter what happens the attacks must look like they came from Iran, not Iraq.

The briefing officer seemed to cover every facet of the operation and as he reached the end of his detailed presentation there were no questions asked by the fishing boat men or the army veterans. Before they departed the meeting all were again warned of the dire consequences of security violation, critical Iranian deception and vital importance of mission accomplishment.

Boat crews and missilemen stared at the other as they left the room, each group clearly wondering if the others would be capable of doing their part as Mossaheb whispered, "Let's pray they're better at running old boats than our navy is," and Moses Farscian agreed even to that prayer adding, "Did you notice that 'we in this room are Operation Najaf' is now only 'we in these six little boats?' I don't see any navy with us."

A month later the six young army veteran missilemen were each assigned to a fishing boat and three of the 60 foot boats departed immediately, two the next day and ten days later the 80 foot fishing boat with Moses Farscian embarked sailed for Diego Garcia.

CHAPTER 9

"What is going on in the Middle East?" Barney asked. "That's what everyone wanted to know. That's always what everyone wants to know, but it's rare that the public knows. Sometimes I think that it's just as rare that our intelligence people know what's going on. There's always great interest though and I recall a segment of a TV show, can't recall whether it was FOX or CNN—."

His wife Jackie interrupted. "What difference does it make, which channel? It was probably FOX. That's the one you watch most of the time. So what was on the TV?"

"Well, there was this interview and as I recall it was just about the time that Martin Shielbrock went to Diego Garcia, maybe a couple of weeks before—."

Interrupted again, this time by his son-in law Steven Shielbrock, "—and was it about my dad's operation?"

"Hold on, hold on. I recall that at the time I realized how much the public wanted to know what was going on and this TV show, this interview, was an example of what the press was doing about it, their pitiful attempts to gather information, but it was interesting."

TV SHOW, WASHINGTON, D. C.

The television network talk show host introduced his guest, "—Doctor Mohammad Al Amaji, Professor of Middle East Studies at the Johns

Hopkins School for Advanced International Studies in Washington, D. C." Doctor Al Amaji was a polished, suave academician in a tailor made gray flannel suit of the finest British wool. Small and slight with dark complexion, he wore a thin mustache similar to that of Jordan's King Hussein and the smile that never left his face showed strong even white teeth as he spoke with the clipped accent of an Arab educated in England, careful to pronounce every word.

"Doctor Al Amaji, could you give us a brief background on Iran to help us better understand what is happening in that area?"

"Yes. I would be pleased to do so. You see, one cannot comprehend the events which are transpiring in Iran today, and their significance, without understanding the history of that area."

The host interrupted. "Well, rather than history, Doctor, perhaps just the background."

Doctor Al Amaji was not to be denied his moment on national TV. "Nooo, no. It is the history of that area which forms the basis of this crisis. One must look at the history," And he launched into a long detailed description of ancient conflict which focused on Persia; the area known today as Iran, explaining that among the earliest evidences of human life in the area was homo erectus, the first man to walk upright, then Neanderthal man one hundred thousand years ago. Then came the origins of agriculture, basketry, textiles, cosmetics, pottery, tools and the development of one of mankind's earliest cultures and an advanced civilization around 2500 B.C.. Migrations and invasions came from Europe and Asia including Aryans upon which the name Iran is based. Tribes were formed then united under the Medes, then the Persians and a progression of kings and conquerors passed across the stages of history. Cyrus, Darius, Alexander and Xerxes are a few of the names linked to the area. At one time the Persian Empire was one of the greatest in the world then, as have others, it was conquered and divided.

As the TV talk show host stared, Al Amaji continued with his explanation that twenty years after Mohammed had unified Arabia and died, his tribe succeeded in the conquest of Persia. Conversion to Islam followed, but the Persians adopted the Shia sect rather than the orthodox Sunni faith of the Arabs. In the eleventh century A.D. the Turks invaded Persia, bringing another Sunni Moslem influence and in the thirteenth century Genghis Khan brought his Mongol horde. But through each invasion, change of rule and imposition of religion the Persians adjusted, adapted, accepted and ultimately conveyed Persian culture to their conquerors. In fact, Doctor Al Amaji explained, in his view ultimately they controlled their conquerors.

As the Mongol dynasty faded during the fifteenth and sixteenth centuries, Turkish influence increased as did conversion to Shiaism and Persia rose in power. By the seventeenth century that status weakened and in the eighteenth century Persia slid into decadence.

Doctor Al Amaji went into great detail to explain that during the nineteenth century what had been Persia lost Georgia, Tashkent, Samarkand and Bukhara to Russia. Turkey took Mesopotamia and the British established Afghanistan as a buffer state. The Kurds, Turkomans and some other tribes formed their own strong kingdoms and the once great Persian Empire was splintered, without effective leadership, a pawn of foreign governments as the twentieth century commenced.

Doctor Al Amaji explained how a commoner, Reza Khan, rose to power in the early 1900s, became Prime Minister in 1923 and Shah in 1925. The talk show host was nervous as over twenty minutes of his half hour show had been taken up with Doctor Al Amaji's history lesson. "That's really fascinating, Doctor, but could you tell us what, in your opinion, is happening in Iran today?"

The smile had still not left Al Amaji's face. "Certainly," And he disregarded the question and continued with his history lesson, explaining that Reza Khan, the Shah, directed that henceforth the country would be known as Iran, and not Persia, and the Shah forced all inhabitants to use family names as was the European practice, and took the family name Pahlavi himself. The Shah embarked on a grand modernization program to recover the lost glory of Persia, called Iran now by official decree, and to bring the people into the twentieth century.

Al Amaji described social, cultural, religious and economic changes decreed by the new Shah, including the elimination of foreign power. He described the influence, wealth, authority and success of the Shah and then the miscalculations which led to disaster for the Pahlavi regime in early World War Two. Then, in 1941, with portions of Iran occupied again by foreign military as it had been at the beginning of the century, the Shah abdicated and turned over the country to his twenty one year old son. The new young Shah of Iran was immediately faced with some of the same problems which had confronted his father years before, and these focused on occupation and influence in Iran by foreign elements, but through negotiation, treaties and alliances, primarily with the United States, Great Britain and the Soviet Union, the new Shah kept his faltering economy alive. At the end of World War Two, consistent with the Tripartite Alliance, the British and the Americans departed, but the Soviets not only remained but created a Kurdish Republic out of part of Iran and made a strong attempt to take over a portion of Iran. When in 1946 the United States President Harry Truman sent a blunt message to the Soviets to get out of Iran or else the U.S. would land troops there, the Soviets departed. The young Shah had succeeded in clearing Iran of foreign military, again, as had so often been the case in Persian-Iranian history.

Doctor Al Amaji maintained his smile as he explained in great detail how the young Shah of Iran continued and even accelerated the modernization programs introduced by his father. "And as we have seen in our own time," continued Doctor Al Amaji, "Shah Mohammed Reza Pahlavi was forced to abdicate and Ayatollah Ruhollah Khomeini took over and has ruled Iran as a fundamentalist Shiite Moslem entity."

"Yes." The talk show host had only ten minutes of his show time remaining, less than that for talk because three of those precious minutes had to be allowed for beer, perfume and sanitary napkin advertisements. "Doctor, this has been very enlightening and now that you have brought us up to the present time perhaps you could connect that background with what is happening today in Iran."

Still with the smile, the doctor continued. "We have seen throughout the history of Iran and Persia that foreign influence; invasions, occupations and migrations are not unusual. They are very common, very consistent with these peoples. One can even plan on or expect that in Iran, whatever is the present status or regime, it will be changed by an outside influence usually accompanied with violence, even brutality. Then we see an accommodation by the people, the culture, to accept the foreign influence, absorb, adjust, reunite and move ahead."

"Doctor Al Amaji, could you be a little more precise as to current events and what they mean?"

"Certainly." The smile remained as did the doctor's disregard of the question. "Iran is a complex area of tribes, factions, varying religious and ethnic groups, geographics, entities and influences. It is not a coherent nation of peoples with common goals and heritage. The history of Iran and before that Persia is filled with cycles of disorder, dismemberment, fractionalization and separation. Only when a powerful leader has been on the scene has there been unity. Cyrus, Darius, Alexander, Xerxes, Genghis Khan, Tamerlane, Shah Pahlavi and Khomeini are but a few. There have been many others who have held this disparate congregation together."

"And today, Doctor, and tomorrow, what will happen now that Khomeini has left the scene? Can Montazeri hold the power that Khomeini had or will it be someone else and, if someone else, what then?"

"What then you ask? What then? Am I a fortune teller? You ask about the future. How can we know that? We can only know what has happened and then project forward. Yes, we can look at the past and make some judgments."

"Such as—?" The talk show host was running out of time.

"Such as, now that Khomeini is gone another mullah will try to take over. If this mullah is powerful and influential enough he may be successful and he may control the country effectively. He could hold it together. If he is weak Iran could either come apart or else a stronger leader might take over. At present Montazeri seems to have taken over. We may see a period of power struggle during which various mullahs may try for power with no one in control. This could lead to division of the country into the various factions. It could even invite foreign interests or occupation. The Soviets and the Turks, for instance, might try to control some of Iran. The Kurds have been trying to establish their own state for a long time." Doctor Al Amaji paused a moment but before the host could stop the history lesson, he continued. "Now, the Kurds, ah, there's a very interesting and important history that reflects directly on what is happening today.

"Did you know that Solomon, the ancient very wise and powerful Hebrew king, found that the magical spirits called jinn were causing too much mischief and too many problems? So he expelled 500 of the most troublesome jinn from his kingdom and exiled them to the Zagros Mountains. These jinn first traveled on their magic carpets to the area now known as Germany, took 500 blond virgin brides on those same magic carpets, went to and then settled in what became what we know as Kurdistan. Jinn is what we know as jinni, or genie; a magical creature that gives three wishes if one were to rub the lamp or bottle to release him. King Solomon's expulsion of jinn is Kurdish legend that explains their origin."

Time for the talk show was running out. "Very interesting, Doctor, and if the Soviets moved into Iran, Doctor, what then?"

"What then? What do you mean, 'what then?' If the Soviets moved into Iran the Soviets would be in Iran."

"But what should the United States do, Doctor, if the Soviets moved into Iran?"

"Do? Why should the United States do anything? What the United States does or does not do will be determined by the President and Congress, I suppose. We shall have to see and then comment as responsibility to act or not to act rests on the leadership of the United States while we, of the academic community, can only observe and critique."

"Well, Doctor, if the president asked for your advice, what would you tell him? Would you suggest that he rub a magic lantern?"

"I wouldn't be asked. The question is irrelevant—."

Time was running out but the host tried again. "So is the lantern, but if he did ask, what would be your advice?"

"I'm not in the business of giving advice—."

"But if asked, certainly you would have advice, in the best interests of world peace or the best interests of the United States, or both."

"Yes. I could, I suppose, if asked, but this is purely hypothetical of course. I could say that occupation or invasion of Iran or before that Persia is always temporary. The occupying force always leaves eventually, departing with Persian culture—."

The talk show host interrupted, "And could you also say that some occupations have been for two to four hundred years and only left when driven out by a more powerful foreign military force?"

Doctor Al Amaji was embarrassed but maintained his smile. "Well, there is the time element, I suppose—."

"Thank you, Doctor, and speaking of the time element, that's all the time we have."

CHAPTER 10

"When Martin Shielbrock retired from the navy, as you know, he took a consulting job with a guy he had known and liked, Herman Reisling." Barney Williams was explaining the retirement of his longtime friend to his wife, daughter and son-in-law. They were sitting on the patio of their waterside condo. "Reisling had been consulting with the navy for many years and Shiel first met him during Shiel's tour on the OPNAV staff and then again with the SSG. It was easy stuff for Shielbrock because it was just what he had been doing during his last three duties in the navy." Barney paused, "No, during all of his time in the navy; coming up with new and better ways of doing things. But most important to Martin Shielbrock, of course, who always had to have things just like he wanted even if it was a little different than others, was the feature in his employment that allowed him to work when he wanted and on the projects he wanted. That meant that he could become part of a navy program that was part of a NATO program that was called 'Convoy Commodore' and it was for retired captains. Now, I had not heard of this program until Shiel became a part of it and I didn't know any others in the navy that had heard of it, but somehow Shiel found it and got into this convoy commodore thing."

Barney stopped and looked at the three others. They said nothing so he continued. "Martin Shielbrock always had these characteristics; he only did what he wanted to do, that is what he thought should be done, and he had to be what we might now call 'total immersion' in everything. He couldn't just join-up for something, sit back and see how it went. He always went full bore or not at all. Boy Scouts, baseball, broads or beer; total immersion.

When it was Navy; total immersion. So when he heard of this convoy commodore thing it sounded good to him, something he should do and he went for it, total immersion. And when he found out that there was a periodic exercise at sea called Rainbow Reef run from Diego Garcia in the Indian Ocean with real merchant ships, he had to be part of it. That's the way he was, total immersion."

DIEGO GARCIA, CHAGOS ARCHIPELAGO, BRITISH INDIAN OCEAN TERRITORY

The trip to Diego Garcia had been the most exhausting journey that Martin Shielbrock had ever taken. He met Captain Joe Farwell of the Military Sealift Command Headquarters at the Baltimore-Washington International airport in Maryland on Friday morning 12 January. Joe was on his way to observe the Rainbow Reef exercise at Diego Garcia because his office was responsible for the training of convoy commodores and Naval Reserve staffs that supported the convoy commodores. Also, he was responsible for the training of the people in the Naval Reserve units that provided Naval Control of Shipping Officers and staffs and as the Rainbow Reef exercises were the best training tools that Joe had for these purposes, he was anxious to see one first-hand.

The two retired Navy captains had decided to travel together and the trip started at BWI with a commercial flight to Norfolk and a short taxi trip from the commercial airport to the Naval Air Station, Norfolk. This put the travelers at the terminal of the Military Airlift Command, where they showed identification, orders and reservation forms and signed up for the MAC flight. Arrangements included paying a token six dollars for three meals to be served during the flight, not bad, two dollars a meal, but the originally scheduled ten AM departure flight was delayed until finally departing at noon.

The C-141 Starlifter is a large cargo plane which, when passengers are to be carried, is fitted with some lightweight airline type seats and nylon strap webbing racks along the sides in which passengers can sit. An hour after departure, over the Atlantic, the pilot announced that the landing gear wouldn't fully retract and he was turning back for his home base McGuire Air Force Base in New Jersey. So, four hours after landing at

McGuire, with a replacement aircraft and a new flight crew, the trip again commenced heading east and Joe Farwell turned to Martin Shielbrock. "Y'know, it's been ten hours since we left BWI and we're about two hundred miles from where they started."

Shielbrock thought a moment. "Gee, that's twenty miles an hour. It's gonna take a long time to get to Diego Garcia." They both laughed.

At Terrejon, Spain the travelers were told to remain close by in the MAC terminal as the flight would continue in two to six hours but it was six rather than two hours and Joe and Shielbrock got to know the terminal very well in that time.

A few hours of flight brought them to Sigonella, Sicily, this time at a Naval Air Station. Stay close, two to six hours, again, but this time Shielbrock and Joe ventured away from the terminal, found a closed bar at the Bachelor Officers Quarters and coerced the duty mess specialist to sell them some drinks. Time had already lost meaning for the travelers but it was early afternoon and two to six hours would be fine, even if it happened to be the low side this time. That was not to be, for having just finished their first beer, the mess specialist came running into the bar reporting that he had just received a phone call from operations and a car was on the way to pickup the two captains as the plane was ready to depart even though only a half-hour had elapsed. What the hell happened to two to six hours? Away they went.

A number of hours flying took them to Nairobi, Kenya, arriving at two AM. The flight from Sigonella had been long and cold as the heating system in the cargo plane was not functioning and at thirty five thousand feet even near the equator it was very cold. A blanket around each foot, another around the hips and a fourth over head and shoulders were necessities and the second boxed meal was handed out on this leg, identical to the first that had been served over the Atlantic. Two slices of white bread supporting a lone slice of bologna was, in fact, a sandwich however simple and a cookie, apple, candy bar, container of milk and one very dry and cold wing of what long ago had been fried chicken came from the box in a two dollar meal. There was no talk as ear plugs were required due to the tremendous noise level in the aircraft, off the scale decibels, thought Shielbrock, damaging to hearing.

Clearly a cargo plane, the C-141 did little to accommodate passengers even though the flight crew did their best with coffee and blankets, but the bone chilling cold, continuous deafening noise, uncomfortable seats and teeth rattling vibration wore away at the travelers as time dragged on; two, three, four, five hours and even the light was so bad that with the vibration any attempt at reading was futile. The stop at Nairobi was welcomed particularly as Joe felt sick to his stomach and Shielbrock ached all over including eyes and head. Two to six hours with no need to say "stay close," as the travelers were not permitted through Kenya customs or immigration and had to remain in a small waiting room with wooden benches, but it was warm and even with the constant ringing in their ears they could at least talk.

After six hours they departed Nairobi on the final leg of their trip, six hours to Diego Garcia and again the cold and blankets, ear plugs and noise, vibration and bad light, and of course boxed meal number three served over the Indian Ocean, identical in content but colder than the first two, the last two dollar meal.

In late afternoon they landed at Diego Garcia with Joe throwing-up sick and Shielbrock's ears ringing in a high decibel soprano, his head and eyes aching from the forty hours elapsed since they met at BWI for that comfortable commercial flight to Norfolk, about thirty six hours of discomfort with two MAC aircraft, three flight crews and three two dollar meals half way around the world in the middle of the Indian Ocean, to the atoll of Diego Garcia, Chagos Archipelago, British Indian Ocean Territory.

A few days after the two captains had landed at Diego Garcia it had still been dark in the early morning hours when Ahmad Bakhari, captain of the 80 foot fishing boat first picked up lights on the horizon. The big fisherman had been at the wheel, the boat rolling gently on the nearly flat calm, the engine droning on at moderate speed. "There, there, see those lights? By Allah's eyes, I told you. Right where I said. That has to be Diego Garcia!"

They all looked as they were all awake and even the two off watch were up for the landfall. Bakhari handed the only pair of binoculars in the boat to Moses Farscian who studied the lights on the horizon carefully. "How can you tell it's Diego Garcia?"

"Goat's ass! I know its Diego Garcia because of the chart and I'm a navigator, that's how. Do you think I've been underway for eleven days to take you to Mina al Bakr, you army mud-rutter?"

"I'd be surprised if you could find your ass with your finger, you dumb fish chaser. You've never been out of the Persian Gulf before in your life. Now that you've gotten us here a full day late, when will we be close enough to carry out our mission?"

"In a few hours, maybe two or three, and then I'm going to put you right alongside a great big ship sitting at anchor. Anyone with half a brain and even less coordination will be able to hit such a target, that's you. Why an army slob instead of a navy man, I'll never know, but you screw this up and I'll cut off your balls."

"You'll never know, is right, fish fucker. You'd never know daylight from a pig's ass. You get me there and I'll do my part."

The three others in the boat kept away and out of the heated exchange between Moses Farscian, the army missileman, and Ahmad Bakhari, the captain of the boat as for eleven days they had listened to the two slash each other with harsh words. Twice they had almost come to blows but were separated by the others and it had been particularly bad when the engine stopped and they lost a full day cleaning fuel lines and filters. Because of that delay they had missed the time for the coordinated attack which was to have taken place in the early morning of Sunday 20 January.

Their 80 foot boat was the largest of the attacking group. Five other fishing boats specially configured for this mission also were to be at Diego Garcia that Sunday morning and the six of them were to sail into the harbor anchorage, attack the big ships anchored there and depart. Their boat carried six TOW missiles for the mission and fifty of the smaller RPG-7 missiles while each of the other fishing boats carried four TOWs and twenty-five RPG-7 missiles.

Bakhari kept the bow pointed toward the lights and the engine droned on as two of the crew helped Moses Farscian set up the tripod base and the launcher for the TOW missile. Bakhari told the other crewman to turn on the small portable VHF voice radio. "Leave it on channel sixteen for fifteen minutes then search the channels all the way up then back down all the way to one, then up to sixteen again and listen awhile." The radio set was a common piece of equipment similar to that used by every merchant ship and fishing boat. It had ninety nine pre-set channels, each a slightly different frequency in the Very High Frequency, or VHF range allocated for maritime use by seamen, just as the citizens band or CB radio was used by truckers on American highways. Channel 16 was the most used frequency on the marine VHF radio.

This is it, thought Moses. Six months ago it started at Basrah and now, today, he would carry out that special mission.

Motor Vessel Corporal Louis J. Hauge, Jr. is the full name of the flagship of Maritime Prepositioning Ship Squadron TWO. The name is too long and complex so sailors call the ship simply, Hauge, pronounced hay-gee, with a hard g. That's probably what the marines called the corporal for whom the ship is named. The title of the squadron is more than a mouthful also, so it's called MPSRON TWO, pronounced empee-es-ron-too, in one word. There are five ships in the squadron, each named for a U.S. Marine Corps Medal of Honor winner, each ship name complete with the hero's rank and each a motor vessel, which means diesel engine powered.

MPSRON TWO lives in the central Indian Ocean at the tiny atoll of Diego Garcia, which is owned by the British and leased by the United States as a naval and air base. Nine other merchant ships call Diego Garcia home and all of them, the five ships of MPSRON TWO and the nine others are part of a maritime prepositioning program which puts military equipment afloat instead of in warehouses ashore. Each of the huge cumbersome ships is a combination parking garage and storage barn, a floating military arsenal and armory. In time of crisis the entire MPS squadron would proceed to a distant port, there to meet sixteen thousand airlifted U.S. Marines, an Expeditionary Brigade, who would use the equipment. Troops could be airlifted but their equipment had to go by ship and without the equipment the troops could not be effective.

Hauge was the first ship underway in the dim light that preceded dawn and she carried the regular navy commodore of the squadron, Captain Donald M. Addington, and his staff of twelve. In the lagoon used as anchorage for the fourteen ships the water surface was like a mirror and even outside the harbor the Indian Ocean was calm, as would be expected in January, the Northeast Monsoon season.

Ten minutes later another ship, Anderson, weighed anchor and got underway, following Hauge toward the harbor channel leading out of Diego Garcia and into the Indian Ocean. Then another ten minutes and Baugh was underway. The sortie plan called for a ship underway every ten minutes and at the Convoy Conference for this routine exercise it had been emphasized that each ship should get underway precisely at the prescribed time. So Hauge got underway at 0530, Anderson at 0540, Baugh at 0550, Fisher at 0600, Bonnyman at 0610 and so on. Proceeding at ten knots, the big ships cued up in a single file to pass through the narrow channel leading from the inner lagoon to the ocean and Hauge was in the channel with Anderson 2500 yards astern approaching the channel, Baugh maneuvering to take position 2500 yards astern of Anderson.

Every month the ships of MPSRON TWO went out for a convoy exercise conducted by their commodore, Captain Addington as these were merchant ships carrying military cargo, ships built for this specific prepositioning program and operated under long term charter with U.S. shipping companies. The ships' masters and mates were good at this as monthly practice made them the most experienced merchant seamen on convoy procedures in the world.

Captain Martin D. Shielbrock stood on the bridge of Motor Vessel Private First Class James Anderson, Jr. watching the ships get under-way, comparing the times with that prescribed for each and watching them proceed to form a single column for transit of the narrow channel. Shielbrock was a retired U.S. Navy Captain recalled to active duty for two weeks as a convoy commodore and he had flown to Diego Garcia to conduct this exercise, called Rainbow Reef by the Navy. This exercise was just like the regular monthly convoy exercises conducted by Don Addington, but for a Rainbow Reef exercise the squadron was turned over to a recalled convoy commodore and a staff of naval reservists for their training.

Ahmad Bakhari had kept the bow of his boat headed for the lights of Diego Garcia and as they drew closer to the island the gray light of dawn showed a small low flat island now with fewer lights. Still closer, he could see with the binoculars the left and right extremities of the island atoll as he found the lighted buoys marking the channel entrance and as he turned toward them his binoculars went back to the other lights. Bakhari studied the lights and as the morning light increased he could make out small shapes. "Allah's eyes, I make out some ships! They are there, our targets." Then he hesitated, studying through the binoculars as the oth-ers stood at the wind-screen staring at the still distant lights and shapes. "Ships, they are there!" Bakhari was not about to give up the binoculars to anyone else at such a time but, again, he hesitated in his narrative.

"What is it? What do you see?" Moses Farscian could tell that the boat captain was troubled.

"The ship, at least one, maybe more—," he hesitated again.

"What? What?" Moses was impatient. "Give me the glasses." He reached for them but the big fisherman pushed Moses' hand away.

"Get out'a here! You wouldn't know what you're looking at." Bakhari continued his study. "At least one, maybe more of the ships are under-way."

"Underway?" Moses was an army man not a sailor. "You mean not anchored?"

"That's what underway means, mud-rutter. It means not at anchor, like moving, dumb-shit."

Moses disregarded the insult. "But we expected them to be anchored, stationary targets."

"Well, some, maybe just one, maybe more, are moving. Can you hit a moving ship?"

"Yeah, I guess so." Moses sat on the deck and looked at the TOW launcher, thinking aloud. "Shouldn't make much difference. Ship moves slow. Big target. Shouldn't matter." He thought some more, staring at the launcher. For eleven days he had planned to cruise into the harbor and shoot at least four individual stationary ships, one after the other, before they could move or shoot back and at the same time the five other fishing boats would be in the harbor and they would all attack. Then the fuel line problem cost them a day so the fishing boats must have attacked yester-day. That's it, he thought, yes. "That's it! The five other boats must have attacked yesterday so the ships are moving around." None of the others replied as now, with some of the ships moving it would be more difficult to take a firing position which would accommodate four targets. Unless, yes, unless they could ride along past a number of targets and shoot them one at a time. "Are they lined up in some way so that we could ride down the line and shoot them as we pass, going in the opposite direction?"

"Dumb mud-rutter! You think they would just keep going past us to get shot? After we hit the first one the others would scatter and we'd have to chase them down."

"I was thinking that maybe they couldn't go far in the harbor. We would be like the fox in the hen house and the hens couldn't go far."

"Goat's ass! If they're underway they're leaving the harbor. They wouldn't just run around in circles in the harbor."

Moses Farscian had seen the harbor chart of Diego Garcia and al-though not a sailor, he knew that there was only one exit and entrance between the inner anchorage area and the open sea. "Don't they all have to go single file out of the channel to leave the harbor?"

"Goat's ass! They—," Ahmad Bakhari hesitated, took his eyes from the binoculars and looked at Moses for a few seconds. "Very good, mud-rutter, very good, they would have to go out the channel and we could hit them there, at least the first two. Then we could be inside and chase down maybe two more. Very good. Let's see." He looked again with the glasses at Diego Garcia. "Ghermeziat!" Bakhari yelled at the crewman who was bent over the portable VHF radio. "Anything?"

Ghermeziat raised his head and shook it in a negative indication. "I'm still working my way down the dial."

"Nothing on sixteen?"

"No."

"Go back there and listen a while. If you hear anything let me know and Farscian, too. He talks American." Ghermeziat bent back to his radio. "They'll talk on sixteen. Everybody uses sixteen. We should have two radios, one for channel sixteen and the other to search the other channels."

One of the other crewmen couldn't understand. "I thought there was only one channel at Diego Garcia."

Bakhari looked at him with disgust. "Pig's-ass! I'm talking about radio channels. What in Allah's eyes do you think Ghermeziat is doing there, fucking a goat? He's listening on all of the radio channels. The ships there," he pointed ahead, "they use the one channel to get in and out of the harbor, not radio channels, a shipping channel." After a brief pause Bakhari spoke again to the unfortunate crewman. "Now see if you can put up the Iranian flag on the stern without getting your balls caught in the rope."

They could all plainly see the island and the channel markers as Bakhari kept the boat headed in and as they approached the beginning of the channel the engines droned on steady, the boat rode smoothly.

Shielbrock raised his binoculars and looked ahead where beyond Hauge, outside the harbor entrance, a boat approached the channel. In most other ports of the world it would be a common situation, at Diego Garcia it was rare. "What do we have here?" Shielbrock asked with the binoculars still at his eyes. The master of Anderson, Irving Cappelton stood next to Shielbrock and raised his binoculars for a look and Lieutenant Tim Smith, a naval reservist on Shielbrock's staff for the exercise, did the same.

"I thought you didn't get visitors here at Diego Garcia, Captain," Shielbrock commented.

"Usually we don't." Cappelton now had his binoculars on the boat. "He's a fishing boat, small. Can't make his flag yet. He's keeping over, outside the channel for Hauge. He'll stay over for the rest of us."

"Wonder why a fishing boat is coming in here," spoke Tim Smith.

The other two also wondered as the Mate on watch gave an order to steer to the helmsman who acknowledged and the pilothouse was silent as the three stood side by side looking with their binoculars at the stranger in the dim morning light. The voice radio between ships was silent as Shielbrock had directed for the sortie which was good training in peacetime to get a convoy underway without radio chatter that could be heard by a waiting enemy. In Navy terms it was called "Silent Sortie." The boat in the channel had moved over as Hauge passed about a hundred and fifty yards abeam.

"There's a big ship approaching the inner end of the channel and I can see another ship just like the first, following." Bakhari threw back his head, laughed and cheered. "We got 'em! We got 'em! Farscian, get ready. I'm going to get over just outside of the channel and slow to put us alongside when the first ship is in the channel. The second ship will probably be in the channel by then, too, so he won't be able to turn away. We'll continue in and shoot at both of them as we pass. How's that?" Bakhari was obviously pleased with his plan.

Moses thought a while, looking ahead at the channel and the ships. "About how far will we be from the ships when we're directly alongside them in the channel?"

"We won't be in the channel. We'll be off a little to the right of the channel. Those ships need the deep water. We don't, so it'll look proper for us to leave the channel for them."

"So how far away from them will we be?"

"Fifty yards, maybe a little less. If your arm was a little longer you could hit them with a hammer." Bakhari was gloating and pleased with his plan.

"Not good." Moses was still looking at the channel ahead.

"What? What do you mean, 'not good'?" Bakhari's self satisfaction quickly changed to anger.

"Too close. The TOW missile needs at least seventy five yards to arm properly."

"Allah's eyes! You fucking mud-rutter, why didn't you tell me before?"

"You dumb fish-fucker, if I told you everything about the TOW you wouldn't need me, now would you?"

"Can you shoot before we get to the closest point, as we approach?"

"Yeah, but then the second ship probably won't be in the channel yet and—."

"And he'll be able to turn away," Bakhari finished the sentence for Farscian.

They thought awhile, now in the channel as the first big ship was easily visible ahead and Bakhari studied the chart. "I can get over, maybe a little more. Seventy five yards, you say?"

"That's minimum. More than seventy five yards would be better."

"Damn you! I thought you had to be close. Now you tell me, 'not too close'."

"Take it up with the American president. It's an American weapon, but even the Soviet Sagger has a minimum range. They all do."

"Okay! How about a hundred yards? I can move out of the channel enough to give you that much."

"A hundred and fifty would be better."

"Pig's ass!" Bakhari studied the channel ahead and the chart. "Okay, but I'll have to go real slow in case we touch bottom."

"That's your worry, navigator." Moses emphasized the last word as if name-calling.

They were well outside the channel, to the right, heading in at five knots and the first big ship was in the channel now standing out at ten knots. At the launcher in the open stern area of the boat Moses Farscian went over the firing procedure in his head and thought about how he had planned to aim the weapon high, well above the target, as Mossaheb, Abolqazeri and he had discussed at Umm Qasr. Aim high and bring the missile down on to the target, all the more reason to have a firing distance more than minimum and a hundred and fifty yards was not much. He would have preferred five hundred, time for the missile to arm, for him to get control of it and for it to drop on to the target. Well, a hundred and fifty should be enough, it would have to be.

"Okay Farscian!" Bakhari yelled from the pilot house, "This first ship is almost abeam and the second one is in the channel. Go on and shoot!"

Moses brought the cross hairs of the optical sight on to the center of the ship then back to the superstructure. He then raised the sight so that he was looking at clear sky with the top of the superstructure at the very bottom of his view and there, high and well above the target, just as he had planned, he pressed the trigger button with his thumb.

A roar shattered the stillness, the dim dawn lit up by a sharp bright flash with a cloud of smoke from the boat and a streak of light shot from the strange boat toward Motor Vessel Hauge. "It's a missile!" Shielbrock was first to yell out.

"Jesus Christ!" "Holy Shit!" "What the hell—!" "Did it hit?" All of them on Anderson's bridge watched the streak go over Hauge a good half mile and splash in the water.

"It missed!" Shielbrock had his binoculars fixed back on the boat.

"What should we do?" yelled the Mate.

The Master turned to Shielbrock, "Commodore?"

Shielbrock glanced around and a second is all it took as they were all looking at him; the Master, the Mate, his senior staff officer, two other staff officers from the other side of the pilot house, even the helmsman. "Speed! Speed! All you've got! Get past him!" Shielbrock pointed toward the boat.

"Speed?" The Master hesitated.

"Yes, speed, God Damn it! What else do you want to do; haul out of the channel and go around? Stop? You can't turn around in the channel, you can't back down to get clear and you can't block it. Get to sea and fast!"

The Master rang up full speed.

Shielbrock grabbed the radio handset. "Team this is Bull. Sortie at maximum speed. Close up and get to sea. Bravo Two, Delta Two, over."

"This is Bravo Two. Roger. Out."

"This is Delta Two. Roger. Out."

The roar and flash had engulfed the stern of the fishing boat and a cloud of white smoke blocked everyone's vision as the crewmen yelled, swore and jumped to get away from the flash, noise and debris. Moses kept his eye to the sight oblivious to the noise and confusion around him and there, the missile came into his view and he immediately lowered the sight so that the superstructure of the big ship was in the cross hair. By his past experience Moses knew that the missile would follow the cross hair on to the target but it didn't this time as the missile kept on a high trajectory over the ship. He had missed!

"Bastard son of a pig fuck! You missed!" He could hear Bakhari yelling at him from the Pilot House as he placed the second TOW missile canister on the launcher. The yelling and swearing continued as Moses again sighted the big ship and moved the cross hair to the superstructure aft. He raised the sight to where he had fired before and thought for a second; more, higher. He couldn't get more range but a higher arc might work as he sighted well above the ship with the launcher at about a forty-five degree angle of elevation and fired his second TOW missile.

Again a roar, a flash, a cloud of smoke and yells from the crewmen as Moses picked up the missile in the sight and lowered the cross hair on to the ship, to the bridge and pilot house area of the superstructure and the missile followed and hit with a flash and a sharp clank.

"You hit'im! You hit'im! Bakhari and the crewmen were shouting, "A hit! A hit!"

As Shielbrock spoke on the radio on board Anderson they watched as another flash, a second missile firing came from the boat, followed by a roar and a streak of light went high into the air, arched high over then down sharply and hit Hauge with a flash. Then a loud crack like a sledgehammer hitting a steel rail reached their ears immediately followed by a muffled explosion.

"Another missile!" "It hit Hauge!" "Holy shit!" "Jesus Christ, it hit aft." "Looks like it hit the bridge." "Maybe the pilot house." "Aft of the pilot house, looks like."

"Al," Shielbrock turned to the staff officers and pointed to a hand-held radio on the chart table in the pilothouse. "Try to raise the base commander or anybody else ashore at Diego Garcia on VHF and tell them Hauge has been hit. Start with channel 22. I think that's the water taxi channel. Stay off channel 16. If you hear the MPSRON TWO staff or Hauge reporting, lay off and let me know. This is no longer a Silent Sortie."

"Yes, sir."

"John," he pointed to the port wing of the bridge. "Get out there. Make up a status board and keep track of who's underway, who's in the channel and who's clear of the channel for as long as you can see."

"Yes sir."

"Tim—." He was interrupted by the voice radio, "Bull this is Bravo One. Over."

"That's Hauge!" Called out Tim as Shielbrock grabbed the handset.

"This is Bull. Roger. Over."

"This is Bravo One. Fairchild here," They knew that Joe Fairchild was Master of Motor Vessel Hauge. "We've been hit by a missile." Before he got any further another missile was fired from the boat, now astern of Hauge and ahead of Anderson, but this time the missile went high toward Hauge and appeared to spiral or tumble as it went over the ship and fell in the water a half mile ahead and off to the left.

Moses had placed the third TOW missile on the launcher and smoke was coming from the superstructure of the first ship as Bakhari was still yelling from the pilot house, "Hit 'im again! Hit 'im again!"

Moses looked further up the channel, "No. Let's get the second ship, as we planned."

Bakhari continued to yell and swear and Moses could see that their boat was speeding up and turning toward the stern of the first big ship. "What the hell are you doing, fisherman? Where are you going?"

"I'm going astern of the first ship, into the channel. Shoot him again."

"We don't have enough missiles. I've used two already. Let's get another ship."

"No!" Bakhari was still yelling from the pilot house. "I want to hit this one again."

"We're too close."

"Goat shit! We're not too close. Shoot him!"

Moses had stepped away from the launcher to yell at Bakhari when the big fisherman came back to the stern as the wheel had been turned over to one of the crewmen. Bakhari held a small hand gun that Moses had not seen before in the boat and the gun was pointed immediately at Moses' head, "Listen mud-rutter, get on that launcher and hit that ship again or by Allah I'll blow your fucking head off."

"I'll shoot, okay," Moses took his position behind the launcher, "But I'm telling you we're too close. It'll never work."

The gun was still at his head, "Shoot it!"

Moses had followed the same procedure as last time, with the forty-five degree elevation, and fired the third TOW missile. The missile went high and when Moses lowered the sight on to the target the missile tumbled and continued well over the big ship.

Fairchild's voice came back on the radio, "That one missed. Bull, are you there?"

"This is Bull, yes. Go on."

"Okay, Bull. We've been hit just aft of the pilothouse. Captain Addington is badly hurt. Berky appears to be dead." Shielbrock looked at Captain Cappelton inquiringly and the Master mouthed silently, "Ops officer, Commander Berkowitz," and Shielbrock nodded. "There's a few small fires but we have them under control. There are at least three other people with minor injuries. A lot of damage in the superstructure but no damage to ship control. No speed reduction. I have to get at least five some medical attention."

"This is Bull. Roger. Keep your speed up. Proceed to—," Shielbrock grabbed a chart from the table, "—point Delta Echo on our exercise chart. I'll arrange medevac. Over."

"This is Bravo One. Roger. Out."

Hauge was increasing speed now and the boat seemed to be dropping back but Anderson had increased speed, was gaining on the boat ahead and they could see a tripod mount and a launcher on the stern of the fishing boat with a crew of three working around it. The boat was about fifteen hundred yards directly ahead of them and all binoculars were on the boat as Shielbrock spoke quietly. "I believe we'll be the next target."

Bakhari had pushed the gun toward Moses' head and hunched a shoulder as if to fire. "You bastard! You deliberately aimed over the ship. You missed on purpose."

"No. No. Wait. Please. That's the way you have to aim this thing. That's the way I aimed when I hit. Really, I'm telling you we're too close."

Bakhari hesitated, looked at the big ship now directly ahead and then lowered the gun. "How about the RPG-7? Are we too close for that?"

Moses breathed easier. "No, the RPG-7 we could use at this range but it's got a very small warhead for a ship this size, y'know."

"Shoot some RPG-7 at this one," Bakhari pointed at the ship ahead. "Then a TOW at the one astern."

Moses started to object but the gun came up again. "Okay. Okay."

Of the ten small missiles that were fired in rapid sequence against the tall stern of the ship ahead four malfunctioned, four bounced off the heavy stern gate and two appeared to be good hits, hits that exploded against the steel gate. "That's enough!" Bakhari was disgusted with the poor results of the RPG-7 hits and Moses threw the hand held grenade launcher to the deck yelling. "Fucking Egyptian El Fateh. They sell us dog shit!"

Bakhari again pointed the gun at Moses and with his other hand pointed at the ship now astern. "Shoot a TOW at that second ship."

A small cloud of smoke had come from the stern of the boat and then a loud popping noise reached Anderson just as a small flash of light appeared for an instant on the huge and massive stern gate of Hauge. "What was that?"

"He fired something else! It hit Hauge's stern ramp."

Another cloud of smoke was seen, then another and another, followed by popping noises as smaller missiles from the boat hit and bounced off the stern ramp of the ship ahead and the smoke and popping continued. Shielbrock had been watching with his binoculars. "I'm not sure, but I think those last shots were rocket propelled grenades, like the RPG-7 they use in the Persian Gulf."

Tim had been watching also. "But a grenade, you have to pull a pin and then it goes on time, doesn't it?"

"No. These are grenades made into missiles for use against tanks. They're armor piercing and designed to start fires inside."

Captain Cappleton had been listening and watching. "Well, that stern ramp is the best place for them to shoot at. It's heavy and strong as hell, like armor. It's the thickest place on the ship."

Tim asked Shielbrock, "What can we do?"

"Until we get out of this channel there's nothing we can do. Just get to sea as fast as we can."

"And he can just shoot at each ship as we pass through the channel?"

"Well, I don't think he'll stay long."

"We don't even have anything to shoot back at him."

"No, and there's nothing at Diego Garcia we can call for."

"But he may not, probably doesn't, know that."

"He's getting ready to shoot at us!"

Moses looked aft, then at his TOW launcher, then at Bakhari's gun. "It's too far."

"What?" Bakhari was again angry as the gun was pointed at and almost touching Moses` head. "First too close, now too far. Listen, Farscian, I don't trust you a bit. Now hit that ship," He pointed aft, "or I'll kill you."

"I'll try," Moses took his position behind the TOW launcher and trained it on the ship astern of them. "Look, Bakhari, you've got to turn the boat. If I fire directly aft the blast will tear up our boat."

Bakhari yelled to the Pilot House to turn out of the channel and as the boat turned Moses brought the big ship into the cross hair of his sight. "It's too far. The missile can't reach that ship." He pressed the firing key anyway and a roar, a flash, a cloud of smoke and then Moses could see the TOW missile in his sight. He brought the cross hair to the ship, a head-on shot, and all he could see was the huge bow of the ship, so he fixed the cross hair on the top of that bow but the missile splashed in the water before it reached the ship.

Bakhari was angry, yelling and swearing, "Bastard, son of a bitch. You didn't aim high enough—."

The Anderson people saw a flash, a roar and then a streak of light coming at them from the boat and a missile splashed in the water five hundred yards ahead of them.

"He missed!"

"Something's wrong with his missiles."

"Let's hope he doesn't find out what it is."

Shielbrock was still watching ahead. "Hauge is clear of the channel and turning right. The boat is going straight ahead. No, he's turning to the left. Okay. Now we find out if he comes back for us, or runs away. Any guesses?"

Tim Smith was about to guess that Anderson would be the next target but instead he noticed something else. "Hey, earlier he had a flag flying from his stern but when he started firing missiles the flag was gone and it's still not there."

The Mate had been looking also. "Yeah, I seen a flag. It was Iran."

"Iran?" They all looked at the Mate. "Yeah, Iran, that's what it was."

As Moses stepped out from behind the TOW launcher the yelling continued and Bakhari was still looking back at where the missile splashed as Moses picked up an empty missile carrying case. Before Bakhari could turn around Moses smacked him on the side of the head with the missile case, sending Bakhari spinning across the boat where he fell unconscious. Moses picked up the gun, put it in his pocket and went forward to the Pilot House. "Let's get out of here," And he pointed out of the channel, seaward. "Get out there and then off in that direction." He pointed left, which was west.

Ghermeziat was the first crewman to speak, "I've got some talk on channel sixteen. American talk, I think."

"What did they say?"

"I don't know. I don't talk American."

Shielbrock looked ahead again, "Well, he's turning to the left and," He paused, still watching as they all watched, "And he's heading off to the left, westward. He's not coming back into the channel, at least for now." They relaxed, smiling, relieved. "Captain, if you please, when clear of the channel proceed to point Delta Echo and keep your speed up?"

"Yes sir," Cappleton responded.

Shielbrock walked out on the bridge wing. "John, what kind of a status have you been able to get?" He looked over the list of ships underway and in the channel and looked with binoculars back into the lagoon. "You'll be able to see them for awhile yet."

Back in the Pilot House, Lieutenant Commander Al Bevins came up to Shielbrock. "Commodore, I was able to get the water taxi dispatcher on channel 22. He said he would relay the report to the base commander."

"Good. Now get back to him and tell him I need a medevac helo immediately for Hauge. He has five people to be evacuated right now and hold him on until he gets an acknowledgment."

"Yes sir."

"Captain," Shielbrock looked at Cappleton. "What do you make of that boat? Could you tell anything about it?"

Irving Cappleton had been going to sea for over forty years. A short fat man whose stomach hung well over his belt, he seemed to have no waist and how his trousers stayed up was a mystery. His khaki shirt was always out of the trousers, always dirty and wrinkled and a coffee cup, full or empty, was always in his hand. Cappleton liked to use the merchant seaman's expression that he had "come up through the hawse," which referred to the hawse pipe through which came the anchor chain, meaning that he had first gone to sea as a deck seaman and had then become a Third Mate, then Second, First and finally obtained his Master's license. Now he held an unlimited Masters license and at 64 was one year shy of retirement age.

Cappleton carefully took an unfiltered cigarette from his shirt pocket, the open pack positioned just right for a cigarette to be lifted out with two fingers and into his mouth went the cigarette, all the way into his mouth, and he chewed on it for a few seconds, paper and all.

"Well, I'd say it was an ordinary old style fishing boat, maybe 80 feet length, small, pretty small for this water, way out here in the Indian Ocean, bit risky y'ask me."

"And the Iranian flag?" Shielbrock asked.

"Could be bullshit," The Master chewed a while more. "Long ways from Iran to here in a small fishing boat. What do you think?" The Master turned to his Mate with the question.

"Y'r right, Skipper, too small fer here. Flag don't mean nothin."

"How fast do you think it can go?" Shielbrock asked.

Cappleton chewed and thought a moment, "Fifteen maybe 18 knots on a good day, Hub?"

The Mate agreed and added, "On a good calm day but she ain't going far at that top speed. She's got to go slow, mehbee 10 or 12 knots t'get some distance, t'have legs." Cappleton nodded agreement.

For the next hour they watched their ships clear the channel and turn east toward the rendezvous point as Shielbrock and his staff formed them in the prearranged broad front rectangular formation.

A call on the voice radio came from the base commander. "This is Base, himself. You are to return to port with all ships so that injured can be treated and ships protected. Over"

Shielbrock thought a few moments. "Base this is Bull. The boat that attacked us is still at large, is probably in the area and is very likely listening to our conversation right now. In the lagoon at anchor we are sitting ducks. At sea he has to find us. There may very well be others like him around. You have nothing to protect us with. We are safer at sea than at anchor. Of most immediate priority, get a helo to medevac the five people from Hauge. Right now! Over."

There was no reply for a few moments, then, "This is Base. Let me make my position clear, sir. I am ordering you to return to anchorage. Your exercise is terminated. You are no longer in command. Acknowledge. Over."

"This is Bull. Let me make my position clear, sir. I am in command of this group of ships. Your authority does not extend to me at sea. You are not even in my chain of command. If necessary we could compare dates of rank." Having retired a few years ago with thirty years of service and now recalled to active duty, Shielbrock was clearly senior to the base commander. "I intend to remain at sea until the situation is clarified ashore. I have one probable dead, one seriously injured and three others injured on board Hauge. Now get off your ass, stop this petty bickering and get a helo out here fast or else you may have another death on your hands. Over."

Another long pause followed and Shielbrock was getting angrier and was about to reach for the radio handset again when the base commander spoke up. "Bull this is Base. The helo is down. You'll have to bring the injured in or send them by boat. Over."

"This is Bull. There are two SAR helos and they can fly if you lean on them. Do so. Those helos exist for Search and Rescue. This is Rescue. Get them going. Have the Det 0inC call me on channel 36 immediately. Over."

A pause, then, "This is Base, Roger. Out."

Five minutes later on another portable radio set on channel 36, a call came in, "Bull, this is Helo 0inC. Over."

There followed a long discussion and then argument focused on material condition of the two Search and Rescue helicopters, safety of flight restrictions, coordination problems and overall readiness. Shielbrock even questioned the personal integrity, dedication and "plain old guts" of the pilots and the conclusion was that one helo would be airborne in fifteen minutes, the other an hour later, with Shielbrock agreeing to accept responsibility for the flights.

"What the hell," Shielbrock thought aloud to his staff. "I either have responsibility for the entire operation or else I have no responsibility for any of it." He turned to Tim Smith. "Come over here and take some notes." They walked to the chart table in the pilothouse. "I've got a big project for you."

Blood was dried and matted in the hair of Ahmad Bakhari and still the gash on his head bled some as he stood against the after bulkhead in the pilot house of the fishing boat. His head had hit the deck edge as he fell and a large red welt curved across the left side of his face where Moses Farscian had hit him with the missile case. They were all in the pilot house except Ghermeziat, who was out on the foredeck searching the radio channels and listening for some information from the American ships. The rag Bakhari held to his head was heavily spotted with blood as he removed it and looked at the fresh red stain. "Still bleeding," he muttered.

"Listen!" They all looked at Moses. "We hit one ship but that's not good enough. Something is wrong with the missiles. I did everything right except we were too close on that third shot and too far away on the last one, but even so I couldn't control the missiles. The others should have hit. The range was within tolerance, the missile flew, I acquired it in the sight but it didn't follow. Three of the four didn't follow. I don't know why." The others stood and sat silently, looking at him, offering nothing, waiting for an answer, for a decision as Moses continued. "We've got to hit them again but I've got to know why those other shots didn't work right. We've only got two shots left and I've got to make them good. Any of you have any ideas?"

They shook their heads, remaining silent, staring at the deck as the boat rolled gently on the flat sea as the engine idled quietly. Bakhari put the bloody rag back to his head. "Maybe you don't know a damn thing about how to use that TOW missile. Maybe you lied all along and never shot one before. Maybe we'd better shove you over the side and head for home."

Moses felt the gun still in his large side pocket. "Listen, damn it, I've shot TOW missiles before and I've hit tanks and trucks with them. They're a lot smaller than those ships." Moses reached out his left hand as a target and pointed at it with the index finger of his right hand close to his right eye. "I've put the truck in the cross hair, raised above it, fired the missile and seen the wire spool off across the ground. Then I've acquired the missile and brought it right onto the target. I've done it before. This time it didn't work but it should have. Everything was the same except the ship target was much bigger." Moses paused and thought awhile. "The bigger target should have been easier to hit. Everything else was the same." He thought awhile more as the others remained silent.

Bakhari broke the silence. "Dumb army bastard. 'Everything was the same' you say. In a pig's ass! This time you were on water where a mud-rutter doesn't belong. If we'd had a navy missile man we'd a'had all hits."

Moses looked at Bakhari and thought a few moments. "On water! You may be right, water!" He thought awhile more. "The wire spools out faster than the missile flies so it lays across the ground. But firing over water the wire lays in the water. Maybe it doesn't work right with the wire in water." Moses became more enthusiastic. "Hey, that could be it. The one hit I got was when I aimed very high. The wire maybe hadn't reached the water at that short range, so—, so maybe that's why I could control the missile. That could be it! The wire has to stay out of the water."

Moses jumped up and ran out to the foredeck. "Ghermeziat, have you heard anything yet?" Then back into the Pilot House. "They went east when they cleared the harbor and we ran off to the west. They have to be east of Diego Garcia. Bakhari! If you're through playing with yourself how about taking us over to the east so's we can hit 'em with the other two TOW missiles?"

A few seconds later the engines increased speed and the boat turned toward the northeast with Bakhari at the wheel as Moses and Ghermeziat sat hunched over the portable radio, listening.

The second helicopter had just taken off from the pad on the after deck-house of Motor Vessel Corporal Louis J. Hauge, Jr. as Captain Shielbrock, watching through binoculars from the bridge wing of the nearby Anderson, spoke by radio with the helicopter pilot. Two people were on board Anderson who had to be taken into Diego Garcia and they had important information that could not be sent by any other means. Yes, the pilot would stop at Anderson and pick up the passengers enroute to Diego Garcia.

Minutes later the H-3 Search and Rescue helicopter settled softly onto the landing pad on board Anderson and Tim Smith and Joe Farwell, both wearing .45 caliber pistols in leather holsters strapped to their waists, climbed on board. Shielbrock followed them on to the helo and as the two strapped themselves into a webbed seat the captain proceeded through the aircraft to the cockpit. The pilot was also the officer in charge of the helicopter detachment based at Diego Garcia.

Even idling, the engines of the aircraft made so much noise that normal conservation was impossible but by hand sign Shielbrock motioned from his own mouth to the pilot's ear and with a brief nod the pilot slid his helmet up, exposing his ear. A peculiar discussion followed between Shielbrock and the helicopter pilot as each spoke in turn with his mouth directly at the ear of the other. At first it was Shielbrock explaining and then asking for something and the pilot responding with a strong negative. Then more explaining and requesting with negative response and more explanation as the passengers watched the two having their bizarre discussion, wondering with some nervousness how long this would go on.

Again, it was Shielbrock obviously asking something of the helicopter pilot and explaining with added emphasis and again a negative reply, this time resembling an apology. Another Shielbrock explanation and request as this time the pilot hesitated. Shielbrock was at his ear again but still hesitation followed by more emphatic discussion by Shielbrock and the pilot asked some questions. After a very strong affirmative reply from Shielbrock with added commentary, they looked at each other and with a questioning gesture from Shielbrock the pilot thought a few more seconds then nodded his head in the affirmative and gave thumbs up. Shielbrock smiled, nodded, slapped the pilot on the shoulder and made his way back through the aircraft. Passing the passengers he gave a smile and thumbs up to Tim Smith who acknowledged with a smile and a nod.

Shielbrock stood on the edge of the helo pad as the engine noise increased to a deafening roar as the aircraft seemed to lean forward and then slowly lifted itself clear of the deck. It went higher, turned abruptly with a smart bank and headed rapidly off toward the west, toward Diego Garcia. Shielbrock picked up his portable voice radio, set it on channel sixteen and listened as he made his way forward to the bridge.

The nonchalance of an aviator's voice came on the radio. "Bird Two, this is one, over."

"Go, one. Over."

"This is one. We'll have a little more shuttle to do after I get back. Fill up and be ready. See you in ten. Over."

"This is two. Roger. Out."

Shielbrock smiled to himself as the helicopter detachment officer-in-charge was cooperating after all.

CHAPTER 11

Barney Williams continued with his story. "So our favorite guy set out to conduct a nice routine convoy exercise in the Indian Ocean with a group of merchant ships and all of a sudden he's in what may be an international incident, what we used to call 'deep kimshi'. And just like he's so often done in the past, when he's told to do one thing, he knows better and he does something else. Here we go again. Authority says stop and he says no and keeps going. That's our Martin Shielbrock. That's Shellback."

Jackie, Ellie and Steven had been listening quietly as Barney described the events that he had been able to put together. He had read all the reports and had spoken with most of the participants so he was probably one of the most informed people concerning the Diego Garcia events and of the actions that followed.

Steven spoke, "I can see that he was faced with a classic military planning process; analysis of the situation, mission, possible enemy courses of action,— all that stuff leading up the infamous 'decision', but it seems like he just went right through the planning process in his mind in a few seconds and arrived at a number of decisions; get to sea, stay at sea and prepare to defend."

"Yes, you're right on," Barney smiled. "Remember, your father was an expert on that full military planning process; Naval War College, National War College, staffs, etc., so maybe he could just shoot right through it and come to the decision, or in this case decisions. Anyway, here he is at sea with a group of big merchant ships and he gets busy trying to keep them safe from he knows not what, with no protection and—."

"And don't forget the woman!" Jackie added.

INDIAN OCEAN, EAST OF DIEGO GARCIA

Late in the afternoon Bird One, the H-3 Search and Rescue helicopter flown by the detachment officer-in-charge, Lieutenant Commander Bob Ryan, settled softly but with the usual loud engine noise onto the landing pad of Motor Vessel Private First Class James Anderson, Jr.. They were forty-five miles northeast of Diego Garcia on a flat calm sea and Lieutenant Tim Smith was first off the aircraft with Captain Martin Shielbrock there to greet him. As he took off his flight headgear the smiling lieutenant leaned over to shout in Shielbrock's ear over the roar of the helicopter engines. "We did good. Got what you wanted." Shielbrock nodded smiling and Tim pointed toward the southwest, "More coming in the next helo."

Shielbrock slapped him on the shoulder and yelled into Tim's ear. "Great. Get these people settled and meet me up in the Pilot House." Tim nodded and went off to round up the others who had disembarked from the helicopter.

Shielbrock got aboard the aircraft and made his way through the cabin to the cockpit where Bob Ryan, the OinC nodded to him, smiling and gave a thumbs up. Shielbrock returned the nod and smile and pointed from his mouth to the pilot's ear. The helmet went up and Shielbrock leaned over to shout, "Hey, you've really done great. I understand Bird Two is on the way, also."

The pilot nodded, pointed at Shielbrock's ear and Shielbrock moved so that his ear was near Ryan's mouth. "That's affirm. Two has the last of it. I'll clear and go home now. He'll be here in about fifteen minutes."

They shifted ear and mouth positions again so that Shielbrock could speak. "Why don't you shut down and stay awhile. We'll fuel you and Two, when he gets here. There's plenty of room for both of you on this pad, isn't there?"

The mouth and ear shifted again, "Yeah, there's room for both of us but I thought this ship couldn't fuel us." The pilot's thought came out as a question.

"The ship's Chief Engineer rigged a helicopter refueling rig just for you." Shielbrock yelled and slapped him on the shoulder, smiling. "C'mon. Have an ice tea while you're waiting."

"Okay." The pilot slid his helmet down onto his head and spoke into his intercom system to the co-pilot directing the shut down and the helicopter engine noise died out slowly and the crewman climbed out to supervise the tie down as the pilots disembarked.

Shielbrock had the aviators accompany him up to the Pilot House where the ice tea waited and they chatted awhile about the attack and the departure of the ships from Diego Garcia. Then Shielbrock asked one of the staff officers to take the aviators on a tour of the ship. As the three departed the Pilot House Shielbrock told the watch officer, "Execute your signal."

"Team this is Bull. Tango zero six zero. Standby," He paused and looked at the Third Mate on watch who nodded indicating that he heard the signal. "Execute. Alpha Two, Bravo One, Delta Two, Echo Three, over," And the four designated ships each replied in order with, "Roger, out."

The Mate turned to the helmsman at the word execute. "Come on around to six zero."

"Six zero, aye," And the rudder was put over as they watched the ships all turn to the new course, a course away from Diego Garcia.

"Okay, Tim. How did it go?" Shielbrock sat in the high chair reserved for him in the Pilot House as Tim unbuckled his holster belt with the .45 pistol.

"Great! To start with, the Purser met Captain Farwell and me at the helo pad. The Britrep got upset over me wearing the forty-five, but I told him what you said, about us being in a combat environment and all and then Captain Farwell picked up on it and so he let me go." Tim referred to the Britrep which was the commonly used term on Diego Garcia for the senior representative of the British government, abbreviated to Britrep with no loss of respect, as Diego Garcia was owned by the British and the Britrep was the law. Carrying a gun, Shielbrock knew, would be objected to by the local authority but it would also attract attention and perhaps increase Tim's influence.

Tim held his note pad, to which he referred as a check-off list as he reported to Shielbrock. "Radios. The Purser got me five hand held VHF radios and a carton of 24 batteries."

"Good!" Shielbrock slapped his knee.

Tim continued, "I delivered your message to the base commander and, uh," He hesitated and looked at Shielbrock who continued for him, "And he was pissed."

"Yes sir, to say the least. He was highly pissed at you so he took it out on me. He told me a whole lot to tell you—."

Shielbrock cut him off, "Don't bother."

"But to boil it all down you should know this; He has talked with his higher ups and through them he has a message, classified, telling him to convey to you that CTF 73 orders you to get all these ships back into Diego Garcia immediately. Relayed down from CNO, he said."

Shielbrock felt a pulling of the muscles along the right side of his back and he thought a moment. "Did he give you a copy of this message?"

"No sir. I asked him for a copy to take to you but he said that as far as he was concerned I was not cleared to carry classified information and you were not in command."

"Didn't you just give him my classified message?"

"Well, I tried but he refused it. He said you were not the task unit commander and so you couldn't send traffic as CTU 73.7.3."

"That asshole!"

"But wait. I did get your message out anyway."

"But how?" You just said he—."

Tim interrupted the captain, "I gave it to Captain Farwell and he took it personally to the CO of the COMMSTA. It went out as 'Captain Farwell sends' and he quoted your message back to his office in Washington for further distribution." Tim's use of CO of the COMMSTA referred to the Commanding Officer of the Naval Communications Station at Diego Garcia and the message was Shielbrock's report of action, his assumption of command and his intentions.

"Did you read or see this message from CTF 73 telling me to get back into Diego?"

"No. The base CO wouldn't let me see it."

"So neither you nor I have seen this message." Shielbrock thought awhile as the muscles on the right side of his back still ached.

"Formation on zero six zero, sir," The watch officer reported.

"Very well, thank you." Shielbrock's thoughts came back to the present and he turned again to Tim. "Who were those others with you?"

"Ah! Good news! I was at the helo pad getting ready to leave when this Marine sergeant comes up to me and asks if I'm going out to the MPS ships. 'Yes', I said, so he says, 'I want to go with you.' Get this, he says, 'I'm in charge of a Stinger training team. We've been up in the Persian Gulf for a month training sailors on how to use Stinger and now we're going back to Pendleton but we're stuck here waiting on canceled flights.' He tells me he heard about the attack this morning, thinks there might be more and he and his team want to be in on the action. I got a four man Marine Stinger training team!"

"That's great! How about missiles, launcher and all that? What do they have and what do they need?"

"He tells me he has two Stinger missiles and a launcher but he hopes to get more."

"More? How can he get more?"

Tim pointed toward the bow of the ship. "From those containers."

Shielbrock looked at the container boxes stacked high on the forward half of the ship. "Jesus, that's an idea! There must be every imaginable Marine Corps weapon in those containers."

"Helo approaching from astern," The watch officer reported.

"That should be Bird Two." Shielbrock picked up his binoculars and looked aft, "Yeah, there it is." Then to the Mate, "Would you please ask your people back there to fuel this helo coming in now?"

"Yes sir," The mate went to the ship's phone and after a brief conversation said, "They're still fueling that first helo. Takes a long time with this system the chief rigged."

"Yes, I know." Shielbrock looked at Tim and then went to the chart table as Tim followed.

"Go back to the helo pad and greet the new arrivals. We'll increase speed. Give the helo crew a tour, some refreshment or whatever to kill some time." Shielbrock was whispering to Tim. "Tell the fueling team to stop at about half fuel. I need some time."

Tim was confused. "What are you trying to do, Commodore?"

Shielbrock thought it should be obvious. "I'm trying to keep these two helos on board with us. If we get far enough from Diego Garcia they won't have enough fuel to get back there and they'll have to stay with us. We'll have our own air wing for surveillance."

Tim looked at the captain in amazement. "Jesus! You're stealing the only two helicopters from Diego Garcia!"

"Well, not steal," Shielbrock smiled. "Just borrow for a while."

Tim shook his head in doubtful amazement. "Okay, if you think we can get away with it." Tim looked again at his small notebook. "Oh, another item, Captain Farwell stayed ashore. He told me to tell you that with the adverse attitude of the base commander he felt he could help you more from there than at sea."

Shielbrock nodded, "Okay."

Tim continued, "He said to tell you he'll be at the COMMSTA. He seems to have a good relationship with the CO there. He was able to get this secret intell message and gave me a copy for you." Tim handed Shielbrock a folded envelope.

"Hey, that's great." Shielbrock started to open the envelope. "Could you see if those two ships were underway or still at anchor?"

"Yes. Green Valley is underway to join us but Overseas Valdez is still there at anchor in the lagoon."

"Damn fool. What's the base doing about providing protection?"

"They've got three harbor patrol boats so they're planning on keeping one underway all the time, but just in the harbor."

"Nothing outside, looking around at a distance?"

"No sir. I heard that the base commander had asked for VP and ship support, like a frigate or destroyer I guess, but nothing yet." Tim's use of VP referred to land based patrol aircraft, the Navy's P-3 Neptune.

"Okay, thanks."

"Uh, Commodore, one more thing, if I may?"

"Yes, Tim. What is it?"

"Sir, with all due respect, I believe what you're doing is right. I think it's better to keep these ships underway than be at anchor in there," He pointed toward Diego Garcia. "But aren't you really disobeying orders? Even though you haven't seen the orders, isn't it possible that you might be in trouble? I mean later, after this, court martial kind of trouble? I don't know much about this stuff and I guess with all your time in the Navy and with all your experience—."

"Well, Tim, you may be right. I may be in trouble but I have to do what I know is right. We'll see how it turns out." They looked at each other for a few seconds. "But, Tim."

"Yes sir."

"Thanks for the thought. I may be breaking orders. I don't recommend doing that to anyone. I have done it before and gotten away with it. We'll see this time, but thanks anyway for letting me know how you feel."

Tim left for the helo pad and Shielbrock sat in his pilot house chair reading the intell message, thinking about what was ahead and of the aching pain running along the right side of his back, and of Stratford, Ontario on that hot summer day.

The base commander wants me back in port and the message he claims from CTF 73 is probably legitimate, but I know it's wrong to go back there and be sitting ducks. It's much safer to be at sea until protection arrives or the threat is neutralized. Well, it's not the first time I've refused to carry out orders. I guess the first time was during the Korean War. No, before that there was that Sunday at Stratford, and then there was the Cuban Quarantine and then on the gunline. I guess I'm in another of those damn situations.

Captain Cappleton had joined them in the Pilot House of Anderson as Bird Two approached from astern for the landing. With trousers hung dangerously below his protruding stomach the ship's Master looked aft as the helicopter slowed, hovered and gradually settled onto the landing pad alongside its' twin. "Well, now we got both of these birdies here. We got to give them fuel enough to get them home, huh?" Shielbrock didn't reply and Cappleton walked over to the chart table, looked at the gyro repeater and then back at the chart. "Hey, Commodore, looks like we're getting quite a long ways from Diego for these little birdies isn't we?"

"Yes, Captain. It is quite a ways for them, but—," He was interrupted by the bridge phone ringing and the Mate answered. "Pilot house." A pause as he listened. "Yeah we saw." Another pause and the Mate frowned and looked first at the ship's Master and then at Shielbrock. "Hold on," The Mate lowered the phone. "Flight deck says there's a woman just got off the helicopter with two more marines."

Tim Smith led the way from the flight deck up to the Pilot House and Bob Ryan followed with Mike Standick, the pilot of Bird Two. A woman was with them and as they entered the Pilot House Lieutenant Commander Ryan went straight to Shielbrock. "Hey, Commodore, we're getting pretty far from home and that fueling rig is so slow—."

"Hold on a minute." Shielbrock interrupted the OinC and turned to the other pilot. "Are you the pilot of Bird Two?"

"Yes sir."

"Why did you bring this woman here?"

"I didn't know who, uh, I didn't know there was a woman or whatever. I took on three marines, or I thought they were all marines, uh, men marines. When we landed and the passengers disembarked we saw one was a woman. I dunno if she's a marine or what. I—."

"Okay. Okay." Shielbrock interrupted him. "No, she's not a marine." They all looked at the woman standing just inside the Pilot House door and even though she was without make-up and was wearing marine utilities they could see that she was a beautiful blonde woman and with her hands on her hips the narrow waist and ample bosom were accentuated.

Shielbrock frowned, "Kim, what the hell are you doing here?"

"Why, Commodore, you know exactly why I'm here. I'm a journalist. There's a story here. That's why I'm here. I tried to get aboard for the exercise but Captain Addington wouldn't allow it but now I have a message from CHINFO giving me CNO authorization to embark for the Rainbow Reef exercise." She held out a message. "Since the ships had sailed for the exercise I took this helicopter to get on board."

"You know damned well this is more than a Rainbow Reef exercise now."

"I only know that if you tell me so. As far as I know, I've got authorization from CNO to embark in an MPS ship to cover the Rainbow Reef exercise. That's what I'm doing. Is there something else going on that I should know about?" She looked around and spoke with obvious feigned innocence.

Shielbrock looked at her hard, without speaking and Bob Ryan broke the silence. "Commodore," He paused until Shielbrock looked at him. "We're getting pretty far from Diego Garcia. That fueling rig," He pointed aft, "is so slow we won't have enough fuel for the distance."

"I'll see if we can speed up the process," Shielbrock, distracted, replied.

"Well, uh, sir, could you perhaps turn toward Diego Garcia so that we'll have less distance to fly when we leave? We're about at our maximum range now."

"Well, I'll take a look at that. We've got to remain clear because of these boats, you know."

"Yes sir." The OinC looked doubtful as did his fellow pilot.

"Look," Shielbrock smiled at them, "Why don't you guys look after that fueling process while I try to figure out what to do about this journalist?" He emphasized the word journalist.

"Okay." "Yes sir." The aviators departed for the helicopter pad.

"Do you want me to turn the formation to the southwest?" Al Bevins asked.

Shielbrock looked to ensure that the aviators had departed. "Not just yet, Al." Then he looked at Tim.

"Commodore, I didn't know she—."

"I know, Tim. It's not your fault." Then to Captain Cappleton," Captain, do you have a stateroom that we can make available for Ms. McManus?"

"I guess I could move a guy, maybe Pritchard, in with Halburt. Can't you send her back on one of the helos?"

"Well, maybe, but just in case she has to stay."

Cappleton looked at him for a moment. "You're not going to let those birdies go, are you?"

"Just for now, Captain, I'd like to hold on to them. You understand?"

"Okay. Lemme check with the Chief Mate."

"Thanks, Captain." Cappleton turned to go but Shielbrock held him. "Captain, would you please tell Sparks that nothing, I mean nothing, is to go out from anyone without me knowing about it before-hand."

"Cappleton looked at Kim then at Shielbrock. "I gotcha, Commodore. Nothing will go out," And he left the Pilot House.

Kim walked over, "Look, Martin, there's a great story here and I'm the only one who can cover it. You can't hold up my story."

"Kim, there's a lot happening and I don't know it all. I've got to do what I can to protect these ships. I can't let you tell the world what we're doing until I figure out if it's safe. Until then I've got to guard our information."

Kim was angry, "Damn it, everyone at Diego Garcia knows that one ship, Hauge, was attacked and there's dead and wounded. You've taken the ships even though you've been ordered to get them back into the harbor. You've refused to obey direct orders. Now it looks like you've taken the helicopters, too. There's a story here and it's got to be told, now or later. Why not let me tell it."

"Maybe later, not now. Look, I can't stop you from writing the story. Write it. I'll tell you everything I know and when it's safe I'll let you send it. But please try to understand that I've got a mess on my hands. There has been an attack, as you say, and there may be more boats around here trying to hit us. The one that got Hauge this morning is still around, for sure. Like I said, there may be others. The only way to protect these ships is to keep them moving at sea. At anchor in Diego Garcia they would be sitting ducks. I'm trying to hide them at sea because we have no other means to protect them. It's hard to hide twelve or thirteen big ships. I can't take the chance that a news story, a press release, on where we are and what we're doing might in some way help the boat or boats trying to find us. After it's over you might have a story. That's up to you, but not now."

She was still angry but managed a smile and shook her head. "It seems like we've been here before, haven't we? Last time I wanted a story from you and you wouldn't give it to me. Then I had a way to file it. Now I want a story and you'll give it to me but I can't file it."

"That other time there wasn't really a story."

"I think there was, but Newport, Rhode Island is far away and long in the past, isn't it?

They looked at each other awhile and Shielbrock smiled. "Yes, far away and five long years ago." She smiled back at him. "Six years."

CHAPTER 12

"Did anyone in Washington know what was going on at Diego Garcia?" Steven asked.

His father-in-law Barney Williams thought for a moment. "Well, yeah, always a bit after the fact. It takes some time to assemble the information, analyze it and put it all together in some form. I was in the Navy command center the morning that the CNO received the first briefing on what was going on in Diego Garcia. I knew that your dad had gone out there for some kind of exercise. I didn't know what it was but I didn't expect that it would be a topic in the morning brief. As you can imagine, a Rainbow Reef exercise was not what the CNO would ordinarily be interested in and so the briefing staff didn't have much on it. To be more accurate they didn't know a damn thing about Rainbow Reef exercises. No one was interested. They called it an 'undistinguished fleet exercise' but with the attacks on the MPS ships it became of major importance and so the briefing staff had to scramble around and get any info they could and fast.

"I was really surprised when I heard the CNO ask about what was going on at Diego Garcia and even more surprised that they had some scraps of information for him. I never expected that Shiel would drag me into it, but that came later."

THE PENTAGON, ARLINGTON, VIRGINIA

On Monday 22 January, Admiral Calvin E. Frost, USN, the Chief of Naval Operations went first to his office on the fourth floor E ring, the outside ring, and then to the Navy command center, located on the same floor of the Pentagon between the C and D rings. The Joint Chiefs of Staff have a larger more sophisticated command center in the basement and most of his time, when there were operational matters to be dealt with, the CNO was in the JCS command center called "the tank", rather than in the Navy command center. But this day he wanted to hear what his Navy had to say before he had to deal with the Joint Staff, a mixture of all services.

The Navy command center staff was accustomed to seeing Admiral Frost's four stars as these were the officers and enlisted people who provided his regular morning briefings. Frost acknowledged their greetings and asked, "Do we know what's going on at Diego Garcia yet?" He went right to the point.

Admiral Frost was liked and admired by almost everyone he had ever worked for or with as he was known to have a lively sense of humor and always demonstrated an awareness of his subordinates problems and sensitivities. Frost was a "people person", but he was also a hard practical executive who could get right to the basis of a problem and take immediate steps and today he was in that hard practical executive role.

The Watch Captain responded, "We have some fragments of information and expect more to follow soon. We've put together, uh, two rough briefings for you, Admiral. These are, uh, not what we usually give you, not as complete as we'd like but if you'll allow us, we'd like to give you what we have from intel and ops so far."

"Okay. Let's see what you have."

Lieutenant Donna Wright was an intelligence specialist, one of four regular intelligence briefers who rotated that assignment every morning. "Good morning, Admiral."

"Good morning, Donna. This makes two in a row for you, eh?" The Chief of Naval Operations remembered that Donna had given the regular morning briefing on Saturday.

"Yes sir, just lucky, I guess. As the Watch Captain said, Admiral, the information we have is sketchy but this is what we know or surmise so far. During sortie of MPS Squadron Two from Diego Garcia at 0530 local Monday the lead ship, Motor Vessel Corporal Louis J. Hague, Jr., the flagship of MPSRON Two, was hit by a missile. The missile was apparently a short range light weight type similar to, if not actually, a TOW missile. It could have been a Soviet Sagger missile. It was apparently fired from a small craft at the harbor entrance. The vessel is most likely Iranian. It escaped after firing four missiles. There may very well be other small craft similarly armed in the area. We have some information on their overall mission."

"How did we get this information? How do we know, or rather why do you say, 'most likely Iranian'?" Asked Frost.

"We're pretty sure of the Iranian part," Responded Donna. "It flew an Iranian flag but also, another similar boat apparently with the same mission was caught in the Seychelles and we obtained some information from that crew. We've put together a likely sequence of the Iranian operation, Admiral."

"Go on."

"The Iranians configured at least six fishing boats at Bandar Abbas for an attack on the MPS squadron at Diego Garcia. By the most direct route that's twenty-three hundred miles." Donna used a long pointer to show the route on the visual display of the Indian Ocean.

"Their plan called for three attack units. I'll refer to them as Eastern, Western and Central." She had a view-graph projected on a screen showing the three units and their composition.

"The Eastern Unit consists of two fishing boats. They transit via the Laccadive Islands, the Maldives and Gan to Diego Garcia. The Western Unit consists of three fishing boats. They transit via Socotra or Masirah and the Seychelles to Diego Garcia. The five boats of the Eastern and Western Units are similar nondescript fishing boats about sixty feet long and fairly common to the area. They are specially configured for the mission particularly with additional fuel and each of these boats carries four or more TOW missiles, or missiles similar to the TOW like the Sagger. The Central Unit consists of one fishing boat or maybe a different kind of boat, apparently larger than the others, about 100 feet in length, also carrying additional fuel and outfitted with more weapons than the others.

The Eastern and Western Units were given about twenty-three days for the transit, while the Central Unit was given about ten days. The attack was to have taken place around Sunday 21 January. Apparently one fishing boat, the first to get there and maybe that was a day late, attacked on Monday morning 22 January. Of the three boats of the Western Unit, one had engine problems early in the transit and either went into Oman or some Iranian port. The other two fueled at Socotra or Masirah and continued toward the Seychelles. One of these two had an engine problem, had to slow, but is considered to be possibly still enroute. The other continued on at planned speed, then also had an engine problem and had to slow. This third boat reached Mahe in the Seychelles late Monday. The local authorities there, having been alerted concerning the attack at Diego Garcia that morning, spotted the suspicious boat. They delayed it, searched it, found TOW missiles, false papers and identified the boat and crew as Iranian. So, of the three boats of the Western Group; one turned back early, one may still be enroute but late and one was apprehended at Mahe.

"We know nothing of the progress of the two fishing boats of the Eastern Unit. They may be enroute still or like the three of the Western Unit they may have had engine problems. We just don't know." Admiral Frost nodded as Donna continued the briefing.

"From reports received describing the attack we're pretty sure that the single fishing boat of the Central Unit, the hundred-footer, was the one that got there a day late and fired the missiles.

"We're told that the fishing boats have only a receive capability on HF radio and each has a battery powered VHF bridge-to-bridge voice radio, standard commercial type, line of sight range. None has the capability to send an HF signal. So, we surmise that these boats have no way to report their progress, problems, success or failure to whatever where-ever is their home base or command.

"Now, let me divert at this point for some information on the TOW and the Sagger. The TOW, of course, is a U.S. army missile. The Sagger is Soviet. They are similar. Both are wire guided. Our information is that the TOW cannot be used over water and probably not the Sagger, either, because the wire shorts-out when it touches the water. Over land that's not a problem. Since this attack, though, early today we checked with the marines in the Annex and there is a possibility that when fired from a low platform over water at a high target, the weapon can be aimed higher and the missile vectored in a high arch trajectory, like 'up and over', and the wire would stay clear of the water long enough for the missile to get to the target. We're not sure of this, nor are the marines, but the Watch

Captain asked them to try to get some tests set up ASAP, maybe nearby, like at Quantico.

"That's all we have at this time, Admiral, and what we have is based on reports from Diego Garcia and interrogations in the Seychelles."

"Have we gotten anything from State, CIA, anyone else?" Frost asked.

The Watch Captain answered. "Well, the information from the interrogations in the Seychelles comes to us from State, and very likely from CIA to State. We don't know that for sure."

"Okay." Frost hesitated then asked the Watch Captain, "Did they or we have anything even hinting at this before? It must have started over three weeks ago with the departure of these fishing boats, maybe even before that with their training and any reconfiguration, anything?"

"Not that we we're aware of, Admiral, then or even now, looking back. We had no hint. If I may, sir, I would assume that work on this kind of insignificant fishing boats and their sailings would not arouse suspicion and that could very well be why these boats were used."

Admiral Frost thought for a moment, "I would assume the same, Captain," And to Donna, "Thanks." Then turning again to the Watch Captain, "What else do you have for me?"

"We have an ops brief, Admiral, but I have to point out, sir, that usually we know more about what our own forces are doing and less about the enemy, uh, the threat, but in this case we seem to know more about this Iranian threat than what our own forces are doing."

"Why is that?"

"Well, we have some, uh, considerable communications problems with the MPS ships and so, uh, actually, that is, uh, we don't really know where they are or what they're doing." Clearly the Watch Captain was not sure of himself.

"Oh?" Admiral Frost hid his displeasure well."Let's hear what we do know."

Lieutenant Woodrow Tompkins had been the Operations Officer of a Spruance Class destroyer until about a year ago and since then he had been on duty in the Pentagon, in OP-06, as it was known. More precisely he was in OP-64, Total Force, Fleet Operations and Readiness Division, as an Assistant Navy Department Duty Captain/Chief of Naval Operations Briefer but as always the Navy had an acronym for that long title; Asst NDDC/CNO Briefer, and an even shorter handle, Ops Briefer. As did the intelligence briefers, Woody Tompkins rotated the regular morning briefings with three other lieutenants, all Ops Briefers.

Woody spoke from the rostrum. "MPSRON Two at Diego Garcia was scheduled for a Rainbow Reef exercise 22-25 January—," Woody stopped as Admiral Frost started to interrupt because he wasn't sure what a Rainbow Reef exercise was but the admiral hesitated, then indicated, "Go on."

"—22 to 25 January and was in the process of getting underway when the flagship, Hauge, was struck by a missile. The missile was apparently fired—."

Frost interrupted remembering about Rainbow Reef exercises. "The flagship of the regular MPS squadron commander or the temporary, what do we call him, the convoy commodore for the exercise?"

"The regular MPS squadron commander, Admiral. He is, or was, no, is Captain Donald M. Addington. He was seriously injured and has been evacuated by helo to Diego Garcia. One of his staff officers Lieutenant Commander A. L. Berkowitz was killed. There are three others with lesser injuries. Here's a list of the casualties with medical descriptions. We got this from the dispensary at Diego Garcia." Frost took the paper and looked it over. "Jesus, what a shame!" After a few seconds Frost looked up from the paper, nodded, and Woody continued.

"Hauge was struck by a missile apparently fired from an Iranian fishing boat. Observers state that the boat was flying the Iranian flag and was approaching Diego Garcia from the outer end of the channel. There were apparently four missiles fired; two at Hauge, one of which hit, and two missed Anderson which was the second ship in line. Hauge was hit in the superstructure just aft of the pilot house. The ship is still fully operational. The vessel which fired the missiles departed toward the west. In the chaos following the attack no one is really sure where the attacking craft went."

Frost frowned as Woody Tomkins continued. "The Rainbow Reef exercise was being conducted as is usual, without protection—."

"Nothing? Surface or air? How about the P-3s from Diego Garcia?" Asked Frost.

"No sir, nothing. Over the past five years there have been twenty Rainbow Reef exercises. In two of them there was protection, two out of twenty. There has not been any simulated opposition. It's always been treated as an undistinguished fleet exercise with very little interest."

"An 'undistinguished fleet exercise', huh? I haven't heard that one before." Frost shook his head.

Woody smiled. "I confess, Admiral. I just made it up this morning because I thought it described the situation."

"And it does, Woody. How about surface ship patrols in the area? I thought we kept two or three of the MPS, or other ships there, doing their own reconnaissance patrol around Diego Garcia."

"We used to but about six months ago those patrols were stopped."

"Why?" The CNO was not pleased.

"I have no information on why, Admiral." The question was beyond that which an Ops Briefer or Watch Captain would have known and Tompkins adhered to the long standing Navy policy of never saying, "I don't know" as the Watch Captain added the appropriate, "We'll find out, Admiral."

"Frost turned to his aide, "Let's find out what happened to those patrols; who stopped them and why." Then to Tompkins, "Go on." Frost sat back frowning.

"The hit on Hauge knocked out the Radio Shack which included loss of secure communications. Hauge, as the regular flagship, is the only ship which had secure comms."

Frost leaned forward again a little angrier. "Secure comms? You mean all or just UHF local stuff?"

The Watch Captain stepped in at that point. "That's what I meant, Admiral, about the, uh, communications problems. They have HF and VHF clear but nothing secure. Not long haul or local. They can't send or receive secure, only in the clear."

Frost worked a little harder at holding his temper and, as was his nature, he was successful as he turned to his aide. "Regardless of these developments, let's find out why each of these MPS ships doesn't have a full comms suite." Then to Lieutenant Tompkins, "Go on. No. Wait a minute." To the Watch Captain, "This was a Rainbow Reef exercise, so we have a convoy commodore in a training role and he has a staff of reservists?" The statement came out as a question.

"Yes sir, a convoy commodore and a Naval Reserve staff. He is in command of the squadron right now at sea. Some of the ships started to turn back, to go back into the harbor and anchor again at Diego Garcia, but the commodore ordered them to get out of the harbor as fast as possible and clear of Diego Garcia. Let me point out that we are dealing here with the five MPS ships of the squadron plus seven other chartered merchant ships of the Afloat Prepositioned Force. A total of twelve ships departed Diego Garcia for this Rainbow Reef exercise. Two ships, the tanker Overseas Valdez and the LASH ship Green Valley, were not scheduled for the exercise and had not planned to get underway. When Hauge was hit the convoy commodore ordered both of them to get underway as soon as possible, clear the harbor and join his group. Green Valley complied and left port but Overseas Valdez stayed at anchor. We sent word to CINCPACFLT, to tell the convoy commodore to get them all back into port but he refused. We'll have to tell you about that."

"That should be interesting, refusing to obey orders. Okay," Said Frost, "Let's get on with what you have and then I've got to go into 'the tank' and see what they're doing."

Woody Tompkins continued his briefing. "As the Watch Captain said, Admiral, the convoy commodore took command and ordered all the ships clear of the harbor. He formed them up and proceeded east with the intention of heading north when out of sight of Diego Garcia. He said that in port they were sitting ducks but at sea they were harder to find and harder to hit. He said he has to assume there are other boats but even if not the one that hit Hauge was still at large."

"Sounds reasonable to me, but you said," turning to the Watch Captain, "that we, I, ordered him back into port—," but as the Watch Captain started to respond Frost continued, "Oh, you said that's for you to tell me another time. Okay, let's go on."

Woody continued, "After Hauge was hit the convoy commodore got a helo from Diego Garcia to do a medevac and the wounded as well as the one dead officer were taken to the dispensary at Diego Garcia."

"I didn't even know there were helos at Diego Garcia," Admitted Frost.

"Yes sir. There are two H-3s there for SAR duty and the convoy commodore somehow has managed to get both of them on board his MPS ships."

"Why didn't he have them looking around, scouting, for his sortie?" asked Frost.

"He had asked but was refused. He was told they were not available for exercises and then when he insisted he was told they were both down." Down was navy talk for not working, as in "broken down". "But later," Woody continued, "after the missile attack he was very harsh on the VHF voice radio and got the medevac done by helo. As we understand it, he sent in some of his people and they procured some resources for him."

"Like what?"

"He was able to get a team of Marine Corps Stinger instructors, a Stinger Mobile Training Team, with two missiles. He took four marines, also, and he took five walkie talkies even though he has some of these already. As a separate problem, and we don't think that he had any control over this, that is, uh, in a stowaway kind of situation, a reporter got on board the helo and onto his ship, a newspaper woman."

"Jesus, a newspaper woman!" Frost repeated as his anger returned. "What is he going to do about that? He's got to get her off, but how?" Frost was asking questions and making statements faster than the command center people could respond.

When he paused the Watch Captain spoke. "Those are problems all connected with our lack of communications, uh, that is secure communications with him, but the reporter can't file a story unless he authorizes the use of his HF comms, which is unlikely."

"Yes," said the Admiral slowly. "So he has maybe better control of the news media this way than if she's put ashore, better than we have here. This guy has put a lot together."

"Yes sir," Came from a number of the people in the command center.

On his way to 'the tank' in the basement of the Pentagon, Admiral Frost reviewed some of the events with his aide, "—and Don, don't forget to have someone look into that communications problem with the MPS and the termination of those patrols."

"Yes sir."

"And Don, did you happen to get the name of that convoy commodore running this at Diego Garcia? I missed it."

"No sir. I don't think they mentioned it. I'll find out, sir."

CHAPTER 13

Jackie and Ellie had gone inside to see about lunch, leaving Steven to further question Barney about the events that had taken place in the Indian Ocean.

"Those boats that had tried to attack the MPS ships at Diego Garcia and there were others, you said, still trying to get at the MPS ships, still at sea, it sounds like they were not very seaworthy. Was it that or were the men not very well prepared, equipped, trained or motivated?" Steven asked.

Barney thought a while and smiled. "Let's see. You asked about; seaworthiness, preparation, equipment, training and motivation, right?" He paused. "I'd have to say they were lacking in all of the above if you measure by our standards." He paused again. "Well, maybe the last one, motivation, most of them had that, most but not every one of them. But those other requirements for success you asked about, let's see; seaworthiness, the boats were not the right ones for the job. Preparation; they were not properly prepared. Equipment; they certainly didn't have the right weapons or enough weapons. Training; they had some but not enough. But I guess they did have motivation and that's what gave them some small measure of hope for success on their part and that's what made them a threat to us, just that motivation.

Barney smiled again. "You know they laughed at the boy with a sling but he slew the giant; motivation, but in that case maybe some divine guidance, too. But motivation has to be taken seriously. These guys had a tough time and they kept trying. Some of them expected divine help, too.

With enough motivation sometimes you can overcome a lot of problems, a lot of shortcomings, sometimes, but not every time."

INDIAN OCEAN, NORTH OF DIEGO GARCIA

Diesel smoke, diesel smell, diesel taste, diesel noise, day after day, hour after hour the engine of the old fishing boat hammered away and smoke stung and watered their eyes. Fumes irritated their nostrils, lungs and throats as they coughed continually and their voices were raspy from sore throats. Food and drinking water tasted of diesel oil.

The exhaust manifold had cracked on the second day out from Al Basrah and that was only the start of their troubles as the cracked manifold got worse and the noise increased as smoke and fumes came out of the engine compartment into the cabin rather than out through the exhaust pipe. They tried to plug the crack with putty but it blew out and wet rags bound with baling wire held for awhile then started to smolder and burn. They poured sea water over the rags, taking turns to keep the rags wet so that they wouldn't burn and it worked for two days. Then the accumulation of salt from the evaporated sea water caused further deterioration of the cast iron manifold, the crack grew larger, the rags smoldered even with the water bath and they had to slow the engine to keep the temperature down.

Mohami Mossaheb, the army missileman, had been to sea before in his uncle's dhow in the Persian Gulf, which was not the same as this diesel fishing boat out in the Indian Ocean and never as miserable and as bad as was the noise, smell, burning eyes, sore throat and headache, the diarrhea was worse. Some how their drinking water had been contaminated with diesel oil, they could taste it plainly, but it was simply drink the contaminated water or drink no water at all. Mossaheb, as did the other four in the boat, drank the water and like the others he too had diarrhea. It was awkward, embarrassing and uncomfortable to drop your trousers, hang your ass over the side of the boat while holding on to the rail and drain your bowels of liquid shit every couple of hours or so, but at least all of them had to go through the same ritual so a tolerance and patience prevailed as they looked the other way.

More serious than the discomfort of frequent hangings over the rail was the draining of energy as each of them grew slowly weaker as the diarrhea took its toll. Mossaheb stood his watch in turn with the others but it was difficult and he ate less because the food tasted of diesel oil as did the water and he grew weaker each day as they all did.

Gholam Ahriman, the assistant engineer, had diarrhea like the rest of them but in addition he vomited a few times a day and the captain of the boat, Ismail Forughi, told them all, jokingly, that they should be thankful for the diesel fumes as it hid the stink of shit and vomit.

At the reduced engine speed it was obvious that they couldn't possibly make the prescribed date for the attack at Diego Garcia and Forughi talked it over with the other four and they decided to go on with the operation. They could have turned back as did one of the other boats but they reasoned that even if late they could possibly locate a target and maybe then they could get their shots and damage or destroy a huge ship. There was a chance, at least, if they continued on but if they turned back there would be no chance at all.

When they stopped for fuel at Masirah they weren't sick yet and the manifold crack wasn't too bad so they fueled and departed quickly so as not to arouse suspicion. With the brief stop Husayn Hadafour, the engineer, managed to get a can of metal sealant, a chemical emulsion of metal particles in glue and he applied the sealant with the engine stopped, but they had to get going and so the glue hadn't fully dried when he started the engine. For almost a day it held, then blew out a little at a time and they had to slow down again. Hadafour and Ahriman tried to apply more sealant with the engine running and they covered it with wet rags again bound with wire but in a few hours the sealant was gone and the rags smoldered. After a couple of more attempts the sealant was used up and the crack was larger than before.

Each evening they listened on the radio for news from Baghdad and most of the time they were successful in getting a station. The same programs to which Mossaheb, Moses Farscian and the other army veterans had listened at Umm Qasr could be picked up far at sea on other radio frequencies and Ali Esfandiari, the deck hand, became the unofficial radioman as he seemed to have the knack of searching the HF dial until the broadcast came in clearly. Forughi had named Esfandiari as the one who would search the VHF radio channels later, closer to Diego Garcia, to help them locate a target.

One evening, before they got to the Seychelles Islands, Esfandiari brought in a clear broadcast from Baghdad that told them the war with

Iran was going very well on all fronts, Iraqi casualties were light, morale was high and all of them, all loyal Iraqis had to be prepared, more than ever, to sacrifice for the Iraqi Republic.

Grand Ayatollah Ali Sistani came on the air and prayed for almost an hour as the five devoted Moslems in the fishing boat on the Indian Ocean enroute Diego Garcia sat silently listening and after the prayer the Ayatollah explained that he would provide guidance from Allah for the beloved Iraqi Republic. Allah had asked him to so serve and had blessed the Republic with successes against Iran, America and Russia and he explained that even as he spoke loyal sons of Iraq, devoted Moslems, were preparing a massive crippling blow against the devils which haunt and plague the true believers.

Four of the five in the fishing boat jumped and yelled with joy. "It's us! He's talking about us! Allahu Akbar."

"We are the ones to deal the crippling massive blow!"

"Allah's eyes! We are on a truly sacred mission. The holy Ayatollah said so!"

Mossaheb sat quietly and listened, watching his boat-mates dance with joy. "I hope so. I hope all this has a purpose," He said quietly so that no one heard him.

Of the three fishing boats that left Al Basra together for the Masirah - Seychelles route to Diego Garcia, one had turned back before they reached Masirah and Mossaheb's boat, with Foughi as captain, had to slow because of the cracked manifold so soon the third boat was far ahead and lost to their view and the five in Foughi's boat watched with a feeling of envy. Those in that lead boat would make the rendezvous in time for the attack and they would join the other fishing boats and fall on the large sleeping ships, firing their missiles at the anchored targets, causing fires, explosions, destruction and death. They in the trailing boat could only hope to arrive a day or so later, with the enemy alerted and the damage already done, but hopefully they could find a target.

Many days later a rope lanyard held the wheel from turning with the rudder amidships and even at idle speed the engine hammered away but there was less noise and smoke at idle. Foughi called the other four to join him at the stern of the boat, around the hatch over the fish bay holding extra fuel in 55 gallon drums. The four were sitting on the deck around the cargo hatch, their heads hung, eyes red, a lethargic group as

Forughi came back from the deck house coughing and joined them as he laid out a chart on the hatch.

"Look. We got to do some talking, cough, some planning." He pointed to a position on the chart, "Here we are." They followed his finger and listened. "Here's Mahe in the Seychelles and here's, cough, Diego Garcia. At the slow speed we been at we'll get to Mahe in about ten days, maybe twelve. That'll be, cough, four to six days after the attack at Diego Garcia. We'll have to fuel at Mahe, cough, maybe we can get the manifold welded, maybe. Then we got to go to Diego Garcia and try to find a target."

Hadafour spoke up, "I'm not sure we can get it welded and I doubt if we can find a replacement there. Maybe a, cough, patch. I don't know." He shook his head as his assistant Ahriman offered, "It would take time to find the right kind of welder, if there's one there. Cast iron is, cough, hard to weld."

Mossaheb had pushed himself up and stepped over to the chart. "Hell! Four to six days after the attack they'll know at Mahe all about it. They'll be, cough, suspicious. Who runs the Seychelles, anyway?"

Forughi had been nodding his head. "I think the British own it, cough, or they used to. That's why, cough, we got to plan this out."

Mossaheb continued, "Allah's eyes! The British! They'll, cough, search us, find the missiles and lock us up. We can't go, cough, into Mahe after the others attack, not that much after."

"That's why I wanted to talk, cough, it over with all of you." Forughi again pointed to the chart.

"From where we are, cough, now at our slow speed, if we headed straight for Diego Garcia we'd get there a day, maybe two after the attack, cough."

Esfandiari interrupted the captain. "How about fuel? I thought we, cough, don't have enough to make it all the way from, cough, Masirah to Diego Garcia even with this extra stuff."

"Right," Forughi continued. "We wouldn't have, cough, enough at the speed we were supposed to make, cough, but at this slow speed we don't use as much. Right?" The Captain looked at his engineer.

"Right. We been using, cough, a lot less fuel than we planned. But—," He paused and coughed. "But, then after the attack, cough, and especially if we use a high speed in the attack or to get away, then—," He paused again. "Where do we, cough, get fuel? We wouldn't have much left." He thought and looked at the chart. Only their sore throat raspy coughing broke the silence.

Forughi spoke, "Look. This isn't, cough, easy. As I see it, if we go to the, cough, Seychelles we'll probably get captured without a chance, cough, to hit a ship. If we go to Diego Garcia, cough, we get a chance at least to shoot one and then, cough, maybe we get caught there, maybe we get away and reach, cough, some fuel or maybe we run, cough, out and, and who knows what."

Mossaheb was an army veteran and had planned attacks before, but on land, and after a fit of coughing he said, "You got to have a plan for after, for getting out, getting away, or else it's, it's a one way thing, cough, like a suicide and I'm not for any suicide mission."

Ahriman stood up and faced Mossaheb. "It's for Allah, cough, cough, you heard the Ayatollah. You heard the radio! We all have to be ready, cough, to sacrifice."

"Sacrifice a pig's ass! Cough, cough. We're all sacrificing! We're shitting our guts out. We're weak. We got headache, eye ache, throat ache and ass ache." Mossaheb paused with a fit of coughing. "I've been in seven years of combat already and the only reason I'm, cough, still alive is I always had a plan of what to do. This plan," Mossaheb pointed to Forughi, "has no way out. We, cough, go to Diego Garcia, maybe we get to shoot." He emphasized the maybe. "Maybe we get shot at and then we try to, cough, get away without enough fuel. That's no, cough, no good."

Forughi pulled Hadafour over to the chart. "Let's me and you figure, cough, cough, out some distances and fuel. Maybe Mossaheb's right. Maybe we, cough, shouldn't go into this without knowing if we have a way, cough, out. But maybe, too, we just might have enough fuel. I was thinking, cough, we might be able to find some little port, an island, a small enough place to get into and out of, cough, even if we have to force our way, just to get some, cough, fuel, maybe."

The captain and the engineer went to work figuring as Mossaheb and Ahriman sat on the deck, their backs against the combing as Esfandiari went into the deck house, revved up the engine and steered a course midway between the headings to Mahe and to Diego Garcia. After awhile Ahriman hung his ass over the side and drained his bowels.

Three hours later Forughi called them to look at the chart again and spoke with continuous coughing interruptions. "Okay, here's how I see it. We'd have enough fuel at slow speed to get to Diego Garcia and then to Mahe—."

Mossaheb interrupted, "But at Mahe we'd get arrested and maybe—."

"Shut up, Mossaheb! To Mahe or to this little place which is even closer." They all bent over the chart to see where Forughi pointed. "That's Gan. Right near it is Addu Atoll. It can't be much but they must have diesel oil. There can't be any protection and at most there might be a policeman of some kind. Our other two boats were to fuel there at Addu Atoll. If we have to, we take the fuel." The captain looked at the other three and then at Mossaheb. "What do you say? Is that at least a chance of a way out?"

"I don't like it." They all continued the distractive coughing.

"Allah's eyes, Mossaheb! What do you want? The only other choice is to get captured at Mahe before we even have a chance to shoot a ship. What do you want to do?"

"I dunno," Mossaheb thought awhile, looking at the chart." Seems like you came up with this little Gan place and Addu Atoll all of sudden, very convenient. I don't trust it. What do you know about it?"

"Not a goddamn thing! I never been there and never heard of it before but it's the place the other two boats were supposed to fuel and it's on the chart. See? It's a chance, maybe not a good one, but a chance. You got any better idea?"

Mossaheb thought awhile more as the others looked at him, waiting, coughing and finally he sighed resignedly. "Fuck it. Let's go for Diego Garcia. You're right, Captain, that's the only thing we can do." It was the first time in their eighteen days at sea that Mossaheb had called Forughi "Captain."

Four and a half days later just past midnight, the start of the twenty third day of January, Ahriman was on watch on the wheel. They had been unable to get any news on the radio during that time. "Hey! Hey Forughi, get up. I think I saw a light."

It only took Forughi a few seconds to reach Ahriman's side at the wheel and the others woke also at the call. "Did you see a light or not? What do you mean, `I think'? Is there a light there? Are your eyes playing tricks like looking at a low star?"

"I don't see it now but I'm pretty sure there was one just off to starboard, almost directly—. There! There it is!"

The others looked ahead toward where Ahriman pointed and it was a light and they all saw it and then another and others as Foroughi had the binoculars on the lights. Mossaheb stood next to him. "Can you tell anything?"

"No. I can just make out the lights but it's got to be land. The lights are too spread out to be a ship. It has to be Diego Garcia. Allah's eyes, I wish we knew something about that attack on Sunday."

"How far would you say?"

"Oh, probably it's ten to twelve miles. We're approaching the north end of the island. That's where the ship channel is, the entrance to the harbor."

"Then we'll be there in about two hours?" Mossaheb's statement came out as a question.

"That's right," Foroughi's eyes were still in the binoculars. "About two hours to the channel. I was thinking maybe we should head for the channel until we pick up the outer buoy then turn east as if we're going to pass by. There's a group of little islands and rocks across the north end of the harbor that form a sort of wall but there's space enough for us between them. The ships can only use the channel but we can slip in between the rocks."

"Sounds good to me." They were all coughing less.

"Okay. Mossaheb, you get your missile set up. Ahriman, I'll take the wheel now. You help Mossaheb. Hadafour, stay with the engine. Try that tin can flattened out over the crack with putty and wet rags cause we're going to have to speed up for the attack. Esfandiari, you get on the little radio and search the different settings for some American talk."

They all went quietly to their tasks as the engine hammered away even as Hadafour tried again to cover the crack in the manifold. An hour later many lights were plainly visible and the missile launcher was set up on the cargo hatch aft with four TOW missiles lined up well away from the launcher and the RPG 7 launcher with twenty missile configured grenades were on the after deck area, ready for use. Mossaheb moved into the wheel house alongside Foroughi who kept his eyes glued to the binoculars. "All set aft."

"Good. How about going over the steps with Ahriman again? You know, just in case we need for him to do some shooting."

Mossaheb understood that "just in case" meant in the event that Mossaheb was shot on the way in, if they met a patrol boat. "He's ready. He'll be holding the RPG-7. He knows how to use them both."

"Okay." Forughi continued to study the lights.

"Can you see any ships in there?"

"No."

"How about the buoy you were looking for?"

"Yeah, I can see the buoy. We're heading for it now and I'll turn away in a little while."

The engine noise quieted somewhat. "Hey," Forughi called to the engineer, "That's pretty good. Think it will hold?"

"Shit, no. It won't hold but maybe for a little while. Maybe it'll help us get in there if we don't make too much noise."

"Yeah, maybe," Forughi looked at Mossaheb. "Let's hope we can get in there."

Mossaheb the missileman added, "And let's hope there's a target for us."

Ahriman had joined them in the cabin. "Allah will provide. He has brought us here and He will give us a target. The rest is up to us."

Before anyone could comment Esfandiari yelled out from the after corner of the cabin that he heard a radio signal on the VHF transceiver, they all heard it, a voice speaking English!

"Could you tell what he said?" Mossaheb was the first to join the erstwhile radioman.

"I just caught the last part. Something about a boat at zero six hundred."

"A boat!" Mossaheb was excited. "A boat would be for a run from the shore to a ship, maybe." He turned to the Captain. "Do you think it means there are ships there?"

"It could. I still can't see anything in there but the rocks and islands may be blocking my view."

As he spun the wheel the boat turned left. "Okay, now let's see if we can get over a ways and find an opening in the rocks."

A half hour later he slowed the engine to idle speed with the boat moving at a crawl. Esfandiari had left the radio and was up at the bow as a lookout as Ahriman and Mossaheb served the same roles on both sides. It was easier than they expected as they were through the rocks and in the harbor. Forughi kept the boat heading south, into the center of the wide lagoon, which was the anchorage area for the dozen or so large American ships as Mossaheb went to the cabin alongside Foroughi at the wheel.

"They're gone. Allah has fucked us over again. Now we'll probably get—."

"Shut up! Before you defile Allah so let's look around some. Get back there and be ready first with the RPG-7. There might be a patrol boat and we may have to deal with that first." He was looking around with the binoculars. "In the meantime we'll—. There, a ship!" Foroughi pointed off to the right and sure enough even in the dark they could make out the silhouette of a ship against the lights on the shore.

"It's a tanker," Esfandiari yelled from the bow.

Foroughi turned the boat, still at idle speed, toward the sleeping ship.

"There's your target, Mossaheb."

"And we're already within range." The Army veteran scrambled aft to his launcher.

"I think there's a patrol boat approaching from the south!" Esfandiari was still serving as lookout. "Fuck the patrol boat! Mossaheb, shoot the tanker!"

A blinding flash lit up the night and the missile roar overcame even the hammering of their engine. Mossaheb had aimed and fired high and then he brought the missile down onto the target. It hit the tanker with a clash of steel and a bright flash and the muffled roar of an explosion reached them a few seconds later as Mossaheb fired again. The second missile hit just as did the first and the boat crew was cheering as he loaded his third TOW missile.

A series of splashes near their boat came closer and then four projectiles ripped their way across the deck house as glass shattered, chunks of wood went flying and fine razor sharp splinters flew everywhere. Ahriman screamed and fell to the deck with his hands over his face, blood pouring through his fingers. Foroughi spun the wheel to turn the boat away from the rapidly closing patrol boat and speeded up the engine. "Hadafour, give me all you've got!"

Mossaheb fired another TOW missile but missed due to the rapid acceleration and turn of the boat. Flames were coming out of the tanker as he fired his fourth and last missile and it hit the burning tanker.

Another burst of fire from the patrol boat tore across their boat and more glass and wood splinters flew around and as Foroughi yelled from the cabin a jagged piece of metal tore open his right shoulder. Esfandiari ran in and took the wheel as the captain fell in a pool of his own blood and more gunfire ripped across the boat.

Mossaheb picked up the RPG-7 launcher and fired five missile grenades at the approaching patrol boat but all missed and another burst of gunfire hit their fishing boat. Esfandiari yelled for more speed and Hadafour was trying to shout back when the cracked exhaust manifold blew off the engine and raw flame shot out across the engine compartment like an explosive, burning and killing Hadafour instantly. Oil soaked wood fed by fresh diesel oil from ruptured fuel lines flashed into a blaze and the boat went up like a torch.

A few minutes later Mossaheb was pulled from the water by the American patrol boat as Esfandiari was already on board and they waited as the patrol boat searched for other survivors, but there weren't any. Even though handcuffed face down on the deck, army veteran missileman Mohami Mossaheb and Ali Esfandiari, erstwhile radioman, could see not far away the burning tanker Overseas Valdez at anchor in the lagoon of Diego Garcia.

CHAPTER 14

Barney's wife Jackie had just brought ice tea for them all on the patio. She set the glasses on the round table under the large umbrella. "You men have been talking about Martin and his convoy thing around this little island in the Indian Ocean and then there's this business in Iran, or is it Iraq. What's the connection?"

Barney and Steven looked at each other and laughed as Barney spoke. "Ah, there's the rub. What's the connection? That's the sixty-four dollar question and we'll get to that, I promise." He paused and looked at Steven and as they both nodded Barney continued. "Before we discuss much more about Martin Shielbrock, the convoy commodore with his baker's dozen at sea trying to avoid a bunch of boats, we have to take a look at the Middle East. We'll connect them soon enough. There were a lot of things going on particularly in Iran that were very important. There were news reports and there were rumors, and there were continuous intell briefings to the highest levels of government and military. That included, of course, the Joint Chiefs of Staff and I was able to sit in on some of those in the tank."

SIX AYATOLLAHS

The regular network news was about Iran. "Reports coming out of Iran are confused, this day, with some indications that the successor to Ayatollah Ruhollah Khomeini is unable to control the country and many thousands of Iranians are in the streets chanting support for Khomeini, with numerous reports of violence against Europeans." The television network news anchorman described the violence and mass demonstrations with a map of Iran behind him.

"In spite of appeals from various influential mullahs for patience and peaceful prayer to support the Ayatollah Montazeri conveyed to the people by radio, television and newspapers, the mass demonstrations and violence seem to be increasing. Information as to the actual events is confusing and disparate as the various communications systems are not functioning. It is impossible, for instance, to get telephone calls into or out of Teheran, all border crossings are closed and air traffic and railroads are at a standstill. The only information on what is happening inside Iran has been obtained by the monitoring of Iranian radio news broadcasts outside the country. We will be watching the Iranian situation closely and will keep you up to date on developments in that area as information is available."

The announcer turned to his co-anchor person, a well dressed, attractive, well made-up blonde. "Jane?"

"I was wondering," Jane asked on camera, if we are getting anything from the State Department. Certainly they have their own communications system and must have information on what is happening in Iran."

"At this point the State Department has not released any information. I agree with you, Jane, they probably know a lot more than we, and there may be a press conference or at least a news release soon. I called Paul Antrim, Deputy Assistant Secretary of State for Middle East Affairs, and all I got was 'no comment'. All we can be sure of at this time is that significant events are taking place in Iran, the Ayatollah Montazeri is unable to control the people and there is considerable unrest."

"Thank you, Paul." Jane continued with the news.

Later that day the television network news had some information on the developing crisis in Iran.

"The State Department has just released information which confirms our earlier reports of unrest and mass demonstrations in Iran. All foreign embassies in Teheran are closed. All diplomats have been ordered to remain in their embassies. Many thousands of Iranians are in the streets chanting support for various ayatollahs. There have been outbreaks of violence and demonstrations against European and American interests. Local radio and television broadcasts insist that the Ayatollah Montazeri is in charge and that he will soon appear in public and restore peace but civil unrest continues to spread in spite of these appeals."

The next day, "The Ayatollah Montazeri is apparently in hiding, this according to an announcement on official government television and radio. Ayatollah Montazeri, the designated heir to the position of Grand Ayatollah as selected by Khomeini, has been unable to get the necessary support to control the country. Who is in charge is not clear as at least two other mullahs have made claims." The newsman described the other two and gave their backgrounds.

"Meanwhile, rioting and mass demonstrations continue to spread over Iran. A period of at least sixty days of prayer and patience has been declared by the mullahs but this does not seem to have had a moderating effect on the people. On the contrary, the announcement of the death and mourning period seems to have ignited increased unrest. There are indications of factionalism, or geographic and ethnic division, working in Iran as various areas and peoples claim allegiance to different ayatollahs. In western terms, we are seeing a huge power struggle in Iran as a number of influential religious leaders compete for control."

Over the next few days the television news reported that the Kurds of Iran's western province of Kurdistan had declared that henceforth Kurdistan was an autonomous state, a nation independent of Iran. The new leader of the Republic of Kurdistan, Abu Al Amuzagar appealed to Kurds of Iraq, Turkey, Syria and the Soviet Union to join the new state. The news reports went on to describe the background and history of the Kurdish people, explaining that the Kurds are descended from the early Medes of the ancient Persian area. Their language is a variation of Farsi, which is the Persian language of Iran. Most significant, Kurds are members of the Sunni branch of Islam, not Shiites as is most of Iran. The Kurds never felt allegiance to the Shah, who tolerated various religions, or to Khomeini, the Shiite fundamentalist.

The Kurds have sought autonomy for hundreds of years, and had been close to achieving it a number of times. During this century, in 1946-47 a Kurdish Republic of Mahabad was established in Iran with Soviet sponsorship, but collapsed when Soviet troops left the area. The Kurds fought Iraq for independence in the early 1970's, but when the Shah of Iran withdrew his support that effort also terminated. Now, with the death of Khomeini and Iran in anarchy and chaos, the Kurds have seized the opportunity for independence.

All this was described by the various news media.

Support and encouragement of the Soviet Union for a Kurdish state, which had been so necessary and available in the late 1940s, is not now available for this new Kurdish nation. The Soviets have their eye on Azerbaijan and Gilan as Socialist Republics, to be absorbed ultimately into their union of other socialist states. A separate Kurdish republic inviting the Kurds of the Soviet Union to join is not in the best Soviet interests. A Kurdistan across the existing Iranian province and into Iraq and Turkey would have been ideal for the Soviets, but Abu Al Amuzagar has clearly exceeded this position and his invitation to the Kurds of the Soviet Union canceled any chances of Soviet support. Rather, it has given the Soviets reason to be concerned over the stability in the area. They might send "peace keeping" troops into and across Azerbaijan, to provide security and peace in an area under anarchy. They would claim, of course, that this action would only be until effective local government function and control was evident.

The TV analyses told of new reports indicating Soviet troop movements along the southern borders of the Armenian and the Azerbaijan Soviet Socialist Republics, on the border with the Iranian province of East Azerbaijan on the west side of the Caspian Sea.

Turkey, a member of the North Atlantic Treaty Organization, NATO, shared a border with the Iranian province of West Azerbaijan and the Turks well remembered the Soviet influence which created independent republics nearby in Kurdistan and Azerbaijan in 1946. Now, with a new Kurdish nation calling for union with Kurds across the borders including Turkey, and the Soviets making eyes at East and West Azerbaijan in Iran, the Turks see a renewed threat to their sovereignty and security from the east and Turkey is reported to be moving troops to her western border.

News reports went on to describe that Iraq had been fighting a debilitating war for many years with Iran and in spite of attempts to limit and to terminate the war by the United States, the Soviet Union and even the United Nations, the war had continued. The death of Khomeini had turned Iran's attention inward, away from the long war with Iraq and with his death Iran seemed to see little reason to carry on the war started by Iraq and pursued by Khomeini for reasons few if any of them understood. Iraq seemed to be satisfied to have a cessation of hostilities, or even a brief respite. The announcement of the establishment of an autonomous Kurdish state and the invitation to the Kurds of Iraq to join was being viewed as a threat to her sovereignty by Iraq. The land most sought after as their homeland by the landless Kurdish peoples was in

Iraq, and the government of Iraq was not about to give up that land to a new Kurdish state.

The news reports continued to explain that although their names are somewhat similar, Iran and Iraq are much different. The name Iraq means mud bank in Arabic and the people of Iraq are Arab or Semitic, whereas Iran means Aryan. Their differences cover Sunni versus Shiite, Semitic versus Aryan, desert versus mountain and centuries of conflict. Over three million Kurds live in Iraq compared to about one million in Iran, so the threat to, or effect on Iraq by the creation of an independent Kurdish state would be even greater than that of Iran. Iraq had already started to move troops from the southern battlefields toward their border of Kurdistan.

Admiral Calvin E. Frost, U.S. Navy, the Chief of Naval Operations, was in the seat designated for him in the Command Center of the Joint Chiefs of Staff in the Pentagon. On his right sat the Chief of Staff of the U.S. Air Force, to his left the Chief of Staff of the U.S. Army. The Commandant of the U.S. Marine Corps sat to the right of the air force general and on the far left was the Chairman of the Joint Chiefs of Staff, General Hugh P. Meckering, U.S. Army. Each of these officers wore four stars; twenty stars between them, and they were the five highest ranking military officers in the United States.

Attention of the five was focused on Air Force Major Donald Thompson, a Middle East intelligence specialist on the joint staff. Major Thompson worked closely with CIA and State and had already covered a brief modern history including the Shah, Khomeini, foreign influences, the war with Iraq, Persian Gulf shipping attacks, the death of Khomeini, unrest that followed and the declaration of Kurdish independence. Now he went on to cover what combined intelligence sources revealed as the current Iranian political situation. "At least six ayatollahs have been identified by the CIA, each claiming to be the rightful successor to Khomeini, each having a geographic area or an ethnic group of support, each representing a different position on the spectrum of east-west, left-right, or conservative-liberal politics. Their differences had been masked in the time before Khomeini died, by an all encompassing passive subjugation of the ayatollahs and mullahs to Khomeini's authority. Now, with the once Grand Ayatollah out of the way, each seeks to establish himself, with his own interpretations of the Koran and based on his own foundation of power.

"Ayatollah Hossein Ali Montazeri is thought of by the western press and middle eastern experts as the one most probably selected as his successor by Khomeini and he has tried to take over. Montazeri is from the same province originally as was Khomeini, the province of Fars. They worked together for many years and Montazeri had been Khomeini's chief contact and spokesman in Iran during the time of exile, when Khomeini was an expatriate in Iraq and then in France. By telephone from near Paris, Khomeini had directed the mullahs in Iran through Montazeri. It was through Montazeri that Khomeini directed the overthrow of the Pahlavi regime. Montazeri had echoed Khomeini's cries from France to the mullahs and throughout Iran. `Death to the Shah. No compromise. Rivers of blood,' until the Shah went into exile and Khomeini returned to Iran in triumph.

"Montazeri has the support of the Shiite leadership of south central Iran, including the very influential provinces of Fars, Yazd and Isfahan. His position is that he has been selected by Khomeini as successor and he intends to continue with the practices and views of Khomeini, which include a perspective that the United States and the Soviet Union are both sinful, evil devils. Both are enemies of Islam and both are to be scorned by those who support Allah. Every soul and all energy should be spent to advance, deepen and expand the interests of Shiite Moslem fundamentalism. There is considerable support, probably majority support in Iran for Montazeri's views. Iranian President Hojatolislam Ali Khamenei has indicated support for Montazeri which brings together some of the strongest political influence and the strongest religious influence in Iran. The combination of President Khamenei and Montazeri is a seemingly overwhelming force for control, but that control does not appear to be effective."

Major Thompson continued with his intell briefing to the clearly confused chiefs of staff.

"Another powerful political force centers around the Speaker of the Iranian Parliament, not an ayatollah, Hojatolislam Hashemi Rafsanjani, who has been known for some time to be a leading candidate to take over after Khomeini and if he can get the support of one or more of the powerful ayatollahs, he could have the clout to take over. But in Iran fact and myth, practicality and fantasy, reality and imagination often blend into one and take a shape suitable for the occasion or the individual's preference. Khomeini may very well have selected Montazeri as his successor, but other ayatollahs and mullahs prefer otherwise and have proclaimed it so.

"Ayatollah Bakhari Zenderasem comes from the province of Gilan near the Eiburz Mountains of northern Iran along the Caspian Sea. His parents had told him of the once grand opportunity their people had for happiness and freedom in 1920 when the Soviet Socialist Republic of Gilan existed briefly. Then Russian soldiers departed and the Iranian harsh rule returned.

"Zenderasem was raised as a devout Shiite, entered the ministry and rose modestly in the hierarchy until he attached himself to Khomeini. Now, as a high ayatollah himself, he sees a means to more power and greater prosperity for the people of Gilan by associating himself with interests sympathetic to the Soviet Union. He has openly courted Soviet support and claims that the United States, Great Britain and France have caused the decline and ruin of Persian and Islamic culture. He claims to represent the best interests of Islam and that which Khomeini would have come around to in a few years, which is the recognition that only with Soviet support can Shiite fundamentalism flourish in an Iran kept free of United States evil influence."

Twenty stars squirmed in their comfortable chairs as Major Thompson continued. "Ayatollah Gholam Fattachian is from East Azerbaijan and was involved as a young priest in the short-lived Independent Republic of Azerbaijan in 1946-47. He had visited the Soviet Union and had welcomed their influence and even the presence of Soviet troops during that time. He sees the Soviet Union first as the great protector against the religious abuses of the Pahlavis, and now against the western immorality of the United States. In his many years of close association with Khomeini, Fattachian always advocated closer ties with the Soviets, while during the same time he talked about an independent nation of East and West Azerbaijan to the mullahs and priests in those provinces. With Khomeini gone, Fattachian sees the opportunity to establish that independent state with himself as ayatollah and, later, after Soviet support is no longer required, to seek union with the Azerbaijanies of the Soviet Union. To accomplish all this, Fattachian is willing to give his support to any ayatollah that would back the independence of Azerbaijan in return for that support. By Fattachian's analysis Montazeri is the front runner, so to outsiders it appears that the powerful ayatollah of East Azerbaijan supports Montazeri as Khomeini's successor.

"From West Azerbaijan comes Ayatollah Borushir Ghormezian, a fanatic Shiite Islamic fundamentalist, more-so that had been Khomeini. Ghormezian advocates even more strict cultural controls. He realizes that only with a strong internal police force and a powerful protector outside of Iran could he impose the strict religious interpretations on a people still soft from the Pahlavi regime and western influences."

The assembled four-stars were having trouble keeping up with the ayatollahs and their complex names and backgrounds but Major Thompson went on. "Ghormezian is determined to take over the position occupied by Khomeini and to establish in a united Iran the strictest Shiite Moslem fundamentalist society the world has ever known. To accomplish this he knows that he has to overcome the ambitions of some of the influential and ambitious ayatollahs and gain the support of others. He is prepared to have those who stand in his way killed and he has organized a number of dedicated people for that purpose. Regardless of his methods, he knows that Allah will reward him for his service in bringing the true meaning of Islam to Iran.

"Ayatollah Jamshid Montaheb comes from the province of Bushehr, along the Persian Gulf. Bushehr is a mixture of many peoples and has been active in trade with the outside world over the centuries. Montaheb's political strength is based on his reputation for representing the beliefs and needs of a variety of ethnic peoples. He favors a relaxation of the hard lines against the United States and the Soviet Union. Probably the most progressive and liberal of the influential ayatollahs, Montaheb is known to have been in ill favor with Khomeini. Because of this, Montaheb is not considered a very serious or popular competitor in his struggle for power, but he is influential and has the backing of wealthy Shiites along the Persian Gulf. He can only be considered a long shot as far as taking over as the Grand Ayatollah of a united Iran, but if he were to give his support to one of the other competitors it would be significant. Also, in a divided Iran he would be the likely leader of Bushehr Province, along the Persian Gulf, which would be very important to U.S. interests.

"Ayatollah Mahmud Shariatavardi comes from the southeast province of Baluchistan and is also influential in neighboring Sistan and Saheli. Like Montaheb, he is a comparative moderate. Unlike Montaheb, Shariatavardi hates the Soviet Union but favors the United States. Shariatavardi would like to see relaxations in the strict Shiite fundamentalism of Khomeini. He sees the Soviet Union as the threat to Islam and to Iran and looks to the United States for support. His areas of influence include the port city of Bandar Abbas and the Iranian coast along the Strait of Hormuz and Gulf of Oman. The people and the mullahs of the north and east would probably not take Shariatavardi seriously as a candidate for the position as Grand Ayatollah of Iran, but his support, if given to one of the others would be significant and, again, in a divided Iran his influence in southeastern Iran would be very valuable for the U.S."

Major Thompson paused then turned from the map of Iran to the view-graph screen which now displayed an orderly summary of the ayatollahs as the four-stars breathed sighs of relief. "So, now it appears from the information available to us that there are at least six influential ayatollahs competing for the position formerly held by Khomeini," and he summarized them from the visual display:

"1. Montazeri, the most likely leader is anti-Soviet and anti-U.S. and stands for a continuation of Khomeini's regime.
2. Zenderasem, not a likely winner, pro-Soviet, anti-U.S., seeks to recreate a socialist republic in the north.
3. Fattachian; an unlikely successor but dangerous planner seeks an independent Azerbaijan nation, pro-Soviet, anti-U.S.
4. Ghormezian; a strong candidate, religious fanatic, anti-Soviet and anti-U.S., the most dangerous of the competitors as he could easily cause bloodshed.
5. Montaheb; moderate, weak candidate, pro-Soviet, pro-U.S., represents a key area.
6. Shariatavardi; moderate, anti-Soviet, pro-U.S., represents a key area."

Major Thompson looked at the military leaders of his country and a few seconds of silence followed until a general asked, "What about this large area in the east including the oil fields; Khuzistan, Luristan, Markazi, including Teheran, and in the west Khorasan? Are there ayatollahs controlling those areas?"

"Not to our knowledge," Replied Thompson. "But, General, please don't let me give you the impression that these ayatollahs control the areas I described. They are from those areas and derive most of their support from those areas. Each has influence in his area, but they have influence among peoples of many other areas of Iran as well. The areas you ask about are not represented by one dominant ayatollah. Many ayatollahs have influence in those areas. For instance Ghormezian, the fundamentalist fanatic from West Azerbaijan, probably has some supporters in distant Baluchistan."

Another four-star commented, "From what you've told us it appears that Montazeri is the only one with any chance of pulling it all together."

"His chances looked good with the support of some of the others, but now that seems to be questionable. Montazeri has tried to take over but he has to deal with separatist movements in Azerbaijan and Gilan, and he has to deal with the Kurdish independence already announced."

Still another four-star added, "And there could be further divisions within the country unless a strong leader comes along, strong enough to hold it together."

A few of them nodded agreement as the Chairman of the Joint Chiefs of Staff rubbed his chin. "We may be seeing the final division of a once great ancient empire, the division of Persia."

Some of them agreed and the Chairman thanked Major Thompson as the twenty stars turned their attention to other military matters.

CHAPTER 15

"So Shellback does what Shellback does best; total involvement, full immersion, doing what he knows is best, what has to be done, regardless of what anyone else, any authority orders otherwise. That's the Shellback style, his pattern. It seems like throughout his life he would find trouble. He never had to look for it because trouble would always find him." Barney was explaining his friend's adventure in the Indian Ocean to the family. "And now that he had this group of merchant ships at sea, trying to evade a threat that he knew virtually nothing about, with nothing to protect them with and no support from any other navy resource, he set about taking care of them himself."

Steven was listening carefully. "Protection, you said. What kind of protection could he provide?"

Barney smiled. "Well, you have to realize that your dad could improvise and knew how to make lemonade from lemons. So, when he needed protection for a group of unarmed ships, ships without any weapons, he reasoned that these ships were carrying hundreds of containers and rolling stock with all the weapons that would be needed for a Marine Brigade. It was only a matter of finding out what they needed and where they were, that is if they could get to what they needed in those close packed ships."

Steven frowned. "Containers, he couldn't go into those containers, could he? That's cargo, and the trucks, and even tanks, I guess. Artillery, there must have been howitzers and ammunition, too, but he wouldn't be allowed to get at that stuff, would he?"

Barney laughed. "Right you are, son of Shellback, but remember who *we're talking about. This is Martin Shielbrock and do you think he would hesitate or seek permission to use anything he needed? Helicopters for example, he felt that he needed them and so, hook or crook, he went about getting them. He hooked them and he crooked them. First he got the use of them and then he, more or less, stole them, but as a result he ended up with a small measure of air support. And weapons? Let me tell you how he got weapons."*

INDIAN OCEAN, EAST NORTH EAST OF DIEGO GARCIA

It was early evening two hours before sunset as Irving Cappleton, Master of the motor vessel Anderson, filled his coffee cup and walked across the Pilot House to join the others as the Convoy Commodore, Captain Shielbrock, had called a meeting on the starboard side. Eight others were already there including the woman and the three reserve officers.

The officer-in-charge of the helicopter detachment Lieutenant Commander Bob Ryan was angry. "Commodore, you asked me to run a few errands and I did. You invited me to stay awhile and offered fuel and I accepted both but now I find that we're too far from Diego Garcia for me to get back and we're not getting any closer. As a matter of fact we're getting further away!"

"Yes, Bob, you're right. We're too far for you to get back there. You'll have to stay on board here, with us."

"Commodore, I get the idea—."

"Yes, Bob, you've got it right. I tricked you."

The OinC was even more angry than before. "I'm supposed to be back in Diego Garcia for my SAR duties. I'm not supposed to be out here."

"That's right. I understand that. The first order of business for which I called this meeting is to clarify your position and mine relative to your being here."

"What do you mean?"

"I want to explain in front of these witnesses that I deliberately arranged for your two helicopters to be stranded here with me. I know you are supposed to be at Diego Garcia and that you want to be back there but I feel that it's more important for you to be here. I accept full responsibility for putting you in this position. There is at least one boat that we know of out here, probably looking for us and armed with missiles. There may very well be others. We have no protection. The only way we can avoid them is to stay on the move. It would be a tremendous advantage for us if we had some kind of area surveillance. The radars on these ships can cover out to fifteen or twenty miles at best. Your helos could give us much more coverage, maybe out to fifty miles. With that kind of alertment we could turn away and run from these boats. If we can come up with some weapons we'd have time to protect ourselves." Shielbrock stopped and looked at the pilot who was still angry. "I'm asking you to join us. Be our air wing commander. Help us put together a protective system. We have weapons on board these ships." The OinC looked at him with doubt as Shielbrock continued, "Marine Corps weapons. I don't know much about them but we have people here that do. We have to figure out what's available and try to arm ourselves."

"How?" The helo OinC asked. "Are you planning to go into those containers?"

"Before we get to the `how' let's take care of the question of your involvement. Will you help us?"

The OinC looked at the other pilot. "Jeff, what do you think?"

"Shit, Bob, why not? We're here anyway and this could be better than watching old westerns on the rock."

Bob Ryan looked back at Shielbrock. "Surface surveillance flights, is that what you want?"

"Yes, but there's more. I'll have some people and messages to move and we'll be looking at ways to arm you."

"Arm me, with what?"

"I don't know yet, but we've got this Marine Corps stinger team,"He pointed to the sergeant who came on Bird One, "And some others who know a lot about the weapons stored in containers in this ship." Shielbrock pointed to a big rough looking man in his fifties wearing coveralls.

"I'd have to know more about what you plan for us before I jump in. I'm concerned about this business of arming us. Our birds aren't set up to carry weapons."

"Okay and I have no idea what if any weapons we have that may be suitable for your helos. How about this? Suppose you agree to go along with us for now. We'll see how the planning goes. If you don't like it at anytime you just say so and that'll be the end of it."

Ryan thought awhile, silent.

"I'll make you a better deal," Shielbrock continued. "You stay with us for twenty four hours from now, work with us, plan with us, fly a little surveillance. If after that time you say you want out, I'll do what I can, if I can, to get us close enough for you to fly home to Diego Garcia."

Ryan looked at Jeff who shrugged with a "why not" gesture and raised eyebrows and the OinC replied, "Okay. We'll see how it goes."

"Good." Shielbrock then turned to the Marine sergeant. "All of you should know Sergeant Kramer by now. He and his team came to us on Bob and Jeff's helos. They teach people how to use stinger. That's a surface-to-air hand-held missile." Kramer was nodding his head. "And he reminded me that there are a lot of the missiles packaged up in shipping containers somewhere in this ship."

Kramer spoke up, "That's right and there's a lot of other stuff, too, in those containers."

"Yeah," Cappleton offered, "but we ain't allowed to break into them containers. That's cargo and we can't touch it."

Shielbrock replied, "Under normal circumstances, Captain, we wouldn't touch the cargo but these are not normal circumstances. We have no protection and we carry a cargo of weapons. I'm sure that if we had a way to ask the Commandant of the Marine Corps, he would allow us to use just a few items to protect all of his equipment."

"No sir. Nobody messes with the cargo." Cappleton was firm.

The others looked from Cappleton to Shielbrock, who sighed. "Captain Cappleton, I take full responsibility for the authorization of the use of equipment carried as cargo in your ship to be used as protection."

Cappleton looked at Shielbrock awhile, slowly took a cigarette from his shirt pocket, put it into his mouth, chewed it up and worked the cud over to one side to speak. "You got that authority, Commodore?"

Shielbrock looked him straight in the eye. "You're God Damn right I have."

Cappleton looked back at him a moment. "Okay, Commodore, your responsibility."

"Okay," Shielbrock continued, "I'd like you all to know Mr. Sawyer." He gestured toward the big rough looking guy in coveralls. "Mr. Sawyer is here on board Anderson in charge of six other men as employees of the Bendix Corporation. Bendix has a contract to provide maintenance and supply support for all the Marine Corps equipment on board all these MPS ships. Before Mr. Sawyer went to work for Bendix he was Master Gunnery Sergeant Byron Sawyer, United States Marine Corps."

The others in the Pilot House all smiled. "The other six of his Bendix team have similar Marine Corps backgrounds. They are all retired Marines with twenty to thirty years service and he assures me that between them they know how to operate every weapon and every piece of equipment in this cargo."

Bob Ryan spoke up. "Okay! Hey, what have we got for my helo?"

Before Sawyer could answer Shielbrock stepped in, "Hold on Bob. That has to be worked out. Now, what I would like is to form a team to determine just what Bob asked and other requirements and capabilities." Turning to the ship's Master, "Captain Cappleton, would you authorize your Chief Mate to work with this team? He has records and looks after the cargo so he seems to be a natural guy for determining what we have and where it's located. Also, he can keep you informed concerning any cargo disruption."

"Yeah, he'll work with them."

"Good. Now, I think Sergeant Kramer should be on the team, Bob Ryan, Tim Smith from my staff and of course By Sawyer." They all nodded as Shielbrock continued, "Let me add, here, that from now on the proper title will be Top Sawyer. Will that be all right, Top?"

"That'll be just fine, Commodore."

"Now, before this weapon team goes off to put their heads together, I want you all to understand what we are up against. We don't want just any weapons or a lot of weapons. I want you to understand that we are dealing with a threat posed by one to five boats with short range missiles. I want to detect them early if we can, evade them if we can, shoot them if we have to from a helo or from our own deck. Keep it simple and easy to man. We only have a few people so nothing sophisticated. Okay?"

They all agreed and Kramer and Sawyer asked questions concerning Shielbrock's understanding of the threat, time of response, ranges, size and speeds of the boats and as most of the information wasn't known, some he estimated as discussion went on for a half hour or so.

They were about to break up and go into their team meeting but Shielbrock wasn't finished. "One other thing," They all looked at him. "You may have noticed this lady taking notes." He indicated and they all looked at the woman. "This is Kim McManus, a journalist. She's here to do a story on whatever this is we're doing." The others smiled. "She has CHINFO approval and I want you to know that she has my full and complete support. We're not involved with anything classified here, so far, just some sensitive information. So, we can all answer her questions freely, anything she asks." Kim smiled at him. Was that a sparkle in her eyes? "She'll be taking notes, using her little recording machine and taking pictures, and all that is fine. Additionally, she'll be performing a very worthwhile function for us. She'll be keeping a detailed log. So, if any of you don't want to talk to her about what you're doing, you will have volunteered to be the keeper of the log." They all laughed.

"Kim, I'm appointing you our official recorder, historian and log keeper. If there's a story in it for you later, you're welcome to it. Just make your team mates here look good."

They all laughed again and Kim bowed to Shielbrock. "I accept the prestigious appointment with all humility and will do my best to justify your trust and confidence, Commodore, and will do my best to make all of you look good." Then as an afterthought she added, "Within the bounds of accurate journalism of course."

They laughed again and were leaving the pilot house as the Radio Officer came in and handed Shielbrock a teletype paper. "I've been copying press for awhile and thought you'd like to see this."

Shielbrock read the paper and handed it to the others. "Iran is in a state of anarchy. There's a power struggle going on among the ayatollahs."

The chart showed a square fifty miles on a side, the southwest corner a hundred miles east north east of Diego Garcia and Shielbrock had directed his three staff officers to keep the formation in that square or on it's perimeter with as little maneuvering as possible. Thirteen ships were now in the formation; the original twelve that were scheduled for the Rainbow Reef Exercise plus the late joiner, Green Valley, and they were in a broad front rectangular formation, the basic convoy formation that had been used for merchant ships in World Wars I and II. Perhaps it was not the most practical formation against a modern threat or even the threat projected in the vicinity of Diego Garcia, as Shielbrock had explained to his staff but in this case he used the broad front rectangular formation because it was well understood by the Masters and Mates of the ships and was easy to form. Later, like the next day, they would put the ships into a random formation but that should be done in daylight and would take about six hours.

Monday night they were formed with the five MPS ships across the front, beam to beam, two thousand yards between ships with each ship identified by its station number and the stations of the first row were lettered, left to right, A through E. Fisher was A1, Hauge B1, Anderson was flagship and guide in C1, Baugh was D1, and Bonnyman E1. Two thousand yards astern of each of the MPS ships was one of the chartered merchant ships forming the second row, identified as A2, B2, C2, D2, E2 and a third row that consisted of the late arrival Green Valley in A3, and chartered ships in C3 and E3. Station keeping was relatively easy in this formation as ships in the first row kept station on Anderson. Ships in the second and third row followed the ship ahead, maintaining their distance.

At twelve knots the formation steamed for about four hours, then executed two forty-five degree turns to stay on the perimeter of the fifty mile square as Shielbrock's staff officers performed this function in his name as Convoy Commodore; "Team this is Bull. Signals follow. Execute to follow. One three five whiskey. Repeat. One three five whiskey. Over."

All thirteen ships answered in alpha-numeric order, "This is Alfa One. Roger. Out."

"This is Bravo One. Roger. Out."

"This is Charlie One. Roger. Out," And so on.

Then the second row, "This is Alfa Two. Roger. Out."

"This is Bravo Two. Roger. Out."

"This is Charlie Two. Roger. Out," And so on into the third row with finally, "This is Echo Three. Roger. Out."

The staff watch officer kept track of the responses to ensure that all thirteen ships had the signal then three to five minutes were provided for the ships to determine their action and the signal was executed with, "Team this is Bull. One three five whiskey. Standby. Execute. Alfa Three, Echo Three, Over."

In this case the officer putting out the signal asked only ships Alfa Three and Echo Three to respond so there were only two replies. "This is Alfa Three. Roger. Out."

"This is Echo Three. Roger. Out."

The signal called for a turn of the formation to the new course, a heading of one three five degrees true using a wheeling motion in which ships in the columns toward the inside of the turn slowed two knots less than the signaled speed, the center or guide's column slowed one knot and the outside columns maintained speed. The ships followed around and remained in the same broad front rectangular formation on the new heading, much like a company of marching troops in a parade going around a corner, "Column left, `harch!" Even though these were experienced Masters and Mates, a "whiskey" turn took about half an hour to complete and required constant attention to shiphandling and careful station keeping. Shielbrock explained to his staff that when they were in the random formation they would make course changes with a "tango" turn, in which all ships came to the new heading at the same time and that would be much faster.

The three staff officers stood with Shielbrock at the chart table on the starboard side of the Pilot House, each with one of the hand held portable VHF radios that Tim Smith had brought back on the helo and Shielbrock took the radio from Lieutenant Commander John Harvey.

"Okay, here's how we're going to put out tactical signals. Let's say for this demonstration John, here, is the staff watch officer."

"I'm on watch right now."

Shielbrock laughed, "Good. It's hard to tell, 'cause the three of you have been up here like you're all on watch, all day."

"Well, this is where the action is," Offered the other lieutenant commander, Al Bevins.

"Right," Shielbrock was pleased with their eagerness. "It may work out that you'll all be up here most of the time but somehow we'll get you some rest."

"I don't think we have to worry about that just now." Al was the senior of the three reservists.

"Fine. Tactical signals. Here's how we'll do them. John, here, as the watch officer will put out the signal on the bridge VHF set as in ATP Two Volume Two." He referred to the unclassified book which contained convoy signals and was held by each ship. "Before he starts talking, one of you out on the port wing, the other on the starboard wing, will start putting out meaningless tactical signals, one on a channel just below, the other just above the channel John is using."

John and Al looked confused as Tim Smith spoke up. "One channel above and one channel below with the designated channel, the real one, in between?"

"That's right. We'll call it the sandwich system. Do you know why we're going to use this sandwich system?"

The three gave negative replies but then Tim offered that it had to be some kind of deception but to what purpose he couldn't tell. "Wouldn't three transmissions be easier to detect than one?"

"Maybe so," Shielbrock gave his reasoning. "We're dealing with a third world low technology threat here. If it were a Soviet threat they might have sophisticated electronic intercept equipment to detect and sort through all our signals. But this low-tech threat I am assuming has nothing more than a commercial marine band VHF transceiver. He'll search the channels up and down until he hears us. Then he'll listen on that channel. At best he might have a frequency scanner. I doubt it, but even if he does, it works the same way, up and down the scale until it hears a signal. Then it stops while the operator listens. In our sandwich system we cover the real signal, the meat, with two slices of bread, one over and one under. We hope that if someone is trying to listen they get one of our covers, a slice of stale bread, not the real meat."

"Hey, sounds good." "Okay." The three officers were pleased.

"Now I'd like the three of you, well—, maybe we'd better let John here look after the flock, the two of you make up some false signals that sound real. False call signs, misdirections, you know and if a course is given always make the false course much different, nearly opposite from our real course."

Bevins and Smith went to work writing out the false signals and Tim turned to Shielbrock. "So that's why you wanted those extra radios."

"That's part of it."

All night they steamed around the square and one of the helos conducted a surveillance flight before each formation course change, seeing nothing on the dark sea as Shielbrock's thirteen were the only ships in that part of the Indian Ocean.

Off to the west, heading east, Ahmad Bakhari at the wheel of an 80 foot fishing boat had decided to stay well clear to the north of Diego Garcia, so the island remained out of sight to the south of them as sunset approached. Ghermeziat was scanning the VHF channels, hoping to get some indication of the American ships and Nafouzi, the assistant engineer, was trying to get some news from Baghdad on the big radio. His missile equipment carefully checked and ready, Moses Farscian went to help Nafouzi with the radio, for news from home, news of the attack. Where were the other five fishing boats? Had they attacked on schedule?

Were they late or lost? How was their country faring in the war against Iran?

But it was Teheran radio that came in with news. That news was not from Iraq, it was Iranian news that they were forbidden to hear but they knew enough Farsi to follow what was being said. "Leave it on," Yelled Bakhari their captain. "It'll be better than nothing and who will know out here?"

It was the President of Iran himself speaking in Farsi, Hojatolislam Ali Khamenei, asking for the people to remain calm, to keep order, to maintain their dedication to Allah and to the Republic and the fishing boat crew looked at each other questioningly, asking what the problems of Iran were. They had missed the first part of the broadcast and were trying to piece it together from what they could hear. Then came, "—and as Allah chose in his infinite wisdom to call the most holy of holy men, our beloved Ayatollah Khomeini to his side, we must now look for a new Grand Ayatollah to lead us."

A new Grand Ayatollah? What has happened in Iran? They don't have a Grand Ayatollah? The fishing boat crew all thought that a Grand Ayatollah ran Iran, so did that mean that no one was in charge anymore in Iran?

The diesel engine of the 80 foot fishing boat droned on as they proceeded east and they sat silently as the radio continued to pour forth pleas for restoration of order, maintenance of civility, loyalty and dedication to Khomeini's principles. The boat engineer Borujerdi came up from the engine compartment and joined the others listening silently. They had been listening to Ali Khamenei for over an hour and they knew not how much longer before that he had been speaking, but finally he finished and a regular announcer of the Iranian News Service came on with a news broadcast.

Fighting was light on the Iraq front but even so heavy casualties had been inflicted on the Iraqis. Losses on the Iranian side were very light. Morale was high among our fighting men despite the reports of unrest in Iran, and so the news went. It was similar in optimism and reported success to that which they normally heard, but this was from the other, not their Iraqi side. At the end of the news broadcast the announcer introduced a holy man, the Ayatollah Mahmud Shariatavardi, whose name meant nothing to the fishing boat crew and a half hour was taken by that ayatollah to describe the credits of the deceased Grand Ayatollah

Khomeini, to continue sympathy to all the people in his loss. "—but, loyal followers of the holy Khomeini, our beloved leader who now sits at Allah's table and feasts on his deserved life's rewards for all eternity, loyal followers, we must be careful of whom we put our trust in as his successor."

The crewmen looked at each other questioningly. "Who's in charge? Do they have a leader?"

The Iranian ayatollah continued, "There are pretenders who have come forth with false claims and ask you to accept them, to follow them, to grant unto them the love, admiration, loyalty and dedication that you have so willingly and faithfully bestowed on the holy Khomeini. Beware of these pretenders.

"There are power hungry men in holy garments who walk our sacred land and talk of divinity but underneath their sacred robes and taut skin are hearts of evil—." The ayatollah continued to warn the public of false leaders and it confused and bewildered the fishing boat crewmen. What did he mean? Who were these so called devils who would try to lead Iran astray and would that not be good for Iraq?

Ayatollah Shariatavardi told them a chilling story, a story of failure, poorly planned, poorly led, poorly carried out; a military-naval undertaking that was shocking in the stupidity of its concept and the fishing boat crewmen listened all the more carefully, pale faced, somber, staring.

Shariatavardi told of a group of men assembled and trained to go forth and strike at enemies of the Islamic Republic. They were given weapons and boats for the task. The men chosen for the task were the wrong men. They were of doubtful loyalty and questionable background. They had no dedication to the cause or expertise in their roles. They received inadequate training. They had no leadership. The weapons with which they were provided were not appropriate for the task. The boats they were given could not reach the target area. The entire operation was a failure, a waste of Islamic lives, a waste of scarce resources, an embarrassment and humiliation for the beloved Islamic Republic.

"Do the Iranians have an operation going just like ours? Nafouzi asked the question that had come to the minds of all.

"He's, he's talking about us!" Ghermeziat shouted.

"Shut up and listen," Bakhari barked as the radio voice of Shariatavardi continued.

"Responsibility for this humiliation does not lie on the shoulders of those who were chosen, tried and failed. They are but pawns of power hungry evil pretenders. The villain of this act is a man who parades himself as a holy man and a loyal former follower of our beloved Khomeini. Actually, this evil man acted in a way that has brought humiliation to the name of the holy one and to all of us.

"The one it is my sad duty to tell you of is a false ayatollah, a man who once was revered but now proves himself to be an agent of the devil. I speak of," He hesitated for effect, "One known to you as Hossein Ali Montazeri—."

"Allah's Eyes, what is he saying? Who are these people?" Moses Farscian asked the question and received a "Shut up" from Bakhari.

Shariatavardi went on to describe the operation planned for Diego Garcia, told of its failure, loss of lives, broken down boats and the humiliation it caused. He told that it made the Americans look and feel invincible, gave them added resolve and anger toward Iran. His talk went on for another hour, ended with a prayer and then there was just radio static as the fishing boat crewmen sat silently in the dim cabin light as they had been while listening until Farscian went over and turned off the radio. Still the engine droned on and their boat headed slowly east in the dark night.

Ghermeziat was the first to speak. "We've been tricked. We've been used. This whole operation has been a farce. We've risked our lives for nothing. We've just—." His voice drifted off into silence until the engineer Borujerdi spoke up. "He said we were bad people, no loyalty, bad backgrounds. He said we weren't trained right, couldn't do our jobs."

Farscian gave his own interpretation. "Look, we're Iraqis sent on a mission by the Iraq navy and army. Remember, we're supposed to pass ourselves off as Iranian and we've got Iranian flags and papers. He said," Moses pointed to the now silent radio, "That there was an operation against Diego Garcia by Iran. That can't be us, but even if he is talking about us, he said there was loss of lives and failure. I guess that means that the others, or some other fishing boats, didn't make it. Maybe ours was the only attack as little as it was."

"I wonder," Ghermeziat thought aloud, "How does this one ayatollah know about another's plans and results."

"Yeah," Nafouzi looked up. "How can this Shariatavardi know that we've or others have failed while we're still out here hunting?"

Bakhari had been silent until now. "Ayatollahs have ways to find out things, ways we wouldn't know about. If he knew the attack was supposed to be on the twenty first and there was no news of an attack then he'd know it failed."

A long period of silence followed until Moses Farscian spoke. "Well, I wouldn't want to make a liar out of a holy man and maybe this entire operation was put together to fail and maybe there's another similar Iranian operation but I say we're out here to do a job, we still have some missiles left, so let's try to carry out our mission."

The others agreed and were discussing their situation as Ghermeziat went back to the VHF radio and started again to search the channels and a half hour later he called out. "Hey, Moses! Come here! I got an American voice," And Moses ran over and listened.

"—I say again, Racetrack this is Delta. Time of entry first ship zero five three zero. Order of entry follows: Romeo Three, Romeo Two, Sierra One, Sierra Two,—," and the voice went on giving call signs as Farscian wrote down what was being said. It was followed by a series of "Roger. Out," Then static as Moses Farscian walked over to Bakhari who was still at the wheel. They discussed the radio intercept and agreed that it was a group of American ships preparing to enter port early in the morning, as the "order of entry" and the "time of entry first ship zero five three zero" indicated, so it had to be their target group. The series of Romeos and Sierras with numbers had to be call-ups for each ship and it made sense as they had seen the big ships depart, now they were preparing to go back into port.

Bakhari slowed the engine to idle speed and looked at the chart with Farscian. "Here we are along the southern edge of the Great Chagos Bank. We've been heading east. The American ships have to be out there," He pointed east, "And not very far from us, maybe twenty five or thirty miles. That's as far as we could hear them on the VHF radio. They're headed for Diego Garcia probably, from what we just heard. It could be one of those freaks of radio, you know, where the transmission carries far over the horizon. I don't know what causes it but every once in a while you can pick up a VHF signal from a ship far away." Bakhari arched his hand in an up and over motion.

Farscian nodded. "The Americans call it atmospherics, I think."

"What's that mean?"

"I'm not sure, but I think it has something to do with the air, the mixture of gases, the temperature and moisture at different levels, something like that. It causes radio signals to go in different directions rather than straight lines."

"Well, I don't give a goat shit what causes it. All I'm saying is that we could be listening to a group of ships far away. Maybe they're not the ships from Diego Garcia."

"What other group of American Navy ships would be here?"

"Who in Allah's eyes knows? The Americans have thousands of ships. They're getting ready to invade us so there might be another group of their ships here."

Farscian thought awhile before replying. "Well, any of their ships that we could hit would be good, wouldn't it?"

Bakhari looked back at him. "I'd be happy to hit their admirals' wives' fishing boat if that's all we could find."

Farscian nodded in agreement as Bakhari continued, "If we keep going we could easily miss them in the dark but we know they're going here." He pointed to Diego Garcia. "That's where we can get them."

"Uh huh." Farscian continued to listen.

"So, what I'm thinking is this; We go back west a ways to Egmont Island here," He pointed it out on the chart." And hide out there until tomorrow night. Then, in the dark, we run over to Diego Garcia and hit them in the lagoon at anchor."

"Why don't we just loiter here? It'll be less distance to get to Diego Garcia."

"Because then we'd be too easy to spot by an airplane or a ship if they send one out. At this little island, it's just nothing but a few rocks, we'll be harder to spot, especially by radar."

"You think maybe they'll have some protection since we already hit them?"

"Maybe, probably not. They probably think we ran away for good. If that talk by that Iranian Ayatollah Shariatavardi gets interpreted and sent to them they'll think for sure that we're finished."

"I hope you're right."

"Hey, Farscian."

"Yes."

"All this time I've been insulting you, calling you names, you know—."

"Yeah, I know."

"Well, I've thought all along that they should have used navy men for this operation. Why army and why fishermen?"

"Well," Moses thought awhile, "I've asked myself the same question, but if what that ayatollah says is so, they picked us to fail."

"Yeah, if its' us he was talking about, but y'know, we didn't really completely fail. We got there. We hit a ship, caused some damage. We didn't completely fail and we're not through yet."

Farscian agreed with a grunt.

Bakhari continued, "Maybe we can show 'em that we're not so bad, after all. What do y'think?"

"Well, I don't like being picked out as an unreliable bad guy. I've served long and well. We've come a long ways and I'd like to do the best we can. That's all we can do." Moses paused a while, "You know, there must be ayatollahs that can't be trusted, too, like everyone else. Who is this Ayatollah Shariatavardi? I can't keep track of all those Iranians. You ever heard of him?"

"No, I never heard of any Iranian ayatollahs except that bad one, Grand Ayatollah Khomeini, but really, y'know you can't trust any of them."

"Can't trust an ayatollah?"

"Yeah, you can't believe all the gossip."

Bakhari turned the boat from the east heading all the way around toward the northwest, toward tiny Egmont Island, sixty miles away. He couldn't have known it but he had been heading directly for Shielbrock's fifty mile square and was thirty miles from the MPS ships when he turned away.

Lieutenant commanders Harvey and Bevins came back into Anderson's Pilot House after the tactical signal for the whiskey turn had gone out and executed. "What did you put out?" Bevins asked.

"I used a series of station assignments that would form us up in a circular formation. What did you use?"

"I put out an order of entry into port. Do you think any of this really does any good?

"Well, I don't know. It can't hurt and it just might confuse someone trying to find us."

"Maybe so." Bevins reply was without conviction.

The sun had not yet peeked over the horizon, but the imminence of that event was clear as beautiful shades of gray, light blue and pink colored the eastern sky and to the west it was still dark, a black sea against a dark gray sky. Gradually the light would spread across from east to west, and the horizon would become more clear. Brighter and more colorful, the eastern sky attracted the attention of Lieutenant Commander John Harvey, the staff watch officer who turned to Shielbrock, who had been dozing in his Pilot House chair. "Red sky in the morning, sailor take warning, isn't that the rule?"

Shielbrock looked east. "Don't believe it. Last night the sky was red and the other half of that saying is, 'red sky at night, sailors delight.' Out here the weather never learned that poem. This is the North East Monsoon season. Its sailors delight every day."

Harvey looked around the horizon, stopping as he faced the darker direction. "Look!" He pointed west south west. "Look! Is that smoke?"

A tall plume of heavy black smoke was on the horizon, far away, but visible against the gray sky as Shielbrock went to the bridge radar repeater. "Take a visual bearing on the base of that smoke and lay it on the chart from our position." Harvey went out on the wing of the bridge and was back in a few seconds as Shielbrock looked up from the radar "Nothing on the radar."

Harvey walked to the chart. "Two four nine," He announced as he plotted the bearing from their ship's position. "It plots for Diego Garcia, hundred and ten miles from us."

Shielbrock checked the chart. "That has to be a hell of a fire if we can see the smoke at a hundred and ten miles."

The Mate on watch joined them as the three looked at the smoke. "There's only two things at Diego could make that kind of smoke." The Mate was looking through his binoculars as he spoke. "The big fuel storage tanks ashore or a ship."

John Harvey offered, "Maybe a terrorist got to the fuel tanks."

Shielbrock replied, "Maybe, or maybe the boat that attacked us went back or another boat got in and hit a tanker like Overseas Valdez."

The Mate still had his binoculars on the smoke. "A tanker like Valdez could put up smoke like that. He's not carrying crude, y'know, like the tankers in Persian Gulf trade. He's got diesel and stuff like diesel. It's easier t'get burnin' than crude. Not that it just goes up, y'know, like gasoline would. It'd take a hot burn to start it and the ship has an inert gas blanket system for protection, but once it gets burnin' y'can't stop it, specially if y'get a rupture of the tank. That gets air to the oil. Y'get air, oil and a starter, y'got a hell of a fire."

Egmont Island was nothing more than a large rock with dozens of smaller rocks nearby and seagulls that had over the centuries covered the rocks with their droppings were the only inhabitants. Drifting at a safe distance off the rocks was the 80 foot fishing boat as engineer Borujerdi and his assistant Nafouzi had been working to clear a clogged fuel line ever since the engine stopped three hours ago, but it was not a crisis for them as they had been dealing with contaminated fuel that plugged filters and clogged fuel lines off and on since they left Basra. This time the boat would loiter away the day near these rocks, a good time to do a thorough cleaning.

Ghermeziat had spent the night, well, most of it, listening on the VHF radio and had slept a couple of hours as Bakhari had dozed at the wheel after they reached Egmont Island. Early dawn and banging on a fuel line fitting by the engineers awakened Moses Farscian and he stretched and yawned as he walked to the stern, looking at the colorful eastern sky as his eyes glanced toward the south east.

"Allah's eyes! Look!" He pointed toward a column of smoke on the horizon. The others heard him but could not see where he was pointing so Bakhari yelled from the cabin, "What? Where? What are you yelling about?" Then he too saw the smoke as Ghermeziat and the engineers ran to the stern joining Farscian.

Bakhari yelled again from the cabin. "That's smoke from an oil fire. You know what that means?" He didn't wait for an answer. "It means one of our boats hit a ship. One of our guys with Allah's blessing got a hit, maybe more than one."

The others cheered, laughed, jumped up and down and clapped each other on the back, except Farscian who went forward to Bakhari at the wheel. "Are you sure? You can't be sure. There's smoke, a fire, there," He pointed toward the smoke," But is that Diego Garcia and is it a ship? We don't know that."

Bakhari was angry like he used to get before their attack. "Look, mud-rutter," He pulled a chart over. "Here we are and here's Diego Garcia, see?" He pointed to the compass. "Southeast of us is Diego Garcia. Our boats should have hit two days ago. We were there yesterday. We were a day late. One or all of them could a'bin two days late. It can't be a coincidence. The direction is right. The timing is reasonable. The result is what we'd expect. It has to be one of our boats or more than one."

Farscian thought awhile, looking at the chart and at the smoke. "You're probably right. If you are it means one or more of our boats were attacking at Diego Garcia last night while we were idling our way here to Egmont Island."

They looked at each other awhile and Bakhari's anger had dissipated. "Maybe so, but we had no way to know that. We have to make our own plans as best we can and hope for Allah's help. Maybe we missed an attack opportunity. Maybe it is for us to serve later. Only Allah knows."

Moses Farscian walked away. "Yeah, only Allah knows." He thought once again that Allah was a great means of explaining away failure. "It was Allah's wish" was always used when things went wrong. How convenient.

CHAPTER 16

Steven Shielbrock sat back and sipped his ice tea. The family had been sitting on the patio listening to Barney Williams tell about the at-sea adventures of Steven's father in the Indian Ocean. What had started with an "undistinguished fleet exercise" at Diego Garcia had developed into a naval action with international ramifications.

The two ladies also sitting on the patio, wives of Barney and Steven, had listened quietly as Barney detailed the sea stories. Earlier, Jackie had contributed to the Shielbrock saga with colorful explanations of the "single girl" days in Norfolk.

Jackie sat back, looked at her daughter Ellie and said, "Let's get some lunch ready and let these sailors tell their sea stories." Ellie agreed and the ladies went into the condo.

Barney watched the ladies leave and turned to his son-in-law. "Well, Steven, they're going to miss some good parts of the Shellback adventure, but that's the way it goes." He thought for a while and before he could start his next tale Steven spoke. "How much of this Indian Ocean situation was known by higher authority? My dad was busy taking steps to avoid contact and to arm the merchant ships but did any one else know what was going on,—the threat,—the protection steps?"

"No, not all of it, just some, but about the time your dad was trying to put together some protection for the MPS ships in his convoy, there were some other developments that had major effects on his situation."

"Like what?" Steven asked.

"I'll tell you about it," Barney answered. "And you should know that

I made it a point to attend all of the briefings that I could in the OPCON center in the Pentagon, so I heard what the CNO heard, and his responses. He knew, that is the CNO, Admiral Frost, we called him Frosty but never to his face, he knew that I was tight with your dad and a few times he would ask me 'What do you think your friend will do now?' I would always say, 'He'll do what he thinks is right, Admiral, and what that is, is anybody's guess.'

"Frosty thought that Shellback was right to keep the MPS ships at sea rather than go back into Diego Garcia and that was important as events developed."

THE PENTAGON, ARLINGTON, VIRGINIA

"—and apparently the harbor patrol boat had just made a sweep from the channel at the northern end, which is really the only ship exit and entrance, down to the southern end of the lagoon. The fishing boat came in through the rocks and shoals on the north end, here." Lieutenant Woody Tompkins pointed to the detailed chart of Diego Garcia. "The tanker Overseas Valdez was anchored here. The fishing boat fired four TOW missiles at Overseas Valdez. At least two, maybe three hit starting a major fire in the cargo of aviation fuel. At about the time the TOW missiles were being fired, the harbor patrol boat attacked the fishing boat. The fishing boat fired five to ten shots from another type weapon at the patrol boat. As a result of the patrol boat firing, the fishing boat burst into flames, burned very quickly and was completely destroyed. Two survivors were picked up by the patrol boat. From information obtained from the survivors there had been three others in the fishing boat. One body has been recovered. Two others are missing and probably dead.

"The survivors are Iranian. They have been at sea at least three weeks and are in poor health. They are talking a lot but have told our people very little of value, but what we can put together matches with our earlier information.

"This fishing boat is one of the three that we earlier referred to as the Western Group. You'll remember that one of them was stopped at the Seychelles. This one; the one that entered the Diego Garcia lagoon, attacked Overseas Valdez and was destroyed by the patrol boat, had to slow earlier due to an engine problem. It didn't turn back nor did it go via the Seychelles as planned for fuel. It went direct from Masirah to Diego Garcia, arriving about two days later than the planned attack date and went right in and hit Overseas Valdez which was the only ship there."

Admiral Frost leaned forward in his chair. "Didn't you tell me yesterday that there was some controversy about the ships leaving or staying at anchor?"

"Yes sir. The convoy commodore ordered all of them, including two ships that weren't in the exercise, to leave port. All of the ships in the exercise had left port. Green Valley, one of the ships not in the exercise got underway, left the harbor and joined the others at sea. That makes a total of thirteen ships with the MPS convoy. The other ship that was not scheduled to be in the exercise, Overseas Valdez, remained at anchor in Diego Garcia."

Admiral Frost completed the thought, "—and got hit by the attacker."

"Yes sir. Also, you'll remember Admiral, that the convoy commodore was ordered to bring all of the ships back into port immediately after the attack, but he refused."

"Yes, I remember. Good for him and for us. Where is he now?"

The briefer, Lieutenant Tompkins, looked at the Watch Captain for help and from the side of the room the captain spoke up. "Admiral, we still have no secure communications with this group of ships, only HF clear—."

"So, are you telling me that you don't know where they are?"

"Well, uh, yes sir, but CTF seventy-two is sending a P-3 down there to find them and communicate with them. CTF seventy-three has ordered them back into Diego Garcia at least three times but we've seen nothing that indicates that the convoy commodore is doing so."

"Well, it looks to me like he's right. The only ship that didn't do as he said got hit and is still burning. A total loss. He's better off at sea until the situation—." The admiral's aide had been called to the rear of the room to take a message, now he leaned over and whispered into Admiral Frost's ear. The admiral looked at the aide and stood up. "I've got to get to the tank right away. Soviet troops have crossed the border into Iran."

Reports, rumors, assessments, suppositions, releases, statements, the network television news and newspapers were filled with Iran, and little of it agreed with any other sources as the only consistency was confusion, confliction and chaos amid rioting and anarchy.

Soviet troops were still moving into the provinces of East and West Azerbaijan, Gilan and Kurdistan, and Ayatollah Montazeri had come out of hiding and demanded over and over again that the Soviets withdraw. In East Azerbaijan the Ayatollah Fattachion welcomed the Soviets and his followers cheered them in the streets as similarly in Gilan, Ayatollah Zenderasem called upon his followers to welcome the Soviets as flowers were tossed in front of the tanks and trucks of the motorized rifle divisions.

Ayatollah Ghormezian called upon the people to resist the Soviets and there were reports of violence with Azerbaijaniis against each other and some against the Soviets.

From Bushehr, the moderate Ayatollah Montaheb was reported assassinated as he had pleaded with crowds for peace and order and Ghormezian's fanatics were being blamed for the death.

Ayatollah Shariatavardi still insisted that Montazeri was not the proper successor to Khomeini and that only he, Shariatavardi, could claim the title of Grand Ayatollah because of the improprieties of the others. In this claim he had the support of the Speaker of the Parliament, Hojatolislam Hashemi Rafsanjani, who had shifted his support away from Montazeri. Even the President of the Islamic Republic Ali Khamenei, no longer openly supported Montazeri but was remaining uncommitted, still asking the people for law and order, for patience, but it meant nothing. Prime Minister Mir Hussein Moussavi was believed to be in hiding or dead, as he had criticized the assassination of Montaheb and Ghormezian's fanatics were after him, or so it was reported.

Lead units of the Soviet move into Iran were crack airborne troops. These were already in former Iran fighting the followers of the President of the newly proclaimed Republic of Kurdistan, Abu Al Amuzagor, and at least twenty thousand Iranian troops had been shifted from the Iraq front to Kurdistan, first to put down the move toward Kurdish autonomy, then to deal with the Soviet para-troops.

Iraq also had withdrawn troops from the battle front with Iran, and these troops were being used to keep order among the Kurds on that side of the border as Turkish troops on their border were in the highest state of readiness.

Soviet news reports indicated that Iraqi and Turkish troops had crossed into Iranian Kurdistan, but these reports were denied by the two nations.

The people of the now divided Islamic Republic which had been Iran and before that Persia, were confused and alarmed with their political leaders non-committal. Their religious leaders were divided, competing for authority, offering no common guidance and the people fought among themselves each following the direction of a different leader. Accept the Soviets, welcome them. Fight the Soviets, resist them. Tolerate Kurdish autonomy, oppose it. Stay calm, riot in the streets. Anarchy prevailed.

In the midst of this chaos, the Ayatollah Mahmud Shariatavardi asked for the United States to provide a means to restore law and order and his request became a plea. He made a direct telephone call to the White House and although he did not get to speak to the President, he begged for the United States to put troops into Bandar Abbas which, he reasoned, would hold the Soviet invasion in the north and would restore order at least to the southern part of his land.

The American President hesitated until he received the same request from the Iranian President Ali Khamenei, then United States Marines of the Amphibious Ready Group in the northern Arabian Sea, about 1500 strong, went ashore at Bandar Abbas. An aircraft carrier battle group was there to support the landing. Marines of the first wave ashore were led by Colonel Don Rogerson. As they ran forward across the beach they were met by Ayatollah Mahmud Shariatavardi himself leading four thousand supplicants in prayers of thanks for an American salvation. That first wave of Marines stormed ashore, then stood silently with their helmets under their arms until the prayer service ended.

CHAPTER 17

Barney Williams leaned back in his patio chair under the big umbrella, took some deep breaths and continued his story. "So the Soviets were moving across the border into northern Iran with division sized military units, 20 to 30 thousand men we estimated, and we responded with 1500 marines in the south. Not enough for serious opposition of course, but maybe enough to prepare the airfield and port to receive a brigade sized force."

Steven responded, "Sounds right, but could we get a brigade there in time?"

"Oh yeah, we could," Barney answered. "We had had plans in place for years for just that sort of thing and that's where the MPS ships at Diego Garcia fit in. That's what they were all about. We can airlift a brigade of twenty thousand troops anywhere in the world, but their equipment; tanks, artillery, trucks, ammunition and all the other heavy logistics has to go by ships. That's why we have those prepositioned ships, MPS; Maritime Prepositioned Ships."

"How about the timing? The marines have to take over the airfield and port facilities and have them ready for the troops and the ships, and the airlift of the troops would be much faster than the ships," Steven asked.

"Right you are," Barney answered. "And that's why your dad's role of taking care of those MPS ships became more important. If we were going to airlift twenty thousand troops to any hotspot they would need those MPS ships to be there." Barney paused. "And in this case there were some boats out there in the Indian Ocean that presented an obstacle for those MPS ships.

"Our analyses, even now after all this time and study, showed that there were six or seven boats that started out for the attack on the MPS ships at Diego Garcia. Where they started out from, who sent them and the purpose of the attack is still uncertain, even after all this time and study." Barney paused. *"But a few things we do know. The men that comprised the boat crews were of a variety of ethnic and cultural backgrounds that made it very difficult to attach to any one country, like was it Iran or Iraq or some other middle eastern country. And in spite of their questionable origins they were a very determined group. They did everything they could to carry out their mission. The boats were poorly suited, the weapons were few and ill suited for the mission, the logistics like fuel and food for the distance and time were bad and even the ethnics of the men didn't match what they were tasked to do. Still, from what we were able to learn they were determined to carry out the mission they were sent on. They overcame a lot of the obstacles they were faced with and did their best to attack those MPS ships. Some day it may make a good study for a war college, a study in motivation. What motivated this group of misfits? Why were they so determined? Maybe we can learn something from them."*

Steven had been listening carefully. *"Well, it seems almost like a small high school team taking on the Washington Redskins, and keeping at it."*

"And keeping at it even if the team bus couldn't get them to the stadium," Barney added. *"They got out and pushed the bus the rest of the way."* Both men laughed.

"You men, you have to relate everything to football!" Ellie exclaimed. *"How about that woman, the journalist that was with those merchant ships, she was with Captain Shielbrock and she was wearing marine fatigues, what was she doing through all this?"*

"Ah yes, the woman Kim McManus, reporter and author. What was she doing?" Barney smiled. *"We'll get to her, but first let me tell you what we learned about the eastern group of attack boats."*

ADDU ATOLL, REPUBLIC OF THE MALDIVES

Three fishing boats lay in the Wilingili Lagoon, one of the smaller atolls of the group known as Addu Atoll near Gan Island in the Maldive Islands. One boat had its anchor down and the others tied up one on each side of the anchored boat. This part of Addu Atoll was a tiny crescent, a few miles across, open at one end, providing a small anchorage area. The Maldives are a group of about two thousand coral islands about four hundred miles southwest of Sri Lanka. Over a hundred and fifty thousand people live in these islands, most of them in the capital, Male, far to the north. Addu Atoll provides little to no livelihood other than fishing so no one really lives on the small crescent where the fishing boats stopped, but people from some of the other islands frequent the place to fish and to trade with occasional visitors.

Army veteran missileman Emani Abolqazeri had been assigned to one of the two fishing boats routed east via the Laccadive Islands and the Maldive Islands enroute to attack the ships at Diego Garcia. Abolqazeri had last seen his fellow army missilemen at Basra, where Moses Farscian had been assigned to the big boat and the others to fishing boats just like his.

The captain of Abolqazeri's fishing boat was an experienced fisherman, Mahmud Ardeshir. Another experienced boat captain Ismail Seyyid ran the boat that they were paired with. The two captains knew each other well and had agreed to stay together, which is why they were still moored near Gan two days after the scheduled attack at Diego Garcia. Everything had gone well, according to plan, until two days after they had refueled at Amindive in the Laccadive Islands. Then Seyyid's engine quit with a broken piston and Ardeshir took Seyyid's boat in tow.

It was slow going and they knew they would miss the date for the attack at Diego Garcia as they crept into Addu Atoll on the day they were supposed to have been attacking. There, anchored in the lagoon was a fishing boat similar to theirs which had been sent out in advance to meet them with drums of extra diesel fuel, so to the crews of the attack boats this one was "the tanker."

Moored alongside the tanker, the crews exchanged information and ideas. The tanker had fuel for them, but did not carry a spare piston for Seyyid's boat and the three captains tried to plan a course of action but could not agree.

Ahmud Bakhtiar, the captain of the tanker, told the other two captains that all three boats should go home. Their operation was over so why continue now? They had failed to be at Diego Garcia in time for the attack and he wanted to go back to Basra. Ismail Seyyid felt otherwise. Regardless of being late, they had been sent to attack the ships at Diego Garcia and that's what they should do. He wanted to switch boats with the tanker crew, leaving Bakhtiar and his men at anchor in the broken boat at Wilingili, while Seyyid and his crew would take the tanker, join Ardeshir's boat and proceed to Diego Garcia. After the attack they would return to Wilingili and all three would go home, taking turns towing.

Mahmud Ardeshir had wanted to stay with his friend and had done so, towing Seyyid's boat to a safe anchorage here near Gan. Now he wanted to take Seyyid's missileman and weapons in his boat and proceed to Diego Garcia for the attack, after which he would return here and they would go home together. Three captains argued through the day and night as they could not agree.

"Allahu akbar, I'm already two days late! If there was an attack at Diego Garcia, I, we missed it. Now I've got to go there alone." Ardeshir had finally lost patience and he stood up to leave the tanker cabin. "I'm going to leave. I can't wait here any longer. What do you say, Seyyid, can I have your mud-rutter and missiles?"

"Just a minute Ardeshir," Seyyid was still hopeful of going also, and he turned to Bakhtiar. "Look, you planned to sit here at anchor anyway until after the attack. All I'm asking you to do is wait here in my boat instead of yours. Let me take yours so I can join Ardeshir. A two boat attack, even late, even after the others, would be much better than him by himself."

"No!" Bakhtiar was adamant. "There is no attack mission. You're too late. We should all go home together. We can take turns," He looked at Ardeshir, "towing Seyyid."

"Pig shit!" Seyyid continued to argue on the basis of loyalty to mission accomplishment and that it was Bakhtiar's duty to support the operation even it meant giving over his boat. The argument continued another half hour as Seyyid excused himself with, "I'll be right back. Ardeshir, please don't go yet. Just give me a little while more," And he went across to his own boat as Bakhtiar and Ardeshir continued to discuss the problem.

A few minutes later there was a scuffle on the tanker stern and the two captains looked up to see Seyyid coming into the cabin carrying a pistol. He went straight to Bakhtiar, shoved him back against a bulkhead and pushed the muzzle of the gun into his cheek. "I hate to do this to you, Bakhtiar, but I'm taking your boat. Get across to mine right now or I'll blow your fucking head off."

Bakhtiar had little choice and as he went across he saw that his crew had also been taken by Seyyid's crew. Seyyid's missileman, Yasir

Ghoroudi, was moving the launcher and missiles to the tanker as Seyyid barked orders. "Modarishar, you and Raslani get those missiles over here for Ghoroudi. Ghoroudi, I want you to stand up there on the fore deck and keep an RPG-7 pointed at that boat." He pointed at his former fishing boat. "Phorishi, get up forward and weigh that anchor!"

Ardeshir had not said a word but went to his own boat, started the engine and got underway. By the time Ardeshir's boat was clear of the nest the missiles had been moved from Seyyid's old boat to the tanker and the anchor was aweigh.

"Modarishar, cast off that boat!"

"You leaving them adrift?"

"They'll have plenty of time to put down an anchor."

"Lines clear!" Modarishar called out.

Seyyid backed clear of his former boat. Then, shifting to forward gear, followed Ardeshir's boat out of the anchorage. "Phorishi, check the engine. Raslani, see what we have for food, water and supplies. Ghoroudi, get your missiles stowed. Modarishar, come take the wheel and follow Ardeshir." With that, Ismail Seyyid went to study the chart in his new boat, the former tanker.

On board Motor Vessel Private First Class James Anderson, Jr., east north east of Diego Garcia, Top Sawyer's weapon team reported to Shielbrock in the early morning, just after the smoke on the horizon had become visible. All night they had been looking over the loading manifests, trying to determine what ammunition was in which containers and if those containers were accessible. They learned what they had suspected; that they could not get to most of the containers as hundreds of the big steel boxes were stacked below decks. Only a few were topside. The containers could be offloaded onto a beach, barge or pier but on board ship there just wasn't any space, there was not enough room to move them around to get to those buried underneath or to open their big steel doors.

Rolling stock in the ship was stored bumper to bumper which left little to no space for movement except off the ship in proper order, and tanks and self-propelled guns were deep inside with artillery pieces also far below. Trucks, jeeps, bulldozers, military vehicles of every type, size and description were nearly solid across and on top, stacked in tighter than a Los Angeles freeway at Friday rush hour. Still, Top Sawyer and his team knew the arrangement, studied the loadout and found an access to some of what they were after.

Top explained to Shielbrock, "We can get to at least ten mounts of Mark nineteen Mod three forty millimeter machine guns. It's a gun that sits on a tripod base. It's air cooled and blow back operated. It uses linked forty millimeter cartridges and the ammo is in a container that we can get to. "The Mark nineteen Mod three fires about three hundred and fifty rounds per minute out to a max range of two thousand yards. Effective range about fifteen hundred yards. Each round is like a small grenade. Considering the small, moderate speed boat as our target armed with a short range missile, this seems to be the best we can come up with. It has good rate of fire and pretty good range."

Shielbrock had listened carefully to the Top's report. "Do we have anything with greater range, maybe with less rate of fire?"

Top Sawyer looked surprised. "Sure. We got one five five self-propelled guns but we can't get them on deck and I don't think we could hit a moving target from this rolling deck."

"I was thinking of some warning shots, to send them a message to stay clear."

"Well, Commodore, I'm looking at this for what's best to protect us not to communicate."

"Okay. What else you got?"

"Well, we got lots of fifty caliber machine guns. They're mounted on a lot of the jeeps. We can get at the jeeps, can put the guns up on deck and we'll be able to move them a little, that is wherever there's deck space. Ammo is no problem. We can get to lots of fifty cal stuff. They have a max range of about twelve hundred yards, effective to maybe nine hundred."

"Okay." Shielbrock thought awhile. "One of the controlling factors is people. We can't man all the guns you can set up."

"How many you want set up?"

"Well, it'll take at least two men to a gun mount. I can plan on twelve people—."

The Top interrupted. "We got more than twelve people, Commodore."

"Yes, I know, but I've got to use them elsewhere. I'll tell you what, set up four mounts on each side, a forty millimeter, a fifty caliber, a forty and a fifty, bow to stern. We'll man three of the mounts on each side and one gun crew will have to shift mounts as needed."

"What are you going to do with the other people, the ones not on the gun mounts?"

"I want to send four of your Bendix former Marines to the other MPS ships, one to each ship. They'll have knowledge of our weapon plan, what containers, which guns, where the ammunition is located, all that, and they'll stay in the other ships to help them get set-up. Also, I want to send one Stinger team guy to each MPS ship. I don't want to use the helos for personnel transfers more than is absolutely necessary so it's best that our people stay on the other ships."

"Aye aye, sir."

It was full daylight now, time to rearrange the formation and Shielbrock worked with his staff officers figuring out the new stations. Most of the day would be taken to put the thirteen ships into a random formation as one at a time each ship would be ordered to leave her station in the broad front rectangular formation and proceed to the newly assigned station. As each ship cleared the group the next would be sent on her way and when finally formed later in the day the MPS ships, armed with their forty millimeter and fifty caliber deck guns, would form a rough outer ring. Inside this ring would be the eight unarmed chartered merchant ships. All of this careful stationing would have a random appearance.

The Third Engineer of Motor Vessel Anderson, who had helped the Chief Engineer set up the jury rigged helicopter refueling capability, was transferred by helo to Bonnyman as Shielbrock wanted a helo refueling capability, however slow, on each side of the formation and Bonnyman would be across from Anderson in the new formation.

All day the activity had gone on with thirteen ships changing stations, the two helicopters transferring people and flying surface surveillance missions and weapons being dug out of cargo storage, moved and mounted on deck. Late in the day it was time to test fire the guns and Sergeant Kramer and his few Marines, and Top Sawyer with his Bendix retired Marines manned the guns. A short burst from each gun was followed by cheers of approval from those on deck and close ties were formed between the older retired Bendix Marines and the young Stinger Marines. A good group to defend the ships, thought Shielbrock. He still had to see if there was a weapon on board for the helicopters.

Messages were stacked on the small steel shelf next to his chair in the Pilot House; weather messages, supply messages, administrative messages and a series of messages from Joe Farwell. Every few hours Joe sent a general information message to the task unit designator that included MPSRON TWO and Shielbrock recognized right away that this was Joe's way of giving him information. Buried in the middle of news events from Diego Garcia would be a peculiar paragraph like, "Late yesterday O. Valdez hit three for four but his Oilers lost the game to the Fishermen, who lost three of their pitchers. The Fishermen got inside with two (garbled) and replugged (garble) sevens, and may have team mates who play with the same game plan."

"What the hell does this part mean?" Tim had brought the message to Shielbrock from the Radio Shack. "It must be a garble. I asked Sparks, but he said that's the way it was sent."

Shielbrock studied the message awhile and smiled. "The smoke on the horizon is from Overseas Valdez. The ship was hit by three of four shots from a fishing boat and the ship is lost. Three of the five in the fishing boat were killed. That means they captured two. The boat got inside the lagoon and used TOW and RPG-7. There may be other boats similarly armed in the area."

Shielbrock looked at Tim and the watch officer, Al Bevins. "This 'fisherman' term may not be the same boat that attacked us. It may be another one."

The two staff officers nodded as they all thought awhile until Al Bevins spoke up. "He used the plural 'team mates' rather than 'a team mate', so he must suspect that there is more than one boat out here."

"Right. We've got to continue to plan for the possibility that there's more than one boat after us."

"Commodore." Top Sawyer and Bob Ryan had walked up.

"Yes. How's the weapon team doing?"

Top Sawyer was unhappy. "We're okay on the deck guns but I've been going over the problem of arming the helos with Lieutenant Commander Ryan, here, and we can't agree."

"What's the problem?"

"Well, I say all he needs is an M-60 in each bird. Its rapid fire, seven point six two millimeter, hand held, y'know, simple and easy t'use."

The helicopter OinC broke in. "Yeah, but its short range, three or four hundred yards. If the boat is carrying any anti-air weapon he'll have greater range than we will."

Shielbrock looked at the two of them awhile. "Well, I'm not sure they have any anti-air weapons but we don't know that. We do know that they are rather poorly equipped, that is they seem to have very few weapons, so maybe they don't have any to use against you. Tell you what, let's equip you with the M-60 for now but we'll keep looking at it. Let's ask Sergeant Kramer if his stinger could be used. Also, Top, give it some more study and see if there's something that can give Bob a little more range."

"Aye aye, sir," And they departed.

"Time for a course change, Commodore. We're at the south east corner of our square. Bird Two reports clear to the north. I'd like to come north with a tango turn." Al Bevins held the radio handset as he spoke.

"Very well. Make it so. Sandwich it."

"Aye aye, sir." Tim Smith went out on the port wing of the bridge. An enlisted Naval Reservist of the staff went out to the starboard side and each put out false tactical signals as Bevins turned the formation.

"Have you been out of this Pilot House since you've been underway?" A feminine voice. He turned to a smiling Kim McManus, pretty as always even in Marine utilities. No, not pretty, beautiful.

"Sure. Lots of times. I've been out on the bridge wings. Good afternoon, journalist. Is that my question for the day?"

"You won't get off that easy, Commodore."

"What other questions do you have for me?"

"Well, before I question you I want to report to you, as your official log keeper and historian, as you put it."

"Okay, report."

"I have made copies of all logs; engineering, communications, ship's deck log and commodore's staff log. I have recorded interviews with everyone on board who saw the attack as you were leaving port Monday morning. I have pictures of the people interviewed and the ships involved. I have copies of all messages relating to this exercise or operation, including those containing the cute informative disguises buried in meaningless text. Also, I have recorded interviews with your air wing commander and your weapons team and pictures of the deck guns being installed and being test fired."

"Hey, that's really impressive! I was thinking that maybe I'd created a monster but then I remembered you do your homework."

"Yes, I do." Her eyes sparkled. "I wondered if you remembered."

"I remembered," He paused, "Everything."

"That's surprising." She took her eyes from his and looked at the horizon ahead. "But I suppose you have to remember everything when you're responsible for thirteen ships and the people in them."

"Well, I have a lot of help with the thirteen ships. Some other things, really important things, even long ago, I have to remember myself."

"How nice for you." She looked back at him. "Having recorded, copied and photographed everyone and everything else, now it's your turn."

"Do you want a picture of me?"

"All in good time. For now I'd like to interview you."

"Why me? You just said you had every log, every message and everybody's comments."

"Everyone but you, and you, Commodore, are the most important one of all."

"You flatter me, kind lady. Actually this role of mine is that of a figure head, a facade. The real tough jobs and the difficult decisions are made by the do'ers. I only listen and say, 'Very well' and try to appear sagely."

"Pardon me for saying this but 'bullshit', Commodore."

"Ms. McManus! How unprofessional!"

"Au contraire, sir. It is very professional journalism to use a term which best describes the situation and I did just that. It's verbally economical. The people in this ship think that you're something close to the God of Naval Warfare, if there is such a thing. You have taken this group of ships to sea, kept them out of harms way, armed them, provided them with helicopters, defied authority and I don't know what else. That's not a facade."

"Sure it is. All those things have been done by people like the mates, the helo pilots, the staff watch officers, the Marines. They're the doers. I just listen and nod." Verbally economical, he thought. It has a familiar ring.

"Nice try. Very modest. Very appropriate. Just like Marshall Matt Dillon in the Long Branch Saloon in Gunsmoke."

"Very good, and who—."

"James Arness, but forget the trivia—."

"You remember too, I see."

"Yes," she said and paused, "I remember everything."

This time he took his eyes from hers and looked at the horizon. "Go on with your questions."

"Okay. To start with, how did you get into this position, this role? What makes you a Convoy Commodore?"

"Our country maintains a hundred and twenty Convoy Commodores for duty in time of war or crisis as learned in the past two World Wars.

It's a NATO quota. The Convoy Commodores are primarily retired Navy captains who have had duties appropriate for this. They are selected by a Navy board and asked to participate. They can turn down the offer if they choose. If they accept they go to a two week training course at Norfolk or San Diego and completion of the course leads to designation as a Convoy Commodore." His voice carried an inflection of simplicity.

"Most Convoy Commodores never have anything more to do with the program because there are very few opportunities to do anything with it after being designated. There are a few fleet exercises each year for the at-sea training of Convoy Commodores, Naval Reserve staffs and Naval Reserve control of shipping people. This Rainbow Reef exercise is one such opportunity. These exercises are held once a quarter; four times a year. I was asked if I would serve as Convoy Commodore for this Rainbow Reef exercise and here I am, so serving."

"You didn't have to do this? You're here as a volunteer?"

"Yes. Once I agreed to do this exercise, I received orders from the Navy, orders calling me to active duty and telling me to do what I had agreed to do. But I could have turned it down and if I had another Convoy Commodore just like me, a retired captain would have been called to active duty for this same purpose."

"And what if you have a job?"

"It's up to the individual. For a peacetime exercise, like this is supposed to be, we have to arrange to be off work. Some Convoy Commodores are completely retired. They don't work. It's easy for them to be available. They only have to explain it to their wives."

"And you, do you work?"

"Yes."

"And you had to arrange time off from work and explain it to your wife?"

"Yes. I took vacation time. This is a nice vacation, isn't it? An ocean cruise, recreation, good food and entertainment."

"And your wife?"

"My wife understands. She's a Navy wife. She's used to me going away in ships."

"Even now that you're retired? I can understand her tolerance when you were in the Navy but now that you're retired, and you volunteer, that seems a bit much to ask."

"Maybe you're right, but here I am."

"Yes, and doing a great job, it seems."

He laughed. "You can get a lot of argument about that. It might take a court martial to determine what I've done."

"Really?" She showed genuine concern. "Do you think you're in trouble?"

"Well, you just don't disregard orders, steal two helicopters, hide thirteen ships and walk away, you know. I don't know if I'm in trouble or not. I can't worry about that. I've got too much else to worry about. I've got to do what I think is right. I can only be honest with myself and so—. Well, you can imagine the rest." He looked at the horizon again.

"Out here, with all your problems, what is your biggest problem?"

"Communications."

"What do you mean?"

"Communications. I can't talk with my ships because any other ship or boat can hear me. Navy ships have secure voice radio equipment but not these MPS ships. I can't talk with the beach because it can be intercepted and the same for traffic from ashore to me. Navy ships communicate ship to ship, ship to shore and shore to ship with secure radio systems. The people ashore, like in Washington and Diego Garcia, know things that I need to know. They want to know what I'm doing with these ships but we can't exchange info because we don't have secure communications."

"Do you think these boats that may be out here hunting for these ships can intercept your communications?" Kim asked.

"The VHF stuff, yes, if they're close enough. Every boat and ship has VHF marine band radio. So we try to deceive them, that is if they can hear us, with code words, signals and our sandwich system. The long range radio, like HF and satellite, I'm pretty sure they can't intercept and use. It takes sophisticated equipment. The Soviets have such equipment. No, I'm not prepared to fight off the Soviets in this case, but I have to recognize the possibility of Soviet intercept and then passing some of the info to whomever they want. That could be to Iranians, then to these boats at sea. That may be far fetched but I can't take the chance. So I can't communicate freely with my ships and the Navy can't communicate with me except if I use these cute tricks as you've seen."

"What's your next biggest problem?"

"Protection. We've got thirteen ships here with very valuable cargo. These five MPS ships carry all the weapons, ammunition, food, fuel and rolling stock for a sixteen thousand man Marine Amphibious Brigade, thirty days worth of everything they would need. But up north in the Arabian Sea is an aircraft carrier battle group and an Amphibious Ready Group. They all have to be protected and we're far away and have the fewest people. So we're lowest on the priority list for protection. A real threat; aircraft, submarine or surface combatant would tear us up. Against this half-assed boat threat we can hide, we can use our light weapons and we can run away. Maybe we can survive until it's safe to go back into Diego Garcia. With just a little real protection I'd feel secure. Without it we can only piece together what we have."

Kim continued recording the conversation. "You said you had disobeyed orders. Can you tell me about that?"

"Yes. I've heard second and third hand that I've been ordered to take these ships back to Diego Garcia. That's the wrong thing to do. I'm doing the right thing. I'm keeping them at sea, on the move, maintaining surveillance and arming as best we can."

"You've spent a lot of years in the Navy. Have you ever disobeyed orders before?"

Shielbrock looked at her and at the recorder, thought awhile and then thought awhile more before he answered. "Yes. There have been some times even before I was in the Navy and then when I was in the Navy when I found it necessary to disregard authority, to disobey orders. It's never easy."

CHAPTER 18

Steven still had not forgotten the earlier story that Barney Williams had told about baseball in Canada. It had been about when Barney was catching and Steven's father Martin Schielbrock was pitching at Stratford, Ontario in the playoffs for the town team league championship. Barney had not finished that story. He had told about the first game, that tied the league lead, and then left off just when they were about to start the second game, the championship game.

Barney's previous story of the Indian Ocean adventure with the MPS ships had ended with Martin Schielbrock making a statement that he had, on more that one occasion, disregarded authority and disobeyed orders. That led Steven to recall that Barney had not finished the story of Shielbrock's defying of authority in Canada that sunny summer day in 1952.

Steven reminded Barney of the baseball story that had not been completed. "And speaking of disregarding authority and not carrying out orders, how about that baseball game in Canada in 1952? You left us hanging with a tie for the championship, your buddy in pain had just pitched a no hit shutout and he intended to pitch again in the second game. You had hit a homer for the game's only run, right?"

"That's right," Barney nodded assent. "Shiel was in pain but neither the manager Dutch Van Rosche nor I could talk him out of it. He was determined to start and he tricked Dutch into letting him start understanding he would only pitch an inning or two, but Shiel knew all along that he was going to do more than that. He had no intention of coming out of that game after one or two innings. He tricked Dutch and he talked me into it."

Steven smiled. "So now after all these years, after hearing bits and pieces and listening to you guys joke about it, can I hear how my dad Martin Shielbrock defied the manager and all common sense and pitched in the second game?"

"Yes," Barney replied. "It's time you heard that full story. Then we can go back to the Indian Ocean and defy more authority." Steven laughed as Barney paused. "But just a minute, did you know what your dad's favorite song was during his later time in the Navy?"

"Aw, c'mon, knowing him it was probably the Star Spangled Banner."

Barney laughed. "No, really, his favorite song was 'My Way.' You know Frank Sinatra—".

"Yeah, yeah, I know that song and I can see why it was a favorite of his. He always did things 'My Way', right?"

Barney laughed again. "That's right, and every once in a while his way was not the right way, but most of the time he was right. At Canada that summer day he sure was right in that first game, a no hit shutout."

A SUNDAY AFTERNOON OF CANADIAN BASEBALL, SECOND GAME

At Stratford, Ontario, on that bright sunny summer day in 1952, Barney and Martin talked over the details of strategy they would use in the second game. There would have to be some new or different pitches, and considerable emphasis on trying to psyche-out the Kingston players who were already angry and humiliated from the first game. Normally Barney did not harass batters but he had seen the effect it had on Branch and Stoddart and he intended to build on what he had started in the first game, so he talked to the other Stratford players and encouraged them to use chatter and verbal barbs to rub the lack of hitting into the Kingston team.

Shielbrock threw his warm-up pitches easily to eliminate the slight stiffness that had set in between the games and he could feel an ache across his shoulders and down the right side of his back. His arm felt heavier than normal but as he gradually threw more pitches his rhythm returned and his muscles loosened. He threw a little harder and could feel a slight pull up and down that right side of his back, so he eased off for a few throws then tried again to throw hard but the pain was still there, a little sharper so he stopped, put on a jacket even in the ninety plus temperature and went to the dugout for a drink.

During his final warm-up pitches the line-up was announced and the crowd roared with approval and encouragement chanting, "Shiel-brock, Shiel-brock,—" again until the first Kingston batter came to the plate.

"Play ball!" Called the umpire.

Barney turned to the umpire, "My pitcher needs more time, sir."

"Wadya mean, more time? He's had all the throws he's allowed."

"Yes sir, but he's a special case like the rules allow for because he just pitched the previous game, and the rules allow for him to ask you for additional warm-ups. I'm asking for him under that rule."

The umpire was not pleased. "Okay, take four more throws."

Now it was the Kingston batter, Le Clerc who was not pleased. He objected and Kingston manager Vic Parcells came out of the dugout to object also but Shielbrock took his four additional warm-up pitches as the argument went on at home plate.

"You ready now?" The umpire asked Barney with a note of sarcasm.

"Yes sir. We're ready, thank you," Responded Barney. "But I don't think he is." Barney motioned with his glove toward the Kingston manager still present at home plate from his argument.

"Wadya mean? I'm ready! I been ready!" Vic Parcells was angry from the delay and now more so from Barney's accusation.

"Oh, did y' find some hitters? I didn't think y' had any hitters."

"You wise som'bitch," Muttered the manager as he headed for his dugout.

Le Clerc lifted a long fly ball to left field for the first out and Shielbrock could feel a pull and stiffness across his shoulder as he pitched. He tried to work the low inside corner on Luca but missed and walked the batter. Buster Branch was next up, still angry from the previous game and he hit the first pitch a mile into right field but it curved foul. The next two pitches were low and inside and again Branch hit a long drive to right that curved foul. Shielbrock tried the low inside corner again and Branch lifted a fly to right, this time not foul but not long and Stratford right fielder John Temple gloved it for the second out.

Big Eric Stoddart spit a big wad of tobacco across the plate, splat, and Barney started on him. "Wipe yourself when you're through."

Stoddart wheeled around and faced Barney. "You're gonna have a thirty six ounce hardwood crease across your fuckin' head."

Barney's face was right up to Stoddart's and he snarled back, "It'd be the first thing you've hit all day, and the last, 'cause I'd shove that stick up your ass right in your brain."

Before Stoddart could reply the umpire barked, "Knock it off! Play ball!"

The crowd loved it and heaped verbal abuse on Stoddart and encouraged Barney. The crowd couldn't hear the dialogue but they could see the confrontation and angry gestures as Stratford's infielders picked up the chatter, dishing out insults to the batter and support for their pitcher.

"C'mon Shiel, baby, lay it in there."

"No stick up there. Big bluff. Big windbag up there."

"You got 'im Shiel."

"Take him out, pitch. No stick."

They kept it up but Shielbrock couldn't catch the corners and walked the big batter. Vito Morabelli hit two foul balls before lifting a high drive to right field that Temple put away for the third out. Shielbrock had walked two but had given up no runs.

Ken Winder pitched for Kingston in the second game; a tall thin right-handed veteran of many years in the minor leagues. His fast ball wasn't much and his curve broke only a little, but he had good control and was strong and fresh as he took his warmup throws.

The Stratford lead off batter, Pollazio, hit a sharp one between short and third. Franko and Barney followed with fly balls that didn't advance the runner but Temple hit a single up the middle, then with two men on base and two out, Hunsey rolled a grounder to the second baseman for the third out.

Dutch had tried to talk him into leaving the game but Shielbrock had insisted he could go a little more even though the muscle pull across the back of his shoulders was there still as he warmed up for the second inning. He walked Arnell to start the inning and then Billy Adrianne hit a perfect double play ball but Fontaine let it go right through, putting runners on first and second. The muscle pull across Shielbrock's shoulders ached as he walked Sam Whipple to load the bases.

Dutch trotted out to the mound as did Barney and Dutch reached out for the ball. "C'mon gimme the ball. You've had enough. I'm pullin' y'."

"No. I'm not through yet. I can get them out. Don't pull me."

"Look, y'got the bases full. No outs. Yer pushin' the ball up there, not throwin'."

"Hey Dutch, with the double play and the next easy batter I'd be out of the inning. Lemme try a little more."

Dutch looked at Barney. The crowd was silent and tense, waiting. "Let him try a little more, Dutch. We got a gift comin' to bat now. Just a little more," Barney offered.

"Okay. A little more," Allowed Dutch as he turned and walked toward the dugout and the crowd erupted in a roar of approval. The roar continued, then grew louder as Shielbrock struck out the Kingston pitcher Winder with three curve balls. Shielbrock could feel the strain on his wrist as he snapped the spin on the ball in each pitch.

Mario Le Clerc hit a fly ball to left fielder Bill Jarelski for the second out but the drive was long enough for Arnell to tag-up on third base and come home with the first run of the game as Kingston fans came to life roaring approval. Shielbrock tried to get John Luca on slow tempting curve balls but Luca waited and walked, loading the bases again with angry Buster Branch coming to the plate.

"Now I get mine, God Damn it," He muttered and Barney countered with, "Yeah, now you get your next big K." But it wasn't a strike out as Branch hit the first pitch sharply at first baseman Jack Moore who knocked it down and as the ball rolled away in front of him the runners advanced; Adrianne scoring, Whipple to third and Luca to second. By the time Moore caught up with the ball even the slow footed Branch was safe on first. The error had scored the second run and left the bases full.

Walking slowly with his head down, Dutch came from the dugout to the mound and Barney was already there. In organized baseball the pitcher has to leave the game if the manager makes two trips to the mound in the same inning, but in the Ontario league there was no such limit. "Okay," Dutch grunted, "Y'had enough. Get outa here." As he reached for the ball.

Putting the ball behind him, Shielbrock stepped back. "No! I'm not through! God damn it we had a couple a' bad breaks. But for the errors we'd be out of the inning." Seeing the refusal to leave by their pitcher, the crowd yelled support and Shielbrock argued, "Listen to them, Dutch. Give me one more batter. One more and we're out a' the inning."

The crowd roared support as Barney implored, "Give him one more, Dutch."

"C'mon. Play ball!" The umpire called, so Dutch Van Roche turned and trotted back to his dugout as the crowd roared even louder approval.

Eric Stoddart pounded his bat on the plate and spit across it. Splat! "I been waiting for this all day. Ducks on the pond and I got the loaded gun," He said to anyone and no one.

"You got shit for brains is all and spitting that little bit out," Responded Barney.

Without turning, Stoddart was still facing the pitcher as he said quietly, "Kiss my ass".

"You're all ass!" Barney wouldn't let go and Shielbrock threw three fastballs to Stoddart, all three knee high on the inside corner of the plate. Stoddart took the first for a strike, swung at and missed the next two.

On each fastball Shielbrock could feel a sharp pain up and down the right side of his back and on each of the pitches he let out a cry of pain which sounded like a grunt of extra effort but they were out of the inning with two runs, no hits. The crowd yelled approval, Kingston fans because they led 2-0, Stratford fans because they had gotten out of the inning with the strikeout leaving the bases loaded.

In the Stratford half of the second inning, Moore struck out and Fontaine went out with a ground ball to the second baseman. Bill Jarelski hit a single to left but Shielbrock grounded out to the shortstop.

Warming up for the third inning, Shielbrock threw easily feeling stiffness and that same slight ache across his shoulders even with an easy throw. A curve ball brought additional pain to his forearm and wrist, and a fastball added the sharp pain up and down his back on the right side. Soaked with sweat, he had to talk to himself. Hold your head up. Stand up straight. Look like a pitcher. Look confident.

He couldn't catch the corners and walked Morabelli to start the inning. George Arnell looked at two bad pitches then hit a grounder which went right through second baseman Roger Hunsey and instead of a double play there were runners on first and second with no outs. Shielbrock tried to throw harder to the next batter, Billy Adrianne, but the pain caused him to put a ball up in the strike zone and Adrianne hit it deep into right center field. Off with the crack of the bat, Pollazio made a beautiful running catch in deep center field but Morabelli was able to tag up and advance to third base.

With runners at first and third and one out, Shielbrock stood on the mound and took the curve ball sign from Barney with Sam Whipple at the plate. Taking a deep breath, Shielbrock let it out slowly, stretched and could feel the muscles pull on the right side of his back. His throw to the plate was well over Barney's head and upstretched arms going all the way to the backstop. Morabelli headed for home as Shielbrock raced in to cover the plate and Barney scrambled back for the ball but there was no play as Morabelli scored and Arnell went to second.

Dutch Van Roche came out to the mound again as did Barney. "Okay, Shielbrock. This is as far as you go. You got nuthin' left." Dutch reached for the ball.

"No," Shielbrock insisted. "You aren't goin' t'pull me. I'm not through!"

"Look," Dutch could also be insistent. "Halloran's ready. You've done enough an'—."

"Halloran's dogshit! I'm not through!"

They continued to argue. The crowd could see the dispute and knew the issue. "Let 'im stay!"

"Leave 'im in, Dutch."

"Stay in there Shielbrock." Then they started the chant, "Shiel-brock, Shiel-brock, Shiel-brock,—."

Shielbrock motioned toward the crowd. "Dutch, do you hear that? I got about five thousand screaming fans over there and the only way you're gonna get me out a' here is t'drag an' carry me. I don't think you can do that but if you even try I can promise that those five thousand angry drunk idiots are going to take you and this ball park apart. They've been drinking beer since about noon. Now get back in that dugout and lemme finish this game!"

Dutch was intimidated but not ready to give up yet as he turned to Barney. "Williams, will you try to talk sense t'yer buddy here?"

"I've tried, Dutch, but he wants t' stay and I don't want to go up against those wild drunks, either."

"Shiel-brock, Shiel-brock,—," The chant continued.

Dutch was red faced with anger as never in all his years in baseball had he seen a pitcher win out over a manager. He turned toward the umpire who was approaching, Dutch knew, to move things along and to get the game going but before Dutch could speak Shielbrock spoke up. "Dutch, those same crazy five thousand will take apart the umpire, too. Want me to explain it to him?"

The umpire heard only the last few words as he approached. "Explain what? What's the hold-up?"

Dutch hesitated and Barney spoke up. "No hold up. We're ready to go," And he trotted back toward the plate and Dutch stood at the mound a few seconds, confused.

"Dutch?" the umpire asked with his hands out to both sides.

"Shiel-brock, Shiel-brock,—."

Dutch turned and trotted back to the dugout as the crowd roared approval.

Shielbrock grunted with pain as he threw a fastball across the knees for strike one to Sam Whipple and the batter never saw the next fastball but heard the grunt from the pitcher. Two outside curve balls brought the count to two and two and brought the wrist and arm pain so Shielbrock waited a long time before throwing the next pitch; a fastball with pain and a loud grunt for strike three. Kingston pitcher Ken Winder was next up and Shielbrock struck him out with curve balls.

In the dugout Barney talked to Shielbrock. "Look, we gotta lay off the fastball. It's killing you. Save it for only strike three situations, "Okay?"

Shielbrock nodded. "Okay."

Barney continued. "Remember when you fooled around with the knuckle ball a while ago?"

"Yeah, but—."

"But nothin'! We gotta try the knuckle ball. It'll be easier on yer arm."

"Barney, the knuckler is a finger breaker for you! Even if I can control it it'll jump around and you'll be trying to catch it with both hands."

"Don't worry about me. I'll handle it. You just serve it up there big, fat and dancing. Listen, Shiel, these guys are all pissed and humiliated at you. You've put them down without a hit for twelve innings and they all know you go for the fastball to put them away. Now, when you pull the knuckler they'll be shocked."

"Okay."

"One more thing," continued Barney. "They know you're in trouble, arm trouble I mean and their weaker hitters will be taking the first two pitches. When I give you this," he wiggled his little finger, "just lay it across in the strike zone, like a warmup pitch, no, like batting practice. Soon as they get on to that we'll knuckle ball them."

For Stratford in the third inning, Pollazio grounded out, George Franko doubled and Barney walked. With men in scoring position Temple rolled out to the first baseman and Hunsey flied out to end the inning so at the end of three innings it was Kingston three runs on no hits, Stratford no runs on four hits.

Struggling through the first two batters, aching with every throw, Shielbrock got the first on a grounder and the second with a fly ball. Then Buster Branch came to bat again. Getting on base in the second inning by way of an error had done nothing to appease his anger and Barney greeted him with verbal abuse as the infield chatter added even more. The Stratford fans gave some of their own insults to the big batter.

Shielbrock's first pitch was a low curve ball that didn't break and Branch blasted it deep down the first base line. The ball was clearly out of the park but it curved foul for strike one. The next two pitches were outside and didn't tempt Branch, but a low inside curve ball caught the corner for strike two. The next pitch was the first knuckle ball Branch had seen all day and it danced up toward the plate as he watched it for strike three and the third out.

Branch yelled at the umpire. "He's doctrin'! I seen it! That ball had sumtin' on it. He was doin' it the last game—," and Branch continued with his angry accusations as the umpire looked at the ball. Barney had handed the ball to the umpire over his right shoulder without even standing up and as the umpire inspected the ball with Branch jawing away, Barney eased out from between them and headed for the dugout. The crowd loved it and even more abuse was poured on Branch as he and the umpire stood there looking at the ball.

"Branch, you couldn't hit a bull in the ass with a banjo."

"Take a good look, Branch, that's all you'll see."

"Show him what the ball looks like, ump."

Then someone came up with, "The Kingston King of K!" Then, "King K, King K," and soon a chant started, "King K, King K, King K,—." Branch was furious, red-faced and he drew back his bat in a threatening gesture to the crowd. They loved it and heaped more abuse on him and roared "King K" louder with more voices, sober as well as drunken joining in. Branch threatened the crowd again with his bat and they roared even louder as he turned and threw his bat into his own dugout as Eric Stoddart had done in the first game. The King-K chant followed him to his position in right field and when he gave an arm-in-the-elbow gesture to the crowd, they roared with delight and shouted more insults.

Back-to-back singles by Moore and Fontaine put runners on first and second in the fourth inning, but Jarelski and Shielbrock grounded out and Pollazio flied out to end the inning.

Leading off for Kingston in the fifth inning was an angry and frustrated Eric Stoddart. Barney threw more verbal barbs at him as did the infield chatter and the fans.

"Kiss my ass, Williams," was Stoddart's greeting to Barney at the plate.

"Your nose is in the way," was the reply.

Stoddart had struck out three times in the first game and again in the second inning of this one and the fans were really on him, yelling more than their usual cruel and unusual personal abuses. A drunken fan came out with, "If Branch is King K, this must be the queen. Queen K, Queen K," and the chant started, "Queen K, Queen K—."

Stoddart was furious as he pounded his bat on the plate, spit out a big dark wad of tobacco, but didn't say a word. Barney kept after him, the chant continued but Stoddart stood ready without a comment. A curve ball caught the low inside corner for a called strike and Shielbrock felt the pain in his wrist, forearm and shoulders. A little later the count was full and Stoddart fouled off the next two pitches. Shielbrock had to throw a fastball and he knew the pain that it would bring so he waited a long time between pitches talking to himself. Get up there and fire it. Forget the pain. Feel it after you release the ball. He fired the ball low in the strike zone, felt the pain, uttered a grunt and saw Stoddart swing too late; strike three. Again the crowd went wild, "Queen K, Queen K—."

Morabelli followed with a fly ball to right. Shielbrock walked the next batter and Billy Adrianne was baffled by curves and knucklers but managed a ground ball to the third baseman for the third out.

In the Stratford half Franko singled, Barney flied out and Temple struck out. Hunsey walked to put men on first and second but Jack Moore grounded to the second baseman for the third out. At the end of five innings it was Kingston three runs and no hits, Stratford no runs on seven hits.

Shielbrock did not feel at all well as Kingston came to bat in the sixth. He had poor control even with the "pinkie" pitch called for by Barney and he walked Sam Whipple, not a good way to start the inning walking a young fast college kid from Pittsburg. In place of the pitcher, Vic Parcells put in a pinch hitter who took the first two "pinkie" pitches for strikes, but the slow throws enabled Whipple to steal second. A long fly ball to right field got the pinch hitter out but Whipple made it to third base after the catch. Shielbrock was covered with sweat and ached all over but knew he had to bear down harder even with pain in every pitch.

Mario Le Clerc hit a drive to left field that would have been long enough to score the runner from third but it curved foul. Amid sweat, fatigue and pain Shielbrock walked Le Clerc and also Luca, loading the bases with one out and Buster Branch at bat.

"King-K, King-K, King-K—," The crowd chanted and through the fog of his fatigue Martin Shielbrock wondered at this wild drunken crowd. We're down 3-0 in the sixth inning of this championship game, their pitcher is a cripple and they're happy!

Barney came out to the mound. "Control, Shiel, control! Remember what I told you about Dietrich? All he gets by with is control. You got more than that. Keep it low and inside and we'll get Branch."

"Okay."

"You all right?"

What a question, thought Shielbrock through a clouded mind. I'm in pain all over, I'm not thinking straight, I'm dog tired and he asks me if I'm all right. If anything, I'm all wrong. "Yeah, I'm all right, Fine."

"Okay. You're in charge. Remember, look like a pitcher. Look confident."

"Let's go," said Shielbrock thinking of those long ago learned lessons from Coach Jordan. Stand up straight. Look the part. He pulled his shoulders back and winced with the pain but held up his head.

Barney went back to his position behind the plate. God, thought Shielbrock, what a tower of strength that Barney is! How tough can a guy be? Here we are into the second game of a double header, the temperature is over ninety and he's wearing that face mask, chest protector and shin guards. Some call it the "tools of stupidity." For every pitch I throw he crouches down, catches it and throws it back, often jumping up and running after foul balls or backing-up plays at first base. He lives in the constant dust and dirt around home plate; face and hair covered and streaked with sweat and dirt and his entire body and baseball uniform are soaked with sweat. In spite of all this he nurses and controls the pitcher, taunts the batters, calls the pitches and knows every hitter's weaknesses and strengths. He hits, runs the bases and is willing to protect the plate with his body if necessary. Shielbrock was to find out again just how tough was Barney.

Buster Branch stepped back just enough on the first low inside pitch to belt a short drive to right field but John Temple came in and caught it on the run. Whipple tagged up at third base and headed for the plate, a strong fast hard runner. Temple's throw went to the plate, a straight hard throw that didn't bounce before it reached the big glove of Barney Williams. Sam Whipple and the ball reached Barney at the same time and Barney was crouched two steps up the third base line. Whipple was determined to run right through Barney. As he received the ball Barney turned toward the runner, protecting the ball in his glove and rose slightly from his crouch. He caught Whipple with his left shoulder, lifting and sending the runner high into a full airborne cartwheel. Over the plate flew Whipple, coming down flat on his back on the other side of home plate. Sitting on his rear end and looking around, Barney jumped up, stepped over the plate, tagged Whipple and looked at the umpire.

"I already called him out up the line. You got 'im there."

Barney smiled. "Just wanted to be sure, ump. Thank you." And he headed for the dugout as the crowd roared. Coming to a few seconds later, Sam Whipple had to leave the game.

"Now it's my turn to ask," Shielbrock went to Barney in the dugout. "You took a pretty good hit that time. Are you okay?"

"Yeah," Barney rubbed his left shoulder. "Just a little sore, it'll be okay." Then to the others in the Stratford dugout he yelled, "C'mon lets get somethin' goin' this time. Let's get this relief pitcher. Let's get some runs!" The others picked up his enthusiasm. And a cheerleader, too, thought Shielbrock.

They did get something going as Fontaine walked and after Jarelski flied out Shielbrock scratched out a single. Pollazio's sacrifice bunt put runners at second and third and when Franko walked the bases were loaded with two outs. Barney worked the relief pitcher for a full count and the crowd roared and came to their feet as he hit a long drive, but Kingston center fielder John Luca went back on the run and falling against the fence he caught Barney's drive. He held the ball though and Stratford ended the sixth inning still without a run.

There was a scuffle in the Kingston dugout between innings and when Eric Stoddart walked toward the plate he turned and yelled some obscenities back to his team mates. The crowd chanted, "Queen K, Queen K—." A couple of young Kingston players responded to Stoddart's yells, came out of the dugout a few steps and shouted at him, but Manager Vic Parcells rounded them up and herded them back into the dugout.

Stratford infielders joined in the harassment led by Barney. "C'mon Eric, are you girls through with yer tea party?"

"Were you girls havin' a dance?"

"Are y'ready to play ball or are you guys going t'play with yer-selves?"

"Is the dance over yet?"

"You girls be careful, y' might mess yer hair."

"Queen K, Queen K—."

The chant and verbal abuse was stronger than before as Stoddart pounded his bat on the plate and spit, splat, and everyone was yelling, mostly at Stoddart. Angry at the crowd, angry at Shielbrock, angry at Barney, angry at his own team mates and angry at himself, clearly Eric Stoddart was a man full of rage and lacking in judgment. In spite of all his years in organized baseball he was not prepared to cope with this humiliation and verbal abuse and as Shielbrock served him a mixture of tempting curve balls and knuckle balls, Stoddart went out swinging.

Morabelli walked and Arnell was safe on an error but Adrianne grounded out and Whipple's replacement flied out to retire the side.

The Kingston relief pitcher made quick work of Stratford, three up and three down to end the seventh inning.

Even the easy going warm-up pitches for the eighth inning sent pains across Shielbrock's shoulders, up and down his back and in his throwing arm. His legs felt heavy. He felt clumsy and lacked the dexterity and grace that marked the motion of an accomplished pitcher.

Kingston led off with another pinch hitter in their pitcher's position which meant that another pitcher would do the eighth and ninth inning. Shielbrock gave him two pinkie pitches that were taken for two strikes. Two curve balls missed, evened the count and brought pain to arm, wrist, shoulders and back, but the pinch hitter flied out on the next curve.

Shielbrock was sweating more than ever now. With the temperature still over ninety perspiration ran down his face into his eyes, blurring his vision and he was tired and ached all over. He talked to himself about disregarding the pain and fatigue, standing up straight and holding his head up but it was very difficult to convince himself. Slow curves he threw to Le Clerc and Luca, all the pitches low, all flirting with the inside and outside corners and pain accompanied every throw, but both batters grounded out to retire the side and Shielbrock shuffled into the dugout exhausted, sat down and hung his head.

Not Barney. Like a man possessed, Barney stormed up and down the dugout yelling encouragement, pleading, calling for hits and runs. "This is our game! Ours! We gotta get some runs! C'mon, let's put somethin' together." Some of the Statford players picked up Barney's enthusiasm and when Fontaine led off with a base on balls the crowd came to life. Noise built rapidly into a roar as Jarelski singled and a weary Shielbrock managed to sacrifice the runners to second and third, so that Pollazio's long fly ball enabled Fontaine to tag up and score Stratford's first run of the game. The crowd was delighted, yelling, whistling and drinking more beer. They were even more pleased when Franko walked and they exploded with delight and hope as Barney hit a long single scoring Jarelski from second base. With two out Temple walked to fill the bases and the crowd roared with anticipation, but Hunsey grounded out to end the eighth inning. Score three to two.

Shielbrock had to face Branch, Stoddart and Morabelli to start the ninth inning and the crowd got on Branch right away yelling insults and chanting King-K. Shielbrock finished his warmup and stood on the mound, ready to pitch, looking to anyone like the epitome of confidence and poise, a polished gladiator who had dueled under the hot sun all day with extraordinary success and was now ready to complete his super-human challenge. Inside, of course, he was considerably different; dead tired and aching all over. He knew that he didn't have the pitches available to him that he had earlier in the day, that determination was all he had and, he hoped, enough control to get through one more inning.

There would be no pinkie pitches to Branch as Shielbrock knew it would take more than that to put away the big hitter. Low and inside, low and inside he could still hear Barney's advice, and low and inside is where he threw as Branch missed the first. The crowd chanted, "King-K, King-K—."

Again, low and inside, and Branch got a piece of the ball but drove it foul as the infield chatter kept at him. "You wave that bat another twenty years and maybe you'll learn to use it."

"No, no. He's been playing with himself for longer than that and still doesn't know how to use it."

"King-K, King-K—."

With two strikes on the batter Barney signaled for a knuckle ball and Shielbrock shook it off, thinking fastball and thinking of the pain it would bring. Again, Barney signaled knuckle ball but this time Shielbrock nodded assent. In the dugout before this inning Shielbrock had wetted a corner of his glove and applied dirt to it. Now he touched the ball to his forearm where the sweat was heavy and then touched the wet spot of the ball against the dirt spot on his glove, accomplishing this with a nonchalance masked amid the nervous gestures of a pitcher getting ready to throw.

The knuckle ball danced toward the plate with a very slow spin, the big brown spot moving slowly around giving a lopsided distorted appearance and Branch gave a tentative swing missing for strike three. The crowd erupted, "King-K, King-K—," and the infielders yelled delightful barbs, hoots and joys as they tossed the ball around in celebration.

"He's been doctrin'd' ball all day, I tell y'. He put sumptin' on d'ball again." Branch appealed to the umpire but by the time the ball made its way around the infield to the umpire a number of gloves had wiped it clean and the umpire showed it to the angry strike out victim. The crowd loved it, the umpire showing the angry batter what a baseball looked like. They yelled and chanted.

Eric Stoddart was next up. Three times he had struck out in this game and three times in the first game; he who had hit against Johnnie Sain and had played in Triple A ball. He was greeted rudely with, "Queen-K, Queen-K—," as he pounded his bat on the plate. Angrier than ever, more frustrated, he issued forth a large dark wad of tobacco, splat, across the plate.

"That's the only thing you've hit all day." Barney started on him.

"Shut d'fuck up!"

"You girls finished dancing in the dugout?"

Stoddart took his position to hit, "Bastard!"

The umpire tried to calm things. "C'mon. Cut it out and play ball."

Shielbrock's arms were like lead. He stood up straight with head back, looking confident, but he felt awful and every pitch he knew would bring sharp pain. He tried to keep it from his mind but his first pitch was higher than he wanted and a little outside and he grunted with pain as he threw it. Stoddart caught it on the end of his bat for a foul ball and mumbled, "C'mon put it up there again, hot shot."

Barney countered with, "He'll put it up there all right, right up your ass, where your brains are."

"Queen-K, Queen-K—."

A knuckle ball was good for strike two as Shielbrock had little more to give. He was finished pitching but had to finish the game even though every pitch was an ordeal of pain. He couldn't afford the throws to set up a batter and he shook off Barney's signal for a curve, wanting to throw a knuckler. No, but again Barney signaled curve. No, and Barney kept him waiting a long time then signaled fastball and Shielbrock nodded.

He put the pain out of his mind long enough to make the pitch and it was as fast as he had thrown all day and as accurate. He fired it across the low inside corner for strike three and as he released it the sharp tearing searing pain on the right side of his back forced from him a combination scream and grunt and the crowd went wild. They thought it was like the cavalry charge yell, the challenge of attack, their pitcher throwing his best pitch and verbally challenging Kingston's most dangerous hitter and Stoddart was out on strikes in three pitches.

Vito Morabelli had walked twice, grounded out twice, hit three fly balls and struck out once. Having put wood on the ball five times all day he came to bat with two out in the ninth.

Shielbrock took a long time to pitch and he wasn't even sure that he could go through a pitching motion. That last strike to Stoddart, he knew, had damaged something but he didn't know what. Long and hard he thought, trying to determine if there was any pitch at all that he could throw. He turned toward the plate where the batter waited and where Barney was ready to signal a pitch. Before he stepped up on the rubber, Shielbrock moved the little finger of his pitching hand. Barney immediately shook his head, no, and sent back the signal for curve ball and Shielbrock shook it off. They waited. Again curve ball. No. Barney kept him waiting then moved his little finger asking for the pinkie pitch which would be served up like a big fat apple just right for a good hitter to bite into. Shielbrock served it up and Morabelli bit, the best opportunity any Kingston batter had been offered in eighteen innings and Shielbrock grunted with pain even on this pinkie pitch, but Morabelli was just a little too eager. Swinging early he tried to slow the swing but still connected and hit a grounder to Roger Hunsey at second base whose throw to first was in plenty of time for the third out.

Stratford now came to bat in the bottom half of the ninth inning trailing three to two with the league championship at stake. The crowd roared encouragement, Stratford fans hoping to score, Kingston fans hoping to hold onto the win. They stamped their feet, yelled and whistled and even more as the Kingston relief pitcher walked Jack Moore to start the inning.

When the next batter, Jon Fontaine, also drew a walk they were all on their feet yelling approval.

Vic Parcells had seen enough at that point and decided to change pitchers. He looked down the dugout bench at Mel Grieves who had pitched so well in the first game. "Mel?" The name came out as a question.

"Not me! I've had mine for today. That's all you get."

"Mel, just three outs and its over, we're at the bottom of their order."

"No! That Shielbrock can leave his arm up here if he wants, that's his business, but not me."

Parcells turned away in disgust and sent for his last available pitcher as the crowd calmed during time to change pitchers.

Bill Jarelski hit a pop up for the first out and Shielbrock's attempted sacrifice bunt was good for a hit, filling the bases, but Pollazio's fly ball was not long enough to score the runner from third.

With two out and the bases loaded George Franko hit a grounder to short stop which should have ended the game but the ball took a last second crazy bounce, glanced off Le Clerc's glove and the tying run scored.

The fans were jumping up and down, screaming, yelling, crying, hooting and whistling. The Stratford dugout emptied onto the field to greet Moore and when some small measure of calm was restored Barney Williams was at the plate with the score tied, bases loaded and two out.

This is what baseball is all about. It's not the action, it's the situation, the drama as hearts were beating too rapidly for good health and adrenalin was flowing. There was tension, excitement, anticipation and all nerves were on edge as thousands of minds and eyes were focused on a peculiar lack of activity as the Kingston pitcher looked in, stretched and threw the ball to his catcher for ball one. Thousands sighed in relief. Thousands of breaths newly held with another pitch. Ball two. Sighs and held breaths, again.

Barney hit the next pitch to deep left center field scoring Jon Fontaine to win the game and the Ontario league championship for Stratford. It went in the score book of that time as a single because the game ended when the winning run scored but in later years the hit would have been something more. It didn't matter then to any of the Stratford players or fans. All that mattered was that Stratford won 4-3, that Shielbrock had pitched a double-header with two no-hit games and that Barney Williams had accounted for the winning scores in both games.

The fans poured out onto the field yelling and screaming, a mob of crazy drunken ecstatic people, people of all ages in all stages of inebriation. It was difficult to tell the drunk from the sober, if there were any sober, they all acted crazy, crazy with joy and excitement. The screaming and yelling, hooting and hollering, back slapping and hugging went on and on.

Shielbrock was caught up by the mob. Fans hugged him and it hurt, shook his hand and it hurt, slapped him on the back and it hurt even more. Pushing and staggering his way toward the dugout, the mob held him. His vision was blurred with sweat, his mind clouded with pain, his legs heavy with fatigue. He knew they meant well but he was in trouble and in pain. With a desperate final effort he pushed his way into the dugout, made it to the washroom and fell on the damp concrete floor. A few seconds later the door banged open and Barney fell alongside him. The bedlam continued outside the washroom as the two gladiators looked at each other, still lying on the washroom floor and each managed a smile, then they laughed.

"Y'know, Barney," Shielbrock spoke in a forced matter of fact manner. "I'm really glad you got that hit 'cause I couldn't go out there for another inning or for another pitch."

Barney replied in the same tone. "Me neither. I think I dislocated my shoulder in the sixth."

The Maple Leaf was closed on Sunday so it wasn't until Monday that Martin and Barney heard about the great celebration party they had missed. Their team pictures are still on the back wall of the Maple Leaf Restaurant and Bar on the corner of Market and First Streets in Stratford, Ontario. Bar habitués over the years have engaged in trivia contests and frequently a question comes up concerning the Ontario Senior Baseball League championship won by Stratford in 1952. The more knowledgeable sports trivia buffs can go to that back wall at the Leaf, point to the pictures and say, "This is the guy that pitched and won both games of a double header that day and both were no-hitters, and this is the guy that got the winning runs in both games." No one can recall a double no-hitter in that league or elsewhere.

Two months later Barney Williams was one of 556 Officer Candidate Seaman Recruits in Class 11 at the Navy Officers Candidate School, Newport, Rhode Island. Two months after that, OCSR Martin Shielbrock was sworn in as part of Class 12. He never threw another pitch.

CHAPTER 19

"So the two of you finish college, have a summer of fun and games in Canada and just before you get drafted you both go into the Navy, right? Steven asked.

"Right," Barney replied. "The draft board was breathing down our necks, both of us, so we decided that we'd be better off in the Navy than in the army and because we had finished college we qualified for officer candidate school. We figured that it would be better to live on a ship than to carry a rifle in the mud of Korea."

"Sounds like a wise choice to me," Barney's wife Jackie offered. "In the Navy you would have a dry bed and food in the wardroom. Good choice."

Ellie had been listening to the stories by her father, Barney, and she asked, "So was it beds, mud and meals that made the difference that led to thirty year careers for both of you?"

"Well," Her father answered. "We didn't expect to make careers of it when we went into the Navy. There was the draft and we didn't want to go into the army, so the Navy was a logical choice, or so it seemed at the time. After we had served the few required years both of us decided, separately, that it would be a good career and both of us 'went regular', that is we requested, were accepted and became part of the regular Navy. That means we were transferred from the reserve to the regular Navy. They called it 'dropping the R', R for reserve."

"And after his Navy career, which we've all either heard about and/or lived through, we then find our hero, who won't tell us his story, out in the

- 295 -

Indian Ocean with a strange group of ships caught up in what is develop-
ing into an international incident." Ellie was trying to get the story telling
back on track.

Barney picked up on his wife's hint. "Right. Lots of people, especially
in Washington, were trying to find out what was happening in the Indian
Ocean and in Iran, and what the Soviets and even what the U.S. were do-
ing or going to do about it.

"I was on duty in the Pentagon, in OPNAV at the time and so I was
able to attend most of the briefings and discussions. Everyone wanted in-
formation. One of the little corners of mystique was this Kurd thing. The
Kurds kept coming up and no one seemed to know much about them. It
was popular to ask, 'What's a Kurd?'
"There was a TV show that Paul Bartolli told me about."

WHAT'S A KURD?

Most of the time when Vice Admiral Paul Bartolli was at his quarters in
Fort Meyer near the Arlington Cemetery all televisions remained on the
full time news channel CNN and only a significant sports event justified
a variation from that rule, like a Redskin game or an Army-Navy contest.
When he was at work in the Pentagon or traveling to the many outposts
of the most powerful navy in the world, Madeline could watch anything
she wished and that was never CNN. Bartolli had changed from Navy
blue uniform to leisure attire and she heard him call out from the den.
"Mad, what was that channel you said had the show about Kurds?"

"It was either Discovery or History, I don't remember which," she
called back from the kitchen, "and it came on a few minutes ago, I
think."

"What numbers are those channels?"

Madeline shook her head and smiled. Her husband knew all anyone
could know about his navy, and probably about every other navy, good
thing as he was serving in a top position, OP-06, Deputy Chief of Naval
Operations for Plans, Policy and Operations, but he didn't know his own
TV channels. "Try 45 and 56."

Paul Bartolli sat back in his favorite soft leather upholstered recliner
chair, TV remote in hand and focused attention on the screen as his wife
joined him in the den. "I thought you'd like to watch CBS news for a change,"

She said as he clicked the remote looking for the right channel. The CBS television network anchor newsman had just finished a segment on the Iranian situation and the admiral's wife offered, "He seemed to have good coverage, good understanding of the Iran situation, don't you think?"

"Yeah," The admiral was still looking for another channel. "You could say that the anchor had a good hold on that ground."

"Oh, gee, a cute nautical quip." The admiral's wife laughed and shook her head in disbelief.

"You know what an anchor is?" He asked.

"No, what?" She humored him.

"A heavy casting that sticks in the mud to prohibit progress." The admiral laughed.

"Does that just apply to the CBS anchor?"

"Every ship and every network has an anchor." Admiral Bartolli found the program he was looking for in progress:

"—and after the Kurds supported Iran in the Iran-Iraq war, Saddam Hussein retaliated, razing villages and attacking peasants with chemical weapons. Approximately 2 million fled to Iran and about 5 million still live in Iraq." Four commercials gave Bartolli time to go into the kitchen, grab a beer and return to the den just as the announcer was giving the ancient Kurd origin.

"Solomon, the ancient Hebrew king, was very wise and powerful. When he found that the magical spirits called jinn were causing too much mischief and too many problems, he expelled 500 of them from his kingdom and exiled them to the Zagros Mountains. These jinn first went to Europe, traveling on their magic carpets to the area now known as Germany, took 500 blond virgin brides and then settled in what became Kurdistan. Jinn is what we know as jinni or genie; a magical creature that gives three wishes if you rub the lamp or bottle to release him. King Solomon's expulsion of jinn is Kurdish legend that explains their origin."

Bartolli announced that he had heard that story a dozen times in the last two weeks and everyone was asking, "What's a Kurd?" as Kurds seemed to be involved in everything that goes on regarding Turkey, Iraq, Iran, Syria and even a corner of the Soviet Union.

"Do you mean, what has occurred or what is a Kurd? Madeline spelled out each part of the question.

"Kurd, Kurd," The impatient admiral spelled it out, his attention fixed on the TV.

Madeline couldn't resist the question, "How about the genie, the beautiful girl from the TV show 'I Dream of Genie', Barbara Eden? How does that fit in?"

Bartolli laughed, "Nice try, Mad, but no. There were no female jinn, or genie, in ancient Arab lore. All of the jinn were masculine. The Arabian Nights genies were all men. Only Hollywood uses a beautiful female and Barbara Eden doesn't fit either in the bottle or as a genie." He thought for a moment, "She might have been one of the beautiful blond brides they took but I don't know about her being German or virgin and she wouldn't have those magical powers.

The TV continued. "Thousands of years later Kurds, living in the harsh mountains straddling the borders of Turkey, Syria, Iraq, Iran, and Armenia (formerly part of the Soviet Union), call their land Kurdistan for 'Land of the Kurds,' but it is not theirs. It is the land of those five host nations, and the problems of Kurds today are the same as for centuries; Kurds living in areas controlled by others. The Kurds have tried to set up independent states in Iran, Iraq and Turkey, but their efforts have been crushed every time. Their struggle for autonomy, sovereignty, independence or recognition is one of the longest—and saddest—of stories. If their jinn forefathers would grant the Kurds but one wish surely it would be for creation of a Kurdish state."

Bartolli exclaimed, "Yeah, that's the problem."

More TV: "Over a period of 3000 years before Christ, Kurdistan was controlled by Persians, Babylonians, Sumerians, Amorites, Kassites, Assyrians, Medes and Greeks. After Christ's time came Romans, Arabs that converted all to Islam, Mongols, Turks and Persians again. Around the time of Christ, Kurdistan was part of the Persian Empire and the people were followers of the Zoroastrian religion. Persian and Zoroastrian legend tells of three priests that traveled west from Urmia, in what is now northern Iran. The priests were astrologers, interpreters of dreams, givers of omens and they were searching for a prophet or redeemer. They followed a bright star and are known today as the three wise men, the magi, who came to Bethlehem at the birth of Christ. They were Kurds and they are part of Kurdish legend."

Bartolli commented, "See they even claim to have been the Three Wise Men."

"During the Crusades, Saladin was the most successful and famous leader of Islam, leading the Moslem re-conquest of Jerusalem in 1187 AD.

Salah al Din Yusuf ibn Ayyubi, known to his Muslim contemporaries as al Nasir, 'The Victorious,' and to an admiring Europe as Saladin, is the most famous single figure in the history of the Crusades, being even better known than his Christian foe Richard the Lionheart. Saladin was a Kurd but his leadership did nothing for Kurdish independence."

Madeline had tried to remain silent but she ventured, "Paul, dinner is almost ready."

"Later, uh, no, how about trays in here?" And Madeline resigned herself to forego the table she had set in the dining room and serve on bamboo trays he had brought back from the Philippines years ago.

The narrator continued, "The 20th Century found Kurds living a nomadic life herding sheep and goats throughout the Mesopotamian plains and the highlands of Turkey and Iran, generally known as Kurdistan but divided between the Ottoman and Persian Empires. Their language was spoken, rarely written, in two principal dialects similar to Persian but related to European. Some looked like Arabs and others were fair skinned with light hair. Kurds had never had their own country but they were a distinct ethnic group existing under their own feudal process with tribal leaders and serfs. After centuries of alien occupation they had absorbed and reshaped cultures from all that had occupied and passed through. When they were not fighting outsiders they fought other ethnic groups in the area, Armenians and Assyrians, or they fought among themselves. Kurds have seldom been united." Old fashioned still photos and brownish stiff movie segments supported the narration.

"World War I, the Great War (1914-1918), gave Kurds an opportunity for autonomy. Ottoman Turkey joined Germany as the principal Central Powers against the Allies led by Great Britain and France. Persia was sympathetic to the Central Powers. By siding with the Allies, Kurds expected to be rewarded with independence as part of an Allied victory and after the war Woodrow Wilson's Fourteen Points included a statement that sizable ethnic minorities of the Turkish Empire would get their own states. This was a direct reference to Kurds, Armenians and Assyrians but Wilson's points never went into effect." The screen showed old black and white file footage of World War I trench warfare and former U.S. President Woodrow Wilson.

"1919 saw the breakup of the Ottoman Empire as a result of the Great War with Mustafa Kemal Ataturk establishing the Republic of Turkey. The 1920 Treaty of Sevres included the guaranteed establishment of a

Kurdish state within one year but it was rejected by Ataturk and replaced with the Treaty of Lausanne in 1923. The new treaty made no mention of Kurds and they received even harsher treatment from the new Turkish government. Great Britain saw to it that the oil rich areas of Kurdistan didn't fall to Turkey, creating Iraq to ensure Arab control of that resource and British control over Arabs. The breakup of the Ottoman Empire created a number of new nation-states but not a separate Kurdistan. Kurds, no longer free to roam, were forced to abandon their seasonal migrations and traditional ways. The Kurds had joined the winners of World War I but gained nothing." Antique pictures of Ataturk were shown.

"During World War II (1939-1945) Iran was sympathetic to Germany and troops from the Soviet Union moved into western Iran to ensure continued Allied access to oil. Kurds had supported the Allies and after the war in 1946 a Kurdish nation, the Republic of Mahabad, was established in what had been the Iranian portion of Kurdistan. As soon as Soviet troops departed Iranian troops eliminated the new republic. For almost a year a Kurdish republic had existed but again, Kurds had backed winners and gained nothing."

Bartolli said softly, "So they actually did have a country, a nation, once."

"A Kurdish hero of the 1946 Mahabad Republic was General Mulla Mustafa Barzani, who fought the Iranians until forced to retreat into the Soviet Union. In 1958 he brought his army back to Iraq following the coup that put Abdel Karim Qassem in power. Qassem promised to share political and economic power with the Kurds but by 1961 Iraq was in chaos with socialists fighting nationalists. Barzani's army, known as the 'Pesh Merga' (Death Facers), fought against Qassem for nine years. At first the Kurds were united but unity was brief. The Kurdish Democratic Party of Barzani wanted the old feudal systems but new left socialists split from this party led by Jalal Talabani."

Bartolli turned to Madeline as she handed him a tray, "You know, that Talibani guy, he has family right here in Arlington and we have people in contact with him, not even classified. There's a cousin who runs a car repair shop right over on Columbia Pike." He seldom spoke of navy business so she was surprised with that information.

The TV show continued, "In 1970 the Kurds of Iraq signed a fifteen-article peace agreement with the new Baathist leader, Saddam Hussein. The agreement included a census to be taken in northern Iraq to determine areas with Kurdish majority. Those areas would be given self-government. Before a census could be taken Iraqis began deporting Kurds from the north into areas of southern Iraq inhabited by Shiite Muslims. If continued, this would have balanced the minorities so that there would be no self-government. No census was taken."

Bartolli offered, "And no self-government either."

"Shortly before the fall of the Shah of Iran, Iraq began a campaign to remove all Kurds from the Iraq-Iran border. All Kurdish villages within 25 kilometers of the border were burned and villagers were driven away. Hundreds fled into Iran where they were attacked by Iranian military forces. In 1974 the Shah of Iran encouraged Kurds of Iraq to start fighting again because of Saddam Hussein's failure to keep his word. When the Shah was overthrown and replaced by Ayatollah Khomeini, the Kurds were left on their own again, and Barzani's army escaped along with refugees into Iran."

Admiral Bartolli thought aloud. "Y'know, I'm not sure now, if it's Talibani or Barzani that has the cousin in Arlington."

"In the U.S., a report by the Pike Committee to Congress on the role of the CIA in covert actions included a brief reference to Kurds as an "ethnic insurgent group." This report said the U. S. and the Shah of Iran encouraged Kurds to begin their 1974 revolution in Iraq because Iran wanted to harass the Baathist regime. The Pike report called it a 'cynical enterprise,' leaving 3 million Kurds in Iraq plus 200 thousand Kurdish refugees in Iran without support. In their recent struggles Kurds have searched for and accepted assistance or promises of aid from any source, including the U. S., the Shah and even Israel, further alienating Muslims and Arab nationalists.

"Mustafa Barzani died in 1979 and his son, Massoud, gathered up his father's army in Iran and led them back into Iraq. Talabani had continued the fight and was a wanted man by Saddam Hussein, with a price on his head. During the Iran-Iraq War both sides at various times courted and fought the Kurds. In 1988 as the Iran-Iraq War ended the Kurds were despised by the governments of Iraq and Iran as well as by Turkish leadership."

"If it's Barzani in Arlington then it's the son not the old Mustafa we're in indirect contact with." Paul Bartolli was confused.

The TV narrator continued, "Ayatollah Khomeini declared Kurds to be agents of Satan and sent a military force after them and Iran's present government has not changed that view. Saddam Hussein of Iraq has fought them including the use of chemical weapons and promised autonomy again. Turkey since Mustafa Kemal Ataturk has maintained a policy of nonrecognition, stating that there are no Kurds, or Armenians, or Assyrians only Turks in Turkey. Within that policy all ethnic groups are outlawed. Turkey does not want more Kurdish refugees from Iraq, particularly with about 20 percent of Turkey's population Kurdish, the largest of Turkish minorities. Syria has few Kurds. The Soviet Union has absorbed Kurds as a small minority in the Soviet Socialist Republics of Armenia and Azerbaijan with ongoing fighting between those republics. These host countries all consider Kurds to be a problem and all do not want to see an autonomous Kurdistan formed across their borders as each would have to deal with their own Kurdish populations' desires to become part of that republic."

The program was nearing the end as Bartolli stopped eating and turned to Madeline. "Do you remember Dave Clifford, army light colonel at the National War College?" When she responded in the negative he continued. "He wrote a paper on the Kurds and what role they could play, how they could be used in any Mid-East venture. Well, none of us paid any attention. Most asked, 'what's a Kurd' and thought it was a waste of time. Well, now people are seeking him out. He's a brigadier now on the Army Staff and even the CIA wants to talk with him."

The TV program ended with, "Kurdish autonomy in Iraq, even if it would come about as a U.S. reward for cooperation will not be enough. Kurds of at least four other states will insist on joining and those other states will not allow such secession or breaking-away of their territory, including the close U.S. ally Turkey. This places the Kurds in the same dilemma they have faced for centuries; siding with a winner and gaining nothing. It may yet be possible that President Bush will be able to give the Kurds what leaders for the past 3000 years have not but achieving Kurdish autonomy will take more than all three wishes the jinn can offer."

Admiral Bartolli clicked the remote, returned to his favorite Fox news and continued eating dinner from the bamboo tray as he opined, "Nice job of answering that question, 'What's a Kurd?'"

CHAPTER 20

Barney Williams sat back and got ready to tell more of the Indian Ocean adventure of his long time buddy Martin Shielbrock. The family listened as he described how Shielbrock had learned that Soviet troops had crossed the border into Iraq and of political unrest along with long standing attempts at Kurdish nationalism.

Barney looked over his audience of three, smiled and continued his story. "So, when we last spoke of our hero, he was at sea with his convoy of merchant ships and we found that he was doing everything that he could to protect them against an unknown number of fishing boats armed with missiles. Maybe there was more that he could do for protection.

"He didn't plan on any change to his basic mission which was survival; survival of those prepositioned ships so that they could be used in any future contingency. And just maybe he would be surprised to learn that any future contingency was not so far into the future."

MOTOR VESSEL PRIVATE FIRST CLASS JAMES ANDERSON, JR.

Every Radio Officer in every merchant ship in every part of the world knows how to copy press and Angie Silverio of the Motor Vessel Anderson was no exception. Actually, it isn't legal but it is done and the Convoy Commodore had asked for it, so why not? In his nineteen years of going to sea as a Radio Officer Angie had learned many of the frequencies used by the various news services; Associated Press, United

Press International, Reuters, even Tass he could pick up. He would try a number of frequencies until he heard a familiar tone, patch the receiver to a teletype and out would come the news of the world printed on endless rolls of teletype paper.

Often if he was busy Angie paid no attention to the teletype copying press as it just clicked away, grinding out the news until he was ready to look it over and at times the signal and the receiver wandered apart due to some interference and many feet of teletype paper showed only garbles. With little to do in his Radio Shack because of the communications restrictions imposed by the Convoy Commodore, Angie was more attentive than usual to the press. Baseball scores, stock market prices were up, hog futures were down, Pittsburg Pirates signed Mel Grieves as new manager, aerospace industry corporate changes, a murder trial in Cleveland, the mayor of Houston accused of fraud, ah, here's some world news of interest.

Angie walked into the Pilot House and saw the commodore in his usual chair on the port side talking to that female reporter who had sneaked aboard. Good looker, he thought, but he had been warned by Captain Cappleton not to send out anything for her. Good thing she hadn't asked, too, because she could get him to do anything for, well, you know what, but for now it was best he wait for the commodore to be alone before showing him this press.

Kim McManus walked away after a while, over to the port side and Shielbrock saw the Radio Officer standing in the after portion of the Pilot House holding the long teletype paper. "Hey Sparks! What you got? Some interesting press?"

Angie walked over to the commodore. "Yes. Thought you should see this." The woman heard mention of press, turned and walked back over toward Shielbrock.

Shielbrock read the section Angie pointed out. "Jesus Christ! United States troops are going ashore at Bandar Abbas."

It looked just like a standard desk telephone on the small table in the Radio Shack. Angie had called the commodore on the squawk box when the call came in by satellite. Just like a regular phone call between people ashore but in this case the base commander from Diego Garcia was calling Shielbrock at sea. It was an open voice circuit and they knew to be very security conscious on this call.

"This is Shielbrock"

"This is Anson. You know who I am?"

"Yes. I know who you are."

"I don't know if you've been able to keep up with the news but if you have you'll understand what I have to tell you."

"Well, I think I know what's happening."

"Okay. The group with you has to be somewhere else very soon. It is of utmost importance that they get there quickly. A leader and staff are on their way here. They'll be here tomorrow. You must bring the group to me so you can turn them over to their new leader."

Shielbrock heard the teletype clicking away, not copying press this time, this was incoming general message traffic. He hadn't noticed until now that Kim McManus had come into the Radio Shack and was recording his conversation and Angie looked at him, then at the recorder, raising his eyebrows in question but Shielbrock nodded with pursed lips indicating that it was okay to record. He thought awhile and Anson spoke again. "Do you understand me?"

"Yes. Yes, I understand you. It's just that I don't see what's changed. The safety issue is as before only now it's more important."

"Listen! Once again I am relaying to you this official order. Bring your group to my place. Do you understand?"

"Yes. I understand."

"Good. When can I expect you?"

"You? You can't expect me. Tell the people in the other place, the somewhere else, to expect me. I'll get word to them on when."

"But you don't understand. You must get back here."

"No. It's you who doesn't understand. Goodbye." He hung up the phone and Sparks terminated the radio connection with the satellite. A slight pain went up and down the right side of Shielbrock's back as Angie handed him a message from the task group commander. A few of the words jumped out at him; "—return to Diego Garcia,—turn over to designated commander—." Shielbrock sat and studied the message but no matter how hard he studied the message it didn't change the meaning or the situation.

A series of computer bleeps sent Sparks to his keyboard, then to his switchboard and he picked up a phone and looked at Shielbrock. "Another satellite call for you."

Shielbrock picked up the phone again and recognized the voice of Joe

Farwell. "Hey Shellback, how's it goin'?" How could he be so cheerful? It was a phony introduction to cover if anyone was listening.

"Fine, fine, Joe, how are you?"

"I'm fine, thanks. Hey there's a big party being planned and its' for you and your family."

"Oh? Where's this party to be?"

"It's at that place where they got a band a bus driver, you know, up in Disneyland. Can you make it?"

"Well, I'd like to but old lady Anson wants me and the family at her place first."

"Yeah, I know that, but if I were you I'd go straight to the party. That's just the way I see it."

Shielbrock thought awhile and Joe's voice came on again, "Shellback?"

"Yeah, Joe."

"That's the way I see it. For what it's worth, go take your family to the party."

"Thanks, Joe. I appreciate the call and the advice, and the help."

"Okay. Good luck."

"Goodbye, Joe, uh, Joe, one more thing."

"Yes?"

"I'd appreciate it if you'd tell your friends back home in the palace that I'm taking my family to the party at Disneyland."

"Yes, fine. I understand. I'll tell them. Have a good trip."

"Thanks, again, Joe. Goodbye."

He looked at Sparks and at Kim who turned off the recorder and repeated Joe's words, "a band a bus drivers?"

"Yeah, Bandar Abbas is where the party is and we're invited."

Shielbrock left the Radio Shack and went to the Pilot House where he spoke to the watch officer. "Come due north with a tango turn. Increase speed to fifteen knots. Sandwich it."

"Aye, aye, sir," Tim Smith on duty as Staff Watch Officer responded.

They were on their way to the party at Bandar Abbas.

"We got a problem." Lieutenant Commander Bob Ryan the Officer in Charge of the helicopter detachment walked up to Shielbrock in the Pilot House a few hours later when everyone in the ship knew they were enroute Bandar Abbas.

"What's the problem, CAG?" The commodore used the Navy expression for airwing commander of an aircraft carrier, derived long ago as an acronym from Commander Air Group.

"Both birds are coming up soon for maintenance time. NATOPS requires a series of inspections and replacements, y'know, after so many hours and we're almost there." NATOPS referred to an official published technical requirement for aircraft safety.

"And we don't have the maintenance support you need, right?"

"Right, we don't have the people, the equipment or the supplies. It's all back at Diego Garcia. Now that we're heading north this becomes a bigger operation and we're not set-up to maintain the helos."

Shielbrock thought awhile, looking out at the horizon and the other ships of the convoy. "Tell you what. Let's talk this over with Top Sawyer. He might have some retired helo guys in his group here or in the other ships. If we happen to have the right guy, he might help us."

"But the parts and equipment?"

"I don't know but maybe there's helicopter support equipment in one of those containers. Now, maybe it won't be for your H-3's but let's see what we have and if we can get to it."

"It won't be the right stuff even if there is a container with helo equipment."

"We'll see. In the meantime cut your flying time in half. Let's save what hours you have left for as long as we can."

"Yes sir," The helo OinC was not happy.

Top Sawyer did have a helicopter specialist in his group and he knew of two others in other ships and he would get on the problem right away. "Oh Commodore, I thought of somethin' else I wanted to talk to you about."

"What is it, Top?"

"You said awhile back you wanted something long range, to send a message, you said."

"Yes, and you told me you weren't in the communications business."

Top laughed. "Yes sir, but I been thinkin' and I talked it over with the Chief Mate, y'know. We went down and looked it over and I think, 'cause now that we're goin' up to Bandar Abbas and all, maybe we can get a self propelled gun moved around some and maybe over to a side loadin' port."

"A side loading port?"

"Yeah, these ships, they got a side loading port up forward on both sides."

Shielbrock looked over with his binoculars at one of the other MPS ships. "I see what you mean and they're high enough above the water so that with this kind of ideal sea conditions we could open the side loading port underway. Is that what you mean?"

"Yes sir. Now, first I'm not sure we can jockey the vehicles around and make the move but maybe, and second, it's not like we'd have a high probability of hitting a boat from this ship, y' understand, but we could send a message with an artillery shot."

"Yes, I understand the message but can we open the port when we need it?"

"The Chief Mate says that's no problem. He can loosen the dogs so's the port's ready to open. If we hit bad weather he'll tighten them up."

"Okay! Sounds good. Let's try it and if it works we'll get the other MPS ships to do the same."

"Yes sir. I'll get right on it."

"Oh, Top."

"Sir?"

"How much range will we have?"

The retired Master Gunnery Sergeant smiled. "Further than you can see a target, Commodore, with eyeball or your radar here."

A few hours later Top Sawyer, Captain Cappleton and the Chief Mate were back in the Pilot House. "We can't get the self-propelled gun up to the side loading port."

Shielbrock acknowledged the presence of the three. "Why not, too much equipment in the way, packed in too tight?"

"Yeah," the Chief Mate replied. "We had a few feet to work with, pushed some things around. Top, here, and his guys started up a few of the vehicles and drove them the little where they could."

Top continued, "We even took six bumpers off and the skip box off a front loader t'get a few more feet a' space, but it ain't enough."

The three went on with their explanation. The vehicles were stowed closely together with heavy construction equipment closest to the side loading port. This was so that in the offloading process the first vehicles out of the ship would be able to make a staging area, a large parking lot, for the vehicles which would follow. A few feet here and there, fire lanes and walk throughs, wouldn't allow manipulation sufficient to bring a self-propelled gun to where it could fire through the port.

"What's the primary obstacle? I mean is there one or maybe two vehicles which if they weren't there you could get the gun up to the port?" Shielbrock asked.

The three looked at each other and the Chief Mate answered. "Yeah, there's two, a bulldozer and an earth mover—."

"A grader," Top Sawyer corrected. "They're both pieces of sea-bee equipment." Top referred to the Navy's Construction Battalion using the CB acronym.

Shielbrock looked toward the forward part of the ship. "How much would you guess they weigh; the bulldozer and the grader?"

" 'bout thirty ton each," the Chief Mate replied. "Ain't no guess. Weight's painted right on the side, if I remember right." The other two agreed.

Shielbrock pointed toward the bow of the ship. "The number one deck crane, up forward there, isn't it rated at thirty tons?"

"Hold on there, now!" Captain Cappleton spoke. "Y'gotta rig them cranes together, that is t'operate as a twin, t'lift up to thirty ton and that's with a direct lift, straight purchase. T'get at these vehicles we'd have t'twin the cranes, reach out over the side and run the whip back into the port. We'd have bad purchase, maybe even chafe on the overhead combing. Then there'd be drag, we'd need restraining wires and—."

The Chief Mate continued, "And all this underway. Even this slight roll here would cause all kinds of problems. We couldn't rig to control the swing along with the ship's roll and then there's the—."

"Okay, okay," Shielbrock interrupted. "I get the idea. I can see that ordinarily this couldn't be done underway but this is not an ordinary situation. How about this? How about the three of you going up forward there again and look it over with the idea of topping up a twin crane, reaching out over the side, running the whip into the port, maybe with chaffing gear across the top combing. Then with a combination drag and lift along with a number of restraining wires, we take out the bulldozer and grader and put them somewhere on deck. It looks like maybe the foc'sle is the only place. What do you think?"

Cappleton shook his head and pursed his lips in doubt but said to the others, "C'mon. Let's give it a look and mebee a try. He ain't gonna be satisfied 'til we try." The three departed.

Two hours later the wire strained and the thirty ton bulldozer edged a few inches toward the deck edge.

"Hold it there!" The Mate called into the phone to his crane operator. Then to his deck seamen, "Check the chaffing gear up there. Ease off the restraining wires. That's well. Hold what you got. Take some round turns." Then to the crane operator, "Take a strain." The wire tightened and the dozer moved a few more inches. "Hold it there!" Again he checked the chaffing gear which was heavy canvas wrapped around the edge of what would be the top of a door frame ashore. The restraining cables were slacked to allow a few more inches of movement on the next pull of the crane and the process was repeated. A few inches at a time the monster machine moved outboard. Then, they could see that with the next strain on the crane wire, the whip they called it, the bulldozer would be lifted off the deck and would start to swing out over the side. Restraining wires, six steel cables each a half inch in diameter, would hold the dozer from swinging outward for without these wires the dozer would swing out then back and would crash into the side of the ship.

"Okay. This'll be yer lift. Take a strain. Easy now!" The whip grew taut. A scraping sound from above attracted their attention as the whip cut through the canvas and rubbed against the steel combing. The dozer lifted off the deck and moved outboard just as, hardly noticeable, a gentle roll of the ship caused the heavy machine to move slightly out and aft, placing more of a strain on one of the restraining wires than on the others and the half inch cable snapped like a thread, causing a torque or spinning motion on the dozer. Another restraining wire parted, then another and all six steel cables pulled apart and unraveled like spaghetti as the huge bulldozer swung and spun away from the ship's side, suspended by the main whip.

"Up! Up! Take it up clear of the main deck!" The Mate called but it was too late and before the twin crane could raise the load the dozer came swinging back into the open side loading port, crashing into the earth grader and bouncing back outboard as if for another swing at the ship. With a snap like a heavy gunshot the main whip parted and the dozer didn't get another blow at the grader, but fell into the blue water of the Indian Ocean, clear of the ship.

Captain Cappleton, Top Sawyer and the Chief Mate explained the failure to Shielbrock in the Pilot House. The dozer was lost, of course, the earth grader was unusable, totaled, in the language of vehicle repair and the forward twin crane was out of operation but could be restored to use with a spare whip.

"I told you it couldn't be done, Commodore."

"Yes, you did, Captain, and I appreciate your advice and your effort. Fortunately no one was hurt."

Cappleton replied with a grunt and a nod of his head.

Shielbrock continued, "Okay. We tried. Now the dozer is out of the way and the grader is totaled, right?" The three agreed. "So now we can shove the grader over the side and get the self-propelled gun up to the side loading port."

"Over the side?" Cappleton looked at Shielbrock in disbelief. "That's still cargo, Commodore. We can't just throw it over the side."

"I told you before, I'd take the responsibility. It's totaled and I want that gun. Throw the grader over the side."

Cappleton shook his head and gave a sing-song, "Okay," as the three departed the Pilot House.

"Three four zero will take us right to Ra's al Hadd at the Gulf of Oman, Commodore." Al Bevins had been working over the chart.

Shielbrock looked at the chart and thought awhile. "Give away a little to the right, Al, say three five zero. If anyone is looking for us they'll search along the straight line from Diego Garcia to the Gulf of Oman. We'll be better off making it a dog leg."

Al Bevins sent his sandwich team out to the wings of the bridge and turned the formation to the new course, three five zero.

Shielbrock continued to study the chart. We'll pass forty miles from Gan Atoll in the Maldive Islands, he thought. That and some of the other atolls would make good hiding places for boats that may be after us. They wouldn't know or expect us to take this route, though. No worry.

CHAPTER 21

"So Shellback is doing what Shellback does so often and does best; doing what he thinks is the right thing even when authority tells him otherwise, defying authority, disobeying orders. Here we go again! He's goin' to the show." Barney laughed and slapped his knees. "Steven m'lad there's a lot you could learn from your dad that would serve you well in your Navy career, but I sure hope that you didn't pick up this defiance of authority in your genes."

Steven laughed along with Barney. "Well, I guess I'll have to find out when and if I find myself in some kind of hot spot. Then I'll know if I inherited that authority defiance gene."

Jackie looked at Ellie and then asked Barney, "So he's headed north, we assume that's toward the Persian Gulf, with these dozen or so ships and he has to avoid a number of fishing boats, you said, that had missiles, right?"

Barney answered, "Right."

"How many of those fishing boats were there in the Indian Ocean? There must be a lot of those boats. Could he avoid them all?" Ellie asked.

"No, no, not all the fishing boats in the Indian Ocean. He didn't have to and couldn't have avoided them all. He only had to avoid those less than ten that we think were fitted out for the attack against the ships at Diego Garcia. But now, you see, instead of loitering in the vicinity of Diego Garcia until the 'all clear' he's on his way to the Persian Gulf, contrary to orders, and he doesn't know what he's up against and the only protection he has is what he jury-rigged."

Jackie frowned, "Jury-rigged?"

Barney laughed again and turned to his son-in-law, "Tell 'em, Steven."

Steven feigned a salute. "Jury-rigged means made up on the spot with whatever you have. It comes from a sailboat term describing unplanned made up sails. C'mon gals, you're both Navy wives, you should know these terms."

Jackie shook her head. "I married him for better or for worse, not for nautical language." They all laughed.

"Back to our story," Barney continued. "Martin Shielbrock the Convoy Commodore is headed generally north from the vicinity of Diego Garcia in the Indian Ocean to Bandar Abbas in the Persian Gulf with thirteen large maritime prepositioned ships. He has been threatened by some fishing boats armed with missiles but has avoided them. He has been ordered back into Diego Garcia but has defied those orders. Soviet troops have moved into Iran. A U.S. Marine Expeditionary Unit has been landed at Bandar Abbas. It is essential that the MPS reach Bandar Abbas in time to fully outfit some sixteen thousand U.S. troops that are on the way.

"We're not sure who sent the attack fishing boats, how many they are or how they are equipped but we do know that they are manned by some very dedicated folk and they are capable of overcoming considerable logistic shortfalls. It seems that dedication and motivation are their strongest weapons.

"And speaking of dedication, motivation and overcoming shortfalls, our hero Martin Shielbrock is no slouch in these matters and must also do some jury-rigging."

INDIAN OCEAN

Just off Egmont Island, Chagos Archipelago, in the British Indian Ocean Territory, five crewmen sat in the cabin of their 80 foot fishing boat listening to an Iranian news broadcast. Unable, again, to get Iraq news they listened to the Farsi language of Iran and all of the news that day focused on their neighbor and war opponent as Soviet troops were in Iran, in East and West Azerbaijan, Gilan and Kurdistan. Iranian leaders, political and religious, were appealing for Soviet withdrawal as fighting was reported in Kurdistan. Turkish troops had crossed the border into Iran, but no, that was a rumor, it may not be so as communications with those provinces had been cut-off.

But then a special new bulletin! United States troops were occupying Iran at Bandar Abbas! In response to a request made by Ayatollah Shariatavardi and President Ali Khamenei, the President of the United States had directed that U.S. forces go ashore in the southern area of the Islamic Republic of Iran. Ayatollah Montazeri and Prime Minister Moussavi have declared the Shariatavardi - Khamenei request invalid as the Iranian governmental control still resided in Teheran with Montazeri and Moussavi, and a public debate and power struggle was going on using television, radio, personal appearances and mob violence. Various mullahs and politicians manipulated their followers in efforts to gain more authority as the country was torn by Soviet troops in the north, Kurdish autonomy, rumors of Turkish invasion, ayatollah assassination, and now, reports of United States troops in Bandar Abbas.

The fishing boat crew looked at each other, listening to the confused reports, wondering what they should do. The news report said that a huge invasion fleet of United States troops was on the way to Bandar Abbas from Diego Garcia and this large force would consolidate and then expand the invasion of the area including their own beloved Iraq. Diego Garcia! Their targets! The crewmen chattered away, wondering, supposing, asking. What should they do? Finally their captain, Ahmad Bakhari, quieted them down. "Listen. The news report said that the ships from Diego Garcia have sailed for Bandar Abbas. I don't know what that radio signal meant, now, the one we heard yesterday about entering port. We must have picked up some long distance accident of radio. Those things happen, y'know, but that's in the past. We've got to find those ships and the news said they're heading north."

Moses Farscian asked the obvious question, "How can we find them?"

"Well," Bakhari laid out the chart on the deck for all of them to see. "I figure those ships are in a hurry, so they'll go at their best speed by the shortest route from Diego Garcia here," He pointed on the chart, "to Bandar Abbas up here. Now, if we lay out that track, get on it and go as fast as we can go, then maybe we'll find them."

Borujerdi the boat engineer, more than the others, understood speed and fuel consumption. "How fast will they be going?"

"I'd guess fifteen or sixteen knots. Some of them can go faster and maybe they will, but if they stay together they'll have to go the speed of the slowest ship. They've got tankers. They're slower than some of the others."

"What if they don't stay together?" Farscian asked.

"Then we'll catch some of the slower ones and shoot them. Does Allah care what ships we hit, slow or fast?"

"No." Moses thought awhile but Borujerdi asked the question. "How fast do you want to go?"

"Well, I just want to go as fast as we can. Maybe we'll catch up to some that fall behind and, just as likely, some of them might have left Diego Garcia later, after the others, and they would still overtake us, but I know, I know, you're gonna tell me we won't have enough fuel."

"Right, we won't have enough fuel."

"So, I say fuck the fuel. We'll do what we have to do to get at those American ships and then worry about the fuel."

"No," Borujerdi objected.

"What do you mean, no?"

"I mean I'll have to figure it out. Give me the distance you plan to go from here to the most likely attack, and then the distance to the nearest fuel, any port where we might get fuel, no matter what else is there."

The engineer and the captain worked over the chart for a half hour, until they had forced the distances to a minimum, giving them enough fuel, and they revved up the engines to maximum speed proceeding north around Danger Island and the Great Chagos Bank toward the Gulf of Oman.

Meanwhile, to the west of the Maldive Islands, with over a ton of extra fuel in the fish cargo bay, Ismail Seyyid found that his newly acquired fishing boat was much slower than was his former boat or the boat of his friend, Mahmud Ardeshir. Both boat captains had heard news broadcasts indicating to them that their target ships would no longer be at Diego Garcia but would be proceeding north toward the Persian Gulf and before they became separated, the two fishing boat captains had worked out a plan to patrol across the projected track of the American ships. From Diego Garcia the big ships would take the most direct course to the Strait of Hormuz, they had reasoned, and those ships were faster than the fishing boats, so Ardeshir and Seyyid knew they must get in position ahead for any chance of attack for once behind, the fishing boats could not catch the American ships.

Communications between the two attacking boats would be by hand and flag signals when within visual range and VHF voice radio on pre-arranged marine channels would be used when beyond visual signaling range. Allah would provide guidance when they were too far apart for radio.

Throw the drums of diesel fuel overboard, Seyyid thought to himself, but no, the fuel was precious and it represented the means to get them home when this was over, directly home or by way of Addu Atoll to retrieve their original broken boat.

So Seyyid put up with the reduction in speed and that meant Ardeshir would patrol to the west, Seyyid to the east of the American track. Twenty hours it took to get into position and once there they could only hope that the big ships hadn't passed as yet, that they could find their prey early enough to get ahead for an attack, and that they could get close enough to score hits, or a hit at least. At Umm Qasr they had been told about these big American ships; unarmed, unprotected, carrying ammunition, fuel, guns, missiles, trucks, they made ideal targets at anchor but underway was another story as their speed advantage over fishing boats was a problem but still, determination and Allah's blessing would prevail.

Bird One was down for maintenance and Two flew one hour in four, providing the MPS convoy with a periodic surface surveillance sweep out to a range of fifty miles ahead. Astern, Shielbrock had reasoned, was less of a threat probability as fishing boats would be hard pressed to catch his ships at fifteen knots and even if they could make a little more than that speed it would be a long tail chase.

Pink, gray and blue streaks in the eastern sky announced the imminent sunrise of Thursday and as Shielbrock picked up his binoculars and looked at the lightened horizon, toward the tiny Atoll of Gan, he thought that beyond sight in the direction of the rising sun, nothing, just open flat calm sea. A few hours further north and they would be abeam of the Equatorial Channel, a major water route for merchant ships crossing the Indian Ocean, a passage through the Maldive Islands right on the equator.

The equator; it seemed like a long time ago but he so clearly remembered his first crossing of "the line," the garbage tunnel, Harkness'vomit, shaved head, his face pushed into a fat belly covered with mustard and catsup. It must have been fun then and he got his nickname at that time and Shellback had stuck with him like it was his real name, but there would be no crossing the line ceremony this time, can't take time off from their readiness. His thoughts were interrupted by the VHF radio in the Pilot House. "This is Bird Two. Got some fishing boats your red four to green four about two zero to five zero. Over."

Tim Smith was the Staff Watch Officer and made the reply with a simple, "Roger, Out."

Bird Two had spotted fishing boats ahead. Red referred to left of the convoy heading, green to right, so that red four to green four meant an arc forty degrees to the left and forty degrees to the right. Two zero to five zero meant twenty to fifty miles from the convoy. Fishermen, thought Shielbrock, they're all over the world's oceans. Rugged men trying to take a living from the sea, but still he couldn't take a chance and he nodded to the Mate on watch. "I hate to call them so early but let's have our gun crews man stations, please."

"Gun crews man your stations!" The Mate put out the order over the ship's general announcing system.

"Checking one. Red four, about four zero. Looks clean. Out." Bird Two was going for a closer look at the boats.

"How much time does he have left?" Shielbrock knew that the helo was well into his one hour flight time and Tim looked at a Pilot House windshield which served as the aircraft status board.

"Sixteen minutes, sir."

"Thank you."

"Checking two. Red three, about three zero. Looks clean. Out." The helicopter continued looking over fishing boats three, four, five, six and his flight time was almost used up. "Checking seven. Red one, about three zero. Looks—hello." Shielbrock, Tim and the Mate looked quickly at the radio, suddenly alert. "Looks like this guy doesn't have any nets on deck—," Bird Two paused.

"Shift his freq!" Shielbrock called to Tim who was standing next to the radio.

"Dodge three. Dodge three. Out." In accordance with their communications plan, a series of automobile names represented certain VHF channels and the number following was added to that channel number. Dodge meant channel thirty five, the three following brought the total to thirty eight as Tim switched a hand held set to the new channel.

"Go Bird. Over."

"Yeah. No nets, no fish, no scavengers following. Different from the others. Whoa! Turning now, all the way around heading your red green."

"Ford, Ford, Out." Tim switched to new channel twenty as Shielbrock took the handset from him.

"Bird. Give him a burst ahead to warn and turn him away. Over."

"Roger. Burst ahead."

Modarishar, the deck hand of the fishing boat that had been their tanker, had been listening on various channels and yelled when he heard an American voice. Seyyid slowed and scanned the horizon with the binoculars. Nothing. No more voice.

"Ghoroudi, get with him," Seyyid ordered the missileman to help on the radio. "Raslani, get up forward and keep looking."

With the engine at idle they could hear it before they saw it. A helicopter!

"There it is!" Seyyid pointed astern as he eased the throttle ahead. "Modarishar, call Ruby and tell him we see a helicopter." Ruby and Sapphire were the voice calls Ardeshir and Seyyid had agreed upon for action reports. The helicopter circled Seyyid's boat a thousand to fifteen hundred yards away.

"Bastard. He's looking us over too carefully." Seyyid continued heading west as before, trying to make his boat look innocent. "A helicopter like that has to come from an American ship. We're too far from any land. Those American ships are here, somewhere. We got to find them. If only they haven't passed us—. We got to get ahead of them, in front of them."

Phorishi, the engineer, had picked up the binoculars and was scanning the horizon.

"I can't raise Ruby," Modarishar called out.

"Keep trying."

The engineer braced his elbows on the combing to steady his binoculars. "I see a mast. Just a little." He was looking well aft on the port side so Seyyid started to turn the boat.

"Send to Ruby, without response, that we've been seen by a helicopter and we see a ship. We're heading east. Send it three times and then start listening on the different channels."

Ghoroudi went over to the engineer who was still fixed on the mast. "I can't see anything."

"Without these glasses you couldn't see it. I still hold it."

"Any others?" Seyyid called out his question from behind the wheel as the boat turned.

"I don't want to take the glasses off this one. It's too hard to find it again. Wait awhile."

The crew of Ardeshir's fishing boat jumped to life with the first radio message for Ruby and each time they heard a report Laborsi answered but it was obvious that Sapphire could not receive Ruby's reply. Ardeshir slowed, waiting for more information, but when the final three notifications came with the sighting of the ship, he turned, speeded up and headed east.

Jeff spoke through his intercom to his helicopter flight crewman. "Okay, Wilson, give him a short burst, ten to twenty rounds across his bow, well in front of him. Don't hit the boat. Just let him see some splashes," and twenty rounds from the M-60 splashed in a line across the water in front of Seyyid's fishing boat.

Allah's ass! They're shooting at us!" Raslani yelled as he scrambled aft.

Seyyid yelled back at him, "Get back up there, Raslani. He's not shooting at us. He's trying to warn us to turn away. He doesn't want us to go east. Well, fuck him! He just told us where his ship is," and Seyyid pushed the throttle to maximum speed. "Phorishi! You still got that mast?"

"Clearer now. If his course is close to north this heading of yours will put us in front of him."

"Good! Give Ghoroudi the glasses and check the engine. I'm going to need everything this tanker can give us." Then to his man on the radio, "Modarishar, you got anything since that one before we saw the helicopter?"

"No and I'm still on that channel."

"Pig's ass! They've shifted channels. Go up and down the dial again." Seyyid paused a moment, "Or maybe they got other radios, other than these marine band channels. Doesn't matter. Keep searching."

"This is Bird. Burst delivered. Boat still heading east. Increased speed. Over."

"This is Bull. Give him another burst ahead and try to talk to him on channel sixteen. Use your other radio for that call."

Tim pointed at the windshield status board in the Pilot House. "Commodore, Bird Two's flight time is up.

Shielbrock again picked up the handset. "Bird, what state?"

A few seconds seemed like a long time. "This is Bird. Low state. Second burst delivered. Trying VHF. No joy. No change."

"Bird's got to come back," insisted Tim.

"I know." Shielbrock spoke again into the handset. "Bird, go parallel to him, easy visual distance. Indicate he is to turn and go west. Point your gun at him. If he doesn't turn away or slow, fire another warning. Over."

"This is Bird. Roger."

Raslani yelled from the forecastle, "He's shooting again. In front of us. Closer this time."

Seyyid didn't turn or vary speed. "Another warning, that's all." He watched the helicopter circle and draw alongside, three hundred yards abeam of his boat, closing to less than a hundred. Clearly visible in the open hatch on the side of the helicopter a man stood, belted in and holding the edge of the opening, his arm waving indicated a circular motion, then the figure in the aircraft pointed ahead, toward the east and shook his head with a negative indication, then pointed west. He then held up a heavy gun, pointed it at Seyyid's boat and fired a few rounds.

"He's shooting at us now!" Raslani yelled.

"No." The bullets landed fifty to a hundred yards short of the boat and a few ricocheted off the water. "He's still warning us."

"What are we going to do?" Raslani was nervous.

"Nothing as long as he just keeps warning us. We're getting closer to a good target!"

"This is Bird. No comms. Fired close warning burst. No change. Very low state. Over."

"Tim insisted again, "He's almost out of fuel, Commodore. He's got to come home!"

Shielbrock turned to Captain Cappleton. "Captain, please alter course toward Bird Two." Then to Tim, "Change convoy course forty five degrees to starboard and designate Baugh as temporary convoy commodore." On the handset he called Bird Two, "I direct you to fire at and hit the fishing boat with a short burst. If he slows or turns away cease firing, if not fire a longer burst. In either case return to the ship. Over."

"This is Bird. Wilco, Out."

Twelve ships of the convoy turned right together to new course zero three five as Motor Vessel Anderson turned left toward the approaching fishing boat and Jeff gave his helicopter crewman instructions on the intercom.

Twenty bullets ripped into the tanker throwing glass shards, wood splinters and metal particles around like shrapnel. Raslani's torso was torn apart, spouting blood and throwing flesh around the forward part of the boat before what was left of the body fell overboard.

"Bastard!" yelled Ghoroudi. He grabbed the RPG-7 launcher and quickly fired three grenade missiles at the helicopter. Harmlessly the missiles fell into the water and a long burst of gunfire came from the aircraft as it roared away toward the south east. Bullets ripped open the length of the boat, smashing what was left of the wind screen and tearing open the engine compartment. Phorishi screamed with pain as his neck and shoulder were torn apart and Modarishar caught a dozen or more fragments of glass, wood and metal in his face and chest. The radios were destroyed.

Seyyid was still at the wheel and he could see the destruction, death and injuries in his boat but still the engine was running at maximum speed, he had steering control and he still had his missile man. "I can see a ship, Ghoroudi! I see a ship. It's headed toward us. The helicopter has gone!"

Ghoroudi went to look at Phorishi in the engine compartment. The engineer's shoulder and neck were torn open and blood was flowing freely over him into the bilge, there mixing with oil and water in a sticky pink mess, and Phorishi was unconscious, so Ghoroudi pulled a handful of rags from a bin near the engine and pressed them against the bleeding neck and shoulder.

Modarishar was sitting on the deck amid the debris in a small pool of his own blood which ran down his body from his face and chest, but he was conscious, so Ghoroudi put a handful of rags in Modarishar's hands and went to Seyyid at the wheel. "Can we get to the ship?"

"Maybe. The helicopter went away. I think your missile shots chased him away. How are the others?"

"Raslani is dead and over the side. Phorishi is dying. Modarishar is bleeding face and chest. He can't see."

Seyyid nodded. "Check the bilges. See if we're taking water."

Off to the west heading east at high speed was Ardeshir's boat. His crew was excited as the man on the radio had picked up American talk and they knew that action was near.

"Bird Two this is Bull. What state? Over."

"This is Bird. Zero state. Red warning light and buzzer. I'm on fumes and coming to you. Over."

"This is Bull. Headed toward you. Out." Shielbrock turned to the Master of the ship. "Captain, I'd like to get two teams ready, please; a rescue detail in case Bird Two goes into the water and a fire fighting team at the helo pad in case he crashes while landing."

"Yes sir."

Then, on the general announcing system of the ship, Shielbrock alerted the gun crews and had the side loading ports opened as he called out the position of the now visible fishing boat and directed his guns to fire when within range.

The tanker was still running at maximum speed but Ghoroudi had found deep water and oil in the bilges as drums of oil in the fish cargo bay had been torn open by gunfire from the helicopter and diesel fuel had found its' way into the bilges. The bilge pump had been destroyed.

Seyyid headed for the big American ship. "The helicopter is going to the ship, probably to land. They have no other protection. Allah's eyes, Ghoroudi! We have a target." He was elated. "We're not going to fail! For Allah and the beloved republic we're going to hit the devil Americans."

A splash in the water ahead surprised Seyyid and Ghoroudi. "What the hell was that?" Ghoroudi looked at the ship in time to see a blast and a puff of smoke from the side. "They're firing at us! Some kind of big gun." A second splash appeared, this time a thousand yards ahead. "That's artillery and not very accurate. I thought these ships were supposed to be unarmed."

Seyyid looked at him, "They weren't supposed to have helicopters either."

Another splash, and another and still another, all hundreds of yards from their boat. "Well, let's hope they don't learn how to aim better." Seyyid kept his boat heading for the big American ship.

Bird Two came straight into the helo pad, hovered only a second or two and landed hard. The self-propelled gun barked out again and again from the side port but the shots were far off target.

"Okay!" Shielbrock was pleased that the helicopter had made it back safely and he looked at Captain Cappleton. "Now, let's go to max speed, turn away from this guy and catch our other ships."

Tim Smith had been taking bearings on the closing fishing boat and now he went to a maneuvering board and plotted the relative movement of Anderson and the boat. "Commodore, we may be able to run away from this guy, but right now he's well up on our bow and about the time we complete our turn he's going to be pretty close, maybe close enough to fire whatever he has at us, if he has anything to fire."

"Okay. Then we'll be able to shoot at him with our deck guns. Maybe we can hold him off until we get out of his range."

"We're getting close now, Ghoroudi. Get ready to shoot. I'll keep going in so after you use your TOWs we can get close enough for the RPG 7."

Ghoroudi had his launcher set up on the after deck and got into position. The artillery shells had stopped. Four thousand yards he estimated as the big ship was turning. Three thousand five hundred, three thousand, he counted down to two thousand then heard and saw the deck guns on the target open fire at him. Hundreds of rounds came at him in rapid fire as bursts hit all around, in the water, in the boat. He heard Seyyid yell but couldn't determine what was being said as the firing continued. Some of the rounds hit the fishing boat and concussion, shock, shrapnel and debris flew all around him as large sections of the boat were torn off and hurled aside, but still the boat kept running, closing the big American ship. Then there was a brief pause in the firing from the big ship and there it was, within range. He aimed above the ship and fired a TOW missile but just as it appeared in his crosshairs the missile tumbled and fell in the water.

Ghoroudi loaded another missile and fired but again the missile tumbled into the ocean short of the target. "I don't know what's wrong, Seyyid. The missiles—." His voice was drowned out by gunfire and exploding shells from the ship and suddenly most of the boat's bow was gone, all of the deck house and the starboard side was ripped open to the water line but still the engine ran. Ghoroudi fired his third TOW missile but never saw it in his sight, never again saw anything, as a grenade blast tore him apart, carrying his pieces across the boat and into the waters of the Indian Ocean leaving a splash of blood as the engine stopped and what was left of the fishing boat drifted, now quiet.

Shielbrock called for cease-fire and all of them in the Pilot House of Motor Vessel Anderson went out on the port wing of the bridge to look at the boat, or what was left of it. "Slow, please Captain, and let's see if there are any survivors." Cappleton expertly maneuvered his big ship at slow speed closer to the smashed boat.

Laborsi hadn't heard anything on the radio for some time but Ardeshir kept heading east at maximum speed while up on the forecastle Jansani scanned the horizon. Emani Abolqazeri, the army veteran missileman who had been at Basrah and Umm Qasr with Farscian, Mossaheb and the others, stood lookout on the starboard side, his TOW and RPG-7 missiles on the after deck.

"There's a ship!" Jansani called out pointing off the starboard bow and Abolqazeri went up beside him. They both saw the ship. "Can you tell what kind? What's its heading?" Ardeshir wanted to take an intercept course.

"No, still too far."

Assuming a northerly course for the ship, thought Ardeshir, at say fifteen knots, that means a course of about due east is still good. Estimating the range of about twelve miles we should be close enough to shoot in less than an hour.

From the port wing of the bridge the people in Anderson could see no survivors.

"Let's get out of here." Shielbrock turned to Cappleton. "Let's catch our other ships."

"Look at this!" Tim Smith had his binoculars fixed on the horizon to the northwest. "Another boat coming our way."

Shielbrock looked at it also. "And this time we don't have a Bird to warn it away. It could be an honest innocent fisherman." He went to the announcing system and alerted the gun crews. Then had the mobile gun fire a few rounds out of the side port. They watched the splashes far off the mark and the boat continued as before. Eight miles.

"Tim, try to raise him on channel sixteen and warn him off."

"Fishing boat on easterly heading, this is United States ship on your starboard bow heading north. Over." No response. Tim repeated the call again and again with no response then added, "For your safety, I request that you turn away. Do not close this ship. This is a warning. Do not close this ship. Turn away. Over." No response as artillery fire banged out from the side of Motor Vessel Anderson. Six miles.

Laborsi called out to Ardeshir when he first heard the American voice. "You hear that?"

"Yeah, yeah, I heard it. Keep listening."

Again the fishing boat radio called out, "Fishing boat on easterly heading, this is a United States ship. Do not close this ship. Turn away. Over."

"Don't answer him, just keep listening. We got all we need to know. 'United States ship' he said. That's what we're after and we see him."

Jansani and Abolqazeri were still up forward. "Hey! He's shooting at us. I saw a gun blast—." A splash ahead of them and then another. "I thought these ships didn't have guns."

"Well, they're not very good with them."

"Maybe not but this is pretty long range. What happens when we get closer?" Another three splashes.

"We'll see. Abolqazeri, get ready with your missiles. Jamshid, get with the engine. I wanna use that lighter fluid in the air intake as we go in to shoot. Gimme that when I call for it."

Artillery fire from Motor Vessel Anderson continued as the fishing boat closed to four miles and the splashes drew closer to the boat. Without an aligned radar and fire control system, the self-propelled gun was being operated by Top Sawyer's retired marines in manual mode and optical sighting and as the boat got closer their gun laying was more accurate but still not good enough to hit a small boat at sea, but soon the deck guns would take over.

"These shots are getting closer," Jansani yelled from the forecastle.

"Yeah, I know," Ardeshir watched the splashes nearby. "And we're getting closer to that ship, too. Go back there and help Abolqazeri." Three nautical miles equaled six thousand yards.

"He's less than five thousand yards now, Commodore. The self-propelled gun will soon cease fire." Tim was on the radar as the fishing boat continued to close but no shots were now being fired and the quiet seemed strange.

"Jamshid, use the lighter fluid! Give me all you've got. Abolqazeri, get ready, we're almost close enough." Lighter fluid injected into the air intake of the diesel engine caused a significant increase in power and the boat surged ahead.

"Three thousand yards," called Tim from the radar in the pilot house as two Mark Nineteen 40 millimeter machine guns on the deck edge of Anderson opened fire together. Fifty rounds came out of each gun in a ten second burst, each round a small grenade about an inch and a half in diameter that exploded on contact, but still beyond maximum range the 40 millimeter rounds fell ahead of the boat.

Soon the fishing boat drew nearer to Motor Vessel Anderson, almost at TOW range as Abolqazeri got ready to fire, when a ten second burst of 40 millimeter, and then another as grenades tore into the boat, exploding and ripping it to pieces. Wood, glass and metal pieces flew around as Ardeshir's head was cut off with blood pouring out of the body trunk. Laborsi went to take the wheel but he too was cut down as rounds also hit the engine, sending heavy chunks of iron and steel in all directions, cutting up Jamshid and Jansani and the boat coasted to a stop, torn apart, slowly settling in the gentle swell of the Indian Ocean.

"Captain, once again please. Let's slow and take a look for survivors." Cappleton directed the helmsman as the big ship turned and circled the silent derelict.

Abolqazeri had been hit in the legs, face and chest. He lay in the midst of debris and his own blood on the after deck but slowly he crawled over to the TOW launcher and pulled himself up. There was his target! Big. Close. Too close but it didn't matter. He could feel the energy, the life, flowing out of him as he trained the missile tube and looked in the sight.

Shielbrock grabbed the electric bullhorn on the port wing of the bridge as he saw the bloody figure raise himself to the missile launcher. "I don't know if he'll hear me at this range." He spoke into the bullhorn, his voice amplified into a yell. "Don't be a fool! Get away from that weapon. Let us help you. We can save your life. Please! Get away from—." A roar. A flash. A cloud of smoke and a missile went high over the ship, falling hundreds of yards on the other side.

"Deck guns open fire!"

This time it was fifty caliber machine guns at close range that tore apart what was left of the boat, leaving smoking debris on the water, a large oil slick and the lingering odor of gunpowder and diesel.

"Let's get out of here, Captain. Once again if you please, try to catch our other ships."

Cappleton acknowledged and as Anderson turned toward the other MPS ships Shielbrock went to his chair on the port side of the Pilot House. He shook his head, "Those poor dumb bastards."

CHAPTER 22

It was getting into late afternoon as the sun was low near the western horizon so that the large umbrella no longer provided shade for those sitting on the patio. Barney had been talking for more than an hour, describing what he had learned about the early part of Shielbrock's transit from the vicinity of Diego Garcia north toward the Persian Gulf.

Ellie had been listening carefully. "Dad, it seems to me that those marines at Iraq must need what's in the convoy ships that Uncle Martin has at sea. How can they be effective, I mean how can they do their job if all their equipment isn't there yet?" She clearly did not understand that the 1500 marines of the amphibious unit had what they needed for a short term operation and the MPS ships carried all of the equipment, the logistics, for a much larger number of troops, a sixteen thousand man brigade sized force. Barney patiently explained the different sizes of the forces, their missions, the process of taking control of an area of operations and the potential for expansion of those operations.

Barney continued, "You see, it's very frustrating for the higher-ups, 'the almighty' sitting in the Pentagon, to order an operation to take place and then not know every detail of every step of the process as it unfolds. All the generals and admirals in the higher headquarters have 'been there and done that' and had to deal with constant demands from their then higher-ups for more information as to what's happening. They complain about it later, after the operation. Then, a few years later, when they've been promoted into those higher positions and find themselves anxious for info on an operation, they do the same as their predecessors, they demand more and more info, all the details.

"At sea and in the field it's simple enough. You know who you work for and he knows who works for him. But once you get into the higher levels it gets complicated. We have operational commanders and we have logistic commanders and we have type commanders and each one thinks he's really in command. He thinks he's important but each one needs the other or serves the other. Does that sound complicated?"

Barney didn't wait for an answer. "That would or should work itself out at those high levels without any concern or involvement of the sailor or trooper, at sea or in the field. But too often one or some of the commanders sitting at a desk far away has to know what is going on and has to put his oar in the water. Then it can get complicated for the sailor or trooper."

The others sitting on the patio were listening so Barney continued. "Now, in this case Martin Shielbrock has this group of very valuable ships at sea and the 'higher-ups' cannot communicate with him. They're not sure who's in charge of him, where he's going or when he'll get to where they think or hope that he's going. The information process is highly questionable and they aren't used to that. The entire chain of command is very uncomfortable."

THE PENTAGON, ARLINGTON, VIRGINIA

The Chief of Naval Operations really didn't, and still doesn't conduct naval operations. Operational control or employment of naval forces, as well as army and air forces, was and still is conducted by joint commanders representing the Joint Chiefs of Staff, including all of the military services. It's difficult to understand and very few people outside the military establishment understand the complex structure of the United States military chain of command, which is all right because most military people don't understand it either, although they don't admit it.

Just as odd is the fact that for many of those in high up positions, this command structure is important, or they think it is, and they don't understand it but they think they do. If they did really understand it they would simplify it, but each level of the hierarchy is afraid to admit to the other levels that he, or she, doesn't understand the structure of which they are a part, so the command process grinds along its cumbersome, unyielding and unknowing way.

It works though, not through any brilliant process of leadership from the top, but because the working level makes it work. The individual ship, the platoon, the aircraft, get the job done, report to their single commander and carry out his orders, so the lowest level of operational command in this case is "where the buck stops," to vary the Truman expression, not at the top. The top is where you might say the buck starts, and stays, knocked around from one to another with no one grabbing it. Down at the lowest operational level is where the action is and must be. While the civilian leaders and multi-starred admirals and generals in Washington discuss the issues, the sailor, aviator and trooper must act, must shoot or be shot, move or stay, live or die. Planners plan, warriors act, academicians philosophize and journalists second guess. It has always been so. Politicians? They try to get re-elected as to them that's all that counts.

And so it was in late January as politicians criticized or supported the administration's actions depending on interpretation of constituency response, with no regard for whether the U.S. had a real interest in Iran or Iraq, and journalists were aggressive in obtaining that information made readily available to them, acted like they had discovered everything they were given and presented the news with smug sophistication implying they would have done better and known more. Professors who were invited to comment on TV or to consult with politicians avoided responsibility as adroitly as their profession demanded, claimed background and knowledge beyond mere laymen, referred to irrelevant historic similarities and left more questions than answers.

Admiral Calvin E. Frost, U.S. Navy, Chief of Naval Operations, met with his key staff officers in the Navy Command Center. Next, he would meet with the other members of the Joint Chiefs of Staff in "the tank", but now he wanted to go over Navy matters before being exposed to the Joint issues, to plan, to find out what was going on, what should happen and what would happen.

Present at the meeting with the CNO was the Vice Chief of Naval Operations, a dozen three star directors and deputies and a legion of two and one star rear admirals and commodores. Together they constituted the senior officers of a vast staff known as OPNAV, the staff of the Chief of Naval Operations, existing to help the CNO provide naval resources to other military commanders and it was those other commanders that operated the naval forces, but still Admiral Frost was interested in how "his" forces were being employed.

Lieutenant Woody Tomkins had been briefing the CNO and the top level OPNAV officers for almost an hour. He had covered the landing at Bandar Abbas, the support being provided by the carrier battle group, the disposition of the amphibious ships in the objective area and the attack by high speed boats of the Islamic Revolutionary Guard.

At least thirty boats, thought to be Boghammer and La Combattant class, armed with Exocet and some type of shorter range surface to surface missiles, had attacked the U.S. Navy ships anchored in the amphibious objective area the day after the landing. Carrier aircraft had destroyed and damaged at least half of the attacking boats and naval gunfire stopped a few as dozens of missiles were fired at the U.S. ships by the attackers. Many of the missiles apparently malfunctioned but three U.S. ships were hit, two of them were heavily damaged and a total of eighteen Navy men had been killed and over fifty wounded, sixteen seriously. The Marines from those ships were all ashore, had moved to take control of the airfield at Bandar Abbas and were being treated as honored guests by most Iranians in the area.

Most didn't mean all, and the Marines ashore were subjected to constant sniper fire and harassment by a small dissident element as three Marines had been killed that first day, seven wounded. The plan was for the Marines of the Amphibious Ready Group to take and hold the airfield. Then the Eighty-Second Airborne Division would land at and take over the airfield from the Marines, who would then move to take the port facilities.

Those port facilities, the piers and adjacent staging areas, would be used to offload the ships of Maritime Prepositioning Ships Squadron Two, enroute to Bandar Abbas from Diego Garcia and sixteen thousand men of the Seventh Marine Amphibious Brigade would be airlifted into Bandar Abbas to join their equipment from the MPS ships. Each step of the operation was planned with precise times for the Marines' landing, movement to the airfield and taking control of it, the arrival of the Eighty-Second Airborne, movement to and taking control of the pier area, arrival and offload of the MPS ships, arrival of the Seventh MAB and finally, consolidation of the area, but timing had gone to hell. Marines landed as planned and took the Bandar Abbas airfield but a heavy snow storm on the east coast of the U.S. had grounded the Eighty-Second in North Carolina.

Colonel Don Rogerson, in command of the Marine Amphibious Unit ashore, had decided to hold the airport with one company and take the other two companies to seize the pier facilities. That seemed reasonable until the Revolutionary Guards attacked the ships and now it appeared likely that there was stronger opposition to the U.S. intervention than was demonstrated that first morning on the landing beach, when Rogerson was welcomed by Ayatollah Shariatavardi and thousands of his followers. Fifteen hundred Marines of the Marine Amphibious Unit held the airport at Bandar Abbas, waiting for support, waiting for the Eighty Second, for the Seventh MAB, for MPSRON TWO and waiting for support to take them past the five days supplies they carried.

Woody Tompkins had briefed all of this and now turned to the MPS ships. "We have information that the MPS convoy was attacked by two fishing boats. The attackers were destroyed with no damage to the MPS ships."

"Where did you get that information? I don't remember seeing it in message traffic." Admiral Frost leaned forward as he asked.

A three star sitting behind him spoke up. "There's a captain ashore at Diego Garcia who has been used by the Convoy Commodore as a communications link. They've been exchanging information in disguised form. He got word of the fishing boats and sent us the information in a 'personal for' classified message through the COMMSTA there."

"How were the fishing boats destroyed?"

"He didn't say, sir."

The CNO turned to the vice admiral who had just replied. "Two fishing boats attack a group of our unarmed unprotected ships. Both boats are destroyed. Our ships are untouched. Doesn't anyone else here but me wonder how this can happen? I find it hard to understand and I have to question the validity of such a report."

"Well, uh, yes sir. It does appear rather questionable but that's the best, uh, the only source of information we have." The embarrassed vice admiral replied.

"And that's the same source, the same unreliable source that tells us the MPS convoy is enroute to Bandar Abbas?" The CNO waited for a response but none came and he looked at a vice admiral wearing Navy wings of gold over the colorful group of ribbons on his left breast. "How about VP, have we looked for these ships?"

"Yes, sir," The land based patrol plane officer replied. "We've had a P-3 flying along the track from Diego Garcia to the Strait of Hormuz for two days but they haven't found the MPS ships yet."

"Rhumb line between Diego Garcia and Ras Al Hadd?" The CNO pointed toward the large chart of the Indian Ocean.

"Yes sir."

"Do you think this guy who's been smart enough to get his ships out of port and hide them at sea, would sail a straight line along a track where anyone could find him? The last place I'd look would be on the rhumb line or the great circle route. He's off that track making it more difficult to be found." The CNO turned to another vice admiral. "How about our space systems? Can't you get photo satellite coverage and locate these ships."

"We've tried, Admiral. I've had photo satellite coverage and electronic satellite coverage. There are a lot of merchant ships and their radars are all the same as other merchant ships."

The CNO frowned, "I suppose, that is we can assume, that the MPS convoy is in some kind of random disbursed formation so it would be hard to pick it out, not like a bulls-eye circular formation." He turned to another three star. "How about HFDF? Any change?"

"No sir. As far as we can tell these ships are not transmitting any HF."

"Any ideas?" The CNO looked around at his staff but there were no responses. "Thirteen big and very valuable ships, our own ships, are at sea and we can't communicate with them and we can't find them. Is that what I have to tell the JCS?" He referred to his next meeting in the tank with the other service leaders, the Joint Chiefs of Staff.

From the rear of the room a hand went up and a tentative voice followed. "Excuse me, sir. You asked for ideas?" A rear admiral stood up.

"Yes."

"I was thinking, sir, that we know the ships have departed Diego Garcia and that they are on their way to Bandar Abbas. Isn't that enough? We heard that the convoy commodore would announce when he would arrive and I guess I'm suggesting that we have all we need to know and it appears that there really isn't a problem. Can you sell that to the JCS?"

Laughter included the CNO, who turned and looked back at the young speaker. "Not a bad idea, as I should expect from a submariner. It's just like sending a boat out on patrol and not hearing from him until he completes his mission, huh?" More laughter. "In this case I don't have that same confidence that you would have with a submarine. The initial information is questionable and—," The CNO thought awhile. "I just don't have confidence that the MPS ships are doing what we want them to be doing. That's all I want, some assurance that these thirteen ships are on the way to Bandar Abbas."

The VP vice admiral spoke up. "If we expand our P-3 coverage off the direct route we should be able to find them."

"I hope so," The CNO looked at him, "and if your P-3 finds the convoy can your guys communicate with a merchant ship?"

"Well, yes. That is I think so, but probably not secure. The MPS ships have no secure comms."

The CNO continued his thought. "Right, and no UHF and won't use HF, only VHF clear voice. Does your P-3 have VHF marine band?"

"I'll have to find out." An embarrassed vice admiral squirmed in his seat.

"And figure out how to talk about classified information on a clear circuit while you're at it. It seems to me that's what this Convoy Commodore has been dealing with since Monday morning."

All of the staff looked uncomfortable as the CNO continued. "That reminds me. Why don't we have secure comms in the MPS ships?"

Another vice admiral replied. "It was in the budget the last two years but was cut out."

"Who cut it out?" Silence. The staff was very uncomfortable as CNO turned to his Director for Space, Command and Control. "Bob, it's a c-cubed system."

"Uh, yes sir, but I haven't had any of the MPS systems."

Still concerned, the CNO looked at his Deputy CNO for Logistics. "Tom, we're dealing with strategic sealift ships here."

"We carried communications improvements for the MPS ships as a line item each of the last two years but it was cut out both years."

"Who cut it out? Was it me?"

"No sir. It wasn't you. It was cut out of the proposed budget before it reached you. I'm trying to find out who or where, but right now I don't know."

"Does anyone know who cut out these communications improvements?" No one replied to the CNO's question. "Well, Tom, please keep looking into it and let me know when you find out."

"Yes sir."

"Another matter, before I run to the tank. We used to keep one or two of the MPS ships at Diego Garcia underway for security of the area. That was canceled." He looked at his aide who gave a negative response. "Can any of you tell me why that was canceled or by whom?"

Silence, again. Finally the Deputy for Plans, Policy and Operations spoke up. "We were faced with a fuel cut a year ago and it was felt that we could save some fuel by keeping them all at anchor in Diego Garcia."

"Fuel cut? It's not even the same budget line item as Navy ship fuel. What fuel did we save? It seems to me we saved fuel costs for Maersk Shipping Company not U.S. Navy. I suppose the termination of the security patrols was directed by CNO, that's me. Who did this in my name?"

Seconds of the CNO's anger were like hours of God's rage for these senior staff officers and finally the Deputy for Plans, Policy and Operations spoke again. "It was an OP-06 directive, sir." He gave his own staff code.

"Who issued it, Paul?"

"I'm OP-06, Admiral."

"I know that. See me later today with the officer that issued that directive for you and for me."

On his way from the Navy Command Center to the tank Admiral Frost turned to his aide. "I asked you this before but did you get the name of the Convoy Commodore with the MPS ships."

"Uh, no, sir." Now it was the aide's turn to be embarrassed. "They didn't have his name in the Command Center. I'll find out, sir."

CHAPTER 23

"So the Washington hierarchy and bureaucracy feels very uncomfortable because they don't know the where, what, why and when of the MPS ships. Your Shellback has succeeded, so far, in hiding them at sea from those nasty fishing boats but, in doing so, he has also hidden them from his own Navy."

Barney was describing the situation to Ellie and Steven when his wife, Jackie, came out of the condo and onto the patio. "Enough, enough of this sea story telling, it's time for dinner. Come in it's almost ready. No more sea stories."

"Just a minute," Barney shook his head and replied, "I'm just about to tell about an interesting part of this drama. There are even girl parts in this story. You'll like this. Even Barbara has a walk on role, and me, too."

"Okay," Jackie yielded, "but as soon as this one is finished you're finished for the day. It's dinner and no more stories, no more Shellback in the Indian Ocean until tomorrow."

MOTOR VESSEL PRIVATE FIRST CLASS JAMES ANDERSON, JR.

Spectacular sunsets at sea are common and this one was no exception as bright red, pink, blue, gray and purple spread across the cloudless sky, the brightest colors centered in the west where the sun had just bowed below the horizon as coffee cup in hand, elbows on the steel combing on the port wing of the bridge, Martin Shielbrock watched the colorful display.

"Fascinating, isn't it?" Kim McManus approached, sharing his study of the sunset.

"It's beautiful. Sunsets at sea are unlike anywhere else. It's one of the little secrets that we sailors keep from the rest of the world."

"I'd think you'd be used to it by now, that the fascination would be gone after all the sunsets you must've seen at sea."

He chuckled, "No. You never get to the point of taking real beauty for granted. It's a rare gift, to have the opportunity to see nature displayed like this. It puts you in your place, sort of shows the power and extent of natural forces. A sunset like this is awesome, like a typhoon. It has power. It can't be controlled. It can capture you."

"Pretty artistic and philosophical for a military man." She smiled.

"Does that surprise you? We learn to respect nature by going to sea. The sea can be very harsh or very kind, noisy or quiet, rough as hell or smooth as a baby's, uh, cheek. You learn to love and to hate the sea; sometimes both at the same time, but always you respect it."

"Will your sea behave herself for the next few days, until we get to Bandar Abbas?"

He laughed, "Well, now that you've given the sea a feminine gender, I'll say it is like a woman. She's unpredictable and you have to treat her with respect, as I said. If not, she'll turn on you, surprise you, shock you and maybe even kill you." He laughed again, "But don't worry. This is the North East Monsoon season and the lady behaves herself this time of year. We'll have beautiful weather."

"What does the good weather do for your efforts to evade these fishing boats?"

"Well, if we had bad weather, heavy seas, strong winds, reduced visibility, it would be worse on them than us. These big ships would still be able to operate but bad weather would make it tough for the boats to find us. So, we may admire the kind lady for her good behavior but she's making it easier for the boats to find us, to attack us."

"Sorry. I'll hope for bad weather." They both laughed and looked back at the sunset.

"Is your husband still in the Army?" Shiebrock asked.

"Yes. He's a lieutenant colonel now and still stationed in Washington."

"Children?"

"No." They both watched the color panorama in uncomfortable silence.

Kim broke the silence. "And your children? You had a daughter in Atlanta and a son in the Navy, is that right?"

"Yes, that's right. My daughter Nancy is still in Atlanta. She's with The Magnolia Store, a department store."

"I've heard of that store. What does she do there? Let me guess, ladies fashions, like your wife, right?"

He laughed, "Very close. She was in the ladies fashions department but has moved up the corporate ladder, as the saying goes. She's in management now, you might say."

"Very nice, and your son is in the Navy?"

"Yes. He's in a nuclear attack submarine home-ported in San Diego."

"I'll bet you're proud of him, proud of them both."

"Yes, I am. I'm very proud of them."

"Are they married, either of them?"

"My daughter Nancy has a romance going but isn't married yet. She's tied up with a guy at the store, seems to be a nice guy. My son Steven is married to the daughter of my best friend." He laughed. "We tell them it's like they're cousins. They've known each other all their lives. She calls me Uncle Martin."

"Navy friend?"

"Yes, and college before that, and high school, grade school, I grew up with Barney Williams and he married my wife's best friend. Now, their daughter and our son are married so after all these years we're related, Barney and me."

"And your wife was with Saks in Washington. Is she still?"

"No, she left Saks, went with Woodies and is now with Nieman Marcus."

"In management, also, like Nancy?"

"No. She has always worked on the floor, as she calls it, and insists on keeping it that way. She has been offered positions up the ladder but has stayed in sales. She likes to sell dresses to ladies and doesn't want the headaches of corporate management."

"Sounds reasonable if that's what she likes."

They looked at the sunset in silence as he finished his coffee.

"Do you ever get any rest?" She asked.

He laughed again, "Rest? Sure, I get lots of rest. I spend most of the day and night sitting in that chair." He pointed toward the Pilot House.

"Well, I meant sleep. Have you had any sleep since you left Diego Garcia?"

"Sure. I sleep in that chair. It's big and comfortable. Also, I go down to my stateroom for a nap and to clean up. I get a few short naps every day when things seem quiet. This lady, the sea, you can't go to sleep with her 'cause if you do she gets nasty and causes all sorts of bad things to happen. So I try to stay up here and awake as much as I can so she won't think I'm neglecting her."

"You're giving her more personality than she deserves."

"No, no. I give her all the respect she deserves." He was serious.

"What you mean is there may be more boats trying to attack us and you want to be up here on the bridge, ready for them."

"Something like that. I go down to my cabin for a nap once in a while. So far I haven't missed anything."

"Those other boats today; after you destroyed those two this morning I think there were maybe three others that you made turn away. Do you think they were out to attack us?"

"There were three others that we turned away. We called all three on the radio. Two of them turned and passed astern of us. The third didn't respond to our radio call so we fired a shot near him. Then he turned away. No, I don't think any of those three were attackers but we can't take the chance. We can't let them get into an attack position. That one we fired at this afternoon, I'm sure he didn't hear us on the radio."

"And the helicopters you so deftly stole, or excuse me, borrowed from Diego Garcia, I understand they can't fly."

"Well, not right now. Bird One is being checked over now and may be ready tomorrow. Bird Two broke some parts making a hard landing and we may have a big problem there. Our guys are trying to figure out if they can repair the landing gear of Bird Two."

Tim Smith stepped out of the Pilot House. "We got a ship bearing zero five three, Commodore, about twelve miles. No bearing drift yet."

"Very well."

Kim listened to the report. "There seems to be more ships around us now than we've had the past few days."

"Yes. We're crossing the shipping lanes that use the Equatorial Channel and the One and Half Degree Channel. Those are two passages through the Maldive Islands used by ships crossing the Indian Ocean, like from the southern tip of Africa and from the Persian Gulf on the way to Japan. There's a series of these passages. North a ways there's Eight Degree Channel and Nine Degree Channel."

"How unimaginative!" Kim shook her head. "Who named these channels One and Half, Eight, Nine? Where's that artistic sea lore, that romance? Eight Degree Channel!"

He laughed, "Centuries ago, the early sailors didn't navigate as we do today. They could tell their latitude from the sun, but not their longitude. We call that latitude sailing. They knew latitudes but could only estimate longitude. So it was very practical for them to know the latitude of these passages. The Equatorial Channel is right on the equator. One and Half Degree Channel is on that latitude. The same for Eight Degree and Nine Degree, it's very practical."

"And ships come through these passages and pass near our group of ships. Is that a coincidence, Commodore?"

"I had hoped that our group, spread out in a random manner would sort of blend in with the transiting ships and fisherman."

"I see," She paused. "Martin, I've got to know more about you, about your Navy career."

"Oh, not human interest stuff this time? Not family, home life and recreation?"

"No, more about your Navy experiences."

"Jesus, you want thirty years worth!"

"Sure, but maybe just the highlights."

"Highlights? Lets see; mostly destroyers, Korea, Vietnam, war colleges, what else do you want?"

Shaking her head in disbelief, Kim glared at him. "Just like before; still the uncooperative interview, still the modest macho refusal to talk about yourself. How can I make you look good in my write-up if you won't tell me about yourself? Do you expect me to use just what your staff officers say about you?"

"I don't know. I guess I never thought about it." He thought a moment. "What do they say about me?"

"I told you a few days ago. They think you're the God of Naval Warfare. One of them told me you sunk a Soviet submarine on the Cuban Quarantine."

Shielbrock threw his head back and laughed, then stretched out his long legs and put his feet up on the Pilot House combing. "God of Naval Warfare, that's pretty good. I've never heard of a God of Naval Warfare. If there was one he'd be a combination of the Viking God of War, Thor, and the Greek and Roman Gods of the Sea, Poseidon and Neptune. No, I'm not the God of Naval Warfare, I just taught him everything he knows," and he laughed more at his own joke.

"Oh, so now the modesty falls away and we go on a hyper-ego trip. You must have convinced them of your deity status long ago."

"Long ago? I never saw them before this exercise."

Kim was confused, "You never saw them—? I thought they were your staff—, that they and you had worked together a long time—, other exercises, or before you retired, even."

"No, no," he laughed again. "We got together for this exercise at Diego Garcia and I went over with them the procedures we would use just before we got underway."

"Then how do they know so much about you?"

"They don't. Its myth, fantasy and reputation. Kind of like the way a journalist puts together a story; questionable threads of information and lots of imagination."

Her eyes sparkled with anger and he remembered and looked away as she asked, "Here we go again! How about the Soviet submarine on the Cuban Quarantine? Did you sink one or is that a myth?"

"Come on, now! Nobody sunk a submarine on the Cuban Quarantine."

"They told me you got a medal for it and I suppose you couldn't admit it even if you did sink one." She pointed to the ribbons over the left breast pocket of his khaki shirt. "What are these for?"

"Were your parents married?" Shielbrock responded.

Angry again and shocked she looked at him, "What kind if question is that?"

"The same kind of question you just asked. You just don't go around asking people what their medals are for."

"Why not? Why do you wear them if not to show them off?"

"Ah!" he held up one finger, "A good question. I wear them because it's required by uniform regulations and my high school coach taught me to look good even when things aren't going well. Wear the uniform properly. Look confident."

"Okay. Let me put it this way, Commodore, would you please excuse my lack of propriety and my imposition of your privacy and tell me what these ribbons represent and what you earned them for?" The sparkle was still in her eyes.

"Why yes, pretty journalist. I will tell you of these awards. Did you know that the plains indians earned a feather each time they counted coup, and some of their coups were mystic with—?"

"Cut the trivia, Martin, and tell me about the awards," she laughed.

"Okay," He looked down at his left chest, awkward trying to see almost under his chin. "Ribbons represent medals and are worn with the most important on top and toward the right, or the inside of the wearer. In this case on top is the Legion of Merit—."

Kim interrupted as he pointed to his upper most ribbon. "What are the little stars and letters?"

Shielbrock stopped and looked at her. "I'll get to that."

From across the Pilot House a smiling Tim Smith came over. "This should be interesting."

"You mind the formation." Shielbrock pointed toward the other ships and Tim raised his binoculars with feigned intensity, still smiling.

Again, Shielbrock pointed to the small magenta colored ribbon with four gold stars aligned horizontally across. "This represents the Legion of Merit and each gold star means a subsequent award—."

"Of the same medal? So you really have been awarded the Legion of Merit five separate times?"

"Yes."

"What did you get them for?"

He looked at her and sighed with resignation. "First, I got one for pullin' a guy out a' the water off Korea. Next, I got one for surfacing a Soviet sub—." Kim started to interrupt but Shielbrock held up his hand in a stop indication. "Third was for developin' c-cubed procedures, forth was for startin' up a tactics school and fifth was for bein' in on the development of a naval strategy. Is that good enough?"

She had been jotting notes in her small book. "No, not hardly enough. What do you mean, 'surfacing a Soviet sub'?"

"Surfacing is bringing it to the surface. It's the opposite of sinking as you accused me of."

"I didn't accuse you. I only told you what I heard. How does one go about surfacing a submarine? Were you in the Soviet submarine and you brought it up? I don't understand."

Tim Smith added, "I don't either."

Shielbrock pointed at Tim, "You! You're just encouraging her. Can't you watch the ships from the starboard side?"

"Yes sir, but its more interesting over here." Tim took one step away and raised the binoculars to his eyes again.

"Shielbrock continued, "I wasn't in the Soviet submarine. I was in a destroyer and we got sonar contact and held it until it had to come up for air."

"How long did it take?"

He paused then said, "About fifty hours."

"Gosh, there must be a hell of a story there." Kim looked at Tim Smith who nodded, then back at Shielbrock. "Tell me about it, please."

"I just did."

"Damn you, Martin! You didn't. You give me a scrap of information then cut me off."

"That's all you need to know."

"Tell me about the others then, the life saving and the other three."

"I helped pull a guy out of the water off Korea. The other three are apologies."

"Apologies? Apologies for what?"

"The Navy has a peculiar perverse use of the Legion of Merit. It's awarded primarily to captains who are not selected for promotion to flag rank. It's an apology for non-selection. 'Sorry, captain, we didn't promote you but here's a nice medal, the Legion of Merit, to retire with.' In my case three apologies. The first two Legions of Merit were as a junior officer, too early for apologies."

"I think you're being cynical. It's not becoming." Kim pointed to another ribbon, "And this one with the letter V and the two gold stars?"

"That represents the Bronze Star Medal with combat V and second and third awards."

"What for?"

"All three for Vietnam. While you and your college classmates were demonstrating against us, I was serving my country shooting ships' guns at North Vietnamese, killing some, firing in support of our troops ashore in South Vietnam, interdicting infiltration trawlers."

"I never participated in a demonstration or went to one, Martin. Were you there long, I mean in Vietnam?"

"I never set foot ashore but I spent thirty six months, that's three years, in four different ships at sea off the coast in the Gulf of Tonkin and in the South China Sea."

"That's a long time."

He was looking out at the horizon. "Yeah, it's a long time but lots of guys spent more than that and saw more action. I don't claim any title. My ships did everything, every job they were assigned and I never lost a man. Naval warfare is impersonal, most of the time you don't see who you shoot at. I fired thousands of rounds, got some good damage assessment reports and my ships were never hit. So, I'm sure I killed some North Vietnamese and Viet Cong, maybe a lot, but they didn't get any of my men. So I came out ahead." He swallowed and stared at the horizon a while then continued. "Well, that's the story of my awards; thirty years, a little excitement, a little action, a few apologies, a lot of good friends and a lot of family separation. I served with a guy once, an old timer, who said, `No matter what they're for, each ribbon represents six months of family separation.' In my case thirteen ribbons, six and a half years away from home, that's about right."

Sparks came out on the bridge wing with a message and cast a brief admiring look at Kim. "Thought you'd want to see this one right away, Commodore."

It was from the task force commander up north. A Navy guided missile frigate was being sent to provide escort for the MPS convoy. Shielbrock was to establish a rendezvous with USS MCCLUSKY (FFG 41).

"But how can we make a rendezvous with McClusky if we can't exchange classified info?" Tim Smith still held the message which directed MPSRON TWO to meet the frigate for protection.

"We'll have to figure out some way." Shellback picked up a pad of lined paper and walked over to the chart table. An hour later Tim was back in the Pilot House and Shellback was just finishing writing a message. "Take a look at this," He handed Tim the message that he had been writing.

Tim studied it and then laughed. "Well, the heading and handling instructions are clear. You're sending this to CNO for someone named Williams and you want him to figure out your code then send a classified message to the info addees. I guess that's supposed to get to McClusky with rendezvous instructions."

"That's right."

"But who can figure out your code?"

"Only someone named Williams."

Half way around the world in a suburban residential area of Northern Virginia the harsh ring of a telephone shattered the late night stillness, awakening Rear Admiral Barney Williams. The Watch Chief at the OP-NAV Command Center apologized for the early hour home call and stated his business. "I have a rather strange message for you, sir. It's unclass immediate, sir."

"Can you read it to me over the phone or is it too long?"

"I can read it to you sir. It's not long but the key part doesn't make sense. It might be a garble but the Watch Captain thought we should get it to you right away to see if it meant anything to you."

"Okay. Go ahead."

"Well first, sir, do you know of CTU 73.7.4 and what that involves?"

"Yes," Barney knew that Shellback was at sea with MPSRON TWO under the operational designator Commander Task Unit 73.7.4.

"The message is from CTU 73.7.4 to CNO info to a number of Seventh Fleet commands. Subject: RDVU. Para one says `CNO for OP-024 paren Williams paren', that's why I'm calling you."

"All right, so far." Barney was writing on a notepad next to the phone.

"Para two reads, `Req decipher and pass as classified to info addees and others as appropriate.'"

"Okay. Got it."

"Para three is the tough part. It reads, and I'll have to spell it out, `MSG: RDVU MYDESRON PLUS VANROSHENR 1200Z TACK YR-CANADA N MYWAIST plus YRWEBORN TACK 00 TACK E.' Does that make sense, sir?"

"Well, not yet but I'll work on it. Is that all?"

"No sir. There's one more paragraph. Para three reads just, `two fingers' and then there's like an add-on, like a signature, `Shellback'."

"Okay. I have it. I'll have to work on it. Tell me one thing just to put this in context."

"Yes sir?"

"Do you know, does he, this CTU 73.7.4, have any secure comms?"

The Watch Chief was hesitant as he didn't want to divulge classified information on the phone, didn't know whether this was classified and didn't want to refuse to answer an admiral. "Well, sir, that question puts me in a difficult position."

"Yes, I see. Okay. Never mind. Look, I acknowledge receipt of the message and I'll work on this and then come into your place with a response. Will you tell the Watch Captain, please?"

"Yes sir. I'll tell him." The Watch Chief hesitated again then continued, "Admiral, may I ask, that is if you don't mind my asking, sir, does this ending indicate that this message is some-how connected with, or from a Captain Shielbrock who used to be called Shellback?"

Barney was surprised at the connection made by this chief petty officer and laughed. "Why yes, it is and he's still called Shellback. I'm sorry, I didn't catch your name, Chief. Do you know him?"

"I'm Master Chief Quartermaster Harkness, sir, and oh yes, sir, I know him real well. We go back a long ways, shipmates in Robinson in '52 off Korea we did a SAR together and he cut himself bad with my Buck knife and then in the Cuban Quarantine in Stickell we were with the Soviet sub. I lost track of him, thought he'd retired, but if you talk to him tell him he can borrow my Buck knife anytime."

Barney laughed again, "I've heard about your Buck knife and I'll tell him. Thanks." Barney hung up and sat back studying the conundrum as a sleepy female voice from the other side of the bed asked, "What is it, Hon?"

"It's Shellback. He's having some problems out in the Indian Ocean." Then he turned to his wife. "I'm going to have to go into the Pentagon. It's nothing serious, though. Go back to sleep, Jackie. I'll be back home soon."

Barney went to the family room and studied paragraph three. Okay, it's a rendezvous. He had command of Destroyer Squadron Twenty three, so that's MYDESRON, Twenty three plus VANROSCHENR? Barney looked at the term for awhile and then it came to him. Van Rosche! Dutch Van Rosche, the manager at Stratford in the Ontario League. Jesus Christ, what was his number? Barney searched his memory and came up empty. He could picture the tough old guy and even hear him swearing at his players but couldn't remember the number on the back of his game uniform or the smaller version of it on the front.

"What city, please," the information telephone operator asked.

"Stratford."

"Yes?"

"The Maple Leaf Bar and Restaurant."

A pause, "Would that be the Maple Leaf Restaurant and Bar?"

"Yes, okay, and the number?" Barney wrote it down, thanked the operator and punched the numbers.

"Maple Leaf." Barney could hear loud music and voices in the background.

"Hello. Listen, I have a peculiar request to make of you. Please don't think I'm a nut and hang up."

"Try me."

"Okay. First, I wonder if George Marcial still owns the Maple Leaf and works there."

A laugh from the other end. "Well, that goes back a ways. George Marcial is my father. I run the place now. I'm Tom Marcial. George only comes in here once in a while."

"Oh. Look, I know this sounds crazy but in 1952 the Stratford Indians won the Ontario League Championship and your place, the Maple Leaf, was the hangout of the players."

"Hey, right man, I remember that. I was a little kid but that was big for us."

"Okay, great. Now, I was a member of that team—."

"You were? Hey, what's your name?"

"I'm Barney Williams, I was—."

"Jesus Christ! You were the catcher! You hit the winning home run and—hold on." Barney could hear the bartender yelling to turn down the noise, he had Barney Williams on the phone. "Yeah, I'm back. Jeeze, Barney Williams. Hey, you're a legend here, you know. You and Shielbrock, the names always go together here, Shielbrock and Williams, a legend. Where are you? What have you been doing? I was the red-headed kid used to chase foul balls and throw them back to the umpire, still have one from that day. Hey man, what can I do for you?"

"Well thank you. It was a long time ago. Listen what I need is simple. Shielbrock and I were sitting here and, well, an argument started over some real petty trivia, like what was the manager's number, Dutch Van Rosche. You should have it on a team picture at your place maybe on the back wall?"

Tom Marcial again laughed, "We sure do. Hold on a minute." In just that time he was back on the phone. "Okay. What did you guys guess his number to be?"

"Uh, I said twenty and Shielbrock said nine."

"Well, you're both wrong. Want to guess again?"

Games! Games! I'm trying to figure out a rendezvous time and position in the Indian Ocean and between Shielbrock and this guy in Canada they're playing games with me. "Uh, no thanks. What was his number?"

"Six."

"Okay. That's great of you. Thanks a lot—."

"Wait a minute," Tom Marcial was not about to let go of a legend. "How about telling me a little about what happened to you guys after you left here in 1952? Did you try to make it in pro-ball?"

Barney sighed, seeing there was no easy way out. "No, we never played baseball again. We both went into the Navy and that's been our life ever since. Shielbrock retired a few years ago and I guess I will soon. He ruined his arm that last day in Stratford and I had a shoulder separation. Mine healed but Shielbrock tore up rib cartilage and his arm. But, hey, that was a great time for us and it's been nice talking to you."

"Say, if you're ever up this way, why I'd, we'd all really like to see you."

"Thanks. That would be nice. Good talking to you."

"Goodby."

Okay, 23 plus 6 is 29, and that's followed by 1200Z. In Navy terms the rendezvous is to take place at 291200Z. That's noon Greenwich Time on the 29th of this month. Now, where? A position has to follow. "YRCANADA TACK N" has to 1952, or in navigational positions nineteen degrees fifty two minutes north latitude. The term "tack" was used by Navy signalmen to mean tackline, which was a spacer in signal flags. It separated signals and was the same as a dash. That's followed by MYWAIST plus YRBORN tack 00 tack E. That has to be an east longitude.

The late night phone call awakened a sleepy Barbara Shielbrock.

"Barbara, this is Barney. Everything's all right, I just need some information." He knew that a late night call from him with Shielbrock out at sea would alarm Barbara.

"Okay, Barney. What do you want to know?"

"What is Martin's waist measurement?"

"Barney! You're calling me at this hour to ask his waist measurement? Have you been drinking? Has Martin lost his trousers?"

Barney laughed, "No Barbara, honest. This is on the level. Martin is trying to get some information on his exercise to me so that no one else can tell what he's talking about. He needed some numbers disguised, that's all."

"Well, his waist is thirty seven inches but I would think you boys have more serious things to do than to play games like this. Is Jackie in on this?"

"No. She's asleep."

"Smart girl. That's what I'm going to do unless you need anymore information vital to our national defense."

"Thanks Barbara and goodnight."

Let's see, waist 37 plus year born, which is '30. So, 37 plus 30 is 67. That makes it longitude 67 degrees 00 minutes east. Got it! Wait. Paragraph four was "Two fingers." Two fingers? Oh! Simple. That's the signal for a curve ball. It means he's going to that position for the rendezvous by an indirect route.

A couple of hours later all involved Navy commands received a classified message giving the time and position of the rendezvous of MPSRON TWO and the ship that would provide protection.

On board Motor Vessel Anderson, Martin Shielbrock read a short unclassified message from CNO that read, "WILLIAMS SENDS. THEY STILL LOVE YOU AT THE LEAF AND HARKNESS HAS A BUCK KNIFE YOU CAN BORROW." He laughed even though he didn't see any relevance to the part about Harkness' Buck knife.

Joined with the frigate McClusky, Motor Vessel Private First Class James Anderson, Jr. cruised along smoothly and Shielbrock studied the chart as he had for over an hour, measuring with dividers, translating to distance on the latitude margin, making notes and just staring, thinking. When they reached the Gulf of Oman all of his ships would have to queue up in single file for the transit through the main shipping channel which would take them from the Gulf of Oman around the northern tip of the Omani Peninsula then across the Strait of Hormuz and into Bandar Abbas. Muscat, Oman and Saudi Arabia would be on the port hand with Iran to starboard twenty to fifty miles most of the way from the Iranian coast. They would be in restricted waters over a predictable path through the strait, twenty to fifty miles from the Iranian threat. Shielbrock reached for the radio handset.

Shielbrock used NATO radio procedures in which the escort commander was referred to as Boss while the convoy commodore was Bull. "Boss this is Bull. I'm concerned about an old 1983 movie which starred

Meryl Streep. It was about a woman who objected to a reactor fuel plant. She lost her job. There was a big trial. Do you know what I mean? Over."

"This is Boss. Roger. Wait. Out," Guided missile frigate McClusky replied.

"What the hell is he talking about?" Captain Martin asked everyone and no one in particular as a few seconds of silence followed.

"Silkwood! That's it! He's talking about the movie Silkwood with Meryl Streep, nuclear power fuel plant, trial - that's it!" came from the Operations Officer. "But what does he mean? Is he worried about nuclear weapons?"

Carson, the Weapons Officer responded, "No, I think he means that he's concerned about the Silkworm missiles. Silkwood - Silkworm. That's it!"

"Okay," said the Captain. "I get it. He's worried about how we're going to deal with the Silkworm missile threat in the Gulf of Oman." Then by radio, "Bull this is Boss. Wilco your movie problem. I understand your concern. I'll look into that and get back to you. Over."

"This is Bull. I hope you understand the reference. Over."

"This is Boss. I understand. It looks like a real wormy-wood Chinese crossword puzzle. Over."

This is Bull. That is correct. Out."

Shellback turned to Tim, who had a questioning look. "The Silkworm missile is a Chinese version of the Soviet surface to surface cruise missile called Styx by NATO. The Styx became famous in October 1967 when it was used successfully by the Egyptians in sinking the Israeli destroyer Elath off the Sinai coast. More recently the Chinese have built their own version of the Styx for use as a coastal defense weapon. We call the Chinese version Silkworm.

"The early Styx had a range of about twenty five miles and was carried in high speed missile boats. The Soviets improved the missile and gave it a range of about fifty miles. The Chinese version gets a few more miles and is portable on land. By portable I mean that it's carried in vans with all the support equipment included. It can be taken down in about two hours, driven to a new site and set up in about four hours.

"A number of these Chinese Silkworm systems have been sold to Iran. Some of these have been set up along the Iranian coast on the Gulf of Oman just south of Kuhestak. With about a sixty mile range, these missiles can cover the shipping lanes used by the big tankers coming out of and going into the Persian Gulf."

"We'll be sitting ducks," Tim offered.

"Well, not exactly. First, they're not very reliable. So a lot of them don't function properly. The Chinese don't build them well and the Iranians don't maintain or operate them well. They did hit a tanker at anchor up north in October 1987, I think it was."

"That's not exactly comforting. They can fire five or six, I suppose, and only one has to fly right to ruin our entire day." Tim was not comfortable.

"That's right. But we've got McClusky sitting over there. He'll probably position himself between us and the known or suspected missile sites, along the threat axis, and he has some systems that can help protect us."

Tim looked surprised, "To shoot down a missile? Jesus, Commodore, with all due respect I hope you're not expecting that!"

"Well, wait a minute. Don't sell him short. He has the capability to shoot down a missile, depending on the situation, but he has some other systems going for him. He may not have to shoot it down."

"What then? How else can he protect us?"

"Well, before we get into what McClusky can do to protect us we have to look at the bigger picture."

Tim's eyes rolled in a non-verbal communication of disbelief as Shielbrock smiled. "Yeah, I know, here he goes again with the big picture, but really there are some practical steps that are very important to us."

"Such as?"

"Such as carrier air strikes to take out the Silkworm sites before we get into their range."

Tim lighted up, "Now yer talkin'! But first they've got to know where they are and then fly through their protection."

"Right. The Enterprise battle group is up in the Arabian Sea. They have access to all kinds of intelligence, from satellites, reconnaissance aircraft, electronics, all kinds of sources. It is very likely they can get exact locations of some, if not all, of the Silkworm sites."

"How about the defense of those sites, wouldn't the Iranians protect them?" Tim asked.

"Yeah, probably they would, but I don't think they have much to protect with and after all, that's what we pay those attack guys for. Really, our attack guys in the carriers just live for this shit. If they have to, they'll take out the defensive systems first but either way they'll go after those Silkworm sites if they're told to."

"The trouble with that, Commodore, is that first they have to get permission and I would guess that would mean something like, y'know, Presidential approval. Then they have to locate the sites which depend on threat intelligence information. Then they have to hit the targets through defensive systems such as maybe fighters or ground to air missiles or both. I can't give that a high probability of overall success."

Shielbrock thought that Tim was correct, of course. Presidential approval for such a strike would be necessary and would be difficult to obtain. Then the detailed intelligence information would be needed and there might very well be protection of the Silkworm sites to consider. If the Iranians could, and did, buy Silkworm missiles from the Chinese they could just as well have procured surface to air missiles from the Chinese or a number of other sources. Most of the F-14 fighter aircraft which the Shah had purchased from the U.S. years ago were no longer usable by the Iranians because high technology systems didn't last long under fundamentalist Shiite Moslem culture and especially so when parts and technicians from the U.S. were not available. F-4 phantom fighter aircraft were still being used by the Iranians but these were few in number and short on sophisticated weapons. Ground to air missile systems operated by the Iranians would suffer from the same lack of ability to maintain and operate high technology. They had some Hawk missiles from the Iran-Contra deals years ago but it was questionable if those systems were still operational. In all, the threat of effective protection which would be presented to U.S. carrier aircraft strikes was minimal.

Shellback discussed all this with Tim Smith along with the possibility of the carrier battle group using Tomahawk cruise missiles in conventional land attack version against the Silkworm sites. If the targeting information was accurate enough the sites could be eliminated without exposing carrier pilots to danger as Tomahawk missiles could be launched from Navy ships a few hundred miles offshore and the missiles would strike the exact point of land targeted.

The Commodore added, "And don't forget bombers. We still have B-52s and maybe even B-1 bombers could be used to wipe out the Silkworm sites. It was called 'Rolling Thunder' in Vietnam. The North Vietnamese really feared those B-52 raids."

A somewhat similar discussion was going on in the Combat Information Center of the guided missile frigate McClusky as Commander Martin had asked Lieutenant Carson, the Weapons Officer, to find out what he could about the Silkworm missile system. The information was scanty. "We had an intelligence message on the Silkworm three weeks ago and it gave the exact locations of some sites but said that they could change in a few hours and probably would. So it's safe to assume that they've moved by now. Basically, the Silkworm is a Chinese version of the Styx with some improvements but probably not as reliable. It's a big missile, about 21 feet long. It flies at about point nine mach at a hundred to a thousand foot altitude. All this is conjecture by our intell people as is the max effective range estimated at about 60 miles. It's supposed to have an active radar seeker in the missile head."

"Can we see it or hit it," asked Lieutenant Whelan the Operations Officer?

"Well maybe," continued Carson. "It's a long bird so with its own radar seeker head it should have good radar cross section. It's a little smaller than a Talos but much slower."

They all remembered that McClusky had fired a few months earlier at a Talos missile, which is a U.S. Navy missile now considered obsolete and just used as targets. The Talos was 38 feet long and traveled at almost two and half times the speed of sound. A very difficult target, McClusky had been able to pickup the Talos on her search radar and lock on with her missile fire control radar but her standard missile shot missed the fast, high flying Talos.

"We didn't do so good against the Talos," offered Whelan.

"Yes, but this guy is much slower and with a decent radar cross section it could be a good target," countered Carson. "On the other hand," he deliberately over-emphasized the dramatics, "the Silkworm flies lower and lower can be tougher. We don't know how low but a hundred feet off the deck can be tough."

"A thousand is better, you said a hundred to a thousand, didn't you?" asked Whelan.

"Yes, but we don't know that. It could be anywhere in between. Also, on the plus side the missile uses a radar seeker and we should be able to pickup the radar on our ECM." Carson was referring to the complex of electronic countermeasures equipment carried by his ship, equipment that detected electronic emissions from ships, aircraft or in this case missiles, and through complex computer programs could analyze the characteristics and identify the type of emitter which in turn could be used to identify the platform carrying the emitter.

"Do we have the fingerprints of the radar seeker?" asked the Captain.

"Yes sir," responded Whelan. "Our EWs have them and are setting them into the slick thirty two." Slick thirty two was ship talk for a sophisticated system of electronic countermeasures equipment with a formal designation of AN/SLQ-32 for which a short title of SLQ-32 was reduced further to "slick 32".

"So maybe we can pick it up on the slick 32," continued the Captain. "At a hundred or so feet it doesn't come over the hill very far away." The Captain's reference to "over the hill" referred to the horizon. As radar energy travels in straight lines, the radar signal from the Silkworm missile, traveling a hundred feet from the ocean surface could only reach McClusky when the missile came over the horizon, about twelve miles from the ship.

"Yes sir," responded Carson. "One minute at best at a hundred feet, maybe three minutes at a thousand."

Whelan continued the thought, "So we can hope for one to three minutes of response time from ECM."

"A truism well spoken, Ops," Said Carson.

"How about targeting?" asked Commander Martin. For the Silkworm to be fired at a ship, some source had to provide targeting information to the launch site because unless the launcher was located on high ground, the same horizon problem existed as with radar signals. The target could be seen visually or by radar at ranges of ten to fifteen miles but more than that range required some other target information and the conferees understood that.

"With a simplistic radar seeker head in the nose of this missile," Carson offered, "it only needs a bearing to fly down. Then, depending on the seeker width, it picks up the first target along its flight path." The Captain continued, "So all the past doctrine calls for the protector, that's us, to be positioned between the protectee, that's the MPS ships, and the threat, so that we can take on or absorb the missile, yes?"

"Captain, 'absorb' is a nice way to put it but let's not plan on that," responded Whelan.

"Exactly right, Ops, so let's plan on how 'not' to absorb the missile.

Let's talk about countering it." The discussion continued along the lines of increased alertness, decreasing response time and the use of various systems and techniques to deal with the Silkworm missile threat.

In Flag Plot on board USS Enterprise, Rear Admiral Frank (Fuzzy) Riendeau was going over some of the same considerations as were being discussed on board Anderson and McClusky. Briefings on the Silkworm missile and potential actions by the carrier battle group had been presented and discussed and the Chief of Staff was summarizing. "So it comes down to a series of actions on our part, Admiral. First we have to task the intell system to give us exact locations and defenses of the Silkworm sites. Then we have to ask for Tomahawk targeting programs and while we're waiting for those we can do our planning for TACAIR strikes."

"At the heart of the whole problem is the issue of `authority'." Fuzzy Riendeau let his staff think about that detached statement a few seconds. "Authority to strike targets ashore rests on very restrictive rules of engagement. Simply, we can't hit a target ashore in Iran unless that specific target attacks us first and even then, no command centers, no support activities. It means we can't attack a Silkworm site until and unless that specific site shoots at us or at one of our ships and then we can only hit the specific site that fired at us. No others. Someone has to eat the worm before we can cut open the apple and then we can't hurt any other worms we find." He liked the metaphor even if it didn't fit.

CHAPTER 24

In Coronado, California, there's a little known feature of weather prediction that greatly simplifies the entire process. Instead of historic record keeping, gathering current information over vast geographic areas and using sagely scientific analyses including computer technology, any "weather guesser" can achieve 80 percent accuracy by predicting, "The weather tomorrow will be the same as it is today." Simple but true, the weather in Coronado is that consistent. Matter of fact, similar consistency exists in many other areas. One such area is the part of the Indian Ocean in which the MPS ships from Diego Garcia were in transit toward the Persian Gulf.

Weather in the Indian Ocean was not a major consideration for the Joint Chiefs of Staff but weather in some other areas was of major importance.

Barney Williams was in his usual seat on the patio in Coronado enjoying his second cup of morning coffee when he was joined by his wife, daughter and son-in-law. On the patio they could all enjoy the 80 percent consistency of fine weather this morning as Barney got ready to tell more of his stories. "Look at this beautiful morning," he pointed out. "It must have been just like this for Shellback in the Indian Ocean during the North East Monsoon season." The others smiled and nodded as he continued. "But it wasn't 'fair winds and following seas' everywhere, especially where the JCS were concerned. Weather, bad weather was causing problems for these multi-starred leaders.

"I couldn't be in on the meeting in the tank but I heard second, third hand how it went with the JCS that morning."

THE PENTAGON, ARLINGTON, VIRGINIA

Five officers each wearing four stars sat at their designated seats in the Command Center of the Joint Chiefs of Staff including General Hugh P. Meckering, U.S. Army, Chairman of the JCS. Being in charge of the service chiefs was not an easy task, considering that the other attendees were all accustomed to being in charge themselves. The leaders of the four military services; Army, Navy, Air Force, and Marine Corps, sat to the right of General Meckering in that order, an order determined by service seniority. There had been an Army at the birth of the nation, then a Navy and following World War Two, about a hundred and seventy years later, the U.S. Air Force was created and service seniority is still based on that sequence of origin, except for the U.S. Marine Corps.

Folklore and Marine Corps legend holds that a group of toughs in a colonial Pennsylvania bar one night declared themselves to be soldiers of the sea a few months after the minutemen fought at Concord and even before there was a U.S. Navy. In spite of that claim, probably due to a much later acceptance as a service separate from the Navy or maybe its small size, the Marine Corps' Commandant occupied the junior position.

General John R. Lundy, U.S. Marine Corps, was known as Big Jawn by his friends, then by the press and then the public. Big he was in height, weight and manner and in a booming Boston brogue he pronounced his name Jawn and the press loved him, a feeling not reciprocated as privately he referred to the fourth estate as "perverse parasitic pussies." A year after playing football at Boston College, young wounded Lieutenant Lundy had led his company of Marines through the snow, carrying their wounded from the Chosin Reservoir in Korea and forever after he was known as one of the "Chosin Few." Four tours in Viet Nam, two shortened by serious wounds, included Tet Offenses, Hue City and the Quang Tri Citadel so covering his big chest were just a few of the ribbons he chose to wear; only the highest ranking awards. There wasn't enough space on his broad chest for them all.

Big Jawn was not happy. "I got fifteen hundred Marines ashore in Iran with five days of supply on their backs. Everyone says support is on the d'way, but where is it?"

The Chairman had just been over a summary of events which traced from a Presidential directive. Marines of the Seventh Fleet Amphibious

Ready Group had gone ashore and the 82nd Airborne Division was supposed to be airlifted to Bandar Abbas. The Seventh MAB also was to be airlifted there to join the MPS ships but deep drifting snow, high wind and cloud cover were holding the 82nd at Fort Bragg, North Carolina. Also, Marines of the Seventh MAB would soon be ready, awaiting airlift at Twenty Nine Palms, California.

General Malcolm S. Vanlandingham, Army Chief of Staff, was embarrassed. "We can't do anything about the weather, John. They're plowing continually but the snow's still falling and the wind keeps drifting across the runways and taxiways. We should be clear by tomorrow." He looked at the Air Force Chief of Staff.

"Uh, there's another problem." Air Force General Silas R. Carter was known as Skip and as a B-52 bomber pilot he had come from command of the Strategic Air Command, SAC, to command the Air Force. It always surprised him that of his entire Air Force; bombers, fighters, missiles and all, the most significant to these Joint Chiefs was the Military Airlift Command, MAC, which was not really under his command. MAC belonged to the Department of Transportation. Still, MAC, with its' flying boxcars, along with air force airborne radar platforms, two of the least glamorous, poorest career enhancing elements of air power got the most attention every time there was a crisis somewhere in the world. He had bombers, fighters and intercontinental ballistic missiles, yet all these other service chiefs were interested in were flying trucks and busses. He had been successful some time ago in having the Military Airlift Command shifted to the Department of Transportation so that his Air Force would not have to deal with it. Still, the Chiefs looked to him for aviation problems. "The problem is fuel. MAC can lift the 82nd and the Seventh MAB to Bandar Abbas but we can't use any of the NATO allies or Saudi Arabian bases to fuel the aircraft for the return flights. Now, there's fuel at the airport in Bandar Abbas but we have to ascertain how much and how good it is."

Big Jawn didn't like what he was hearing. "I can have Rogerson find out about the fuel."

"That would be fine, John, but with all due respect to your men there, do you think they have the expertise to determine the quantity and quality of aviation fuel?"

"Does it take some kind of fucking technical expert to sound a tank and see if the fuel is okay?"

"Well, there's more to it than that, John. The tanks at a foreign airport, like at Bandar Abbas, can't be just sounded, and yes, it does take a certain technical know-how to test the fuel."

"We've got people just offshore in the amphib ships who know how to test aviation fuel and how to sound tanks, too," The Chief of Naval Operations, Admiral Calvin E. Frost spoke up.

The Chairman, General Meckering, always tried to keep his JCS discussions on a high level but here they were, the twenty leading stars of the U.S. military, discussing fuel testing. "Look, gentlemen, the fuel will be measured and tested if we so direct. John, would you ask your people to do that and if necessary get help from Frosty?"

"Yes sir."

"Thank you. Now, Skip, we'll need to know your requirements because if there isn't enough aircraft fuel at Bandar Abbas we'll have to get some there. J-4 is already working on it." The Chairman referred to the logistics section, J-4, of the Joint Staff.

Admiral Frost spoke up, "As you are aware, Hugh, as all of us are aware, a ship loaded with JP-5 was lost at Diego Garcia a few days ago. That's a very big part of the aviation fuel that would have been available to us. MSC is trying to get a short notice charter on a replacement." MSC meant the Military Sealift Command and JP-5 was aviation fuel.

"Yes, Frosty, we're aware of that loss and we'll have to wait and see about the replacement of that fuel," the Chairman acknowledged.

Skip Carter liked to have things neatly packaged and in order and unless every item on his bomber's pre-flight list was checked off, he didn't fly. "Hugh, we can't ask MAC to commit to an airlift unless we are sure of this fuel issue. I realize J-4 is looking at it but I'm telling you it won't go unless we are assured," he emphasized the word assured," that the fuel is there in quantity and in quality."

"We understand, Skip." The Chairman replied and then he was interrupted by Big Jawn.

"Skip, I just said a little while ago I have fifteen hundred Marines at Bandar Abbas living on what they carried in. They're being sniped at continually and intell says there may be a big hit coming at them. They're holding that airfield and they still have to take the pier facilities for the MPS ships. Now, unless you get the Eighty Second and/or the Seventh MAB in there, and soon, my people are going to have to walk back across the beach and leave. Once, just once, Skip, I'd like to see the fucking Air Force make a contribution to carrying out national policy."

"I object to that!" The Air Force Chief of Staff was enraged as he stood and faced Big Jawn. "That's a God Damned insult—."

"It's the fucking truth!" The Marine Corps Commandant also rose and faced his neighbor.

From the far left the Chairman could do little to intercede. "Gentlemen, please—."

"I demand an apology!" raged Skip Carter.

"You'll get shit," Big Jawn barked back. The two generals faced each other, the taller marine glaring down at his shorter air force counterpart. "And I'll tell you something else, Skippy, you can dance around all you want but when the Seventh MAB is ready to move, they'll move, and if your Military Airlift Command won't fly I'll charter commercial aircraft to move them."

"That's insulting, cruel and unfair. I object to your implications and your—."

"Gentlemen, gentlemen, please! Please sit down and calm down. Insult, anger and innuendo will get us nothing." The Chairman finally brought the situation under control. "John, I'm sure we're doing everything to get the airlift going." The Marine general looked away. "Skip," the Chairman continued, "I'm sure your people are doing everything they can but if you can't lift them as John says, we may have to find other means."

An insulted and embarrassed Air Force Chief of Staff glared at the Chairman, who had been an airborne trooper himself long ago and had experienced the frustrations of dealing with the Air Force.

General Meckering brought the attention of the Chiefs to Major Donald Thompson who had just taken a position at the briefer's rostrum. An intelligence specialist, Thompson had given the Joint Chiefs a view of Iran's internal situation just a few days ago. Now, events had unfolded rapidly and another briefing was in order so today he would provide the Chiefs with a summary of his previous information, a look at what had now developed and some interesting insights and estimates.

Thompson spoke, "I'm going to cover what we know, what we suspect and what we guess-timate." They knew that "we" meant the intelligence community and a "guess-timate" was the product of careful analysis, experience and crystal ball fortune telling.

Six Ayatollahs was the heading on the view graph which showed the geographic area, degree of fanaticism and Soviet or U.S. leaning of the principal religious leaders and Thompson discussed each as he had before, pointing out that Ayatollah Jamshid Montaheb, the Bushehr moderate, had been killed, presumably by Ghormezian's fanatic hit squads. The next view-graph was entitled Areas of Influence and Thompson described the ongoing power struggle by regions.

In Teheran, Ayatollah Hossein Ali Montazeri, who had been identified earlier as the heir to the position of Grand Ayatollah, was struggling to maintain control of the country. Also in Teheran, the extremist fanatic Ayatollah Borushir Ghormezian campaigned for the position of absolute power, announcing that only he represented the future of a true Shiite fundamentalist society originating out of a decadent Iran to spread ultimately across all of Islam. Openly and publicly he had stated that opposition must be removed by any and all means including physical force including death to Ghormezian and his followers. Opposition included moderates as well as any who favored east or west, Soviet or U.S.

Thompson explained, "On a more local level there is Ayatollah Gholam Fattachian, a pro-Soviet seeking to establish an independent State of Azerbaijan with Soviet support while similarly, in the province of Gilan, Ayatollah Bakhari Zenderasem hoped to establish that province as a Soviet Socialist Republic.

"This now brings us to the Ayatollah Mahmud Shariatavardi, a moderate pro-American from the Bandar Abbas area." Thompson continued as the Joint Chiefs smiled, "Shariatavardi is the latest darling of the American press. They've even started to refer to him as 'Shari' and we have seen media pictures of him leading thousands in prayers of thanks, welcoming United States Marines as they came ashore. He is the one who requested, pleaded for, begged the President of the U.S. to send help to keep his country from being over-run by the god-less communist tyrants of the Soviet Union.

"Shari convinced political leaders such as the leader of Parliament, Hashami Rafsanjani and the President of the Republic, Ali Khamenei that only with American intervention could the Islamic Republic be saved from Soviet domination. He is why we have U.S. troops in Iran today and why more are enroute." Thompson paused and looked at the Joint Chiefs.

"What do we know of Ayatollah Mahmud Shariatavardi? Let me share with you some very recent intelligence information."

The Chiefs looked at each other as this was rather dramatic for an intelligence briefing, generally dry and factual, as Major Donald Thompson continued. "Shariatavardi would like to be recognized as the Grand Ayatollah some day but the cards are stacked against him. Montazeri holds that position. Ghormezian has a widespread fanatic following. Fattachian and Zenderasem have strong but localized followings.

"To gain strength, Shari must figure out a plan to weaken the others and focus attention and success upon himself. He has done this. The assassination of Montaheb is blamed on Ghormezian. We have reliable information that Shari directed it and was the first to blame Ghormezian."

The chiefs looked at each other.

"Rioting and anarchy has demonstrated lack of effective control by Montazeri and has caused foreign intervention by the USSR and the U.S. We have reliable information that Shari encouraged and caused much of this disruption, deliberately, to provoke anarchy and then intervention.

"Also we have reliable information that Ayatollah Shariatavardi encouraged Abu Al Amuzagar to move for Kurdish autonomy and that Shariatavardi promised his own support, Iranian military support, and even United States military support to the Kurds.

"Now, gentlemen, if you get the idea that Ayatollah Shariatavardi, the great friend of the United States might be a rogue, please let me continue. Shari might also be the instigator of a complex plan that started at least six months ago, a plan which sent a group of poorly prepared fishing boats to Diego Garcia to attack the Maritime Prepositioned Ships there. Our analysts are still researching this, we can't prove it yet and we are holding this close, highly classified. We have indications that this operation might have come out of Iraq but made to look Iranian so that the blame could be attached to others but the action would help bring the U.S. into Iran."

The Chief of Naval Operations interrupted at this point. "So the attack at Diego Garcia that hit Hauge and killed an officer, and the attack that destroyed Overseas Valdez, might have started with Shari?"

"Well, yes sir, but 'might' is the key word. We don't know for sure and as to the details of this plan, the extent of the operation, uh, we really don't know where they came from or how many boats are involved. One was destroyed at Diego Garcia after hitting the tanker and we think two were destroyed by the MPS convoy. Earlier we were told by the people in the one stopped in the Seychelles that another had turned back. So we know of six fishing boats and there may be more."

"And you think that Shari staged this attack to make Montazeri look bad?"

"That may be, yes sir. He, that is Shari, was on the radio and TV blaming Montazeri before anyone knew the results of the attack. The boats we know of were still 'at large' at the time and it worked. The people were, or are, still angry at Montazeri for trying such a foolish operation even though Montazeri keeps insisting he knows nothing about it and we think that he may be right."

Admiral Frost shook his head in disbelief as did the others. "Jesus Christ and he's supposed to be on our side, our friend."

Major Thompson was not finished, "There's more, Admiral."

"Oh, I'm sorry. Go on, please."

"We have reliable information which indicates that Shari convinced Mohsen Rezai, the head of the Iranian Revolutionary Guard, to attack the U.S. Navy ships off Bandar Abbas with Boghammer and La Combattant boats. Then he alerted our people when and from where the attacks would come. There were more boats than we expected but our battle group was able to chop them up pretty well."

"We still had a couple of ships hit and a lot of people killed," the CNO contributed.

"Yes sir. The Revolutionary Guard lost a major part of their force, though, and Shari blamed Montazeri for that, too. So, he stages an operation and doesn't care if it succeeds or not because if it fails, he blames Montazeri and we suppose that if by accident it would succeed, he would take credit."

General Meckering commented, "With friends like this, do we need enemies?"

"And for the likes of this bastard we're risking our people." Big Jawn thought aloud.

Thompson continued with his briefing, giving political issues and describing what was left of Iranian military resources. As he concluded, Admiral Frost was handed a note by his aide.

"Well, here's an interesting item." Frost looked at the note awhile, then at the vertical chart of the Indian Ocean on the side wall. "USDAO Columbo, Sri Lanka, reports a complaint from the government of the Maldives that, let's see it would be two days ago, one of their fishing boats was fired upon at long range, doesn't say how long, by a large black hulled merchant ship believed to be a U.S. ship." USDAO stood for United States

Defense Attaché Office. In this case the U.S. had no such office in the Maldives so the Sri Lanka office took care of that business.

Before the CNO could continue Big Jawn spoke up, "That could be an MPS ship."

The CNO smiled, "Must be, John, the report goes on to say the ship was one of many, all heading north. This happened west of Nine Degree Passage." They strained to read the fine print on the chart until an army sergeant walked to the chart with a pointer and indicated the location.

"Okay! Heading north, good, and John, it says the boat was fired upon at long range. That means they're using your artillery."

"Good!" The Commandant of the Marine Corps looked at the Air Force Chief of Staff. "At least someone is doing everything they can to get to Bandar Abbas."

Skip Carter looked away still embarrassed and angry.

General Malcolm S. Vanlandingham, the Army Chief of Staff had spent most of his career years in Washington and was more sensitive to political issues than the others as he addressed the Chairman. "Hugh, this business with Shariatavardi has very serious implications. I hear in this some echoes of the past, unpleasant echoes, sounds similar to Watergate and Viet Nam, sounds like cover-up. There is a very serious ethical issue here and it is imperative that we know, at this point, if this duplicity is real and, if so, who else knows of this? Specifically, does the President know about this double crossing bastard? Who else knows? Are we backing a dead horse? Will we find ourselves next week or next year fighting to survive as occupation forces in a hostile environment, maybe fighting to keep an unpopular regime in place? Does all that sound familiar?"

"Mal, I can't answer all of your questions," The Chairman replied, "and I'm quite sure no one can. One question I can answer is that the President does know what we suspect about Shariatavardi, he is aware of the sensitivity and is going over the problem with his council. I'll be a part of that study."

Vanlandingham responded, "That's fine Hugh but I want this clearly understood by all here. Call it a classic 'cover your ass' move if you will. I am today sending you as Chairman a personal memo and putting a copy in my records, stating that I have just learned of Shariatavardi's duplicity and that the U.S. military has been placed in an untenable position. We are backing a person who clearly cannot be trusted and unless some more stable reliable Iranian leadership comes on the scene I will support the

War Powers Act and speak publicly for withdrawal of U.S. forces from Iran."

The Chairman spoke as he looked directly and hard at the Army Chief of Staff. "I'm sorry to hear you say that, Mal, because I think you are acting prematurely. We all want withdrawal as soon as possible. Also, I believe you are placing your position here as a member of this staff and as a service head in jeopardy. The present administration, any administration, cannot tolerate threats from their own senior advisors. I recommend that you couch your memo in terms of constructive advice rather than in tones of ultimatum."

"Thank you for your recommendation, Hugh, but I intend it as an ultimatum." The Army Chief of Staff got up and left the command center.

CHAPTER 25

"So while the generals and admirals are arguing back in the Pentagon, Uncle Martin has to get those ships to Bandar Abbas, right, and he has to get through some obstacles, right?" Ellie asked.

"Right," her father replied, "and as you might expect, whereas anyone else would take those big ships through the deepest widest channels, this is Martin Shielbrock, who doesn't do anything like anyone else would. He does things 'my way' remember, and that means 'his way'.

"Now he has to get his ships through what he thinks is the safest route, which is a narrow passage that will take him past the shore based missiles but with the least exposure to those missiles. He has an escort but he's still in charge."

GULF OF OMAN

Thirteen ship Masters listened carefully to the Convoy Commodore on their VHF marine band radios. Channel seventy was sandwiched between tactical chatter on channel sixty nine by Tim Smith and John Harvey on channel seventy one. It was to be a long radio transmission, longer than Shielbrock liked, but he considered it necessary. "We've come a long way together and we've been fortunate so far. Ahead of us is the passage through the Gulf of Oman across the Strait of Hormuz and into Bandar Abbas. Most of that transit will be the most dangerous part of the trip for us because we not only have this continuing threat from fishing boats, but perhaps better equipped, higher performance Revolutionary Guard boats. Also, there are shore based missiles along the Iranian coast that may be able to reach us if they get the proper targeting information.

"Here's what I intend to do. I'm ordering all of you to follow me in two columns close along the coast of Oman, through the Inshore Traffic Zone, across the main shipping channel, behind Larak Island and into Bandar Abbas. I know that each of you is responsible for the safety of your individual ship and I have taken away your means of getting approval of your owners by HF radio. I accept that responsibility. I will share my reasoning with you.

"The Iranians will expect us to transit the Gulf of Oman into the main shipping channel. Their missiles are along the coast south of Kuhestak. If we proceed at night close to the Oman coast they'll have a difficult time locating and targeting us and they may be reluctant to fire missiles at us with Omani land in our background. We can duck behind the As Salamah and Didamar complex of rocks and cross perpendicular to the main shipping channel. That will minimize our exposure and we'll be at long range for those missiles until we get behind Larak Island.

"So, standby to write and to use your recorders. Point Alfa is at latitude twenty five north, longitude fifty seven east. From there we go on a course of three three zero, fifty seven miles to Point Bravo, twenty five degrees fifty two minutes north, fifty six degrees thirty minutes east. Then zero zero three for nineteen miles to Point Charlie, twenty six degrees eleven minutes north, fifty six degrees thirty one minutes east. On course zero one two we steam fourteen miles to Point Delta, just off Bu Rashid, twenty six twenty five north, fifty six thirty five east. When you plot that you'll notice we're in the territorial waters of the Sultanate of Oman from just before Point Bravo until after Point Delta. That may cause some problems for the State Department but that will be after the fact.

"From Point Delta we go through and across the Inshore Traffic Zone on a course of three zero five, close to Ennerdale Rock, nine miles to Point Echo at twenty six thirty north, fifty six twenty six east.

"Then we have to cross the main shipping channel. There'll be heavy outbound traffic on the south side, a neutral zone, and then heavy traffic inbound. This is our most dangerous leg. We'll be on course three three nine for twenty two miles. That's an hour and twenty minutes of exposure. The guided missile frigate USS McClusky will be between us and the shore based missiles. Have your Stinger team in alert during that time."

"Point Foxtrot is close to the western end of Larak Island, twenty six fifty north, fifty six seventeen east. From there we take course zero two three for ten miles to Point Golf, the entrance to Clarence Strait, twenty six fifty nine north, fifty six twenty one east. The Bandar Abbas anchorage area is seven miles from Point Golf on course three one four.

"I hope you understand my reasoning and see that this route minimizes the chances of our being detected and minimizes our exposure to those missiles. I think this plan gives us the best chance of arriving safely at Bandar Abbas. Over."

Thirteen ships promptly acknowledged the Commodore's plan with snappy, "Roger, Out," including Irving Cappleton standing alongside in the Pilot House of Motor Vessel Anderson. Shielbrock turned to the ship's Master. "Well, Captain, what do you think? Can you take us that route?"

Cappleton chewed a cigarette, "Shit yes, Commodore. I like it. You got a real feel for this stuff, n'I think we just might slip right past them bastards the way you got it figured."

"Thanks, Captain. I hope so."

Kim McManus had been recording the long radio transmission "That sounds good, Martin, but what about that business of being in Omani territorial waters?"

"Well, Kim, I'll tell ya'," He stopped and thought awhile. "It'll be at night so maybe the Omanis won't even know we're in their waters. But really, legally, we aren't supposed to intrude into their waters without their approval. Maybe they would grant approval. Maybe they don't care. I don't have time to find out. What's the worst that could happen? A diplomatic protest? The U.S. apologizes and the commodore who ordered the intrusion gets punished. What can they do to me? Add this to my long list of offenses and put me in jail? I think not. Maybe they'll take away my command and put me ashore," he laughed. "What I'm more concerned about is the liability of the Masters of the ships. That's why I said, 'I'm ordering all of you—.' Each of them is responsible for his own ship but I'm hoping that if there is trouble over this later, my ordering will help get them off the hook."

"And you'll be left with the blame."

"Well, maybe there won't be any blame."

"But you've got that destroyer here now, protecting us. Isn't it up to the captain of that ship to get us to Bandar Abbas?"

"Yes and he's a good man. It's a guided missile frigate, incidentally, not a destroyer. We call it a fig seven, for FFG-7 class ship. The CO is Jim Martin. He's a commander now. A few years ago he was a lieutenant commander when he attended my tactics course but we didn't cover protection of merchant shipping."

"So, he's a Shellback trained man and you think he needs another lesson in tactics."

"No. He's a big boy now and on his own but we all need help whenever we can get it. So, we worked out this inshore transit scheme. He'll be between us and the Silkworm sites all the way. I don't envy him that role. He has to try to shoot down any Silkworm missiles that come our way."

"Can he do that?" Kim McManus asked.

Shielbrock looked at her a moment, "Well, let me put it this way, it is possible for a fig seven to shoot down a Silkworm missile and if he gets one it'll be the finest performance by a missile ship I've ever seen."

"So you're saying there's a low probability of success in that frigate shooting down a Silkworm missile."

"Well, it's all relative because there's a low probability of Iranian success in locating us, targeting us and getting complete performance from their missile."

"Isn't this something like that ship Stark a few years ago in the Persian Gulf? It was a fig seven, too, I think, and it got hit with a missile. Why is this any different?"

Shielbrock shook his head, "This is a lot different. Stark had different rules of engagement, different alertment, different geography to deal with. Here, McClusky is dealing with a slow surface-to-surface missile. Stark was hit with a fast air-to-surface missile, an Exocet, more sophisticated, a harder target. McClusky stands a much better chance of success than did Stark."

Kim looked doubtful, "If you say so."

Al Bevins, John Harvey and Tim Smith had been working up the tactical signals which would change the spread formation they had been in since Diego Garcia to the two columns for the Oman transit.

After four hours of careful signals and more careful ship handling the convoy was arranged in two parallel columns. Anderson and Baugh, two thousand yards apart, each led a column. Anderson's column, to the right of Baugh's, consisted of seven ships. Baugh's column had six ships. Ships astern followed in the wake of the ship ahead at a distance of two thousand yards, which is one nautical mile, making a formation six miles long.

Darkness fell over the Gulf of Oman as the convoy passed Point Alfa with about a hundred and forty miles to Bandar Abbas and at seventeen knots, barring unplanned diversions, they would arrive at the anchorage at about 0300. McClusky, the guided missile frigate, maintained station five miles to starboard of the convoy, in international waters.

Three hours and twenty minutes later, in the territorial waters of Oman, the first of the convoy ships passed through Point Bravo and changed course to zero zero three. Lights on the shore were clearly visible only four miles away on their port side. Ras Limah was cleared by two miles twenty minutes later and then Ras Sarkan also close; two miles. Between the tiny island Um al Fayyarin to starboard and the mainland to port it was like threading a needle with big ships going seventeen knots. Fishing boats and dhows scattered out of their way, at times causing quick alterations of the convoy's course or swerves by an individual ship which then hustled back into column position.

Clearing Point Charlie, the convoy changed slightly to the right, to zero one two encountering more fishing boats, causing other quick course changes to avoid a large dimly lighted group of boats.

"Fuckin' ay-rabs! We ought'a just run the bastards down." Cappleton was on the bridge of his ship all this night, looking ahead into the darkness, studying the chart, watching the radar and the fathometer.

"No, no, Captain. Please don't. I'm in enough trouble for just intruding into Omani waters. Wiping out some fishermen would put me away forever," Shielbrock uttered a weak false plea.

"Aw shit, Commodore. Them big brass Navy guys ain't gonna fry you. They're gonna give you another big medal for this. You're savin' their ass! Y'know, these MPS ships'd still be laying at Diego Garcia or some other place if it weren't fer you. You just keep callin' the shots, Shellback, and we'll make it."

Cappleton's encouragement and use of the commodore's nickname was noticed with some satisfaction. Shellback smiled, "Well, thanks, Captain."

At Point Delta the convoy came left to new course three zero five and entered the Inshore Traffic Zone, south of the Didamar and As Salamah Island complex, also known as As Salamah wa Banatuha. Passing close to Ennerdale Rock, the island complex now lay between them and the Silkworm threat. McClusky continued due north, exposing herself to the

Silkworms as she passed east of the Didamar and Salamah Island complex and west of the Main Shipping Channel. Passing fishing boats and dhows, more fishing boats and more dhows, the big merchant ships of Shielbrock's convoy steamed through and across the Inshore Traffic Zone, dodging the small boats while maintaining their double column formation.

Point Echo, the most dangerous part of the transit was just ahead. Changing course to three three nine, the convoy had to cross the main shipping channel while exposed to the Silkworms from south of Kuhestak, less than forty miles away. Silkworm time of flight at that range was about five minutes. Thirteen big ships would show their full length and high freeboard sides as fine radar targets for the missiles for an hour and twenty minutes.

"Here's how I see it." Shielbrock had called his staff and advisors together in the Pilot House at 0100. "From all the reports in the press the past year or so, as I recall, the Iranians have installed Silkworm sites along their coast here, south of Kuhestak. There's a fairly even coastal section with some high flat ground running about fourteen miles. I hadn't seen it before but from this area they have clear firing arcs across the main shipping channels from two seven zero in the south to three five five in the north. This covers the channels and, and this is very important, they would have no land, islands or rocks in the background, just open water. Their missiles could fly maximum range looking for targets and if they didn't hit a ship they would splash in the water. Any other firing bearings would be out of the channels and toward Iranian territory to the north or toward Oman to the south. I don't think they'd want to hit Oman.

"So, it seems to me that the most likely part of our track for the Iranians to use Silkworms against us is this section of our Echo to Foxtrot transit as we cross the main shipping lanes, including this neutral area between the in-bound and out-bound channels.

"As soon as our last ships clear Point Echo I want to execute a tango turn with all ships turning together left to two nine four. This will be a deviation from our track but I want to extend our distance from those Silkworm sites. The greater the distance, the more warning time we'll have. Also, at near maximum range their missile reliability, or better put missile unreliability, works for us. Any weakness in their propulsion system or battery life for their radar seeker heads could cause them to miss. When, and hopefully if, we get a warning of an actual Silkworm firing I want all of our ships to turn together again by a tango turn to the east—."

"East?" Tim and Al both questioned the direction.

"Yes, east. I'll tell you why. I want to present as small a radar cross section, a radar target, as possible. With these big ships a beam target is seven hundred and fifty five feet long with forty to over a hundred and thirty feet of freeboard, all nice flat radar reflective surfaces. Bow-on we present a ninety foot beam with a pointed bow, still a good radar target but not anything as lucrative as our beam."

"Now, we could present our stern toward the threat, as we have a big heavy ramp back there, like an armor shield." A few of the staff nodded in agreement. "But the ramp doesn't cover the full width and it's a good radar reflector. Also, and most important, the ship's control, propulsion and personnel are all aft. That's us folks, so all considered it would be best to put our bow toward the incoming missiles." They all smiled in agreement.

"The Silkworm radar seeker head has to search back and forth ahead of and across the flight path. Beam to would be offering just too much. Bow on would show much less to the missile." He paused awhile and looked at them. "Any questions, comments?"

Al spoke up, "How much warning time do you think we'll have?"

"I don't know. If there is some preliminary or pre-firing warm-up and if our guys have the right kind of aircraft in the right place, we may hear about that. That's a lot of 'ifs'. It may be that our first warning is from McClusky, that he's picked up a missile on radar or he's intercepted the missile's radar on his electronic intercept equipment. He has slick thirty two for that purpose. That's pretty 'iffy', too. Or it may be that we see, in the dark, the rocket motor in the sky, low and fast, like a small jet plane near the deck. Maybe our own Stinger missile guys can get a shot at the Silkworm. We've got to be ready for that."

"Yeah," Sergeant Kramer was with the group. "We'll be ready. I'll be up on the bridge here and my guys on the other ships will be ready, too. This is what we came along on this ride for."

"How will the Iranians at the Silkworm sites know we're crossing the shipping channels?" Tim was still studying the chart with Shielbrock's markings.

"Good question. I'm guessing that some, maybe just one, of these fishing boats and dhows we've been dodging, will report us and that'll get to the Silkworm sites. We may have complicated things for them with our coastal and inside run, but I figure that with a few sighting reports they'll have us figured out, maybe not as good a set-up as they'd like but maybe just enough to try a high risk firing."

Kim was, as usual, recording the conversation. "Will they fire just one missile at us, see if it's successful, and then fire more?"

"Hey, Journalist, that shows you're thinking, but no, I expect that they would fire a salvo on their best information because they probably expect to be hit by aircraft as soon as they fire. If I were them I'd shoot and run like hell."

They continued to discuss the situation for the next fifteen minutes and after the last ship cleared Point Echo the convoy turned together to the new heading, increasing distance from the Silkworm sites.

"Shellback this is Big Mac. Over."

"This is Shellback. Roger. Over."

"This is Big Mac. The zombie's head is up. Electric six bird has testy indications from noisy isometric quadrangle cravat. Bird farm you used to habitate has sue-cap on station numbering a third of a dozen. They are foot and a half type and eager. We'll have to eat before they deal. Over."

"This is Shellback. Roger all. Bon appetite. Out."

Tim, Al Bevins and Kim were listening and looking on in amazement to the radio conversation as Tim spoke for the group, "Pardon us, Commodore, but what the hell was that all about?"

Shielbrock laughed, "Well, let's see. He's using unauthorized voice calls to tell me, that's Shellback from Big Mac, that's McClusky—."

"Yes sir. That's the only part we could figure out."

"Okay. After that comes 'the zombie's head is up.' That's a soft heads up on a zombie, which means anti-surface missile. In this case, he's telling us there's some activity among the Silkworm installations."

"How do you know its Silkworm? It could be other missiles, couldn't it?"

"No. The next thing he said had to do with electric six, testy indications and noisy isometric quadrangle cravat. That means an electronic intercept aircraft, an EA6B, has indications of testing the Square Tie radar. That's the NATO name for the radar used with the Silkworm."

"What did the rest mean?"

"He said Enterprise, that's a carrier he knows I spent some time aboard, has sue-cap, that's anti-surface combat air patrol, four A-18 aircraft on station ready to strike the Silkworm sites. But the rules of engagement won't let the aircraft hit the sites until they fire. So, we have to eat the Silkworm before the attack aircraft can neutralize the launch sites."

CHAPTER 26

"So how did they get through to Bandar Abbas, or did they get through?" Steven was eager.

Barney smiled, "Not so fast, young man, we'll get to that. There are some other matters that bear on your dad's situation that I have to tell you about."

"What could be more important than this transit to Bandar Abbas?"

"Nothing, but you have to hear this. There's a lesson here that you should learn."

Steven frowned, "What lesson?"

"Well, I haven't thought of this before, not in this context, but you must have heard some career people say things like "it's a small navy" and "something or other will come back and bite you.""

Steven nodded, "Lots of people say things like that."

Barney went on, "Yeah, and that's what I want to tell you about, now, before we go on with the story of your dad's action adventure. Remember, 'it's a small navy' and 'come back and bite you' and that's behind this story. A couple of years after this happened I heard about it from a guy who had been aide to the CNO."

THE PENTAGON, ARLINGTON, VIRGINIA

E-Ring offices on the outboard side of the Pentagon are the most desirable as there are windows to the outside world while all other offices look across small open spaces to other Pentagon offices, an incestuous view. From the office of the Chief of Naval Operations one can look out across a corner of the vast parking lot, further across a busy interstate highway and finally into the rolling green hills of Arlington National Cemetery, dotted with thousands of white markers, each marker indicating service to country.

Vice Admiral Paul Bartolli, Deputy Chief of Naval Operations for Plans, Policy and Operations, more easily known as OP-06, waited in the outer office with one of his assistants, Rear Admiral Dan Dawson and the nervousness that showed in both officers did not subside as the Executive Assistant finally sent them into the CNO's office. Some called it "the igloo," as rumor held that in this office, Frosty, the CNO, made raw meat out of subordinates and froze them stiff and this thought did not entertain Bartolli and Dawson, nor did the view of Arlington National Cemetery's rolling hills please them. In fact, the small white markers seemed closer than usual.

Admiral Calvin E. Frost looked up from his desk, took off his glasses and went right to the matter without pleasantries or greeting. "What can you tell me about this lack of communications thing with the MPS ships?"

"To start with, Admiral, let me say that this was done with the very best of intention and motivation and—."

Frost interrupted Bartolli, "I wouldn't question that, Paul. It's judgment that I question."

"Yes sir. Well, at this point, where we are today and what we know, this matter of, uh, judgment may seem questionable but at the time, under the sterile conditions of budgetary restraint in which we process each budget proposal, it seemed logical and clear that rather than expend scarce resources on low visibility, low priority projects, we should utilize those funds for more demanding higher priority projects. We didn't have money for everything so we deleted those items that we felt were less urgent, less important. Now, if we had known that the MPS ships would be called upon to respond, well, that urgency would have been much higher."

"Uh huh. Let me ask this, and I assume that your presence here Dan indicates you have been involved with this?"

"Yes sir," an unhappy Rear Admiral Dan Dawson replied.

"Okay. Tell me this, either or both of you, what possible scenario can you give me for employment of the MPS ships in which they would not need secure communications between themselves, with escort or with the beach?"

No response came from either flag officer so Frost rephrased his question. "Can you think of any operation we would send these ships on in which you as OTC would agree to not needing secure comms between the ships, and ship to shore, and shore to ship?"

"Admiral, the flagship did have secure ship to shore and shore to ship capability," Bartolli ventured a reply.

"Fine, and in peacetime that would be sufficient, wouldn't it? Do you know what we pay to keep thirteen MPS ships operating forward deployed for readiness in event of hostilities? How much do we pay?"

Both flag officers indicated a lack of such knowledge.

"And how much did we cut out of the budget to save scarce resources and to deny adequate communications to these ships?"

"Uh fifty mum mum—," Dawson mumbled a reply.

The CNO's voice level rose, "I didn't hear you, Dan."

"Two hundred and fifty thousand dollars."

"Two hundred and fifty thousand dollars! What the hell is two hundred and fifty thousand dollars for adequate communications when we spend a billion dollars a year to charter those ships? A billion dollars every year, gentlemen, for twenty years. Twenty billion dollars just for the charter. Then there's a billion dollars worth of equipment in those ships and we pay for the upkeep and maintenance for that equipment as well as that of the ships, and we pay for the personnel—.

"Do you get the idea that we are dealing with a very expensive, extensive and high priority program here? And for a one time cost of two hundred and fifty thousand dollars you wipe out the very basic requirement to provide adequate communications. Two hundred and fifty K in this program is like a fart in a windstorm. We spend more on toilet paper in this Navy."

After staring at the two for a few seconds the CNO continued. "So, with your presence here Dan, I assume you recommended this budget deletion and," he turned to the vice admiral, "you went along with it, eh Paul?"

Dawson was quick to respond, "Yes, sir. I recommended it."

Bartolli was upset, "Admiral, it was an OP-06 action so it was my responsibility and I take responsibility for it."

"Very gallant and proper of you Paul but I must point out this to you, it is my responsibility and I take the blame for it. Not Dan, not you, but me. You take action in the name of CNO. That's me. I haven't seen a message or a letter go out of here from OP-06, have I? No. Only from CNO, and CNO cut out the communications from those MPS ships. Now, I have other three star staff officers, deputies like you and some of them, one to be specific, OP-04, wanted those communications and he put that item in the budget. How in hell can you reject a request of one of my other deputies without telling him or me?"

"I'm sorry, Admiral. I—."

"Sorry, bullshit. Sorry doesn't cut it, Mister." The CNO was really angry now. Mister, as a title in the Navy had referred in past years to officers lieutenant-commander and junior. Bartolli hadn't been called Mister even by his mailman in twenty years.

They sat in silence awhile until the CNO spoke. "I don't know how long this Iranian goat-grab is going to last, but right now, today, I want steps taken to get adequate communications into the other two MPS squadrons. As soon as the ships are free I want that same communications enhancement in MPSRON Two."

"Yes sir."

"Now, what's the story on those patrols we used to have, the requirement for one or two of the prepositioned ships at Diego Garcia to be underway?"

Bartolli glanced at Dawson and then answered the CNO. "Those patrols were stopped about six months ago as a fuel conservation measure."

"We've already been through that. The fuel for those chartered ships is a part of the contract with the leasing companies. It's not the same money as our Navy ships' fuel. So what did we gain by stopping those patrols? What did it cost us? Who ordered it?"

"That also, Admiral was an OP-06 directive, so I am—."

"No! No! God Damn it, you aren't responsible, I am. It was not an OP-06 directive, it was a CNO directive. It may have been an OP-06 initiative but the directive was issued by CNO, that's me in case you've forgotten. Now, who issued that directive for me?"

"Well, sir, it came out of OP-06, so I'm responsible—."

"Who, Paul, who?"

Vice Admiral Bartolli hesitated to answer, then after looking directly at the CNO a few seconds he glanced at Rear Admiral Dawson and sat back in his chair.

Dawson spoke up, "I sent out the directive after I came back from a fleet familiarization trip that included Diego Garcia. I felt that we were wasting fuel patrolling the waters around Diego Garcia and providing the Brits with free island surveillance. I meant it as a fuel saving for us, Admiral, and I admit I didn't know it was different money."

"Well it is different. We didn't save any Navy fuel money and we took away the only area surveillance. That surveillance might just have, just maybe, detected that boat or boats coming to attack. We'll never know."

The CNO turned to Bartolli again, "Now that we've denied those ships communications and surveillance, they're attacked by a boat or boats, they get underway and we order them back into port, which is probably the dumbest thing they could do. Fortunately for all of us, a reserve or retired guy, temporarily and accidentally in command, wisely disregards our stupid orders and keeps the ships safely at sea. Who sent that CNO directive?"

Bartolli leaned forward in his chair again. "I did, Admiral. OP-06 sent the CNO message to the Naval Facility commander there, the base CO, telling him to get the ships back to port. CTF Seventy Three and COMSEVENTHFLT then did the same. He refused to obey the orders and then, later, took the ships toward Bandar Abbas when that was ordered."

Adding to Bartolli's comment the CNO said, "And the one ship that remained in port was attacked, hit and destroyed."

"Yes sir."

"It was a weekend, Sunday, Washington time when that happened, wasn't it?" The CNO asked.

"Yes sir."

"Were you here that day, Paul?"

Bartolli hesitated, "No sir."

"Then who sent that CNO message?"

Again Bartolli hesitated, looked over at Dawson and sat back.

Dawson sighed deeply, "I was in the Command Center that Sunday, Admiral. I sent the message. I wanted to get a regular Navy officer in command.

"Did it occur to you, Dan, that this task unit operating at sea was under a joint command structure and not under the Chief of Naval Operations, that I did not have operational control of that unit and that certainly the CO of a Naval Station did not have that authority, that any such order should have originated from a joint command?"

Rear Admiral Dan Dawson indicated negative and the CNO continued. "Jesus Christ, Dan. If those ships had been in port they all would have been sitting ducks. There's no protection there. Instead of just the one ship we might have lost a bunch of them, maybe all. If it hadn't been for this guy with some real tactical savvy and a lot of balls we could have lost our ass! This guy saved—, what the hell is his name?"

Dawson started to reply but the CNO held up his hand in a sharp stop gesture as he spoke into the intercom. "Did you ever get me the name of that Convoy Commodore from the Diego Garcia attack?"

Smartly back came the aide's voice, "Yes, sir. It's Shielbrock. Retired Navy Captain Martin D. Shielbrock, recalled to active duty for an exercise. His name is spelled—."

"I know how it's spelled." Turning toward Bartolli and then Dawson the CNO spoke quietly, "Shielbrock. That's Shellback. Shellback has been in command of this MPS convoy all this time. Do you know him?"

Bartolli and Dawson both nodded an affirmative reply.

"Did you know that he was in command, that he was the Convoy Commodore?" Frost asked both and Bartolli's head movement indicated negative but Dawson didn't move.

"Dan, did you know that Shellback was the Convoy Commodore?"

Dawson swallowed hard, "Yes, sir."

"Did you know it that first day, Sunday, when you ordered him back into port?"

Another swallow, "Yes, sir."

Standing, then walking across the office to the window looking out at the parking lot, highway and cemetery, the CNO folded his arms in front. "Shellback. Martin Shielbrock is probably the finest tactical mind in or around the Navy. Active or retired, whatever, I can't think of anyone at any rank whom I would prefer to have in command of those ships. He started TACTRAGRUPAC, you know, and I was one of his first students. Long before that, on the Cuban Quarantine, when you and I, Dan, were on the CARDIV staff, he forced a Soviet submarine to the surface. Did you know that during the Korean War he saved the life of a squadron-mate of mine?" The CNO turned toward Dawson.

"Yes sir. I knew he saved a pilot during the Korean War. I was on the same search mission."

More intense than ever, Admiral Frost glared at Dawson, then pointed at him, "Laffey! You were in Laffey searching to the north of Shellback's ship. Weather got bad. You terminated the search. Shellback refused to quit the search, went north and found Dick Taylor in your area!" The CNO emphasized 'your area'. "I read the investigation report. He got a medal."

Dawson swallowed again, "Well, that was a long time ago. The weather was very bad. It was dangerous, uh, in a whale boat. There were lives to be considered, safety. We couldn't see, uh, anything out there in the dark, in that boat. It was very rough."

Frost walked over and stood beside Dawson's chair. "And years later on the Cuban Quarantine, when you and I were on the CARDIV staff, he was disobeying everyone's orders and finally forced that Soviet sub to surface. You tried to get him relieved for cause. You volunteered and wrote the relief message, but he wasn't relieved. He held the sub to exhaustion and it was kept quiet."

"That was a long time ago too, Admiral. It has nothing to do with today." Dawson stared at his corfam black shoes, very highly polished, just visible between his knees.

"Oh, but it does. It does have a great deal to do with these recent events."

"What do you mean?" Dawson managed to raise and turn his head toward the CNO who then walked around behind his desk and sat down.

"A few years ago you were on the flag selection board."

"Yes sir." Dawson again swallowed hard.

"I was surprised that Shellback was not selected. A lot of people were surprised. Board actions are held in strictest confidence but I heard that there was one black ball, and from his own community, the surface warfare community."

Dawson sat in icy silence as the CNO continued. "I suggest that what we have here is jealousy, pure and simple but deep and costly. Jealousy has caused you to act against Shellback for over thirty years. He made you look bad in saving a man's life and you've been after him ever since. You tried to hang him on the Cuban Quarantine. You black-balled him on flag selection and you wanted to get rid of him at Diego Garcia even at the risk of the ships. You cost the Navy a valuable flag officer."

Not another sound in the igloo as Frosty continued. "Let me tell you this, Dan, Shellback's ten times the officer you are. You aren't worth a pimple on his ass. You couldn't carry his jock. He gave us our carrier battle group command and control concept, he developed naval gunfire procedures off Viet Nam,—."

Bartolli contributed to the listing. "He wrote a book on shiphandling and developed procedures for integrating direct support submarines into battle groups." Frost looked at Bartolli with surprise. "I didn't know that. Jesus, I wonder how much else Shellback has contributed."

Bartolli supplied another, "He was with the first Strategic Studies Group when they developed the Naval Strategy."

"That's right!" Frost then looked at Dawson. "What the hell have you ever contributed to this Navy, Dan? Seems like Shellback has contributed more in any one year than you have in your entire career and all I can think of you doing is rejecting the ideas of others. You've never done a single God Damn positive thing. He knows more, can do more, can motivate people better than you ever dreamed of. I'd push you over the side without a blink to get ten minutes of his—."

"Bullshit!" Dawson was on his feet, livid. "He's a, a, God Damn pushy Jew bastard. He, He, He never does what he's told. Everybody, uh, fawns all over him, covers for him. He never does what, never does, never, he's always done his own thing. No discipline. No background. No—," Dawson's voice trailed off as he sat.

Again there was silence in the igloo until a very calm Admiral Frost spoke. "Admiral Dawson, you are as of this minute relieved of all duties. Your security clearances and message release authorities are canceled. I want your request for immediate retirement on my desk in the morning. Admiral Bartolli, I believe Dawson's former desk is in a secure office?"

"Yes sir," This time it was Bartolli who swallowed hard.

"He is not to enter that or any other secure space again. Do I make myself clear, ever again?"

"Yes sir," Bartolli breathed easier.

"Please have someone sort out the official and personal items in Dawson's desk and send the personal items to him. Please provide him with clerical assistance in the preparation of his retirement request."

"Yes sir."

"You are excused, Admiral Bartolli. Dawson, get out of my office."

CHAPTER 27

"Aha," said Seven. "So now we find the reason, the probable cause of this negative undercurrent, this dark cloud that seems to have followed Dad through his Navy career. This guy Dawson was always—."

"Hold on there, Steven." Barney interrupted him. "It might look like Dawson was always there, always in a position to foul up a Shielbrock operation, but it wasn't always Dawson. He, that is Dawson, couldn't have been in the right - or call it wrong - place every time your dad got himself in a tight spot. There would have been too many tight spots for any one man to cover. It always seemed to me that over all those years, whenever I turned around I would hear that Shellback's in trouble, or maybe I should say that whenever Shellback turned around he was in trouble. Either way, Dan Dawson certainly damaged your dad's Navy career but your Martin Shielbrock had a way of doing things, you know, 'his way', and his way could and did get himself in trouble without any help from Dawson or anyone else."

Barney's wife Jackie had been listening carefully, especially to the part of Barney's story about the number of Shellback's accomplishments and of Dan Dawson's interference. "Barney, couldn't the CNO undo those wrongs after he found out what this Dawson guy had done?"

"No," Barney shook his head. "Those things were past. Nothing could be done about them.

"The CNO fired Dawson and was now prepared to give any help he could, any help that he could get the JCS to give, to Shellback. But remember, Shellback is at sea, in a very tight sea and with very limited communications, assets and time, very little time, so with the best of intentions there wasn't much the CNO or even the JCS could do at that moment. Shellback was on his own."

Steven agreed, "Yes sir, he's on his own you might say but now he has this destroyer, err, frigate as protection. One small ship with one missile launcher and one or two guns to protect thirteen big ship targets against at least six mobile missile launchers. That's just a little protection, but better than nothing, right?"

"Right," Barney nodded, "and remember, there may still be some of those fishing boats armed with missiles still chasing him and his thirteen big targets."

STRAIT OF HORMUZ

Pale green light from computer screens reflected on the intent faces of McClusky crewmen in the Combat Information Center, CIC it is called by Navymen, or often just Combat, the shipboard space is the command center of the ship. Here is displayed the vital information of naval warfare; contact with enemy or suspected enemy, locations of friendly forces, courses, speeds, altitudes, fuel and ammunition status. Maintained in darkness, the status boards, blue radar screens, green computer monitors and dim red lights cast futuristic eerie pastel shades of color on the inhabitants.

Under the condition of General Quarters all battle stations were manned, putting the ship in its' highest degree of readiness for any type of warfare, ready to fight a submarine, surface ship or aircraft.

"All stations manned and ready. Condition Zebra set throughout the ship." The report reached Commander Jim Martin in CIC and by habit he looked at his watch, noting with satisfaction that three minutes to be at GQ was better than the Fleet Training Group standard for a FFG-7 Class ship. "Good. Main Control status?" He asked.

"Both gas turbines on the line. Ready for max power." The Officer of the Deck's voice from the Pilot House over the intercom was crisp and sharp.

Captain Martin, like most Commanding Officers of modern combatant ships, preferred to be in CIC rather than in the Pilot House for GQ and he turned to his Weapons Officer, Lieutenant Charles Whelan, "See-wiz in auto response."

"See-wiz in auto, aye aye, sir." Whelan repeated the order, pushed two buttons on his attack console and waited for the computer response. See-wiz was the distorted acronym for the Close-In Weapon System, abbreviated with the letters CIWS, and nautical imagination and thirst for brevity carried CIWS to be pronounced see-wiz. Vulcan Phalanx was another name for the system, a high speed, short range twenty millimeter defensive installation that included gatling gun, radar and fire control system in a single package. In "auto" the system would acquire and shoot at a target without human control so only when attack was imminent would the CIWS be put in auto response.

Warning of attack had been conveyed to the guided missile frigate McClusky from an electronic intercept aircraft flying high over the Strait of Hormuz. This same aircraft was in direct communications with the flight leader of four attack aircraft in assigned stations ready to strike the Silkworm installations if, and as soon as, Silkworm missiles were fired.

Commander Jim Martin stood back, watched and listened as his General Quarters CIC team received reports that each weapon system in the ship was operating properly. Gun mounts and missile launchers were cycled through their processes up to the "ready to fire" situation and all consoles reported green boards. His ship was ready.

The Tactical Action Officer was a key role in the GQ team being filled by Lieutenant Nevil Carson, known better as Knees Carson, a nickname that went back to his days at the U.S. Naval Academy where, it was rumored, he used bad knees as a frequent excuse for getting out of the big Wednesday parades. Knees was seated in front of the TAO console, from where he could direct the various combat systems of the ship. Just a few minutes ago the electronic intercept aircraft, a specially configured Grumman EA6B Prowler from the carrier Enterprise had alerted guided missile frigate McClusky to the Silkworm warning and now, with a green board, Knees Carson was a part of the ready team. From the missile console he directed a warshot to be run out on the launcher rail, noting that the Captain saw his action and nodded agreement. Long and white, with small fin-like wings, a Standard Missile, known as SM-1 type, slid out of the missile magazine onto the launcher.

Five minutes they waited, then another five and then ten more minutes elapsed seeming like an hour with men's eyes fixed to radar scopes, to computer screens and to electronic intercept displays. Radios were silent as radar surface contacts that were transferred to a navigation plot showed the last ship of the MPS convoy clear of Point Echo. Now they were all exposed, all thirteen big targets were in the most likely Silkworm missile firing arcs and so was guided missile frigate McClusky.

"The Iranians will never have a better chance to have at those MPS ships," Jim Martin thought aloud for the entire CIC team as two more minutes dragged by.

The UHF secure voice radio cackled to life. "Zombie! Zombie! Zombie! Zombie away. Multiple launch sites Alfa One and Two, Bravo Three, Charlie One and Three, Delta Two. Roll Hornets, roll." It was the EA6B Prowler aircraft reporting that Silkworm missiles had been launched, their sites identified and FA-18 Hornet aircraft were being directed to strike the launch sites.

Tension in the McClusky CIC increased as Jim Martin spoke quietly. "Okay, let's all keep our heads and do what we're trained to do." He looked toward the electronic warfare corner of CIC called "EW", where sailors studied their displays, waiting and hoping for an intercept of the missile seeker head radar, known as Pigeon Pie. Nothing.

Over in the surface warfare section of CIC sailors had their eyes figuratively glued to radar scopes, looking for a low flying missile, low enough to be seen on the surface search radar. Nothing.

Air search radars are designed to detect small fast high flying aircraft and McClusky sailors studied those scopes. Nothing.

It had only been fifteen seconds but it seemed much longer when a thin line of light showed up on the TAO console screen just as from the EW section a voice called out, "Pigeon Pie radar bearing zero nine zero."

From the surface warfare section a voice almost walked on the EW report with, "Radar contact bearing zero nine one, range sixty thousand four hundred yards." A light blip showed on the TAO scope and slowly the indication grew a tail, indicating course and speed. "Bearing steady, range sixty thousand two hundred."

Captain Martin reached for the squawk box. "Bridge, Combat. Increase to max speed. Maneuver to unmask. Target bears zero nine one."

"Aye aye, sir," Came the reply as Martin watched the engine order repeater go to flank speed and the rudder go over 30 degrees. Thirty miles away and coming toward us, he thought, at nine miles a minute, three minutes and about twenty seconds.

From the surface warfare radar and control console the target was processed to the missile fire control radar. "Designating to foxtrot charlie," announced the radar operator, foxtrot charlie for fire control.

A few seconds more, "Zombie Alfa bearing zero nine one. Fifty nine K. New Zombie, designated Zombie Bravo bearing zero eight six, six zero K."

Knees Carson moved his cursor with each report, pressed a button on his console and without looking away from the screen announced, "Designating all three to foxtrot charlie."

The Captain looked at the fire control console operator just as the report came out, "Locked on and tracking." Without waiting to be asked, Jim Martin pushed a button on his console and called out, "Birds free on Zombies Alfa, Bravo and Charlie."

The TAO, Knees Carson, turned to another console operator. "Fire four rounds of chaff." Then back to his own console, Knees pressed the firing key and called out, "Shoot-shoot-look, Zombie Alfa."

A roar from aft on the ship told them as the missile officer reported, "Bird away." Another roar, another report and two standard missiles were on their way toward the first Silkworm.

"Zombie Bravo status?" Knees moved his cursor and punched a button.

"Locked on and tracking Zombie Bravo."

With quick response from the fire control console, Knees punched his firing key and called out, "Shoot-shoot-look, Zombie Bravo."

Shuddering with the roar of two more standard missiles the reports followed and in quick order Knees directed four more chaff shots, received a report of good tracking on Zombies Alfa and Bravo and asked for the status of Zombie Charlie. Before he could get the report, EW and Surface reported new Zombie Delta and then Zombie Echo. McClusky was being saturated.

"Ten seconds to intercept Zombie Alfa. Bravo drawing right. Charlie drawing left. Delta and Echo steady bearing." Five Silkworms, three coming at the guided missile frigate, two others probably toward the MPS ships!

"Chaff!" Captain Martin called out, "Give me a line of continuous chaff between the zombies and the convoy. Keep it seeded."

"Yes, sir."

Both the Captain and the TAO were giving orders. To an outsider it might have been confusing but this well trained team knew that now the TAO was directing the missile firings and the Captain was trying every other method and system to lure, attract, seduce and destroy the Silkworms as a blend of orders came out from Captain and TAO.

"Standby to refire Alfa. Status Bravo. Standby for Charlie."

"Reseed chaff starboard. Bridge, come left more. That's good. Standby gun barrage Zombie Alfa. EW!"

"Yes sir."

"Can you jam Zombie Alfa Pigeon Pie at this range with slick thirty two?"

"No joy yet, Cap'n."

"Go to max power."

"Shoot-shoot—."

"Bird away—."

"Re-seed chaff—."

"Zombie Charlie drawing left."

Five miles to the west on board motor vessel Anderson, Shielbrock and his team watched in the darkness as the single frigate fired missiles and chaff. "He's firing two missiles at each Silkworm, then he watches for success or failure and if necessary fires two more. It's called a 'shoot-shoot-look' policy. We've seen four pairs of shots so far, so he's either taking on four Silkworms or else he's re-firing at the first of three."

"What's the high arch of bright lights?" Kim asked.

"That's chaff. It's a rocket launched package of metal foil ribbons that blows open. The ribbons spread apart and drift slowly in the air to form an attractive target for the missile seeker head. He's trying to lure the Silkworms to a chaff cloud, away from him and away from us."

McClusky lighted up again as two more standard missiles roared off, up and then toward the east.

"Sergeant Kramer? You all set?" Shielbrock barked.

"All set, Commodore. With no radar to alert us we'll all have to keep our eyes peeled."

"We're all watching."

Kramer stood aft of the starboard bridge wing with his Stinger missile launcher on his shoulder, peering through the viewer, looking eastward but offset from the frigate.

"How will we know if you're on a missile?" Al Bevins asked the Marine.

"I'll tell you but even if I don't, you'll hear a buzzing from the receiver. That means I'm tracking a heat source."

On board McClusky, "Ten seconds to intercept, Zombie Alfa," The missile console operator called out. "Five, four, three, two, one." The entire CIC team held their breath.

"Missed intercept both birds!"

"Shoot Zombie Alfa!"

"Shoot-shoot-look, Zombie Alfa."

Two more roars from aft told them that another pair of standard missiles was on the way.

"Status Bravo and Charlie?"

"Re-seed chaff."

"Twenty five seconds to intercept Bravo, fifteen seconds to Charlie."

"Zombie Delta drawing right."

"No Pigeon Pie Zombie Delta." From EW the report meant that at least one Silkworm missile was not indicating radar. It could mean a faulty seeker, which posed no threat, or it could mean that one missile coming at them was an infra-red variant. Instead of relying on radar to acquire a target, the IR variant needed a heat source to home on and a ship was a good heat source. Chaff and jamming had no effect on IR missiles.

"Deploy torch starboard," Jim Martin ordered. Torch was a rocket launched heat source designed to decoy an IR missile.

"Ten seconds to intercept Zombie Bravo." A brief pause, "Five, four, three, two, one." Breaths again held. "Splash Zombie Bravo!" Murmurs of excitement were cut off. "Seven seconds to intercept Charlie. Three, two, one." Would it be?

"Splash Zombie Charlie!"

"Hey!" "Okay!" "All right!" "Yeah!"

"Knock it off! Status Delta and Echo?" The Captain put them back in the serious business of dealing with the other Silkworm missiles.

"Echo drawing left, still broad seeker sweep. Delta drawing right, no seeker."

"Status Alfa?"

"Zombie Alfa, steady bearing, range twenty K, fifteen seconds to intercept."

From EW a call came out, "Alfa seeker changed to short sweep. It's locked on to us!"

"Commence gun barrage on Alfa."

"Deploy super-are-bock." Super RBOC was a set of large canisters of heavy chaff known as Super Rapid Blooming Overhead Chaff. Rocket propelled, they went a short distance over the ship, then burst to form a large cloud of metal foil ribbons intended to confuse the radar seeker of an incoming missile.

"Ten seconds to intercept Alfa."

"Standby to shoot Delta."

"Delta's drawing right, no seeker radar, no threat to us," The Weapons Officer, Charlie Whelan, reminded the TAO.

"Our job is to protect the convoy," Captain Martin reminded them with no time to argue.

"—three, two, one." Held breaths.

"Missed intercept!"

"Oh, oh." "Jesus Christ."

"Zombie Alfa, still steady, ten K."

"Holy Christ!"

"Max speed! Guns! Chaff!"

"Zombie Delta status?"

"Red board. Delta is out of envelope."

"Echo status?"

A tearing, ripping noise with similar vibration was heard and felt through the ship, like a chain saw blade hitting a nail, but it kept on, kept ripping for five seconds, ten seconds. "C'mon see-wiz!" Someone called out. The Vulcan Phalanx gatling gun spewed out thousands of twenty millimeter bullets, heavy bullets, each of depleted uranium and if only one of them could hit the Silkworm—.

A shock wave slammed into the side of the frigate McClusky like a big sledge hammer and books, papers, coffee cups tumbled across open areas. Light equipment jarred loose and a few men fell as all felt the jolt and hung on as a loud explosion was heard.

"What the hell happened?"

"Lost air search radar."

"Lost EW."

"Echo status?" repeated the TAO.

"Out of envelope. Red board."

"What happened?"

"Combat, bridge. The see-wiz hit that missile. You felt the shock of the missile exploding. We got hit with a lot of pieces, like shrapnel, but the missile went off before it got to us. We're still getting reports but it looks like no serious damage to us."

Captain Martin reached for the intercom. "Roger. Thank you, Bridge. Let me know status when you get all reports."

"Yes sir."

The TAO was still at work. "Captain, Zombies Delta and Echo are out of our firing envelope. Both are heading for the MPS convoy and we can't do anything—."

Jim Martin was on the marine band VHF radio. "Shellback, this is Big Mac. Two hot burners coming your way, one toward lead ship, one toward third or fourth ship. Out of my envelope. Over."

"This is Shellback. Roger. Out." He replaced the radio handset and called Sergeant Kramer, "Silkworm coming our way. Another toward Bonnyman."

"Don't see it yet, Commodore. Grannelli is in Bonnyman. Good man. Granny can handle it." Kramer spoke as if thinking aloud, without taking his eyes from his scope.

"Anyone see anything?" Negative responses as Shielbrock walked back toward Sergeant Kramer who still held his launcher, still scanning the eastern horizon just as a buzzer sounded and Kramer yelled, "Hey! Here's a heat source!"

"Are you clear of McClusky and the torch floats?"

"I'm clear. This is a Silkworm." A bright flash blinded them and the roar deafened them as Kramer's Stinger missile went off toward the incoming Silkworm.

"There's the Silkworm!" Tim Smith pointed to a red glow just above the horizon and Kramer's Stinger was heading straight for it.

"Look at Bonnyman." Kim pointed two ships away at a streak of light, just like their own Stinger missile was on the way toward another red glow near the horizon. They watched both missiles, first their own, then Bonnyman's and in a few seconds the red glow coming at Anderson went out. Nothing. Kramer's Stinger kept flying. Nothing.

Bonnyman's Stinger, fired by the Marine called Granny, hit Zombie

Delta and a bright flash lighted the dark sky and moments later the sound reached them.

"What happened?" Tim asked.

Kramer had lowered the viewer but still looked in the direction of his shot. "I dunno. It was there. I shot it and it disappeared. I don't think I hit it."

Shielbrock offered an explanation. "It might be that the Silkworm you shot at lost propulsion and went in the drink as your Stinger was approaching it."

Tim Smith provided comment, "Instead of shooting it down, you scared it down." They laughed.

Kim was recording the conversation. "It looked like the Stinger fired by Bonnyman hit a Silkworm. Is that right?" They all agreed.

"Are there any others?" Al Bevins asked.

Shielbrock reached for the handset. "Big Mac this is Shellback. What score? Over."

This is Big Mac. Electric six tells me all clear. Splash five. Sail on. Over."

"This is Shellback. That's a great performance, Jim. What do you do for an encore? Over."

"This is Big Mac. It's all in a days work. Thanks, Professor, thanks for everything. Out."

Shielbrock replaced the handset. "Al, lets get them turned north again, toward Point Foxtrot."

Kim walked over to Shielbrock. "'Thanks Professor, thanks for everything.' He just saved us and he thanks his professor for everything."

"He was a student of mine. I told you that."

"Yes, and he certainly remembers being your student. In his moment of greatest glory he defers to you as his teacher."

"Oh come on now. There you go again stretching truth and innuendo, mixing in fantasy and imagination. He did a fantastic job. I complimented him and he took a modest and humble position."

"Maybe you taught him that, too."

CHAPTER 28

Steven was the first to speak after Barney had finished his description of the missile engagement in the Strait of Hormuz. "That's some story, some great shooting by that frigate. I don't think that there are now, or maybe even back then, many ships that could handle a missile shoot like that."

"You're probably right," Barney replied.

"How did you find out about those details?"

Barney smiled, "Remember I told you that the CNO asked me to stay close to that situation as it was unfolding? Well, after it was over he asked me to stay with it and work with the people who were putting together the official after-action report."

Steven nodded and asked, "So were you able to read all the reports?"

"Not only did I get to read all the reports including all the reports of interviews with the participants, I was able to travel and to talk with most of the participants."

"Really!" Steven was impressed.

Barney continued, "Yes, for example I went to Norfolk and spent some considerable time talking to Jim Martin, the CO of that frigate McClusky. Boy, if you think that he did some great work, you would have been amazed at the kudos that he threw at your dad."

"Well I gathered from your story of the battle that there was a lot of admiration there and—."

"Just a darn minute," Jackie interrupted the men's discussion. "So you've had your big missile battle and now all's clear, right?" The two men looked at each other and were about to say something like "not quite" but Jackie

continued. "If my judgment of the timing of your story is correct, and I think it is, you're just about at the time I went to see Barbara. Remember Barbara fellas? Barbara Shielbrock? The wife at home while her man is on the other side of the world in this drama? Well, let me tell you a little about that."

Barney and Steven both smiled as Steven asked, "Is it going to be as spicy as your other 'keeping the home fires burning' stories?"

Jackie shook her finger at Steven, "Just you pay attention to what the wives go through, young man."

RETIRED CAPTAIN'S WIFE, ALEXANDRIA, VIRGINIA

Fresh brewed coffee aroma filled the kitchen as Jackie Williams refilled her cup while Barbara Shielbrock waited with her coffee mug in hand, and then the two went back into the den, continuing their talk. Jackie had come over to Barbara's Alexandria house. Barney had told them both of Shellback's exercise in the Indian Ocean and how it had changed from a simple undistinguished Rainbow Reef fleet exercise to a vital real world operation. Now Shellback was in command of a large group of merchant ships, including the five Maritime Prepositioning Ships, enroute from Diego Garcia to Bandar Abbas, Iran. There was danger, Barney had told them, but so far Martin was fine and they would all have to wait and see, and hope.

The night before, the house had been quiet and dark as it was unseasonably warm for February and even the furnace blower was silent. Barbara had listened in her bed to the soft sounds of the Northern Virginia suburban night as a small car with a high pitched engine passed along the street, rare for two in the morning.

After receiving the information from Barney Williams, Barbara couldn't get back to sleep as she thought of Martin, half way around the world, away again at sea. There had been so many times over the past, let's see she thought, thirty or thirty three years, that he was away and it had never been easy for her and it didn't get easier with time. It's just that she developed a tolerance, an acceptance as it had to be, and so it was, because for twenty-eight years of their marriage while Martin was in the navy, it seemed that he was away participating in almost every world crisis, and missing almost every family crisis, and now, after he had retired from the navy, he was away again, this time as a Convoy Commodore.

He had sailed away for the Cuban Quarantine, Lebanon Crisis and

Viet Nam a number of times. Then there were Haiti and the Dominican Republic, or was it twice to both? She couldn't remember them all. There were peacetime deployments of six months or so and a continuous sequence of peacetime exercises with strange names that became familiar; READIEX, FLEETEX, COMPTUEX, RIMPAC, TRANSITEX. They only meant to her that he would be away, she would be lonely and she would have to deal with the family problems alone.

Five years ago he had retired from the Navy and had gotten a job as a civilian consultant on Navy matters. No more deployments or sea duty and no fleet exercises. He would be home to deal with the family problems. No more periods of loneliness. She had been wrong for soon after he retired Martin signed up for a special program with the Navy, special for retired captains, in addition to his regular job. His employer gave him time off to attend a two week training course in San Diego and he became a Convoy Commodore, then later went off to a fleet exercise. Then there were conferences, meetings, more training, another fleet exercise and it all seemed to fit in well with his job as a consultant on navy tactical development. He used the acronym TAC D and E. She thought it stood for Tactical Development and Evaluation and she was right.

She had noticed shortly after they met that Navy people had always sought Martin's views and ideas. He had that charisma, an air of self-confidence and professionalism that other officers seemed to respect and now, even after he had retired, they still sought his advice. To maintain his credibility, he had explained to her, he had to keep in contact with the fleet and this Convoy Commodore program was one way to do that, and so now he was away again at sea.

Barbara had decided not to go to work today. Perhaps, she explained to Jackie, it was time to quit work altogether. She didn't need the money and there were other activities; golf, tennis, bridge, which she preferred. Age was a factor, too, after all, she was almost sixty now.

"Barbara, don't be foolish. If you want to quit work, go ahead and quit, but don't blame it on age. My God! You look twenty years younger than you are and you're just as healthy. If you want to play, do it, but don't blame it on age."

Both ladies laughed and they discussed the cosmetic surgery Barbara had undergone two years before. Clearly, it had done a great deal to preserve her beauty.

Today Barbara would stay at home, listen to the television and radio news, and wait for word of Martin's convoy. Barney would call, she knew, if he heard anything, anything he could tell them. Admiral Frost had asked Barney to look after Shellback's convoy so Barney was spending most of his time in the Pentagon, at the OPNAV Command Center.

Jackie had joined Barbara to wait and to hope for the best. "Have you called Nancy?" Jackie asked.

"Yes. I called her last night. She'll be here this weekend and will be listening to the news. She asked me to let her know, of course, if I heard anything. She'll call me every day now. You know her."

"Yes. I'm sure she will. How about Steven?"

"He's at sea. I told Ellie about it and told her not to worry. She told me Uncle Martin will be just fine, she knew it." Ellie was Jackie and Barney's daughter, and was married to Steven. They had two children and were expecting a third soon and the two mothers-in-law discussed their children and grandchildren.

"Is Nancy still seeing that young man from the store?"

"Yes. She's still going with him. I guess that's how to put it. But with her virtually owning the store, you know, it's a little bit difficult maintaining a romance with a young man whom she had dated when they were both sales clerks."

"But he's an assistant manager or something, now, isn't he?"

Barbara laughed, "Assistant Manager of the Menswear Department. He's doing fine and is a very nice young man, as I've told you, but he has a difficult time with the thought of marriage to the owner of the store. It's one of those double standard situations. It would be a nice acceptable romantic story if a girl from Ladies Fashions married the store owner, but a man from the store marrying the lady who owns it just doesn't set well with a man's image of himself, with his masculine ego."

"That's too bad."

"Well, yes, and it's something they'll have to work out. If not, I told Nancy to pay a little more attention to some of those wealthy men she knows because money isn't intimidated by money."

"Barbara, you're awful!" Jackie laughed.

"Why awful? It's just practical. She can find a rich man to fall in love with just as easily as a poor one."

"Well, he's not exactly poor, is he? He just works for a living like most."

"Yes and he's doing very well. He's good looking, intelligent, well educated and charming. He's just not rich." They both laughed.

Jackie sipped her coffee and a few moments of silence followed. "Barbara, I've often wondered, and I know this is sensitive, but after all our time—, that is after all the time we've known each other and as close as we've been—," She hesitated.

"Come on, Jackie, out with it. What could possibly be too sensitive for us?"

"Well, I wondered how Martin took it. That is how he and you dealt with the question of Nancy's inheritance, Loffman and all. That must have been very difficult."

Barbara got up from the overstuffed chair with her coffee mug still in hand and standing at the window with her back to Jackie, she opened the sheer drapery slightly with a movement of her fingers and looked out for a few seconds. "Yes, it was very difficult for me. I agonized over it for a long time, or it seemed like a long time. Martin was at Newport with the Strategic Studies Group so I saw him only on weekends, most weekends, not all. I had a few days here at home to think about it, to work out in my mind how to tell him. I couldn't figure out a good way, not even a good lie." She laughed, "So I decided to tell him the truth."

"And did you tell him the truth?"

"It was easier than I had hoped. I told him what had transpired at the attorney's office, Nancy's inheritance, my bank account, and all—." She paused.

"All?" Jackie asked.

Barbara was still at the window. "All that was said in the attorney's office." Again Barbara paused. "He was sitting right here in this room, in that chair, and he didn't say a word. I told him everything that was said by Donald Brown in Norfolk and he just listened. I told him that I had been in love with Jules and he with me, the manipulation of the will, the claim of Nancy's paternity and the bank account in my name. I ended the whole explanation with 'and now Nancy and I are millionaires'." She paused again.

"And he didn't say anything?"

Barbara turned, facing Jackie. "He looked at me with those eyes, Jackie, and those eyes of his can go right through you! He looked at me and asked, 'And who is Nancy's father?' I said, 'You are Nancy's father.' He looked at me a few seconds, it seemed like hours, with the most intense look I've ever seen on a man. Then he said, 'Jules Loffman had excellent taste in women.' Not another word has been said about it."

The two ladies looked at each other a few moments and Barbara returned to her chair.

"Barbara, that husband of yours has to be the most amazing man in the world."

"He is, Jackie, and he's the finest man in the world." She fought back the tears. "And, oh God, I hope nothing happens to him."

CHAPTER 29

Barney thanked his wife Jackie for letting them in on the wife's perspective and of the sensitive area of concern in the family. He looked at Steven, "So we find out a little more of home life and family strife.

"Now Shellback has brought his baker's dozen, that's thirteen, big MPS ship convoy through the Strait of Hormuz. It's a straight shot across the Gulf of Oman and into Bandar Abbas. Simple. Easy. They've passed the Silkworm threat, evaded and outran the fishing boats and all they have to do is deliver the goods, right?"

Steven was not so easily taken in. "Hold on. You described that one of the fishing boats in the Indian Ocean had decided to go straight for the Gulf of Oman while our convoy commodore was taking a circuitous route to avoid detection, right?"

Barney smiled, "Right."

Steven continued, "So even though the MPS ships could go faster, their longer route would take more time. Maybe enough more time for the slower fishing boat to get to the gulf in time to intercept the convoy."

"Maybe," Barney replied.

Now Steven smiled, "Maybe like the hare and the tortoise."

GULF OF OMAN

Long, slender, black, silent and slow, for centuries the dhow had glided in, out and around the Persian Gulf and as their fathers had before them, sailormen in dhows had seen strangers come and go. Sailing ships they had seen and multi-tiered oared ships, ships of steam, coal and oil, but still that most important oil, the black liquid gold that had changed the outside world, had changed nothing for the dhow sailormen and life went on for them as it had for their fathers; slowly. A flotilla of low black hulled dhows glided slowly along the western side of the big ship channel as immense tankers carried precious liquid out of the Persian Gulf to far ports of the world. Empty they would return, thirsty for more oil and eager to run again to the other side of the globe.

Dhow sailormen didn't care, tankers were familiar strangers, here this century, something else the next, fishing boats, too, varied some over the years and next century they would be changed, but not the dhow. A different boat joined their group, so what? Soon it would pass along, leaving the dhow as before and this stranger was a longer than usual fishing boat in need of care. Bleached and streaked, clearly neglected, she drifted along with them, seemingly in no hurry.

At the wheel, Ahmud Bakhari guided the 80 foot fishing boat slowly in among the dhows. An hour ago a low slow patrol plane had passed near and continued on and they could see the upper works, radar and radio antennae of a combatant ship on the horizon. Too far to distinguish them in the multitude of black boats and soon it would be dark. They would feel safer in the darkness.

Moses Farscian stood next to the fishing boat captain. "How much further you think we have to go?" The veteran army missileman asked.

"Only Allah knows but in the dark we can drift along with this bunch of Arabs. If we get far enough north before daylight we might see some ship lights off Bandar Abbas. Then we can run for them at high speed, shoot and get away."

"Have you thought any more about where we should go after the attack? They had discussed the problem a great deal over the past days since the Iranian news told of that ayatollah inviting the Americans into Bandar Abbas.

"I've thought about it," Bakhari was silent awhile. "I don't know, uh, I still can't see where we would be accepted other than back at Basra, if we could make it there.

Moses Farscian's mind went back to seven years of Army combat duty. "Who is our commander? Who are we serving?"

Ghermeziat looked up from the dial of the VHF radio to which he was listening, hoping to hear an American ship. "Allah, we serve Allah, that's who we serve, and Allah will show us to a big target and take care of us after."

Bakhari and Farscian looked at each other with doubt, saying nothing until Moses offered, "I hope so, but maybe Allah wouldn't mind if we helped him a little with some planning."

Hours later in the dark, still among the dhows, they moved faster as ahead they could see lights.

Borujerdi came up from his engine into the cabin. "Everything all right below?" the Captain asked.

"Yeah, fine."

Five of them stared ahead into the darkness trying to determine what was in the spread of lights ahead. Across the shipping channel, they had left the dhows behind and now were alone, moving on the dark smooth sea, Bakhari studied the lights with his binoculars with Nafouzi, the assistant engineer at the wheel.

Ghermeziat saw it first, "Masthead and range lights, red and green running lights!" He pointed ahead, just off the port bow. The pattern of lights meant a ship coming straight at them.

"Right! Come over to the right, Nafouzi. Keep the same speed," Bakhari called to the man at the wheel.

Even in the darkness they could see the silhouette. "Navy ship of some kind," Ghermeziat offered.

"Destroyer or frigate," Bakhari had the binoculars on it. "About three miles now abeam. They have to see us on their radar."

"Allah will hide us," Ghermeziat was praying, "La-ila-ha Il-lah-lah." There is no god but Allah.

They slid past in the darkness as Bakhari directed, "Come around now and head for the center of those lights, that spread of lights ahead." The destroyer had continued on. Allah had hidden them.

Tim Smith brought the message from the Radio Shack to the Commodore. It was from the task force commander and Shielbrock glanced down the sheet, handed the message back to Tim with a brief thanks and went to his familiar chair on the port side of the darkened Pilot House.

"Congratulations—, safe and timely arrival—, through adversity—, cargo preparation and offload team to board—, anchor as directed—, order of ships to offload—, relieved of command—, joins me in extending best wishes—, job well done—."

Kim McManus was there in the Pilot House along with the three staff officers; Al Bevins, Tim Smith and John Harvey. Bob Ryan was there, too, and Jeff, Sergeant Kramer and Top Sawyer, all laughing, joking, looking over the message, talking about it and about their adventure.

Angie Silverio the Radio Officer joined them as Irving Cappleton lifted a cigarette from his left shirt pocket with two fingers of his right hand and into his mouth it went. Soon he was enjoying the chew, having worked the paper away and up under his gum with his tongue. Pritchard, the Mate on watch directed the helmsman as the ship made her way toward her assigned anchorage. Shielbrock sat in the darkness, listening to his shipmates celebrate, aware of the dull pain running up and down his back on the right side, rubbing his right wrist and forearm.

Lights now extended all across in front of them, hundreds of lights as the five fishing boat sailors studied them, searching for a target. "There! There's something ahead." Ghermeziat again saw it first.

Bakhari pointed binoculars in the direction Ghermeziat pointed and yelled. "It's a ship, the stern of a ship. I see the stern light and from the silhouette it's big and broad."

A few seconds later Ahmad Bakhari, Captain of the 80 foot fishing boat, spoke again, "This is it. We're gonna attack it. Borujerdi, give me full engine speed. Farscian, get your missiles ready."

Ghermeziat went to the bow as lookout and Nafouzi aft to help the engineer. Soon the diesel engine was running at maximum speed and the boat surged forward. When the target was two thousand yards ahead, Bakhari veered to port enough to give Farscian a clear arc of fire from the stern of his boat.

"Fifteen hundred yards," Bakhari called out.

"I'm within range," Moses agreed.

"Go ahead and shoot."

They were still talking, laughing and joking in the darkened Pilot House when a missile flash lighted their world for an instant and there was the bright flash, a roar, a crash and a deafening explosion. Chunks of metal and plastic flew in all directions as everyone in the Pilot House was knocked to the deck, some were thrown around, cut, torn, bleeding and yells and cries replaced the laughter. A fire burned on the port side.

Cappleton spit out his cigarette and struggled to his feet. "Pritchard?"

"I'm okay, Cap'n."

"Good. Check yer steering. Check for damage."

The helmsman was still at the wheel. Tim Smith was on top of Bob Ryan, both bleeding as they unpiled and got to their feet. Harvey was all right and Bevins was cut up some but not bad.

Another flash lit up the night as a missile hit on the main deck, throwing sections of pontoon causeway around and smashing one of the landing boats. Kim, Angie Silverio and Sergeant Kramer were in a pile, covered with blood. Struggling free, Kim pulled Kramer out from under poor Angie. The Radio Officer was dead and Kramer was badly cut up and bleeding, barely conscious. Top Sawyer tried to get to his feet but had a deep head wound and broken arm so he sat back down on the deck. Bob Ryan and Al Bevins went after the fire with extinguishers.

On the port side of the Pilot House where the Commodore's chair used to be, amid shattered plastic and metal, Tim Smith found Captain Martin Shielbrock lying in a pool of blood. At Smith's yell, Kim ran over to find the lieutenant holding a barely conscious Shielbrock, whose head was cut and bleeding. The right side of his back was torn apart. It wouldn't hurt anymore.

The Commodore's eyes opened and a half smile showed across his bloody face as his eyes went toward the stern then back at the lieutenant. "Get him, Tim."

Tim's questioning look up at Kim was answered with, "I'll take him. You go ahead," and they exchanged places.

The boat which had fired the missiles was now close enough off the port quarter to be visible even in the dim gray night as more flashes, smaller, popping noises and a series of smaller missiles came at the ship, some hit, some missed and some bounced away.

About 18 knots the boat was moving Tim Smith judged, and close now, maybe two hundred yards.

Tim yelled to the ship's Master, "Captain Cappleton! Come hard left now, hard over with all your speed. Now! Now!" Cappleton understood, ordered the rudder hard over and rang up full speed. Gradually, slowly, Motor Vessel Anderson came left, then a little faster and still faster the big ship swung left.

Bakhari didn't see it because in the dim dark and with his interest focused on Farscian firing the RPG-7 missiles, he didn't notice the big ship start toward them. Ghermeziat yelled and then Bakhari saw what was happening but it was late, maybe too late. The big ship was swinging toward them rapidly as Bakhari spun the wheel and backed the engine full, but the engine stalled.

"Borujerdi! What the—."

"Fuel lines! The fucking fuel lines are clogged again."

Without power the 80 foot fishing boat coasted slower as a wall of steel closed. Ghermeziat and Nafouzi dove over the port side and the boat heeled sharply to port with a loud wrenching screech and crash, rolling over on top of the two that had tried to swim clear. Rolling over and over, the boat was finally forced under the big ship's side in a tangled mass of twisted steel and shattered wood and only debris remained on the surface.

Moses Farscian, the last of a pure Kurdish family reaching back over a thousand years to Saladin and before that to the magical jinn expelled by Solomon, died in the waters of the Strait of Hormuz along with his four shipmates.

Smoke and smell from the extinguished fire hung in the air of the shattered Pilot House, but opened from the blast, the night breeze was clearing it quickly. Shielbrock's blood was all over Kim as she held him, sitting on the deck and he was talking but she couldn't understand.

Shielbrock was muttering with difficulty but it sounded like, "—don't take me out,—you can't take me out,—search north more,—never mind the plan,—God the water's cold,—it's a submarine,—him against me,—a few more hours—."

Heavy chain rattled from far forward as Motor Vessel Private First Class James Anderson, Jr. anchored off Bandar Abbas.

He looked up at her, "Kim. Hey." His voice cleared. "You should get a story out of this, huh, a good one?"

"Hang on, Martin. They've radioed for a helicopter and some medical aid. You'll be all right. Help is on the way."

"Not this time. Not for me." He drifted off then came back. "I've used up all the good luck anyone is entitled to in one lifetime."

"No you haven't. Hold on."

"Thanks, Journalist, you've been a good shipmate." His eyes moved toward where the others stood or kneeled, watching, some crying.

"Hang in there Commodore."

"Commodore! Hold on. You can make it."

"Hang on Shellback!"

A faint smile again. "All of you, all good shipmates. We did pretty well, didn't' we? Pretty good for a bunch of retireds and reservists. I'd take you guys up against the Soviet Northern Fleet if we had to. You're, you're—a great—." He drifted off.

"Martin!"

"Shellback!"

CHAPTER 30

Barney Williams, his wife Jackie, their daughter Ellie and her husband Steven Shielbrock sat in silence around the patio table as the sun moved low toward the western horizon. They had just heard the story of the final phase of Shellback's voyage and of his demise.

After a while Steven raised his head. "Yeah, that was tough on us. Mom first heard of it from you," he nodded toward Barney, "when you came over and then she received the official notification. A few days later we learned more about it and even more details came out later in that Kim McManus book. That was pretty good, I thought. What did you think of that book?"

Barney looked at Steven. "Yeah, it was good. She gave a very accurate and very detailed description of what she saw and what she was able to learn from interviews after the action. But she didn't, she couldn't have access to the classified intelligence information and that means she couldn't write about where those fishing boats really came from, who sent them and why."

Steven asked, "Did anyone know?"

Barney frowned, "Well, the various intelligence communities developed a number of theories; I think there were five theories. I was working on loan with Naval Intelligence for that operation, you know, and a sixth theory was developed."

THE SIXTH THEORY

"We still don't know." Vice Admiral Robert Tracy walked into the office of the Chief of Naval Operations, The Igloo, and sat without being asked, facing his service chief and opening his briefcase.

"Morning Dick," Admiral Frost responded using the nickname long attached to the navy's leading detective, Dick Tracy. "What do you mean, 'We still don't know?' It's been over six months and you mean to say we still can't find out who sent them, who they are, or were, or why?"

"That's right. There are a number of theories, each with indicators or evidence, but none of them can be proven and each has holes so none of them really holds water." The intell leader found the paper he was looking for. "Most likely it was Iranian, as we first reported, but then these other possibilities have come up and they might have some validity." He paused, "Our analysts are still working with the CIA and State and even FBI. They've chased down every potential and keep coming up with more questions, more doubts. At this point all I can tell you is we still don't know, for sure."

"Well," Admiral Frost hesitated with his icy stare at Tracy then continued. "For sure Dick, that's not at all reassuring, that the full resources of our national intelligence, diplomacy and police can't solve the questions of why a bunch of rag-tags in a few spit-kits sailed a couple of thousand miles to try to kick us in the ass, or who sent them, or from where, or why and this while we have in our hot little hands half a dozen or so of the survivor rag-tags and two of the actual spit-kits and the wreck of another, half of their force we think. That's not at all reassuring."

Tracy was uncomfortable but proceeded. "Yes sir, but here's what we have. There are five possibilities or theories that explain the attacks against MPSRONTWO.

" First and most likely, and consistent with our first analysis, is that the attack was organized, trained, equipped and sent to Diego Garcia by followers of, and under orders of either Iranian Ayatollahs Fattachian or Zenderasem so that the U.S. would be unable to have a prompt credible military on-the-ground response to the Soviet move into Iran. Fattachian and Zenderasem are both known to be strong Soviet supporters, both strong anti-American. If this is how it went down, it was not an act of the legitimate Iranian government. That's our leading theory and there's lots of support for that, such as original statements of the survivors, the captives, and the fishing boats, all of this seem to be, or were, Iranian."

Frost interrupted. "That's what we all were led to believe but then there were questions and doubt."

"Yes sir," Tracy continued, "Theory Two is that the attack was put together by the Iranian Navy acting under orders of Ayatollah Montazeri, who seems to be the legitimate Iranian leader, that's not much different for our purposes because Theory One and Theory Two are Iranian, and who ordered it is an internal matter of Iran." Tracy paused as Frost added, "All sounds reasonable."

"Theory Three takes a little more imagination." Tracy leaned forward as he spoke. "It's interesting that of the participants, the crews of the fishing boats, there were some Farsi speakers of course as we would expect from Iran, as we might expect all of them to be Iranian, but the majority of them seem to other than what we might call pure Iranian. There were a number of Shiite Arabs and an even more disproportionate number of Kurds, quite a few, and even Turkomen and Armenians. All of them are of backgrounds other than Sunni Arabs. The absence of any Sunni Arabs raises a flag." Frost's raised shoulders and hands asked why.

"Well," Tracy hesitated. "It's a stretch, maybe, but in this area there are many Sunnis and Shiites among the various Arabs and Persians, and if one were to put together a group for this it seems like you would have some sort of cross section that might include some Sunni Arabs, maybe just one, by accident. There are too many of them in the area and why so many Kurds and no pure Iranians or Sunni Arabs?"

"So what could it mean?" Frost asked.

"We don't know if it means anything but it raises eyebrows in the intelligence community. It could mean that whomever formed this group didn't want his favorite ethnic or religious group involved were it to go bad, to shift the blame elsewhere, and so your next question should be, 'Who's favorite group is Sunni Arab?'" Frost nodded as Tracy continued, "And I would give you the answer to that question that you already know," he paused, "Saddam Hussein."

The two admirals sat looking at each other until the CNO broke the silence, speaking slowly. "Do you mean to tell me that Saddam Hussein in Iraq put together this attack to make it look like Iran and," he hesitated not wanting to believe, "and we fell for it?"

"I'm not telling you that, Admiral, what I am telling you is, that is

Theory Three, it's a possibility and there are other indicators leading there, but it gets more complicated."

"Tell me more."

Tracy started then stopped, thought a moment and said, "Before I go into Theory Four and while we're on Saddam, let me give you an aside but a key factor in this."

After the CNO nodded Tracy continued. "Saddam Hussein has for years been talking about taking over Kuwait—."

"Kuwait? What do you mean, 'Taking over Kuwait'?"

Tracy raised his hand indicating patience and continued. "He's had his eye on Kuwait for years as has every Iraqi regime ever since Kuwait was partitioned into a separate kingdom. Kuwait was a part of old Iraq and Hussein would benefit himself and his nation by grabbing Kuwait."

As the CNO shook his head in denial Tracy added, "You mark my words. Someday and soon Saddam Hussein will make a move on Kuwait. He'll have to time it right. It will be when he thinks that Iran and Saudi Arabia, or even the U.S. won't do anything about it, nothing to stop him, and he'll snatch it fast with his huge military and hold it as a fait accompli while the rest of the world, even the Arab world does nothing but complain."

Frost scratched his head. "Well, I don't think so. That's really a stretch, taking Kuwait. I think he would know that the other Arabs and the U.N. and the U.S. wouldn't stand for it, but maybe." The CNO thought a while, "Maybe."

"Let's see what else you've got."

The Director of Naval Intelligence continued, "Well, that's Theory Three, Saddam Hussein, but Theory Three really lacks motive. Why would Saddam Hussein do it?" Frost nodded, enjoying the mental exercise as Tracy continued. "Theory Four, however, still looks at Iraq but maybe without Saddam Hussein knowing anything about it." The CNO tilted his head in question as Tracy continued. "Maybe the pitiful Iraq Navy, what? A dozen antiquated boats and less than a thousand people, a disregarded forgotten extension of the army, never to sea because hemmed in by choke holds between Iran and Kuwait, desperate for attention, for status, finally decides to take on what to them would be a daring act of naval warfare. But can they do it with their resources? No. Just a look at the map and anyone can see that their navy boats couldn't even get out into the Gulf and couldn't survive there, but innocent fishing boats could get out into the Gulf. Fishing boats or navy boats would have a tough time getting at a worthwhile target far away because they don't have the legs and their navy boats would be recognized long before they could get close enough for any attack. And over-riding all considerations is their own fear of failure which would be the end of them. So what do they do?" The CNO was nodding as his navy's leading detective continued. "The Iraq Navy leaders put together a bunch of rag-tags, as you say, that could not be traced back to them but that have as close as they can get to the appropriate experience, and put them in fishing boats that could not be traced back to them but can go anywhere unsuspected. They provide fuel at a hidden-away place, provide weapons that anyone can get on the arms market and they send this formidable naval force to do battle under their enemy's colors."

"Brilliant!" The CNO exclaimed with raised fist.

"Brilliant enough," Tracy continued, "that if successful the Iraq Navy leaders are indeed brilliant heroes to their leader, their personal futures assured and their navy gets notice, funding, more ships, more men."

"I know that situation," The CNO offered smiling. "I go through it every year in the budget process. All of us Navy leaders have the same situation and—." Tracy interrupted him, "And in this case, Admiral, if the operation fails the Iraq Navy leaders can claim that they had nothing to do with it, that they knew nothing about it. Their hands are clean, no blame to Iraq Navy, no blame to Iraq, all Iranian fault. But if successful, ah, 'Look what I did!' Nice?"

"Very nice." The CNO agreed.

Tracy was not finished. "Then there's Theory Five."

The CNO asked, "What else can there be?"

"We can use similar reasoning to Theory Four and double back to arrive at Theory Five." The CNO shook his head not understanding as Tracy continued. "If we take the absence of pure Iranians from the mixed crews and ask ourselves, 'Why no pure Iranians?' We can go through the same logic as we did with 'no Sunni Arabs' and arrive at a possibility that the Iranians might have put this together but with the deliberate intent that it would fail and would, after analysis, point to Iraq." Frost still did not understand and Tracy took a different approach. "Look, say the Iranians want to hit our MPS ships at Diego Garcia but they don't want to be blamed for it, so they put together an operation that looks at first blush Iranian, knowing that we would dig into it deeper, and in the digging we would see that it was Iraqi, poorly disguised. Our MPS are stopped and Iraq gets blamed. That's Theory Five."

"Five theories, yeah," the CNO shook his head, "and each with some measure of credibility or each a long stretch of maybe." He paused. "Tell me again what you've been able to learn, or what the whole intell world has been able to learn from these survivors. They're still being held, right?"

"Yes sir. The two that were taken, that survived at Diego Garcia are being held there in our custody with British authorization—. "

"Yeah I know about that," the CNO interrupted.

"And the five who were originally being held by local authorities at Mahe in the Seychelles are now in our custody also, now at Diego Garcia and with the same arrangement with the Brits. You know the diplomatic process that was used to make that happen." The CNO nodded and Vice Admiral Tracy continued. "So we have seven in custody."

"And are they talking?" the CNO asked.

"Are they talking?" Tracy laughed. "They're talking too much! Every one of them has told us a number of different stories and in different languages and dialects. They claim to be Iranian, Iraqi, Arab, Shia, Kurd, Turkoman, Armenian, Saudi, Somalian, everything. We can find support for every one of those five theories somewhere in the things that have been said and we can find evidence that erases any of the theories. The more we talk to them the more confused we get." Both admirals shook their heads. "One thing becomes clear though, as we try to sort out facts from their fictions." Tracy leaned forward to make his point. "These were low level ranks and civilians that knew virtually nothing of higher level involvement. They were kept isolated from information above their pay grade and any information on national intent, anything regarding navy leaders, ayatollahs, Saddam Hussein or Montazeri is not going to be learned from them or any analysis of what they can provide. When it's all over, whenever that might be, we may never know who or why."

"Maybe so," The CNO thought a moment. "How about the boats? What can we learn from them?"

"Common fishing boats, 60 foot, diesel engines, too small for ocean work, never before out of the Gulf, too short range for this mission, 4 to 5 man crew. We're told that one was 80 feet and could make the full trip but that must have been one of those sunk, if it's true."

"How about the engines? The CNO asked.

"German diesels. The CIA chased down manufacturer and serial numbers and learned that they had been sold to equipment brokers. That led them to Iranian purchasers ten years ago so the boat engines lead to Iran."

Frost repeated, "Iran."

Tracy continued, "But from Iran, fishing boats could have been confiscated, stolen or even purchased by any Persian Gulf state or fisherman. No yardage gained there."

"And the weapons?" The CNO was running out of questions.

"One other piece of the puzzle regarding boats." The Director of Naval Intelligence held up a finger as he continued. "A couple of weeks after the Diego Garcia attack, a frigate of the Indian Navy on routine patrol looked into the atoll of Gan and found a disabled fishing boat with questionable papers. The crew was in bad health, bad water, bad food and couldn't give a reasonable explanation as to why they were there with a small boat and broken engine. Clearly their boat had not been doing any fishing. The boat and crew were taken to India, questioned and released and some time later someone on the Indian Navy staff realized that there might have been some connection to our MPSRONTWO attacks. Now we feel that this boat was part of a logistic support system for the attacking fishing boats, another piece of the operation that went bad. There may have been other hidden support out there but the Indians couldn't help us with who these people were or where they were from, other than they had false papers."

"Too bad they didn't hold them for us but they couldn't have known. And weapons?" Frost asked again.

"Common on the arms market. Everyone that wants them has them. Our only foot in the door there, maybe, is that some of our captives seemed to have a high respect for the TOW missile. They talked of it as very valuable and told us that it was very scarce and therefore was to be used only under the best of conditions. The boat apprehended had only four TOW missiles and an RPG-7 with about 80 grenades, but only one man with army experience knew how to use them. Of the two survivors taken at Diego Garcia, one was also an army man with TOW experience and he was a Kurd."

"Kurds again, huh?" The CNO paused seeing that the briefing was over, then he continued. "Well, you may be right Mister Dick Tracy, this case may never be solved and I thank you for giving me all that. Keep your people on it though and let me know if you learn anything new, if the fog clears."

The Director of Naval Intelligence was not finished. "But there's more, Admiral, a very important additional piece; Theory Six."

"Theory Six!" Frost exclaimed, "You said there were five theories! What else can there be?"

Vice Admiral Robert Tracy, more often called Dick Tracy, the Navy's top detective, had been Director of Naval Intelligence long enough not to be cowed by CNO's anger, surprise or even the well known rage in the igloo from icy Admiral Frost. Tracy had a report to make and he was going to make it whatever the CNO said or did. "Yes, sir, I did say there were five theories and there are five confidential theories, classified only confidential because they're already being discussed openly and most of them are based on open literature. Any analyst could come up with the same possibilities. But," he emphasized the word, "our intell people working together, cross agencies, all sources, have come up with what they consider a sixth theory and maybe the most likely, and it is classified Top Secret because exposure of some of the sources could impact on our national interests if they became public."

Frost calmed and murmured, "Go on."

"First let me repeat from an earlier statement. I said that these people we hold from the fishing boats were low levels, that they knew virtually nothing of higher level involvement and that any information on national intent, anything regarding high level involvement would not be learned from them or any analysis of what they can provide." Frost nodded and Tracy continued, "True, but only to a certain extent, an analytical extent. Apparently they know nothing other than what they were told by a major, and remember that Iraq's navy is a very small insignificant part of the army. So, all we can get from them is through an analysis of (One) who they are, which takes us back to the absence of certain ethnic and religious backgrounds, and (Two) what could be a motive for these fishing boat attacks on our MPS shipping."

Frost nodded and Tracy continued. "We already pointed out the absence of Sunni Arabs and what we might call real Iranians among the fishing boat crews that raised eyebrows of our intell people. Also, we did learn from the survivors that at Basra and Umm Qasr they were not treated well. They were virtually ostracized by almost all of the navy people, bad feelings, and they could not figure out why."

Frost again nodded, "Could have been jealousy."

Tracy continued, "Now, if we search for a motive, why would anyone want to send six fishing boats on what would appear to us a foolhardy mission? We have to ask who would have something to gain. It's hard to pin down because all of the potential villains would gain something." Tracy emphasized the words all and something, "but also to lose. It's like a lottery but with everyone a winner, except us, and except maybe one bad guy potentially wins more than the others and losses less."

The CNO was frowning. "I don't follow you there, or, I don't know where you are."

Tracy continued, "Let's look at it this way; from our list of high level potential and perhaps involved bad guys, if we can find one likely to benefit from this attack then, if we can find a path that leads to sending fishing boats out on this mission, then that might be our man, the source, the instigator."

It takes a lot of intestinal fortitude, some call it guts, for a person in a high position of authority and responsibility to admit to a subordinate that, regarding an issue of intelligence, he is somewhat behind that subordinate. Still, no one had ever questioned Frosty's guts and so the CNO did not hesitate to ask Tracy, "Can you show me how this is going? I'm just a Texas Aggie, you know, and I can't see anything different from those other five theories and I can't keep up with the complex names."

Ivy League educated Tracy smiled with tolerance and went on. "We, that is the combined intell analysts, looked at each one of the potential bad guys and tried to find, for each one, the classic police procedure of crime solving; who would have opportunity, motive and means? All earlier theories started at the fishing boats and tried to work upwards. This time we started with the top people and looked for an opportunity, a path down to the boats. Motive meaning what they could gain but also what they could lose, and we tried to find how they could get it accomplished, that is by what avenue of associations, influence, even coercion, including others who might also benefit, there-by providing a path of least resistance. We looked for who would want it done and how he could get it done. We did this analysis for the so-called six ayatollahs plus four other influentials of Iran and we did it for five Iraqis including Saddam Hussein."

Tracy paused causing Frost to ask, "And what did this analysis give us?"

"It gave us Theory Six. One individual stands out with opportunity, motive and means and because of who it is, why he did it and how he did it, this is classified Top Secret."

"And who is this individual?"

"Ayatollah Mahmud Shariatavardi, from Baluchistan, hates Soviets, loves the U.S. and is considered to be our best friend in the area. He personally welcomed our troops on the beach with hugs, flowers and prayers of thanks to Allah." Tracy raised his voice in falsetto, "We are saved, the Americans are here," then returned to his normal voice. "He sent the six fishing boats to attack our MPS ships at Diego Garcia."

Frost added, "Yeah, and he convinced the head of the Iranian Revolutionary Guard to attack our ships at Bandar Abbas then alerted us to the attack. Nice guy."

"Yes, he is supposed to be our best friend and oh yes, he has demonstrated that he can do such a thing, he's proven that. Let me try to explain why." Vice Admiral Tracy continued, "Ayatollah Mahmud Shariatavardi is our strongest—."

Frost interrupted, "I've heard a lot about him in the tank and look Dick, let's use the short handle for this bastard. The intell briefers in the tank cut his name down to 'Shari' so we could keep track of him, like Shari Lewis the puppet girl, y'know?"

A tolerant look by Tracy indicated that he, too, could use nicknames as he started again. "Shari is our strongest supporter in Iran and because of that he must get help to overcome the anti-U.S. ayatollahs and political leaders, strong help, military muscle, because the most valuable influence in this area is force, that's all the people understand. He has no para-military or militia or even military followers so the best support he can have, really the only support, is to have U.S. troops in Iran. He has to find a way to get the U.S. into Iran and he knows that just asking won't do it." Frost was listening intently.

"Shari is closely associated with Ayatollah Mohammed Sadiq al-Sadr—." Frost interrupted with, "Do I know him? Doesn't sound familiar. He's not one of your six ayatollahs, is he?"

"Very good, Admiral," Tracy smiled as a teacher satisfied with student progress. "No, you haven't heard of him and the reason you haven't heard of him is that he's in Iraq. He's an important anti-Saddam Hussein, anti-Sunni cleric in Iraq and he has close ties with Shari. We'll just call him 'Sadr' to make it easy on the names, but most important it gives us a path, that is, it gives Shari a path of influence from Iran into Iraq. Shari is the only one of the six ayatollahs, or other Iranian men of importance with this kind of connection. Once we get into the politics of Iraq we find this strong Shiite cleric, incidentally Saddam Hussein had a price on his head, and we have an influential dissatisfied leader that would be very willing, even anxious, to weaken Saddam Hussein or to cause him to look bad." Frost nodded.

"So Sadr uses his channels inside Iraq and finds an ally in a very dissatisfied leader of the insignificant Iraqi navy, a brand new guy just put in charge and looking for some way to bring attention to his neglected navy and bingo, along comes Sadr with a great idea. This new navy leader is Abdul Tryak abd al Razaq, a major replacing a fired colonel, fired along with four of his top lieutenant colonels, and this new leader is promptly promoted to colonel and good things start happening to the Iraqi navy, like Osa boats from USSR with STYX missiles."

Frost was still nodding and offered, "And that takes us back to Theory Four."

"Right." Tracy was clearly pleased with the CNO's understanding as he continued. "Just like in Theory Four but with a touch of Theory five for the ethnic and religious cross-section, the navy puts together a plan that if successful they can claim credit within the military of Iraq, while placing public blame on Iran, enhancing their image with their military, more money, more boats, and if unsuccessful they could deny any involvement, and Sadr in Iraq would see to it that either way, successful or not, Saddam Hussein's military tried a very ill-conceived mission and Saddam could either admit that he didn't have control over his own military or that he had ordered the foolhardy operation."

Tracy continued, "Meanwhile, whether the operation was successful or not Shari, back in Iran, would see to it that the Americans thought that it was Iran that had attacked them and that Iran needed American troops to restore order. Just what Shari wanted."

The two admirals stared at each other until Frost spoke. "That's fantastic. I never heard of such twists and duplicity." They were silent again and then the CNO continued, "Dick, that's the most fantastic, the most magnificent stretch of logic and imagination that I've ever heard. If you were writing a fiction it would be too far-fetched to sell and I find it hard to believe. You're calling our closest supporter in the area a double-crosser and claiming double-crossing all across Iran and Iraq. I don't know—." Silence prevailed.

Finally Vice Admiral Tracy replied, "Yes sir. It is a stretch. It's hard to believe, but if you're trying the time-honored American process of looking to identify good guys in white cowboy hats and bad guys in black, let me assure you that in this part of the world there are no good guys. They all wear black hats. They're all bad, and all we can search for are some, or maybe only one, that isn't just quite as bad as the others. Any of them would stab you in the back, but maybe we could find one who would use a shorter knife."

Frost looked at the Director of Naval Intelligence, "And maybe Shari uses the short knife, eh, is that what you're trying to tell this naive Texan still looking for guys in white hats?

"That's one way to put it Admiral, but not the naïve part, not you." They both laughed.

As the Director of Naval Intelligence left the CNO's office Admiral Frost said aloud to himself, "We still don't know. We've got six Iranian ayatollahs and another in Iraq, and can't trust any of them. We've got five confidential theories and a top secret sixth, and the guy we're backing has stabbed us in the back at least twice. We still don't know what the hell happened, is happening now or will happen in the future," as he shook his head in disbelief, "and probably we never will know."

CHAPTER 31

CALIFORNIA LADY

Across the shipyard they walked, from the building ways where ships were constructed, past the machine shops toward the parking lot. Normally a noisy dusty area, there was no industrial activity late on this late Saturday morning. She was a regal woman, almost six feet tall in heels, and she always wore heels. "Heels and hose, and turned up nose," he had described her and even in her sixties she was an attractive woman, an elegant woman in designer clothes, modest appropriate jewelry and most striking of all, an air of feminine self-confidence. Walking beside her was a tall Navy officer in pure white starched uniform with choker collar and gold buttons, the gold of his shoulder boards bright in the sunshine, he asked, "How did you like the ceremony?"

"Nice and simple as you said it would be. Not much to it, is there?" She spoke with a soft southern accent.

"No. Keel-laying is the most simple of the ceremonies for a new ship. They get progressively more elaborate. Next comes launching. That can be a big deal, depends on the builder. Last is the commissioning ceremony. That's the big one, probably because the Navy people do it; the PCO and the other plankowners."

She knew that PCO meant prospective commanding officer and a plankowner was a Navy person attached to a ship at the time of its commissioning. "Well, I've seen one launching and a number of commissionings but this was my first keel-laying. What now?"

"We can go home or if you feel like it there's a reception at the o'club at Long Beach. You said earlier that you'd see how you felt after the ceremony."

The Long Beach Naval Station was just across the bridge from Todd Shipyard in San Pedro and they could be at the officers club in a few minutes. "When does a Shielbrock ever pass up a party?" She replied. "Let's go to the reception."

He held the passenger side front door of the cream colored Mercedes for her. The car had California license plates that read SHLBCK. She sat first in the seat and then lifted in her long legs, a smooth lady-like movement. After closing the door he went around to the driver's side, got in and drove out of the shipyard and on to the freeway that led across the bridge to Long Beach.

In front of the officers club at Long Beach were parking spaces marked Flag/General, Capt/Colonel, and CO Afloat and they pulled into one of the captain spaces. Next to a Flag/General space was one marked Bull Ensign.

"You know," Barbara said, "The first time I heard the expression 'Bull Ensign' I thought it meant the young officer in a ship who talked the most, told the tallest tales, you know, full of the most 'bull'."

"You should have known better than that."

"Oh, I found out soon enough that it meant the most senior ensign in a ship, but of all the ensigns I ever met the one that was the most 'full of bull' was the Bull Ensign of the destroyer Robinson."

"And that, dear lady, would have been none other than Ensign Martin D. Shielbrock back in, let's see, nineteen hundred and fifty four A.D."

"Fifty three. Tell me, do you suppose they still make ensigns with lines as corny as that one had?"

"I doubt it. They're smarter now. Maybe not as bold, but smarter," replied her tall escort.

As they entered the club she excused herself and in the ladies room just off the lobby, settling in one of the soft lounge chairs, she lit a cigarette. Better to smoke in here she reasoned, then out in the reception amid talk, drinks and hors d'oeuvres, besides, she needed a few minutes to get herself together and sitting in this small lounge with a cigarette would do nicely.

How many officers clubs had it been in almost forty years? Beyond count.

Norfolk, in those early years for her, had at least five o'clubs and she knew them all well. Since then she had been in officers clubs all over the country and in some other parts of the world. Newport, Charleston, Jacksonville, five in San Diego, five in the Washington area, Annapolis, Philadelphia, Long Beach, at least four in Japan, a few in the Philippines, Thailand, Singapore, England, Canada—, too many to remember. But it started in Norfolk, where a good looking girl just out of college had no problems getting dates and, if anything, her problems in those days were because of too many men in her life. Then there was Martin Shielbrock and her life focused on him and on his Navy. It was always 'his' Navy and to be with him she had to be a part of his Navy, like at Monterey.

Many years before it had been the grand ballroom of the Del Monte Hotel in Monterey, California, but then, as part of the U.S. Naval Postgraduate School, the room was rather austere as Rear Admiral James G. Parker, U.S. Navy, Superintendent of the Naval Postgraduate School and his wife stood in the reception line near the entrance, greeting the newly arrived officer students and their wives with introductions provided by the Aide and Flag Lieutenant. The young officers in service dress blue uniform and their wives in cocktail dress wore nametags to help with the introductions and as each approached the aide would turn to the admiral and give the rank and name. The admiral would shake hands, welcome the young officer and introduce Mrs. Parker who would then introduce Mrs. Montgomery, the wife of the Deputy Superintendent, who would introduce Captain Montgomery and the process continued for each couple and the numerous bachelor officers.

"Lieutenant Shielbrock." The aide introduced him and the admiral's eyes flicked over the ribbons on Shielbrock's left chest and caught the Legion of Merit, rare on a lieutenant.

"I've heard of you, Lieutenant. Welcome to Monterey."

"Thank you, Admiral," and he passed along the line to the deputy who asked, "Where did you leave the ship?"

"I stayed on board until we got back to Norfolk then had just enough time to get out here."

"Glad you made it."

"Me too." They both laughed.

"Mrs. Shielbrock." The aide introduced her.

"Welcome to Monterey, Mrs. Shielbrock. This is Mrs. Parker."

"Thank you, Admiral. Good evening Mrs. Parker."

"Good evening—," The admiral's wife hesitated, looking at Barbara, still holding her hand. "Shielbrock—," she thought a moment. "Isn't your name Barbara?"

Each recognized the other at the same time and Barbara nodded, laughing. "Yes."

"You're Barbara from Loffman's in Norfolk. You ran the ladies department and helped me on so many occasions." Then to her husband who was already greeting the next student, "Jim, I've told you about this girl." Then back to Barbara, "I'm just delighted that you're here. We need you to teach in our wives club fashion and charm programs. I must get together with you. When can we get together and talk?" She hadn't given Barbara a chance to respond but continued. "Will you help with the wives program? Oh, I'm so pleased to see you here—."

The reception line backed up but Barbara finally got to say, "I only worked at Loffman's, Mrs. Parker. I didn't run the department. I'd like to help in any way I can. I'll call you tomorrow," and she moved along to a smiling Mrs. Montgomery, to the deputy superintendent and then to a waiting Martin Shielbrock.

"Hey," He said with obvious pleasure. "You were a big hit with the admiral's wife."

"You weren't exactly a stranger to the people in that line yourself, Shellback." Arm in arm they walked across the room laughing to join a group of students and wives.

For their two years at the Postgraduate School, Barbara was known to her friends as "Mrs. Parker's Aide." She ran the fashion show, taught the charm course and helped the admiral's wife with a myriad of social events and in later years, in later tours of duty in Martin's ship and staff assignments that followed she was just as active with wives' activities, the classic naval officer's wife.

Well, enough reminiscence, she thought. Best to face the reception here at Long Beach, meet those she had to meet, exchange pleasantries and listen to more accolades. Putting out her cigarette, she went back into the lobby and to the reception, to introductions, greetings, men in uniform, men in civilian suits, only a few women, she moved among them. All wanted to meet her as talking briefly she moved from one to another.

"He was really a great officer, you know, and if he hadn't gotten those ships to Bandar Abbas three years ago we'd have been in an awful mess." A marine three star general spoke but Barbara didn't catch his name.

Another marine, this one Barbara knew. "Don! How nice. It's been a long time and I see its' Brigadier General Rogerson now. Congratulations." She acknowledged his new one star rank.

"Thank you Barbara. It's nice to see you and thanks for the congratulations. Shellback had a lot to do with this promotion, you know."

"No, Don," She laughed. "He may have caused a lot of things to happen but not your promotion. I'm sure you got that on your own."

"No, really, Barbara. If Shellback hadn't of gotten all of those MPS ships into Bandar Abbas our troops wouldn't have had enough equipment to chase a rabbit. The Soviets wouldn't have believed we were serious and they would have over-run Iran, or at least a part of it. Without those MPS ships we would have had to airlift right out of there. So there's a lot more at stake there than my promotion, but I know I wouldn't have been promoted after coming out of a walkaway, a failure. So, you see, his success led to my promotion."

Barbara smiled. "Well, if you say so—. Anyway, I know that he would be very happy to see you wearing that star."

"Thanks Barbara. What's more important is that the Soviets stopped in East and West Azerbaijan and didn't go into Kurdistan."

"Well, Don, I'm glad it worked out well and that you were able to get out of there without any great loss or extensive time.

"Yes, I was glad to get out of there and we've had some relative stability there since that Iran-Iraq War ended. Maybe it will last."

"You're an optimist, Don, but I hope you're right."

A civilian interrupted them. "We're going to build a fine ship to carry his name, Mrs. Shielbrock." The executive of Todd Shipyard shook her hand.

Senator Jack McLain was with the shipyard exec Dick Murphy. "Barbara, I was a classmate of Shellback at the National War College."

"Why yes, Jack, how nice to see you again." She really didn't remember him.

"And you remember Dick Murphy from the Strategic Studies Group years ago?"

They shook hands smiling. "From Newport, certainly, and congratulations, Dick, I read that you will soon be the Secretary of the Navy. That's marvelous. Martin said a long time ago that you should be SecNav."

"Thank you Barbara. That's very nice of you and of him. You know, he was my favorite Navy officer."

"Mine, too." They laughed. It was good to laugh. Let's not make this a wake, she thought.

"Dick and Jack, I'd like you to meet my son, Steven."

"Well, a submariner, I see. Not a black shoe like your Dad?" Dick Murphy acknowledged the gold dolphin badge on the chest of the tall young officer with Barbara.

"He forgave me for what he called a minor error of judgment." They all laughed, and the future Secretary of the Navy discussed the lieutenant's submarine life as Jack McLain took Barbara aside.

"I'd like you to know that I intend to support a move by Dick Murphy to have Martin promoted posthumously to the rank of Commodore. As you remember, the Navy had that rank at the time Martin retired and since then they've gone to this Rear Admiral Lower Half title. But in Martin's case we'd like to see him promoted to Commodore. There will be a bill introduced in Congress to accomplish that."

"That would be very nice, but isn't it a long time ago? Three years? I mean, why now?"

"Well, yes. It has been a long time. You know that Frosty, when he was CNO, saw to it that Martin was awarded the Navy Cross and that led to the ship being named for him. Speakes, that retired rear admiral, was instrumental in the ship naming process."

Barbara interrupted the senator. "Martin served under Steven Speakes three times, you know. Our son," she nodded toward the lieutenant still in discussion with Dick Murphy, "is named for him."

"Oh. I didn't know that. Well, that does help to understand Speakes' interest, doesn't it?" The question didn't need answering as the senator smiled and continued. "But as you ask, why now, the belated promotion?" He hesitated, "I suppose it has something to do with the book that woman Kim McManus wrote. It was a top seller for a time, you know."

"Yes, I know. I really enjoyed it. It was a fine book."

"Have you ever met her?" the senator asked.

"Yes. She came to see me in Alexandria just after she got back from the Iran thing and told me all she could about it and actually asked me if I thought it would be all right if she wrote the book. I was flattered, of course." Barbara smiled. "It was like she asked for my permission to write the book. Of course I agreed. She's a very bright woman and good looking, too. I'm glad Martin was so busy with his convoy when she was aboard his ship." They both laughed.

As she talked with Jack McLain, Barbara caught snatches of Steven's conversation,—he served in a 688 Class submarine homeported in Pearl Harbor,—just returned from an exciting patrol,—third officer,—Chief Engineer,—married, three children, expecting another,—father-in-law Vice Admiral Williams. Murphy knew him.—sister Nancy Lived in Atlanta,—soon to be married,—mother had winter home in La Jolla,—would be there a few weeks then back to her real home in Alexandria. Yes, he knew that his father had command of a destroyer as a lieutenant, laughter. Nuclear power training was discussed.

"Barbara, I'd like you to meet someone." Leaving Steven and Dick Murphy talking, Jack McLain guided her a few steps. "Barbara, this is Senator John Dillingham. John this is Barbara Shielbrock."

Dillingham was a sixty-five year old very distinguished senator from Alabama. Tall, handsome, with gray hair matching his expensive flannel suit, the senator looked at Barbara and smiled. "Why yes, of course. You are the widow of the very gallant officer for whom the new ship is to be named. My congratulations to you and to your family. He must have been a very fine man."

"Yes, he was. Thank you. You would have no reason to know this, Senator Dillingham, but I am originally from your state of Alabama." She used her best southern accent.

The senator laughed. "You are wrong, dear lady. I knew that you were from Alabama and I used that as my excuse to have Jack McLain introduce us." They both laughed. "Please call me John. All my friends do, and I hope that you will be my friend."

"All right, John." She noticed that Jack McLain had wandered off.

"This is awkward, but I should explain to you that my wife passed away some years ago."

"Well, John, I'm sorry, but I knew that and I don't see why you should feel awkward, or have to tell me."

"Oh, you knew about my wife?" The senator was puzzled.

"You're in the news, Senator, and I have to keep track of those I vote for. Shouldn't I?"

"Why, yes. Of course you should. Well," he hesitated, "the reason I wanted to tell you, I wanted you to know, is because I wanted to ask you to have dinner with me, that is when you're back in your Alexandria home near Washington." The senator was clearly in an awkward situation which was very rare for a man of his self-confidence. He was embarrassed but continued. "You still have a home there, haven't you?"

Blue eyes, with those beautiful blue eyes he looked at her and she heard herself reply in her best cultured Alabama southern accent, "Why John ah'd be delighted to have dinnah with you. Ah'm goin' back to Alexandria tomorrow."

Edwards Brothers Malloy
Thorofare, NJ USA
June 20, 2012